SICOLA
The
PAPAL BULL

A Fantasy on the Escapades
of an Itinerant Pope

John A. Vitello

Our Sunday Visitor, Inc.
Huntington, Indiana 46750

Lyrics on page 31 are from "They'll Know We Are Christians by Our Love," words and music by Peter Scholtes, © 1967 by F.E.L. Publications Ltd., Los Angeles, Calif. All rights reserved. Lyrics on page 121 are from "I Am Woman," words by Helen Reddy, music by Ray Burton, © 1971, 1972 by Buggerlugs Music (BMI), Los Angeles, Calif. All rights reserved. Thanks to the weekly Catholic magazine *Twin Circle,* Los Angeles, Calif., for dialogue suggested by its interviews with children on the existence of angels in the chapter "Like Echoes . . ." on pages 359-361. Finally, and importantly, the author is indebted to the late great stand-up comic Charlie Manna for the name and comedic traits of the title character, "Pope Sicola."

This is a fantasy, a work of imagination, and all characters, events and situations portrayed herein are purely imaginary. Any resemblance to actual people, living or dead, is strictly coincidental.

ISBN: 0-87973-646-1
Library of Congress Catalog Card Number: 78-71420

Cover design and illustration by James E. McIlrath

Published, printed and bound in the United States of America

646

To Monsignor Arthur E. Ratigan, who started this book more than forty years ago without knowing it . . . and to my wife, Jean, whose sacrifice made it possible.

CONTENTS

"All men whilst they are awake are in one common world; but each of them, when he is asleep, is in a world of his own."

Plutarch, *Of Superstition*

Part I
IN ROME

The Election

Giuseppe Cardinal Sicola had been surprised when he was named a cardinal, and when he received the news his face colored and he coughed from the saliva he had breathed into his windpipe.

He turned to his friend and seminary classmate, Monsignor Tommaso Del Vecchio, and stammered, "It appears that the Pope has lost his senses. *Mannaggia*! I am to be a cardinal! The last time His Holiness spoke to me he was most severe, most severe. As a matter of fact, Tommaso, do you know what he said to me? He said, 'Giuseppe, you will never amount to anything in the Church because sometimes I can hear the marbles rolling in the vacuum between your ears.' But then he said a strange thing, most strange. He said, 'I am angered by your methods, my Son, but when the anger subsides I find myself smiling and the thought crosses my mind briefly — very briefly — that there is room in the Church for your light-heartedness. You are a lovable knave, Giuseppe. Go, before I box your ears.' Tommaso, I wasted little time in getting out of the room. I think he would have bounced his crozier across my skull."

That had been only three years ago and now he sat in his office, dazed and saddened by the news he had only moments before received by telephone. He was silent and uncharacteristically morose for a time, then he turned to Tommaso, who had since become his secretary. "The Pope," he said, "is dead. Last night. In his sleep. Where will we find another so competent, so good, so able to cope with the enmities within the Church? He permitted, it is true, the polarizations to continue, but only in the name of charity. Always, all he thought of was love, and because he loved as Christ loves, he was patient."

Tommaso also was saddened by the news, but having learned many of Sicola's ways of lightening heavy occasions, he added, "Si, Giuseppe. He was a very holy man. But you need not be concerned about his successor. It will not be you. The Papacy has known all kinds of jackals — from whose turpitude the Holy Spirit has preserved the Church — but never has a jackass occupied the Chair.

He ducked his head adroitly, from much practice, as Sicola's paperweight skimmed past his ear.

"Small chance, Tommaso. I have not endeared myself to the members of the College. Whoever is chosen, however, I pity him. We should pray for him, Tommaso. The ground on which the Pope walks is slippery. It is all the more astounding that when he slips and falls it is not the Church that is fractured, but only the tailbones of those who failed to hold him steady. Though I would flee from the position myself, even a buffoon like me could not harm her."

"Ah-men!" Tommaso agreed.

"Go pick your nose, Tommaso, you ingrate."

Although the method for electing a pope had earlier been changed, no longer permitting secretaries and servants of the cardinals to be admitted to the proceedings, in the last months of his reign the Pope had mysteriously decided to restore the centuries-old format. There had been many rumblings of subdued dissent, and conjecture was rampant. Many saw the reversal of procedures and locale to their original design as an act of senility, but others detected in it a sign that the Pope had worried over the direction of the Church and intended to signal that the time had come for some return to tradition, a braking of the pell-mell changes without substance. True, they said, he had initiated many of those changes himself with good intention, but now second thoughts had characterized many actions as precipitous, and this symbolic gesture should show that acceleration was not the watchword in the Church. So in effect the Pope was warning his successors to find in the tradition of the Church its greatest strength.

Sicola knew that the rites surrounding the death of the Pope would continue for nine days after which time he would join the other cardinals in conclave to elect a new pope. He would be allowed to take Tommaso with him since each cardinal was permitted a secretary and a servant, and once in the conclave they would be locked in, from the inside by the Camerlengo or presiding officer of the conclave, and from the outside by the marshal of the conclave. He would not be allowed to leave until a pope was elected, no matter how long the procedure lasted.

He suggested, in view of the circumstances, that Tommaso bring a sufficient change of underwear for two weeks, or the equivalent: one can of Ban Basic. "The air could become foul," he pointed out. "And if the procedure is a long one and we cannot quickly agree on a new pope . . . well, I leave it to your imagination. And one more item, Tommaso. The aspirin, much aspirin. It could be put to good use."

"I am happy to see, Giuseppe, that you are already concentrating on who will get your vote at the conclave," Tommaso smiled wryly.

"I have read a great deal about these conclaves, Tommaso. Did you know, for example, that when Gregory X was elected in 1271 it took over two years and nine months?"

"And were the cardinals locked up all that time?" Tommaso asked.

"No, Tommaso, but just imagine if they had been. That was when Gregory decided that it was a disgrace to take such a long time, so he decreed that in the future the electors would be locked up in order to hasten the process. Still, in all honesty, it would be possible to be closeted for a week or two."

"I apologize, Giuseppe, for my earlier remark. You are merely being practical. But ... about the Ban Basic, would it not be better to recommend to the Camerlengo that all the cardinals come so equipped. One never smells himself, it seems, hence it is from the offensive odors of others that we must be protected."

"Good ... good, Tommaso. And perhaps it would be symbolic, in a way, if all were to use the product which is purported to bring with it an 'invisible shield.' "

"Now we are getting down to the essentials, Giuseppe. *Buono*! I will mention it to the Camerlengo in your name."

"You are so very modest, Tommaso."

"No, your Eminence. Merely apprehensive."

Sicola took his seat in the Sistine Chapel where the cardinals came together after Mass to cast their votes. Over the chair of each cardinal was a baldachinum, a small canopy, and the expansive room was lined row on row with these hyphens of regality. There was a sense of decorum and dignity mixed with awesome expectation.

Despite Tommaso's remarks that Sicola was concerned with externals, his superior had given much thought to the possible candidates to fill the Chair of Peter. There was the old and venerable Pietro Cardinal Malvasi, who had been Secretary of State, a shrewd politician who, they said, had a pass key to the inner chambers of the Politburo. There had been no question of his loyalty to the Church, but there had often been criticisms that his policies seemed at times to emphasize coexistence with a nation whose political philosophy made it a natural enemy of the Church. In the minds of some this was no hindrance, for if Russia was to be converted there would have to be access to her people, dialogue with her leaders. But to others, like Sicola, temporizing with the truth would be to make the Church a bedfellow to evil, and this sort of appeasement had already permitted the suspicion that some of Holy Mother Church's priests and hierarchy had taken the full route and gone completely over to communism under the euphemistic title of Christian Marxism, as if it were possible to link the two contradictory words. No, Sicola thought, Malvasi meant well, but it should not be he who would succeed to the throne.

Then, of course, there was the fat one, Gasparo Cardinal Pelledura. His specialty had been the liturgy and everyone knew of the chaos following the recommendations he had made to modernize the liturgy. Even Pelledura had been stunned by the extension of his ideas in practice, and the Pope had more than once turned to him and muttered, "What a can of worms we have opened, Gasparo. We cannot retreat, however. Still, we must contain the aberrations that flow from these changes." Gasparo had rung his hands in dismay, but he seemed powerless to stem the tide of creativity on the altars of the Church throughout the world. If, Sicola thought, he could not do it as a cardinal with the backing of the Pope, the chances were slim indeed that he would have any effect if he himself were to become pope.

But if it was not to be Malvasi or Pelledura, then perhaps, Sicola considered, we should look to the right. What of the Frenchman, Pierre Cardinal Bouvret? He was a skilled diplomat, an accomplished theologian, a pious man and he had earned the sympathies of Sicola himself on many occasions for his stand against some of the reforms, but here, too, Sicola hesitated. Bouvret had expressed some sympathy for the renegade Archbishop René Desfeux, who had been suspended for his opposition to the new Mass and the changes of the Council. If Bouvret were chosen, what would be the reaction of the sincere progressives who had believed that certain legalisms had taken the heart out of the Church? Granted, the changes had been fractionating and for some had gone too far, but to what regression would Bouvret take the Church? Schism on the left was to be avoided as much as schism on the right. He trusted Bouvret, but the uncertainty nagged at him all the same. Besides, he was French and the Church was not yet ready for a non-Italian pope. France would take it as a blessing of her own hierarchy, and it was common knowledge that the Pope had, on one occasion at least, singled them out for rebuke.

Who then?

Perhaps there was a need for an interregnum pope, a caretaker who would occupy the Chair only long enough for the dust to settle, for the polarities to become fewer; then when the situation was calmer the next pope would be a truer reflection of the body of thought in the Church. That was, perhaps, the way to go. Alphonso Cardinal Cosenza was in his early seventies, maybe seventy-one. He was calm and unflappable. His theological background was solid, having sprung from the Thomistic seminaries prevalent in his youth. He had on many occasions shown himself to be capable of a vision that showed remarkable balance, a sense of compromise, while always affirming with resolute determination that the Church must maintain the view of eternity. That would be his choice: Alphonso Cardinal Cosenza.

The balloting commenced. On the first day, two ballots were cast in the afternoon. On neither ballot was there a clear-cut two-thirds winner. On the second day Malvasi seemed to creep ahead, but he was far short of the necessary two-thirds. The cardinals were obliged to have no discussion among themselves in private, so there could be no lobbying for specific candidates.

Tommaso, on the third day, whispered to Sicola, "Your Eminence, I begin to see the wisdom of your concern."

"What concern, Tommaso?"

"The 'invisible shield,' Eminence. It is a shame that the Camerlengo brushed off the suggestion. Some of them perspire their garlic."

"*Pazienza*, Tommaso."

On the sixth day, Sicola was stunned to hear his own name called, having received three votes. He grinned and turned to Tommaso. "Some of them believe that a little levity will lighten the mood." He had been too busy with this thought to take note of the buzzing consternation in the Sistine Chapel as the other cardinals reacted to his name.

After the ballot, the cardinals adjourned to their cells, where they would take supper and meditate.

The cardinals returned for the evening balloting, grave and tired. The Camerlengo announced that the balloting would begin.

Once again Sicola cast his ballot for Cardinal Cosenza. He had tried to read the faces of the cardinals about him, but they were masked and none returned his stare. Tommaso whispered to him, "I sense something strange, Eminence. There is a tenseness that was not here this morning, even a grimness. I believe that we will come close tonight."

"You are getting tired of the reduced rations, Tommaso. This is a subtle way to hasten the vote. As Teresa of Avila has said, 'Let nothing affright thee.' The Church moves slowly, but its decisions are those of the Holy Spirit."

The names began to be read aloud. There was a sprinkling of ballots for Cosenza, for Pelledura, and for Malvasi, but Sicola's name was called with greater frequency until toward the end the name "Sicola" was intoned by the Camerlengo with excitement, as if he sensed the inevitability of the outcome.

Sicola shrank in his seat, he too aware for the first time that the voting would lead to his election. His tanned face lost its color, and he suddenly took on the green patina of a bronzed statue, equally frozen and inert. At length he found his voice and he wheezed softly, "I will not serve . . . I will not serve. Count them again. I will not serve."

Tommaso, now overcome himself, sought to control his own quavering voice. "You must . . . you must, my friend. Recall who it was who said these words first. Lucifer! 'Non serviam,' he said. Would you deny the call?"

"*Mannaggia*, Tommaso! Who ever heard of a pope with the name of a soft drink? 'Pope Sicola!' *Mannaggia*! How they will make capital of it."

" 'Let nothing affright thee,' " Tommaso reminded him.

"Si, Tommaso, but we forgot to bring one thing, with all our planning."

"What was that . . . Holiness?"

"The Kaopectate. *Mannaggia*, I feel most peculiar."

Without a Paddle

Since his accession to the throne of Peter, Sicola had changed outwardly hardly at all. He had become even more unorthodox in his methods than his predecessor had imagined possible. From the Chair he was a bulwark of authority, but he had been known to resort to his buffoonery on more than a few occasions, even at times deserting the hallowed confines of the Vatican in order to mingle with the people, always incognito.

It is true that he was now Pope, but in other ways he was like all men. The pressures of his office sometimes disturbed him, so disturbed him that he would dream fitfully. But his dreams had a reality that did not seem at all like his dreams of former times. Then he would dream as most people do, in symbols of the subsconscious flashed like so many hieroglyphics on the screen of his brain, and when he would awake in those days he would muse on the esoteric quality of the dream world. Now it was as if his dreams were visions of bilocation in which he could hear, read thoughts, touch and smell, in which there was a realness and a wholeness that was vibrantly alive, and frequently clairvoyant.

There was one such dream. . . .

Marilyn MacDonald O'Gare stood before her full-length mirror as she checked the length of her dress, patted her hair, and creased her mouth to even the spread of lip rouge.

This would be her finest hour, she thought. After all these years of fighting him in the press, in the courts, in the legislatures, now she would be face to face with her adversary. She had never met him, nor his predecessors, but she despised what he stood for: an organized set of pious myths. And to think that she had once been a member of his Church.

But if he wanted to believe in these myths, let him. She was all for a pluralistic society. "Just don't get pushy, Bub," she thought. "None of this mumbo-jumbo for the civilized people of the world."

She surveyed her image in the glass and then decided to wipe off the lipstick. "When in Rome . . ." she thought, then laughed to herself at the unintended joke. She took three long strides to her closet as she wriggled out of her print dress and reached finally for the black dress with the long sleeves.

"Stuffy S.O.B.!" she said aloud. "But, hell, it is *his* house, *his* rules." She stood by the closet for a long time, holding the dress to her shoulders to measure its length. "Just below the knees. Well, they're coming back, anyway. But, God, how I'd like to show up in a bikini, just to defy him."

Then she considered the rolls of flesh around her waist, the thickness at her hips and thighs, and muttered, "Damn! The joke would be on me, not him. Oh, God! (Strange how I keep using that word.) Let's get dressed and on with it."

Sicola dreamed on as if he were having a vision of events in which he was slightly above them, more as an observer than a participant. Here he was in her very bedroom, and he felt embarrassment at dreaming like a Peeping Tom. He found his gaze sweeping every corner of the room to determine the presence of witnesses who would blab about his presence to the press. Imagine the headlines in the secular press, he thought in his dream: "Separation of Church and State Caput in Bedroom Drama." Or worse still: "Peripatetic Pope Plays Peekaboo in Picaresque Play." Perhaps, though, they would compromise with "Peeping Pope in Potbelly's Pad."

He strangled at the thought of it, and the reality was so great that he saw himself muffling his mouth with the sleeve of his white cassock, fearful that O'Gare would hear him.

Then he spied a letter opener on the dressing table, and as he looked at it, it seemed to rise from its place, hang in mid-air for a moment, then suddenly it was in his hand, and he seemed to hear his own voice as it squeaked, "Joosta one jab inna *la ponza*." He brushed his hands in horror but the letter opener had evaporated and returned to its place on the dressing table.

Sicola awoke and pondered over the dream. He remembered reading about the well-known atheist in the newspapers, and he was certain that he had taken his anger with him to bed. It was the only explanation. Certainly he pitied her. Certainly he had prayed for her. But most certainly also he was concerned for her influence on the pliable minds of the religiously uncommitted, and he ground out an expletive aimed more at her effect than at her. He did not wish her dead, but how, oh how, he thought, he would enjoy puncturing her and watch the air go out of her so that she would be reduced to her true stature before God.

He dressed quickly, ate a simple breakfast and went to the Papal Court for the scheduled general audience. He delivered a short homily in which he discussed the theological concept of God's loneliness. Though God was not truly lonely, because in Him is contained all things and hence He has no need of anything, He is nonetheless so filled with love for all men that there is still a longing for all men to return to Him totally and completely. And, Sicola continued, because of this longing we impute to Him the idea of loneliness, for He cannot help but be offended, not merely by those of us who sin but even more by those who ignore Him, who take not a moment to think of Him, who are unsure even of His existence. It is agnosticism which is a far greater danger to the soul than atheism, he said, for if it is true that atheism is but the other side of love, then he who hates God presupposes His existence, else he would not hate Him so. And in this presupposition he is attracted to that which his soul yearns to love even in opposition to his will.

The faithful filed before him and he extended to them the papal blessing as they knelt humbly to receive it. The group filed out and he sat alone with Tommaso, or so he thought.

"The homily, Holiness," Tommaso said. "It was very good."

"I wonder, Tommaso," the Pope sighed. "I wonder if they heard in their hearts. The world does not wish to hear. They await a miracle, some of them, to turn the wicked and the indifferent. But this does not seem a time for miracles. The cross weighs heavily, Tommaso. Perhaps a younger man . . ." he trailed off, sick with the hopelessness of his prayers, of his pleading, even of his teaching. The dream had left him morose and he felt ineffectual.

Then he heard a shrill voice: "No . . . no . . . no! You mustn't speak so!"

Tommaso and Sicola looked up, startled, as a barrel of a woman plodded from the half-light of a remote corner of the court. She walked directly to the dais and said again, "You must not tire of the fight. You must lead."

Sicola turned to Tommaso, and in unison they shrugged as if to emphasize their surprise at the intrusion, even of such an example of faithful Catholicity.

"Wotta must I lead, my daughter?" Sicola asked her.

"Your people. For when you have given up the battle, then they will also give up, and matters will become uncomfortably easy for me. Oh, how I have enjoyed the fight. Victory has never tasted so sweet because they continued to fight me at every turn. That I also continue to win is only as it should be, but to win without a fight — even dogs do not enjoy that kind of a skirmish!"

"Ah-h-h, so!" he said slowly. "So it is the fight you like?" He knew her now, and he prayed for the letter opener.

"You are the American . . . wottsa your name . . . Maddalena Garo!"

"I am not Italian, sir. Thank God. O'Gare is the name, Marilyn MacDonald O'Gare."

"Okay, O'Gare! Wottsa you beef?"

"I do not believe in God!"

"Thatsa too bad. He's a believe in you."

"I believe in me, too. But I am not God."

"Thatsa good. For one a minoote, I am not so sure."

"Do not humor me, Sir. It would take a mighty act for me to believe in the supernatural, and I do not think you have it within your power to summon God to prove it, assuming that there is such a God."

Sicola closed his eyes and turned his head to the ceiling in prayer. As he did so, he peered at her through slits that screened his view of her through the lashes of his eyes. Her expression was hopeful, almost hungry, as if she awaited a bolt of lightning, and the presence of a radiant figure beside her.

After a very long time, Sicola said to her, "Onna you dresser inna hotel room you have a letter opener. The handle is black, it is made of a wood. And inna the handle issa setta you initials, MMO. Inna you closet you have a bright dress, flowers printed on it. The neck she is low. The dress is, how you say, decolleté. You were going to weara when you come a see me today. But you change a you mind. Instead you weara black."

Her pencilled eyebrows arched in surprise, but she recovered and said, "In my country and in others as well, Sir, many people have psychic abilities. I have been impressed, but I do not see that this qualifies them as extraordinary emissaries of a nonexistent God. If you are what you say you are, show me a miracle," she demanded almost hungrily.

Sicola kept his eyes closed as she spoke, then he said, "Yes . . . yes . . . and there is the thin scar onna you stomach, onna the right side."

"Oh, my God!" she blurted.

"No, my daughter. Joosta His friend."

"This is all nonsense. A charade. The same kind of mumbo-jumbo you practice at Lourdes and your other *holy* places."

"*Mannaggia!*" the Pope thought. "Just give me

the letter opener for a moment. I will not miss another chance. Just a slight touch in the fat belly."

Then in the hidden ear of his mind Sicola heard another voice that came to him as if it echoed through the cosmos, thundering and yet gentle.

"Leave her to Me!" the voice commanded.

Sicola was overcome with a kind of serenity he had never known before. The anger was gone, and in its place came a quiet, peaceful acceptance of a will greater than his own in operation.

He looked at her kindly, and the tranquility seemed to cross the space between them and enfold her. She was strangely entranced. She began then to talk as a child and recited a form of patriotic verse unfamiliar to Sicola.

"I pledge allegiance to the flag of the United States of America, and to the republic for which it stands, one nation, under God . . . under God . . . under God . . . under God. . . ." She could not seem to go beyond the phrase "under God."

Sicola looked at Tommaso, who said, "This is a most unusual occurrence, Holiness. She seems to be a child who has forgotten her lesson. Speak to her, Holiness. Perhaps you can awaken her."

"My daughter. . . ." Sicola started.

"Yes, Daddy," she replied. "That horrid lady said that we must not pray in school, but I showed her."

Then just as suddenly she awoke and continued without any knowledge of her regression.

"Not only Lourdes," she went on, unaware of the gap, "but I understand you are peddling a story of the Mother of Jesus appearing to three children in Fat-*teem*-a, Portugal, with all sorts of superstitious manifestations."

"FATima . . . like in O'Gare," Sicola corrected her.

Again Sicola heard the voice within him, "Patience, my son. Leave her to Me."

"I am here," she went on, "to serve notice to you, Sir, that through every court in America I will pursue you. I will shred your belief so that it has no meaning, no value to any but the most ignorant. In the courts I have an ally. Look to the record."

"What is it you want?" Sicola asked her, confounded by her threat.

"As the head of the United Federation of World Atheists I am here to demand that the Church pay one hundred million dollars in retribution to atheists and henceforth stay out of our bedrooms."

"*Mannaggia*!" Sicola thought. "She could not possibly have known I was there."

"We demand one hundred million dollars for the atrocities perpetrated against all atheists during history. And let me warn you that the fate of the Church is an atheist-dominated culture tomorrow depends upon the action of the Church today.

"You can make your existence more tolerated in tomorrow's world, first, if you surrender the crown given to the papacy by Ferdinand and Isabella of Spain, which is a symbol of one of your tyrannies, the Spanish Inquisition.

"Second, we further demand that the Church stay out of the bedroom and not concern itself with the wombs of women.

"Third, that the Vatican Museum prominently display, for all to see, the iron maiden, the rack, pulleys and other instruments of torture by which you stifled dissent.

"Fourth, that the Church publish its financial and business assets throughout the world.

"Fifth, that the Church withdraw from intrusion into the schools and stop forcing upon the minds of undeveloped children the psychopathological precepts of Christianity.

"Sixth, that the Vatican return all looted art objects, antiquities, statuary and rarities now illegally and immorally in its possession.

"And, seventh, that you assist in dismantling the Church and thus cleanse the world of a fetid wound."

Sicola ignored her demands. "Atheism," he berated her, "is a philosophy of loneliness, for it was your own beloved atheist Heidegger who said, 'He who does not know what loneliness is cannot philosophize.' And in your loneliness for the embrace of God — from whom you are alienated — you choose the arms of Lucifer, and your loneliness, like his, only deepens."

"That," she exploded, "is ridiculous! There is no capital "B" in being because all being is measured in and by existence. There is, therefore, no God."

"You only affirm the words of that faithful apostle Fulton Sheen that an atheist is a person with no invisible means of support, and your tirades are exercises in the hidden faith of faithlessness."

"You persist in baiting me, Sir, but your words can have no effect on one who does not share your belief in the hereafter."

"You have," Sicola interposed, "an American humorist, Woody Allen by name, who avers, 'I do not believe in an afterlife, although I am bringing a change of underwear.' I suggest that this is the beginning of belief and it would be well for you to ponder the question: suppose the Church is correct? What then? Can you afford not to know?"

"I know all I need to know. Where Mr. Allen

leaves the door ajar, I have closed it tight. Besides, Sir, you only quote Mr. Allen in part. He also said that if God exists, He is an 'underachiever.' "

As if coming from the great domed ceiling itself, each of them heard a sonorous voice intone with exasperation, "ATTSA TOO MUCH!"

Sicola and Tommaso gasped at what they beheld. The woman was in levitation with her hindquarters up, her legs hanging down and kicking. As they watched there was the sound of a staccato thumping that coincided with undulating impressions being made on her buttocks. She screamed shrilly, "No . . . no . . . no . . . I'll be a good girl!"

Then the two men heard the voice again, "I am very sorry, Giuseppe. Even God loses His patience! In the kennel there are studs and bitches. In deprecating their union, you refer only to the sons, but why do you not give recognition also to the daughters of bitches?"

"It is a very interesting question, Lord," Sicola mused.

Then the Lord seemed to pummel O'Gare once again, and through the Vatican could be heard the baying and yelping of a trapped hound wailing, "Ah-o-o-o-o-o . . . Ga-a-a-w-w-w-d . . . A-a-a-a-h-h-h!"

Sicola smiled and said, "Give me the paddle, Lord."

What a Little Love Can Do

Sicola sat on the papal throne, anticipating the arrival of his renowned visitor, hero of heroes among Church liberals, but a thorn in the throne of the Pope.

Fathers Hans Kugelfinger entered the court and he strode the length to the dais with a majesty and a hauteur that would seem to suggest that he was the Pope and Sicola the visitor, an attitude that did not escape Sicola.

The Pontiff's eyes turned from the theologian in revulsion as he looked down at his white cassock and flicked at a tiny red spot on his breast. He flicked at it again with annoyance but the blot remained as a tiny mockery against the purity of his robe and his office. Then he remembered the pasta at lunch and he recalled how it had slithered and whipped and undoubtedly spattered in its descent into oblivion.

"We must not let that beega mouth Kugelfinger see it," he thought, nudging his mozetta over to cover the red spot. Then, as if to prepare himself to adopt a friendlier disposition toward the theologian, he thought, "I will be pleasant with him, but I will come immediately to the point."

Kugelfinger now stood before Sicola, a look of intellectual detachment — or boredom — sending out infuriating signals. Kugelfinger ignored the Pope's extended hand, and fury mounted within Sicola. "He stands there like a *cafone*, not bending to kiss the ring. Not even so much as the smallest courtesy." There was a grimace behind his smile, and he considered how it would be an inordinate pleasure to "give him a shot in the head."

"Ah-h-h, Kugelfinger!" he smiled benignantly.

"How's mit you, Joe?" Kugelfinger asked, purposely omitting the title "Holiness."

This omission also did not escape Sicola, who spread his index and middle fingers behind his back, tempted to thrust them into the eyes of Kugelfinger. Charity reigned once again, however, as the Pope considered with some melancholy, "It would be a shame to soil him further. I must admit that he cuts a handsome figure, but there is something incongruous about the dappled gray beard coming to a point above the roman collar. The image would be complete if the ears also came to a point."

"Very well," Sicola finally answered the question. "And howsa you wife and kiddies?"

Kugelfinger's eyes narrowed, offended and angered. "But you know, Sir, that I am not married. I am but a humble priest."

"Not mar-r-ried? But, Hans, my good friend, how come? Ah-h-h, you mean, not yet, no?"

"I mean no, Sire, not at all."

"Ah, well," Sicola sighed and picked away with enjoyment, "Do not give up hope. The right girl will come along soon. Now, Hans, let us arrive immediately to the point. This book you have written, I'ma not so sure I like it. You tella the people that I'ma not the boss. That's a no-no!"

"You seem to miss the point, Sir," Kugelfinger interposed. "I'ma no tell . . . that is, I'm not saying precisely that. What I am saying is that you are not the whole Camembert."

"O-o-o-h-h-h, thatsa different!"

To his secretary, Tommaso, Sicola whispered an aside, "Wotsa dis 'Camembert'?"

"Formaggio, Holiness."

"Ah, Hans," Sicola smiled angelically, "so you do not think that I am the whole cheese, yes? Why you say that?"

"Because, Sir, while I embrace the notion of the kerygma, exegesis indicates that there is some grave doubt with regard not only to apostolic succession but to infallibility as well."

"Ah, I see-e-e-e-e."

"Tommaso," he whispered, "Wad-he-say, wad-he-say, wad-he-say?"

"He said, Holiness, you are not the whole Camembert."

"What, again? How many ways can he say it?"

"His book has six hundred and fifty pages, Holiness. They all say: 'The Pope is not the whole cheese.' "

"Tella me, Hans," Sicola asked, still smiling, "You papa. What was his name?"

"Hermann."

"Yes. Hermann. Good name. Strong. He was a good man?"

"Yes, Sir, he was. A very kind man, a good father."

"You ever naughty with you papa?"

"Yes, on occasion."

"You papa get mad?"

"Yes."

"But he still good man, yes?"

"Yes."

"You ever breaka the window?"

"Oh, yes, Sir, I did, indeed."

"Me too! Holy Smokes! Me too! You papa? He get mad?"

"Very angry."

"Ah, so. But he is stilla good man?"

"A good man."

"Hans. I like you. I'ma gonna give you present. Behind you is box. Please to bend over and pick it up."

"Oh, *thank you*, Holiness!"

"*Mannagia! Now* he calls me Holiness," Sicola grumbled inwardly.

So Hans Kugelfinger, eminent Swiss theologian, turned and stooped to pick up the ornately decorated box to which Sicola had pointed. As he did so, the Pontiff felt welling up inside of him all of the love and charity of a father who must temper all of his actions with justice. As Kugelfinger walked toward the gift and bent to pick it up, Sicola rose from his dais and walked the three steps to him. On his slipper toe there was a pointed ruby that shot irridescent patterns on the walls around him as the sun struck it. He brought his foot behind his robe to keep the sun from reaching the jewel, and somehow it came forward and met Kugelfinger's pant seat with a force that was unintended, accidental, and certain to be misunderstood, for Sicola was truly filled with love for this man. Then, somehow, his voice raised to a shout and he shrieked at Kugelfinger with such majestic force that even Sicola would have cowered at such ferocity. "OUT . . . OUT . . . OUT! *I* am you Papa. I am the whole cheese!"

Kugelfinger glided out backwards on his knees,

his head bowed, and he said unctuously, "Yes, Holiness . . . Yes, Holiness . . . Yes, Holiness!"

"You see," Sicola said to Tommaso, "what a little love can do?"

They Kicked the Habit

The Sisters of Mary the Liberator (formerly Liberatrix) were having their general chapter in Rome, only a fling of the bra from the Vatican. Sicola's calendar showed no audience scheduled for any of the leaders of this community. That no move was made to visit him was a matter of great concern. Were they not his beloved children, coequal with the Jesuits in his heart? Had he not permitted them liberties beyond toleration? Why, now, this snub to his Holy Office? Alas, there was but one gesture of charity remaining. It was to go to them.

They were meeting in the Soporific Room of the Hotel Viva Femmina, one of the newest structures in all of Rome. It rose above old Rome like a spire, straight, unembellished, pragmatically unadorned with the symbols of the past. The Soporific Room was at the very top of the building, providing an unimpeded view of the world for as far as the eye could see, and below was Holy Rome itself — never surveyed because the wider view was indeed more breathtaking. From the penthouse one would naturally have that feeling of elitism that permeates the heart through the eyes. For the view is most assuredly magnificent in its breadth.

Sicola made the ride to the hotel in seclusion.

27

There would be no "Viva il Papa" this day. He was dressed as a simple priest. As he ascended to the heights in an elevator, the air seemed to grow thin. He understood the euphoria that embraced him as the doors parted from the middle like the Red Sea. The air was indeed different, but having been a montanaro in the north of Italy, he soon became adjusted. Yet for just a moment there was this urge to fling off the roman collar, wear a bright Indian tunic, and hear jingling from his neck the copper bangles of the new rosary.

He looked about the Soporific Room, but he saw no nuns. He was ready to leave, believing his information on time and place to be unreliable. It was true that he saw women only, but these could not be nuns. At the long bar the women were lined up abreast (as the phrase goes immodestly), and the air was heavy with a gray haze of cigarette smoke, while the chatter and giggles competed with the clinking of glasses.

It had been many years since he had seen a woman's knee, so he felt a strange queasiness when he saw thighs, a whole sea of thighs, crossed over the tall bar stools. "Holy Mary," he muttered, "this cannot be the place!"

As he was about to turn in haste to leave the room, he was approached by a svelte, long-stemmed woman who seemed to step out of a vodka advertisement, her blonde hair coiffed in a high, lacquered billow with a pasted curl, like an upside-down question mark, stuck to her cheek. Her lips were full and painted with a brush. Sicola was certain that the sheen around her mouth had been heightened by a second coat of high-gloss varnish, but the effect gave the impression that she had been licking her lips with the sheer delight of tasting herself. She wore a blouse that opened in a V to the mammaries as if to permit verification that there were indeed two of them. It had never occurred to Sicola to question the fact until it was called to his attention. She held in her left hand a shallow bowl-shaped glass on a long stem, a skewered olive nestled at the bottom. In her right hand a one-hundred-twenty-millimeter cigarette extended by a six-inch mother-of-pearl holder. She puffed but did not inhale.

"Father!" she said as her thin eyebrows arched in surprise. "How may I help you?"

Before he could think, he blurted out, "Go washa you face!"

She was at first startled, then angry. When Sicola realized that he had offended her, he said meekly, "You mascara is onna you nose."

"Oh!" she said, "I didn't know. You're a dear for telling me. Thank you. I'll go to the powder room directly. But, Father, are you in the wrong room? This is for women only . . . in particular, the Sisters of Mary the Liberator."

He groaned inwardly and thought: Dis-mus'-be-de-place!

A dumpy little woman with her hair in an Afro approached, and even the muu-muu failed to hide her obesity. In the old habit she would have been described as the Mother Superior type, but now she was just another fat woman.

"Sister Helen," she addressed her associate. "What seems to be the problem?"

"No problema," Sicola interjected. "You are also the nun?"

"Yes, Father. I am Sister Brunhilda."

Perfetto! he thought. Wagner would have been pleased. But where is the helmet with the goat horns?

"I am you Papa," he continued.

The rolls of flesh under her chin shook and rippled as she laughed. "What do you mean, my Papa? He has long since departed, rest his soul."

"You no unnerstan'," he pointed out. "*Il Papa*! How you say . . . the *Pope*." Then he held out his hand where the Papal ring could be visible to her.

She viewed it icily, made no move of obeisance, and asked curtly, "Who sent for you?"

It had been difficult for Sicola to go to the nuns, but the hostility now served to increase his discomfort. "You knowa," he stammered nervously, "whenna the mountain a no go to Mohammed . . ." He looked at the huge woman and thought, what a terribly appropriate analogy. The mountain! O, joy, thatsa gooda one!

The simile was not wasted. The jowls did not ripple, but the lips began to quiver. Then, as if an idea began to break through to her, she smiled, turned to the chattering assemblage and called for attention.

"Girls . . . girls . . . let me have your attention, please." The laughter, the tinkling, and the buzz ceased, and she said, "We have an unexpected guest with us today. You'll never guess who it is. Well, dears, I won't keep you in suspense."

She turned toward Sicola with a wave of her fleshy arm and raised her voice an octave, "I give you . . . the Pope."

There was a gentle smattering of applause, as ear-shattering as a trickle of water from a commode whose valve has not completely shut.

"And as long as he is here, I think it would be very nice if he would come to our speakers' platform to answer questions concerning the direction the Church is taking in these post-Vatican II days."

Now the applause was thunderous, and he thought to himself, "You sonofagun. Nowa you gonna get it!"

Sister Brunhilda took him by the arm and led him through the maze of tables on the way to the lectern.

As she did, a young nun wearing a tattered denim skirt, with a guitar strapped around her shoulders and resting on her exposed thighs, sat before a microphone. She began to strum and to sing in a manner most angelic in its untrained, youthful sweetness. He would have bet the Sistine Chapel that she would lead them in "For He's a Jolly Good Fellow." But he wasn't really surprised when they sang, "They'll know we are Christians by our love, by our love. Yes, they'll knew we are Christians by our love."

He threaded his way to the stage and glanced at the young nun, legs straddled, thighs exposed, and thought with no little charity, You better be careful, bambina, or you gonna get in lotsa trouble witha you love.

Sister Brunhilda ushered him to the lectern, then bounced away, pleased with herself. He addressed the convened nuns with all the dignity he could muster and he decided that he would speak to them in the papal "we" so that they would recognize that the Pope spoke *in loco Dei*, that he was really at one with them in heart and spirit.

But he botched it.

"Why a you no come to see me?" he wailed. "You no like a you Papa?"

The audience was hushed. He recognized the boner immediately, and suddenly the severity of his tone softened. He smiled as if it were all a joke and said, "But that's hokay. I come a see you." Then he blessed them and continued.

"We welcome you to Rome. Alla Rome welcomes you. The Churcha, she looksa to you to helpa feed her lambsa, to feed her sheepsa." Then he paused and looked at them piercingly. "Joosta be careful you no feeda the wolves, too."

That did it. In the middle of the room a petite woman smiled blandly and raised her hand. "Holiness, do I infer from that that you disapprove of our life-style? How do you feel about today's nuns?"

He waited for a few seconds as he studied her expression. Was it angry, baiting, academic? Would she be pliable? At length he hunched his shoulders up under his ears, extended his hands palms down, then teetered them as he murmured, "*Mezzo-mezzo.*"

"Letta me ask a question," he went on. "Why you become a nun?"

"To serve God, Holiness."

Holiness, she says two times. Thatsa ni-i-i-ce.

"Good. Now make a believe we no talk about God. We talk about chef in the kitchen, and you are the waitress. Howa you serve a the chef?"

"By catering to the needs of his patrons, by seeing that they are fed without delay."

"Ve-r-r-y good!" he commended her. "But howsa the patron gonna know you the waitress? How come he no say to another patron waiting for place at table, 'Hey, Wallyo! Feeda me!' "

"Because, Holiness, my uniform tells him that that's my role."

"Ah, so-o-o-o-o? How come it's a no sauce for the gander with God's patrons? Howsa people gonna know you nun? Howsa God gonna know you nun?"

"Because, Holiness, He knows what is in my heart."

Thatsa very sharp kid, he thought to himself. "Thatsa good. Very good. He's a know what's inna you heart. Tella me this. You prouda what's inna you heart?"

"Most assuredly, Holiness."

"Then why you no weara you pride? *Mannaggia*! WEARA YOU PRIDE! WEARA YOU HABIT!"

The Sister flushed, and about her the buzzing began anew and rose to a clamor. Sicola was not able to make much of the noise, but occasional words came through, like "male chauvinism," "out of the dead past," "reactionary," "rank conservatism." The din grew louder and he was unable to hear even a few words.

Sister Brunhilda came to the lectern and smiled that ingratiating smile that said, "You boob! Now you've done it. But I knew you would." He had hoped that he could talk about self-abnegation, about losing sight of words like male and female and be concerned with obedience, loyalty, and quiet service, but it was apparent that this was not to be.

Sister Brunhilda hushed her Sisters and thanked him for coming. She took him by the arm with outward deference and humility, but the pull at his elbow was firm.

He was licked, and he knew it. Hell hath no fury . . . he thought to himself. How would he ever be able to reach them now? Only with kindness and charity, he thought.

As he passed the denim-skirted guitarist, he smiled broadly at her, raised his hand in benediction, and touched her head. She bowed demurely.

Then he whispered into her ear, "Go home and putta you clothes on!" Ah, charity, he thought, it is the only way. But he would have to contrive other devices that would show them how deeply he cared and how concerned he was for their vocation, their commitment, and their ultimate sanctity.

He left the hotel in a state of agitation and telephoned Tommaso. Perspiration formed in his heavy eyebrows and cooled him as if menthol had been smeared into the follicles. Tommaso answered the phone, and Sicola gushed out his plan. "Do not question me, Tommaso; simply do as I say. It is to you that I charge the responsibility of seeing that the lights are controlled, and the other mechanical details. I will handle the Sisters. *Sta te buono!*"

Then he hurried off to the Carmelite Monastery in the hills outside Rome where he asked to speak with Mother Ignatius, the superior. The Carmelites had given the world Teresa of Avila, St. Thérèse of the Child Jesus, known as the Little Flower, and hundreds, no, thousands of uncanonized saints. These were the women who, through their contemplation and prayer, their simplicity and sanctity, had controlled the spiritual destinies of whole legions of once-errant souls. They had shut themselves off from the world to pray, neither seeing life outside their walls nor permitting persons in the material world to see them. Even Sicola addressed Mother Ignatius through a veiled and grated screen.

He related to her the story of his constant worries over the direction of the secularized orders; how they were for the most part inhabited by good women intellectually committed to a new life-style, sincere in their belief that God wanted, not the immolation of their personalities, but the ascension of their individuality and their womanhood. He ended with his experience at the Hotel Viva Femmina this very day, and how he had left in abject defeat. He needed help, he pleaded, and the Carmelites could provide it.

"Your Holiness," Mother Ignatius spoke through the screen, "we will pray day and night."

"You do not understand, my child," the Pontiff interrupted. "We need the prayers, yes. But we need more." He outlined his plan to her, and he could sense the astonishment on the holy woman's face.

"But Holiness," she said, deep concern in her voice, "how can we do such a thing? It would be a break with the tradition of centuries."

"My devoted friend," Sicola pleaded firmly, "I will stand before God Himself and assume full responsibility."

"We will do it." Mother Ignatius said firmly after a moment's thought. "And may God help us to do His will."

"Good, Mother! Good! I go now."

Sicola returned to the hotel, where he passed Tommaso in the lobby and winked at him. Then he took the elevator to the Soporific Room and burst in during a discussion of catechesis. Sister Brunhilda was at the lectern, and she spoke of the need to "mold these delicate minds with the social gospel as the highest commitment to the brotherhood of man." Was this not the greatest prayer one could make of his life, she said fervently . . . to do . . . to act . . . to bring joy to the joyless? Then she saw Sicola striding down the aisle to the stage, and she stood dumbstruck, joyless herself.

At length, there was a lessening of the constriction she had felt in her vocal chords, but it was only enough to permit her to gasp, "But wha . . . what is the meaning of this?"

Sicola took a position beside her, then gently, but commandingly, pushed her aside. "As I was saying earlier, my children . . . it is good that you have come to Rome, for Rome is the seat of authority. It is from Rome that God directs His Church." He was smiling, but there was a firmness in his manner, a quiet persuasiveness that combined the tenderness of a loving parent with the deeper wisdom and insight of two millennia.

"There is great need of the love of which you speak. The children of the world cry out for it, and the children of whom I speak are young and old, for they are all of the people of God. But there is no love without law, no law without love, and all law stems from God, who is the beginning of love and the ultimate law. That popes have erred in the political affairs of the world, even in the conduct of their own lives, is open to no question, for it is a fact. But that popes have treasured the deposit of faith and have guided the destiny of the Church without error is equally open to no question. For it, too, is a fact.

"And it is this pope who says: 'Enough!' It is this pope who reaffirms what the Church has known for two thousand years, that all commitment to Christ begins on the knees, and in such a position of humility one begins to see that emergence of self is but a euphemism for abandonment within the Sacred Heart of Jesus. Those who would choose the religious life have opted for sanctity, and true sanctity requires the shedding of one's self so completely as to be lost in the one identity which is God. Lose yourselves, and you find Him. I say to you . . ."

The women had been listening attentively, some rapt and eager, some with condescension, but suddenly all concentration was lost as there was heard the gasps of a hundred nuns. The lights had flickered and then gone out. The room was in total darkness.

Sicola grumbled, "Tommaso, you donkey, you could have let me finish first."

Then the women turned as they heard the *a capella* strains of Gregorian chant coming to them from the foyer near the elevators. Twenty voices blended, high and sweet, rich and resonant, in the chanting of Lauds from the Little Office of the Blessed Virgin Mary. In single file, twenty Carmelite nuns walked in procession, each holding a lighted candle. The tapers flickered and painted golden auras of warm light on faces whose piety made them aware of nothing but their prayer, rising to God in a melody of humble gratitude. And those faces — framed in the soft whiteness of their wimples, the brown veils catching the radiance of the candles — seemed translucent, with a glow coming from within. The world mattered not the least to them, for they were on fire with a love so magnificently consuming that it destroyed concerns that were not centered on the effulgence of Christ's own love.

Their voices rose in the glory of their joy as they praised the Mother of God: "*Beata Dei Genitrix, Maria, Virgo perpetua, templum Domini, sacrarium Spiritus Sancti. . . .* O blessed Mother of God, Mary ever Virgin, temple of the Lord, sanctuary of the Holy Spirit; you alone, without example, were well-pleasing to our Lord Jesus Christ. Pray for the people, mediate for the clergy, intercede for the consecrated virgins."

The procession neared the stage and took a position behind the lectern as the Carmelites continued their chant with a kind of passionate serenity. Their robes rustled, and there was a softness even in the movement of the long beads that hung from their cinctures. Then as they gathered at the center under the proscenium, their candles cast a glow above them that reached up to light a suspended replica of the Pietà. There was a murmur of awe and pleasure from the nuns in the audience.

There it was in summary, it seemed. The body of Christ, broken, bloodless, beaten, held in the comforting arms of a sorrowful mother, a mother sorrowful for the needful pain and death He had suffered for all who came before Him, all who would follow Him. She knew His divinity. She had known it in her womb, and she knew that even now, in her sorrow, He had gone to prepare a place for her, unique in heaven and on earth. But this did not assuage her human torment. She had loved Him with a passion never known by mothers and never again to be known, for hers was complete, undenying, unselfish. Only such a love could have made her worthy to be the co-redemptrix of all mankind. Nothing less than total love is what He demanded, and nothing less than total love is what He gave in return. To emulate her was to emulate perfection. To seek less for those committed to more through their vows was to deny the purpose of the whole divine drama, which bore within tragedy the essence of joy and hope in resurrection. But the Resurrection contained in it only promise. It is total all-consuming love of Him, before all others, that gives reality to the promise fulfilled. And the Pietà hung suspended before them as an invitation to fulfillment.

The Carmelites remained for a few moments, then turned and filed up the aisle to the foyer, and soon they were gone, their chant trailing in the distance, yet leaving the melody behind.

There was silence, stark and penetrating, for five minutes. The lights went on again. The replica of the

Pietà was gone. And so was Sicola. Sister Brunhilda stood at the lectern alone, bowed, somehow at peace. After moments of wordless meditation, she glanced up, then looked out at the sober faces of the nuns before her.

"Sisters," she said, "I think we should go home now."

The Lost Shepherd

Giovanni Martocchio looked across the dinner table at his wife, Jenny, and their three children, a boy aged 4 and two girls, 3 and 2. It was a good family, he thought, and Jenny was a loving wife. He had much to be grateful for, so why this vague anxiety, this haunting sensation of fear that settled sometimes around his intestines, sometimes in his groin?

Then he glanced to his right at their dinner guest, a man he had only recently met. Giovanni had felt something about the man that made them kindred spirits. He wasn't quite sure what the quality was. He just knew that there was an immediate attraction when the man came into his shop one day for some provolone, a loaf of bread, and some red Italian wine. They had chatted about nothing in particular and everything in general, and what should have been a business transaction lasting but a few moments had stretched into an hour.

He was cultured, Giovanni had thought as he sliced the provolone, and serene, yes, serene — even though there was a touch of the comic about him. He seemed to make everything a joke, but there appeared always to be a point to his humor, as if speech was not to be wasted, even when it seemed inconsequential.

The stranger had also a habit similar to his own,

40

the shopkeeper remembered. When Giovanni had picked up the sliced provolone to stack it for wrapping, he had suddenly noted his own way of picking things up by using the last three fingers of each hand and holding the thumb and index finger together in a kind of "o." And, most peculiarly, when Giovanni had handed the package to his customer, he noticed that he, too, held his canonical fingers together. Strange, he thought, it had been years since he had referred to them that way.

Perhaps it was this act of their commonness which had prompted Giovanni to invite the stranger to his home for pasta. He was a man like all men. His clothing was like Giovanni's, simple but clean, perhaps that of a tradesman like himself. He was tall, taller than Giovanni, maybe six feet, and his hair was wavy and full, black except at the sides where it seemed to accent his cultured face with white sideburns and silver streaks in the fullness above his ears. The nose was not at all like Giovanni's, not even Roman for that matter. It was more patrician, somewhat aquiline, and it was that one feature that permitted him to be described as handsome. When Giovanni had asked his name, he had said simply, "Peter." No more.

Now they relaxed at the table. Dinner was over and Jenny had placed anisette before the two men. The rich odor of tomato sauce and cheese and garlic lay heavy on the motionless air. Giovanni extended to Peter an Italian cigar. Peter hesitated for a moment, then said, "Why not!" as his host struck a match to light it. Peter sucked on the black, rope-like cigar and choked and coughed until the tears came to his eyes.

Carefully, with the last three fingers of his right

hand, he placed the cigar in the ash tray before him and then wiped his eyes with his napkin.

"Attsa too much!" he choked out. "Howa you smoke such a rope? It is made from the droppings of the chickens, no?"

"One becomes accustomed," Giovanni smiled. "Perhaps we sit in the parlor and talk, eh? Jenny! We go in other room. You come a soon, too."

Peter towered above Giovanni as they passed through the stringed curtain that separated the dining room from the living room, and went immediately to the chair near the open window where he gulped in great breaths of air. Gradually, the grayness of his face disappeared and the color returned. "I suppose," he sighed, "there are some things one does not wish to become accustomed to."

"So be it," Giovanni said with resignation. "Sometimes a man looks back at his life and says to himself, 'If I had not picked up the first cigar, I would not have become enslaved,' or 'If I had not done that, this would not have developed from it.' It is the way of life, the curse of hindsight."

He stopped for a moment and thought to himself, "Here I go again. It seems like a small thing, but I am beginning to talk to this man of inner things. What is there about him?" But now he had started, and he found himself revealing more and more to Peter.

"Sometimes," he continued, "I often wish that I had not left my former occupation, for example."

"You are not happy, Giovanni?" Peter asked. "Jenny is a good woman; the children are beautiful and well-behaved. Why you say that?"

"It has nothing to do with Jenny and the children. It simply has to do with me. I am — somehow — a fish out of water."

"You do not like the store?"

"Si, I like the store. I like the customers, even the complainers and the hagglers. I like them all, and I see something of the angels in them, even when I am aware of the devil that comes out of them."

"I think, Giovanni, you are a good man."

"You too, Pietro. But I speak only of myself. You are not married?"

"No."

"You have a no interest in women?"

"At one time. *Mamma mia*! At one time, yes."

"How you turn it off?"

"The cold Tiber puts out the hottest fire."

"You take lots of cold swims?"

"Si! In America I hear of a this Mr. Clean. He is as nothing compared to me."

"Why you fight the fire?"

"Because I tenda the sheep, anda the sheep needa me."

"You are a strange man, Pietro. Sometimes you answer me in riddles, and I'ma no understand."

"Onna the lasta day you will understand all things."

"Son of a gun! See — you do it again!"

Peter laughed a quiet, throaty laugh, and Giovanni knew from the gentle eyes that there was warmth and tenderness in the laugh. Then he said gently, "And you, Giovanni, what troubles you? You are, it seems, two people. Sometimes you are like the shepherd, sometimes like the sheep, but when you are the sheep you seem distressed, lost. Letta me helpa you."

"You cannot, my friend. But it is most interesting that you touch nerves when you speak, even in jest. For you see, I too was once a shepherd with a very small flock. I was happy atta first. I would look at my sheep and think that thissa was God's way of sharing with me the joy of heaven. Atta night, I look at the stars and count them, and with eacha one there would be spoken an Ave Maria. For the big stars, a Pater Noster. Of the stars I made a rosary, and I would see the stars as a cincture around the waist of the Queen of Heaven."

Peter listened, and the tiny laugh lines around his eyes were gone. There was a sorrow in Giovanni he wished to assuage. "To make the stars your beads, Giovanni, is high prayer indeed. The Mother of God was pleased, be assured."

"Ah, yes, Pietro. I am assured. But one day I grew tired of this. Perhaps tired is not the proper word. I began to believe that there were other ways to pray, better ways to pray, and they were with deeds, not beads. So I left my sheep in search of a more noble flock, a bigger flock. And I found them. Some of the sheep were black, some were covered with the mange, some bleated all the day in their loneliness. These would be my new flock, and each would become a prayer in action. There was no longer a need to look at the stars and see the Virgin, no longer a need to look at the Virgin and see the Father. Was I not tending the most needful of His sheep? Was this not the highest form of prayer?"

"So you stopped, Giovanni?"

"I stopped, Pietro."

"And soon you left the new flock also?"

"Si, Pietro. I needed no cold baths when the stars were my beads, but now I found a certain delight in the fantasies of the mind. I began to envy the sheep that found their warmth with one another. I saw new life coming from the flock and I wished that I, too, could propagate myself. And in this, too, I saw the infinite mind of God at work, for I reasoned, what greater prayer than the creation of new life? Would I not find more blessedness for this supreme prayer than for the star-studded rosary, for the afflicted flock to which I had next administered? Now it was one and one, not one and many. And in this couplehood there would settle a concentrate of all piety."

"But this, too, failed in its fulfillment for you, Giovanni?"

"This, too, failed."

"Why, Giovanni?"

"Because, Pietro, I think you know very well. Once a shepherd, always a shepherd, according to the order of Melchizedek."

"Si, Giovanni. But at least you can again turn to the stars," Peter said softly. He was no longer the clown, for there was no humor in the piercing pain that struck his breast. He looked at the ashes of the burned-out cigar, then at Giovanni, and there was a catch in his throat as he said, "Remember, my son, we love you still."

Of Rabbits and Asses

Rome had become accustomed to the eccentricities of Sicola, therefore it was not any longer unusual to see him flitting through the streets of the Eternal City riding a Honda motorbike, his white cassock speckled a foot above the hem from his gleeful and deliberate splashing through the puddles of the city.

Old Italian women would watch from the curb, and their expressions of dismay were perennial. They would never get used to the sight of the Pontiff straying from the confines of the Vatican, much less playing the role of a circus chimpanzee. "The clown," they would mutter, "will tear down the Church with these childhood regressions." And it was almost prophetic, this observation, as Sicola, charged with glee, headed for a black, murky pool alongside a group of chattering wastrels who played *Morra*, a guessing game of numbers with the fingers, as they shouted and argued, "*Cinque!*" or "*Due!*" or any given number that made the competition so enormously emotional. The muddy water gave way to his zoom-zoom in a spraying V, covering the young men with a fetid shower. As he drove away, Sicola turned his head to enjoy the soggy fury of the men. One of them curved the index finger of his right hand and bit at the knuckle, while with his left hand all his fingers but one were grasped in a fist, the second finger pointing upward in a recognizable sign of defiance. Another slapped at the junction of his upper arm and forearm as his fisted hand swung upward. The Pope read the obscenity on his lips.

Sicola grinned with satisfaction, and thought, "You *cafoni!* Now taste the filth you speak with your tongues."

He wove through the traffic to the beep of horns and the animated gestures of motorists. At the intersection, a *vigile* stood on his platform directing traffic and exchanging insults with drivers. He held up a gloved hand for traffic to "*alt*" on the street being traveled by Sicola, but the Pope continued through the intersection, careening and jazzing his engine as he narrowly missed the Fiat coming toward him, ultimately to slither off the unbalanced bike on his tailbone. The policeman blew his whistle, threw down his hat and stomped on it in anger as he approached the Pope, who rubbed his elbows and smoothed his aching gluteus muscles with a gentle massage.

The policeman, in a banty-rooster strut that seemed to reincarnate Mussolini, strode toward the soiled Sicola, his hands on his hips and his chin jutting out beneath lips that turned down in an air of resigned superiority.

"Ah'm a gonna get it now," Sicola thought to himself.

The officer finally reached Sicola, and he seemed to take pride in his composure, his air of authority, and his detached objectivity. But he was a boiling kettle, and his control suddenly deserted him. His face puffed, his eyes grew large beneath his shaggy brows, and Sicola could almost see the steam jetting through his ears and his nostrils. "Idiot!" he screamed.

"Keepa you toy forra St. Peter's Square. Get offa my street."

"Peace, my brother," Sicola smiled amiably. "Do not speak to me of excommunication. It is a tool no longer in favor."

"Attsa whatta you think!" the policeman screamed. "Inna my house, you breaka the law, and you getta you fanny slapped."

"Gooda point," murmured the mollified Pope. "Mebbe you come a my house a some time and tella my people."

"What I tella you people?" the policeman asked, beginning to see possibilities in this conversation.

"Tell about the law."

Now a crowd had gathered around the Pope and the policeman, among whom were the spattered, angry young men who had been victimized by the papal cycle. They intruded into the argument and their hatred was undisguised. "We are the law," they said to the policeman.

"Who'sa you?" the mystified policeman asked.

"We are from The Committee of Forty-One," the leader said, "and we say that Sicola is guilty of doing injury to us, and to alla the people. Putta him away."

"Why you say that, my sons?" the Pope asked in mock innocence and wonder.

"Because a you sit onna you throne and you tell us how to play the game, but you never playa youself. Thatsa why."

"Gimme for instance."

"Well, I tella you, Mister Poop."

"Ah, no, my son. It issa 'Pope.' "

"Hokay, uppa you poop, Pope!"

"*Mannaggia*! Whatta kinda talk you calla this?"

The policeman's head bobbed from side to side, trying to follow the argument. "*Basta*! Enough!" he blurted. "Whatsa this to do witha traffic? What am I got to do witha you fight? I'm a got trouble enough of my own." And trouble he had indeed, for by now traffic in the intersection was jammed; horns blared, and temperaments flared. In desperation he turned to the crowd, blew his whistle and screamed, "*Sta te zite!*"

But quiet they would not be. It was not within the temper of an excited Italian to remain quiet when he could be a part of the excitement. Motorists left their cars and descended upon the small circle of combatants in the center of the intersection. The cacophony of an Italian multitude without order or unison is like a thousand bells chiming with overlapping bongs.

The Chairman of the Committee sensed that he would now have Sicola where he wanted him. The crowd would most certainly be on his side. He ascended the officer's traffic podium and shouted above the babble of the crowd.

"This, my friends, is *Il Papa,* Pope Sicola. He chooses to leave the safety of the Vatican to be among us. Therefore, must he not answer to us for the crimes he commits in the name of God?"

"Si . . . si . . . si!" the crowd shouted in concert for the first time. It would not have surprised Sicola if they had answered, "Barabbas!"

"From his womanless apartment," the Chairman shouted, "he writes letters to us and he say, 'Footsie is a no-no. Bambinos, a yes-yes. But footsie is a yes-yes if you play for bambinos.! Now what kind of talk issa that? I ask you. He say, hokay, you play, butta you gotta play roulette. You wanna play roulette? I'ma no wanna play roulette. I'm a joosta wanna play! Play! Play! Thatsa nice. Joosta play!"

"Si . . . si . . . si!" the mob shouted.

The Pope stood in the center of the clamorous, surging circle, his head bowed, his arms to his side. He thought, "Next, I will hear the words, 'Crucify him!' "

It is a truism that truth is stranger than fiction — and who would say this is fiction? — for as the Pope began to feel that all was lost, a giant rabbit, walking on its hind legs in human fashion and muttering excitedly, stepped from the crowd into the vortex of the circle of hate. The figure stood three feet above the crowd, a most imposing figure. That so large a rabbit should appear walking as a man was, in itself, startling, but that he should speak was so astounding as to bring silence to the crowd.

They drew back, then froze, wondering what hostility lay buried in the breast of this giant remnant of prehistoric man. Was he there to consume them as if they were mere cabbages in his patch? They were unprepared for so gentle a monster, it turned out, but their fear made them better prepared to listen . . . to a rabbit with a Sicilian accent, no less.

"Go backa to you hutch," he exclaimed to the awestruck Romans, "and throw away you notions that the deeds of rabbits are for the birds. The time from conception to birth is nine months for humans, but for us it is but twenty-eight days. Have we taken over the world? I say, no. If you do not outnumber us, you control us. Perhaps, even, we *do* outnumber you, but do we drive your automobiles and pollute your air? Do we build our hutches forty stories into the sky? Do we deposit our droppings into your rivers and oceans? Let this man be." And with this, he took

Sicola by the hand and walked him through the crowd, which parted as if Moses himself had divided them for his path.

Struck dumb, the Italians stood and watched as the nine-foot rabbit and the six-foot Sicola walked arm in arm off into the distance. They turned a corner, and both the rabbit and Sicola slapped their thighs and bent over choking in their laughter.

"Gooda work, nice a job, Tommaso," the Pope finally giggled to his faithful secretary.

"The rabbit and the jackasses, we should call the next encyclical, your Holiness," Tommaso grinned, skinning out of his warm costume, and stepping off his stilts.

Sicola couldn't miss the opportunity. He stepped back into the street where the mob stood frozen and speechless. With his open palm and a twist of the wrist, as if he were scooping up a section of air in a quick jerk, he shouted: "Eh-h-h! That for you, donkeys!"

Then it was Sicola's turn to freeze in his slippers. For the picture that confronted him as he said "donkeys" amazed even him.

Protruding from the heads of the people in the crowd were ears a full foot long. They tried to curse him, but all that could be heard was the braying of many asses.

This is how The Committee of Forty-One came later to be known as "The *Ass*ociation."

A Carbuncle on the Neck of Humanity

Alfredo S. Smegma was the publisher of *La Parata dell'Erotica*, Italy's most widely read (or looked at) magazine, whose lubricity was known to titillate even the Prime Minister, though he was given to hide each issue under his mattress. Journals of public affairs ranked far below it in circulation, and the charts gave ample proof of it, proclaiming the dominance of Smegma's magazine like a phallic symbol. The circulation of religious magazines was, of course, a mere speck in the sea of printer's ink that flowed about Italy's readers.

To now, Smegma flicked at any threat of moral suasion on the part of the Catholic periodicals as one would brush a fly from the nose. "They are of no consequence," he was heard to tell one of his lieutenants who called to his attention a particular piece in *L'Osservatore Romano*. "Who reads these things?" A fistful of traditionalists in an age of liberals, and those who read are silent, and even if they had a voice, it is a voice without power. Smegma is king."

At least this was his view before Sicola, chatting extempore in audience, had delivered a scathing reproach of eroticism in general and *La Parata dell'Erotica* in particular. In his uniquely discursive manner, he had spoken of the curiosity of the young and the frustrated passions of the old, of their link with the depravity of hell through the ill-conceived media emphasis on the salacious, the lewd, the pornographic. "And," Sicola continued, his voice rising in a fury that sprayed spittle before him, "there is that cyst, that carbuncle on the neck of humanity, Alfredo S. Smegma, whose initials bespeak his position in the hierarchy of the animal kingdom. It is he who sucks at the blood of our children, weakening their wills, enervating their purity in the face of his explicit delineations of that which should be a private affair even among the sinful — and a sacrament of married love among the chaste children of God."

The Pope's words were carried throughout the world, for it was one thing to speak in generalities and quite another to single out one man as the personification of evil. Smegma was distressed, not so much because he feared a drop in readership, but because Sicola was imputing to him a depravity which was not, he believed, wholly warranted. Did not his magazine attract the writers who were, indeed, the very cream of literati in literate society? Were not these pieces contributing to the world of letters? And as for the pictures, Sicola was simply behind the times. Sex was no longer what the Church had painted it to be. Now it was open, an expression of nature itself, which the Church continued to use as its basis for morality. Oh, the clown! He would expose his circulation list and show that the magazine was mailed even to priests, some in the Vatican itself. It was time for a confrontation with this man who played God. Smegma would not tolerate this affront to journalism and to freedom of the press. He would write to him this very day and establish his position and, moreover, would print his letter in the next issue of *Erotica*, with all due promotion in advance of publication, of course.

"Take a letter, Miss Loveless . . . baby," he said to his secretary.

"*Si Signore . . . caro*," she replied in a deep-throated voice, quivering with excitement in the very depths, even beyond the uvula. Was it a joy she derived from the sound of her lover's voice, or was it from a sense of satisfaction in knowing that the Pope would soon be exposed for the meddlesome buffoon he was? It is uncertain. What was certain was that she sat, her legs crossed, and raised the pencil to her lips as she waited for Smegma.

"Dear Sir," he began. "It is with a certain distaste that I reply to the statements you have made in your recent audience concerning this publication as well as the inaccurate description of my function as its editor and publisher. Your personal references to me as a 'carbuncle on the neck of humanity' was a most libelous statement, and unless an apology is forthcoming, you may be certain, sir, that you will be hearing shortly from my attorneys, whose talents in court are without peer, and whose arguments time and again have caused the highest court in the land to look with disdain on those who would inhibit the liberty of a liberty-loving people, especially in such matters appertaining to freedom of expression. I will spare no expense, sir, for it is within my means to purchase that which serves me best, and be assured that victory will be mine, for I and this magazine represent all that is truth in society while you, sir, represent all that would return man to the darkest depths of the Middle Ages.

"It has been said, in whispers and without evidence, it is true, that you have been known to take leave of the Vatican for long periods so that you can mingle incognito among your people. Certainly, these excursions must have been the occasion for your enlightenment as to what is taking place in the world today. What is transpiring before your very eyes, sir, is a vindication of one of your nobler spirits, whom your Church has seen fit to banish to the dungeons of theological odium. For, sir, you are aware that this angel of light saw what you have not seen, namely, that as man has evolved and continues to evolve to a higher state, so, too, does morality evolve. And I submit, sir, that what is occurring in our times is man releasing the shackles that bound him, and now he rises to sing paeans of praise to God in the fulfillment of the selfhood of man. For that which God created is noble in its essence, in its use, and in its display. Shame, shame, shame! That you should seek to inhibit man in the expression of the fullness of his love for his fellowman, that you should look upon nature as foul, that you should see in the efforts of this publication a perversity, is to look into the face of creation and to spit upon it.

"I am enclosing herewith a prepublication copy of a forthcoming issue of *Erotica*. I would call your attention to the young man and the young woman in the picture series beginning on page 53 of this issue. See with what tenderness he embraces her. And take note, sir, of the ecstasy that overcomes her. She is limp before him, her eyes closed in the filmy dream world of her love. Their bodies glisten with the perspiration of their passionate love for each other. The touch? It is not enough for them. The kiss? It is only a canapé before the sumptuous repast that calls to them. They will be restless until they give to each other the fullest expression of their love, a mechanism created not by this magazine but by God Himself. Now you have it in the final photograph. Fulfillment. Complete. Rapturous. The final step. Heaven! And, sir, let it be known that the young man in the photo sequence spent some time in the minor seminary, while the lass came from good, hardy peasant stock, churchgoers on numerous occasions. This, sir, is what you demean.

"Apologize, or suffer the consequences.

"Yours,

"Alfredo S. Smegma"

Sicola received Smegma's letter with its enclosure. It was Tommaso who handed it to him, all the while dousing the envelope with holy water. "As is my custom, Holiness, I took the liberty of reviewing the contents of this package that generates so much heat with so little light. I hesitate even to subject your very human passions to it. Because, however, Signor Smegma raises points of some importance and because the enclosed magazine is a further illustration in support of his letter, I am duty-bound to submit it to you with a prayer to St. Michael for protection against this instrument of Satan."

Sicola took the package silently and, distrusting his own emotions, which would be improper for Tommaso to witness, he merely said, "Leave me alone to study it."

"I understand, Holiness," Tommaso replied as he turned and left the room.

Sicola first read Smegma's letter, and he was happy for the privacy which permitted him to swear under his breath so that only he would hear. That God heard him also he was aware, but, he reasoned, his swearing must be as nothing compared to the curses from the tongue of God Himself. Then he studied the article on page 53, and thereafter Tommaso, in his anteroom, heard the steady s-s-s-h-h-h of the hard, needlespray shower from which Sicola could be heard to emit a very loud "BR-R-R-R-R-R!" as the cold water pierced his skin with a thousand stabbing pricks. He dressed quietly and returned to his desk, where, once again, he picked up the letter and studied it, but not before burying the magazine under a pile of papers. Then he grasped the pen in its holder before him and began to write.

"Dear Signor Smegma," he began. "We have before us your recent letter defending yourself against our criticisms of you and your publication. There is no philosophical nor theological critique we could give you that would alter your life-style, no objective rationale that would have the slightest effect on the thrust of your magazine. This is not to say that such arguments do not exist; it is only to say that one does not vanquish the devil with logic, for there is no predisposition to belief. He is defeated only by prayer, only by holiness and sanctity in one's daily life, only by creating in the soul such a longing for God that no bad seeds can be permitted to take root, only by entwining one's own will with the One Will. That this may not at some time happen to you, I would not predict. That it is most unlikely, given your present imprisonment, I would not hesitate to aver.

"But the sin of Smegma would be a sin committed in privacy were it not for the fact that there is a greater sin that stalks the macrocosmic soul of humanity. Because you operate in concert with Satan, you have been made aware that his evil is so great that it has permeated the world, even among those good souls who are unaware of his influence. Were you not to succeed in your work, it would not lessen your sin, but your sin is made greater by its effects, just as God's goodness is made more knowable by His effects.

"We invite you, therefore, to consider that no retraction will be forthcoming from the Vatican. You may do as you wish in the matter of your threatened suit. But you are urged to bear in mind always that there is a Judge greater than any who might be asked to rule on the matter of libel. It is to Him that the Church is bound, and it is to Him that you will be asked one day to present your case. We have no doubts concerning the outcome of this confrontation.

"We also return your courtesy and enclose herewith a rosary blessed solely with you in mind. It would be too much to expect you to use it, just as we have no use for your enclosure, but it will tend to support this letter in much the same way that your enclosure supports your letter. It will proclaim to you, sir, that this is our sword. Bow before it.

"Yours in Christ,
"Innocent XIV"

When Smegma received Sicola's letter he was furious. "The fatuous bull!" he exploded. "All he does is pontificate. He will not argue with me. One would think a Churchman who has been so careful to document doctrine would do me the courtesy of providing arguments with chapter, case and verse to substantiate his stand. He treats me as one not worth saving. Is it not his job as Supreme Pontiff to give as much attention to a single soul as to the multitude of souls?"

His secretary, at first elated, now seemed perplexed. "But, Alfredo, my dear, you seem so disap-

pointed — as if you seek the honor of personal conversion by the Pope himself. I understand your anger,
but I do not understand the reasons you give for your
anger.''

Smegma picked up the beads Sicola had sent
him, studied them carefully as he ran them through
his fingers. He looked at the crucifix and noted that
the workmanship on it, as well as on the beads themselves, was extraordinary. They were not cheap beads
turned out by the hundreds. This set was handcrafted
with care and affection, and perhaps very old. There
was, at least, some honor in this. Then he tossed them
into his shirt pocket where he kept his cigarettes, and
turned to Miss Loveless. "Don't be ridiculous! I
wrote him a learned letter, referring to the new
process theology, and one would expect that he would
provide me with a theological treatise in return. In ad-
dition, he as much as tells me that I am controlled totally and completely by the devil. If I were not educated, urbane, objective, I would be frightened by such a
thought, but as you can see, I am not. He only irri-
tates me more and increases my anger.''

"But why?" the woman asked him. "You have
no need of him. Your wealth cannot be affected by
him. You prosper. You will continue to prosper. And
remember, my darling, you have me.''

"Of course, you are right," Smegma retorted with
irritation. "He cannot hurt me, and as you say, I have
you, at least for the moment — until you tire of me.''

"Nonsense," she pouted. "I shall never tire of
you, *tesoro*, though I will admit that something troubles your performance of late.''

"This is precisely what I meant. It is as if one
becomes lost in the page on page of flesh that passes
across the mind, as if there is a satiety that strikes one

not entirely according to the rules of the Marquis of Queensbury. It is as if the desire of the mind is short-circuited. What has it been like for you, my pet?"

"Not as before, bambino. But it will pass. Meanwhile it is kind of you to allow me my excursions with the others. It is good that you understand my needs for fulfillment."

"Understand? Hah! Only too well. But there is no enjoyment in understanding." He pounded at the desk top, and lay back limply in his chair, as his eyes looked beyond the walls of the office, reflecting a moment out of the past. "Often," he said dreamily, "I recall Gina. She was what Sicola would call a 'good girl,' so pious, so eternally peaceful, so ravishingly beautiful. I was a virgin and I was overcome by her desirability, so aloof and unattainable, that I wanted her desperately. I failed! Oh, how I failed. She would not listen to me. She looked at me with such tenderness, such love, and yet such hurt when I did all but tear off her clothing. I would not, I could not bring myself to violate her, and I never saw her again. But it is interesting that I have seen her many times in my mind since, and most especially at my moments of greatest triumph with you. But of late, even that has not returned me to the full vigor of masculinity."

"It is no compliment to know, Signore," she said icily, "that you see someone else when you look at me."

"Why does it disturb you? We both know that as long as the empire grows, you will continue to love me. No?"

She turned her back to him and said nothing, as if she were hiding the hurt on her face, but it failed to move Smegma.

"Enough of romance!" he shouted as he sat forward in his chair again. "There's this matter with Sicola, and how to best him. Ah! I have it! One cannot do in a letter what he can do face to face. I will request an audience, and we will meet in the ring, so to speak." Then he leaned back in the chair again and reached in his breast pocket for a cigarette. His fingers touched the beads for a moment, and he stroked them absentmindedly as he felt an emptiness and a hunger once again for Gina. "You were so lovely," he thought. "So damnably and beautifully chaste."

Sicola fingered Smegma's request for a private audience and smiled at Tommaso. "So the devil has come to raise me up to his mountain with promises that all will be mine if I but bow down and worship him. Perhaps he will come in his birthday suit that I may observe how he lets it all hang out, or perhaps he will approach the Vatican lance in hand as he rides a great black steed to do battle for his fallen angels. It will be interesting to see. We will meet with him, Tommaso."

"I will inform him today, Holiness."

"Request also that Miss Loveless, she of the lascivious larynx and amorous alimentary canal, remain at home among her throat sprays."

Tommaso paled and exclaimed, "Holiness! How do you know of such things?"

"Tommaso . . . does Macy's tell Gimbels? It is enough to know that there is a Pope who knows. Go!"

Smegma could not understand the feeling of excitement that seemed to overcome him as he entered the Vatican. It reminded him of the time when, as a boy, he was asked to recite a passage from Dante for Cardinal Guardino. He remembered with what awe and trepidation he had contemplated the look of a prince of the Church, and on him a mere peasant child. The Cardinal, too, had been a peasant, he was told, so there was nothing to fear. But he trembled, all the same, and he was sure that the Cardinal would detect the quaver in his voice. So, he thought, here he was now approaching the Pope himself. It was said that Sicola had also come from peasant stock; no doubt he had been sired by a bull, he smiled to himself through his nervousness. Well, this is what he had wanted. A confrontation. And now he was here. He would argue that the Church had been so preoccupied with procreation as a part of the marriage bond that it had lost sight of the pleasurable aspects of marriage that need have no tie to increasing the population of heaven, or of hell for that matter. That's where it all had started, he would say. And when mankind began to consider the Church wrong in this view, then it was only a small leap to contraception, to the pill, and to a whole new enlightenment about sex itself. This was proof, indeed, of man's ethical and moral maturation, of his evolving soul. Given these initial premises as being false, then it was also false that premarital and extramarital sex, incest, profligacy were merely extensions of this belief. And if all sex was permissible outside of marriage, then its promulgation was equally valid. And, moreover, if this was also true, then there need be no sense of responsibility for the accidents of profligacy, which was birth. For if one were answerable solely to oneself in such matters of morals, was there not a further implication that one was the owner of one's own body and all rights impinging thereon, including not only the right to bear no children but to destroy those children *in utero* who were not intended to flow from seminal pleasure. The outline grew in his mind, and who was to say that this meeting would not result in a new encyclical abrogating all those which preceded it? The passion for debate became aroused within him. All he needed was a strong punch line, some startling statement at the end of his talk that would underscore his sincerity with quotable memorability. He saw himself before Sicola, slapping the Pontiff's desk for emphasis as he said, "*These things I believe so deeply that I would be willing to distribute the magazine to the public without charge!*" He mulled the line over in his mind for a moment, then quickly discarded it. There had to be another way of summing up, he thought. Doubtless it would come to him at the time.

Suddenly he became aware of his leather heels making a click-clack on the marble floors of the Vatican corridor, and he came out of his reverie, conscious of others passing him in the hall. Approaching him with a graceful stride, and a muffled swishing of her black habit, came a nun whose apparel in itself surprised Smegma. They still wear the habits? he asked himself. As she drew closer he felt a surge of tenderness, a vague feeling of familiarity. Was this, too, a hearkening back to childhood memories of nuns who taught him? No, no, he muttered, there was something else. Something in the expression, so peaceful, so uninvolved with secular matters, so radiantly contented, and all of this showing in just a portion of her face which was cropped close for emphasis by her veil. He knew her, but how? . . . from where? She came close to him now, and he stopped and touched her arm on the pretext that he needed directions to the Papal Chambers. As he touched her, he became more certain that he knew her. He looked into her face. Absolutely beautiful, he thought. Marvelously formed. So white and clear. The eyes, blue and gentle. And no nun should have lips so sweetly ripe. "Can you direct me to . . . ?" he started, then stopped and simply looked into her eyes with an expression of unembarrassed questioning.

"Hello, Alfredo," she smiled. "I would know you anywhere. Even after all these years. It is so good to see you."

It was the voice, like a gentle breeze rustling chimes in a summerhouse. Now he knew. And his eyes filled with pleasure and longing. "Gina . . . Gina . . . Gina. It is indeed you. And you are a nun."

"Yes, my dear Alfredo. But it is not Gina any longer. It is Sister Maria Goretti. Come, let us sit for a few moments."

"My God in heaven, Gina," he said as they sat on the plain marble bench nearby, "how I have remembered you, recalled you night and day in these long years." He took her hand in his and she made no move to restrain him or to withdraw it. She merely smiled with that openness, that manner of inner generosity, which had but a friendly spirit to share with people, and she was sharing it again with Alfredo. She asked about his career, and he dismissed it as of no importance. "Only an editor," he said. He parried her question concerning the name of the magazine. "It is only about you I wish to speak, my dear Gina. My life has been of no consequence."

She spoke of her work as a teacher, then as a writer of children's stories and ultimately of her assignment to the Vatican in the Office of Catechetical Studies. "So that is all there is, Alfredo. Now I am just Sister Maria Goretti, and most happy, I assure you."

"How did you happen to choose the name Maria

Goretti? Was she not the child-saint who was mur-
dered in an attempted rape and who prayed for him
who assaulted her before her death?"

"Yes, Alfredo. The same."

"But, Gina, do not tell me! You? Were you
raped?"

"Heavens, no, Alfredo. But there was one who
wished to do so one time. And at that moment I was
aware of graces in such abundance that it did not happen. Indeed, the graces were so great as certainly to
have touched him also. Shortly I entered the convent
and took this name. Not a day has passed — not a
night, not a Mass, not a rosary — when I have failed
to pray for him. I pray unceasingly that he will be
united in his lifetime with the Sacred Heart of Jesus
and will give to God his great talent."

"Gina . . . Gina . . . Gina. What can I say to you
after all these years? That I am sorry? There seems little need to do so. You are the happy one. While I?
Well, dear soul, the graces of which you speak did not
touch me, not at all."

"It is a cliché, Alfredo, that God works in
strange ways. But it is also a truth. You were, indeed,
touched with graces. You do not know it. But I know
it. There is pain in your eyes, Alfredo. The lines on
your face tell me that it has not been easy. Perhaps you
have followed the wrong star, or perhaps it was the
right star whose pursuit has left you its victim. I do
not know. But of one thing I am most certain. You
are singularly loved by God. He merely waits for you
to return His love. . . . But I must go now, dear Alfredo. All the days of my life you are with me in my
prayers for the one thing that matters most to you
and to Him . . . that peace of the soul which is fully
possessed by Christ." She grasped his hand in both of

hers, squeezed it tightly, and said softly, "Goodbye, Alfredo. God bless you."

Then she was gone. Alfredo sat on the marble seat exhausted, wanting very much to let the tears flow out, yet restraining them. There was a tightness in his throat that came close to choking him, and around his chest he felt a band that tightened and relaxed and tightened again. He reached for his cigarettes, and as he removed the pack the Pope's rosary beads, entwined about the package, spilled out on his lap. He replaced the cigarettes in his pocket and held the beads in his hand as he walked down the long corridor to the Papal Chambers.

Tommaso greeted him, and Alfredo announced quietly, "Alfredo Smegma to see His Holiness." Tommaso ushered him to Sicola's office and closed the door, secluding the Pope and the apostate.

Tommaso, now back at his desk, leafed through a mass of papers stacked there, trying not to listen for sounds coming through the door. Suddenly his head jerked with a start as he heard the explosive voice of Sicola coming to him as if it would shake the whole building. "Confession? Confession? *You* want to go to confession? *Mannaggia*! Holy Cow!"

Too Much With the World

Sicola sat on the park bench and looked out over the rolling green knolls laced with gravel paths. He stretched his legs and threw his arms over his head, loosening the taut muscles in his midsection, then he relaxed again into a slump on the bench. The sun sank into his pores like soothing water in a tepid tub bath. It would be pleasant to doze, but then he would miss the glorious spectacle of a Roman spring, which announced to him that life was indeed an unfathomable miracle.

A child of four or five played with a puppy in the soft grass, while off to his side his young mother lay prone, squinting from the reflected light bouncing off the open book she was reading. The child muttered unintelligible commands at the dog with feigned and practiced irritability, then he swooped it up in his arms and nuzzled it joyously.

The very music of God's glory was in the air, for above Sicola and off to his right there was the happy twitter of birds, and as he watched, he was warmed and pleased by the takeoffs and return flights of a mother bird to her nest. Each time she came with a morsel her head would bob and dip into the teeming, chirping life of the nest. Once Sicola chortled as the hungriest, or perhaps the most assertive, of the brood stretched above the rim of the nest like a ball on a rubber band, its beak opened in a wide Y stuck into its bare, ball-like head and its elastic neck secured firmly to its base in the nest. In a mock representation of the birdling in the act of swallowing, Sicola said aloud, "Gulp!"

Suddenly he was aware of the young man beside him. True, he had been there throughout Sicola's preoccupation with ornithology and emerging life, but the soporific sun and the projection of his thoughts to the life around him seemed to exclude all awareness of things immediate or proximate.

The man chuckled at Sicola's emphasized gulp, for he too had been studying the in-flight delivery service that was as frequent as the courses of an Italian meal, a ritual more than a formal necessity.

"Ah!" the man smiled, "the bird is on the wing."

"No," Sicola replied, "the wing is on the bird."

"That is a very old joke, Signore."

"I am a very old man, my young friend, and I keep hoping that one day I will meet a man who has never heard it. But it is not to be," he sighed, undisturbed.

"You must keep trying, then," the man grinned, "and one day you will succeed."

"Yes," Sicola agreed, "I will, indeed. If one tries hard enough, whether it is for heaven or hell, he can be assured of getting that for which he seeks. Let us hope that more seek to play among the harps than before the furnace."

"Now you turn philosophical, Signore. I suppose spring does this to some."

"You mistake philosophy for another attempt at humor, for which I seem to have no gift today. Yet I do not retract it. So. We call it philosophy to please you, but may it endure into the fall and winter also, lest you continue to confuse it with the flow of sap."

"I have offended you?"

"Sir, you are singularly without humor, and I begin to be less offended by your lack of it as I recognize it more. Look at the brightness of this day, feel the gentle warmth of the sun, which brings just a trace of sweat to the skin, only to be soothed by the caressing breeze that cools in a counterbalance to the sun. How can one be offended over trivial affairs on such a day? And does it not induce in you the slightest sense of giddyness that permits even feeble attempts at humor? I twit you, my boy."

The young man flushed slightly. "I am sorry, sir. I suppose your reference to heaven and hell, though spoken innocently enough, touched a chord within me which does not vibrate to the pitch of religion. My métier is science and I find your allusion — and its implications — incompatible with observations, which are all I can trust, you see."

"Ah, so you are a scientist?"

"Yes, sir, Jean-Paul Bouchard is the name."

"Simon Petrus," Sicola introduced himself. "Then you are an admirer of Albert Einstein, yes?"

"Most certainly!"

"But you do not claim to be greater than he?"

"No, of course not."

"That is good. So perhaps you can learn from him, then. For it was he who said, 'Science without religion is lame; religion without science is blind.' Does this not permit you to look at the nest in the tree and observe that which falls within the province of science, while seeing also that there would be no science without creation, which is reflected in the birdlings as well as the child on the grass? . . . Now, *Mannaggia*, you have made me turn serious, when that which occupied my thoughts most was light and buoyant."

"The word 'creation' disturbs me, Signore. With all respect to Dr. Einstein, I recognize the need for man to manufacture religion because something within him cries out for it, and therefore he sets up an ordered process of thought in harmony with his desire, but for me, I do not have need to establish such an ethical and moral order. I see man as having evolved from a cell, ever-expanding and dividing and joining into a complexity of cells which became known as fish, horse, bird, man."

Sicola threw his hands up in seeming despair. "How can one attempt to play the comic with one who persists in playing Hamlet? You are too much with the world, and for such a one the denial of the supernatural finds a home. Seek instead to develop that sense of intellectual intuition in which the essence of Being arrives on a beam of light, not from without but from within. You wish for the 'why' of creation to be demonstrable as scientific phenomena, through the eye, the touch, the sound, the smell of experience, and because you seek on a material plane, you are blind to what lies behind it."

Sicola reached into his breast pocket and drew out small note cards on which it was his habit to write those memorable passages of books he had been reading. "Let me read you something on this topic from the scholar Frithjof Schuon:

"When intellectual intuition is operative, there is no problem of Being, and assertions considered to be 'summary' and 'dogmatic' are in fact sufficient; but when the intellect is paralyzed, every effort to define 'Being' is vain, for it is obvious that one cannot define what one does not know. If for some people the idea of 'being' is 'the most obscure there is,' this is certainly nothing to cause surprise; but what is disturbing is when blindness poses as light, or as 'leading to light,' which amounts to the same thing. Intellectual intuition cannot be created where it is absent from the essence of the individual, but it can be actualized where its absence is only accidental, otherwise it would be senseless to speak of it; knowledge, as St. Augustine maintained, with Plato and many others, is not something that is added from outside; teaching is only the occasional cause of the grasping of a truth already latent within us. Teaching is a recalling, understanding a recollection. In the intellect, the subject is the object, 'being,' and the object is the subject, 'knowing' whence comes certitude."

"That is all very well and good, but I am afraid that 'intellectual intuition,' as your friend describes it, is fundamentally absent from me; therefore it cannot be actualized."

"I agree," Sicola muttered. "A *cafone* is a *cafone* is a *cafone* is an intellectual *cafone*."

"That is a word I do not understand. *Cafone*?"

"Let it pass," Sicola said dryly.

"Let us try anew, my bench companion. For too long men have argued Creation versus Evolution, and the arguments are all material arguments. That Signor Darwin's theory remains only that, a theory, that there remain gaps in the evolving ladder of the amoeba to man, is generally understood and accepted. But it is not on this level of experience data to which we must address ourselves. One must not, then, probe into exterior matters when the answers he seeks lie within himself."

"Does this not strike you as ridiculous, Signor Petrus? How can I study science from within when science is based upon observable phenomena not heretofore known by the observer?"

"Si. This is true, if all we are interested in knowing about is the material world. But we seek to find the commonality between the material and the immaterial, between the accident of evolution and the design of creation, between the absence of God in the universe and the presence of God in the universe. As a scientist, you owe it to yourself to overlook nothing. It is your very rationalism which limits your vision, for again it is Schuon who tells us that 'there is a close relationship between rationalism and science; the latter is at fault not in concerning itself with the finite, but in seeking to reduce the Infinite to the finite, and consequently in taking no account of Revelation, an attitude which is, strictly speaking, inhuman. . . . A science of the finite cannot legitimately exist outside of the spiritual tradition.' "

The young man laughed. "That is so much mumbo-jumbo. The mystical is not a factor in scientific investigation."

"What a pity. What cannot be touched has as much reality as that which can be touched. 'A scientist,' Schuon tells us, 'may be capable of the most extraordinary calculations and achievements but may at the same time be incapable of understanding the ultimate causality of things; this amounts to an illegitimate and monstrous disproportion, for a man who is intelligent enough to grasp nature in its deepest physical aspects ought also to know that nature has a metaphysical Cause which transcends it."

"I do not humor you, my elder, so let me ask how one begins to develop this intellectual intuition about which your philosopher speaks with such conviction."

"First, *desire* it."

"That simple?"

"That simple."

"We seem to go back to what started our discussion, Signore. You said that if one tries hard enough, whether it is for heaven or hell, he can be assured of getting that for which he seeks. And that, I would suspect, presupposes desire."

Sicola smiled as he studied the man. "You begin to prove the accuracy of Signor Schuon's observation. The absence of intellectual intuition in you is *only* accidental; therefore, it *can* be actualized."

"But how can one receive a desire for which there is no *a priori* desire?"

"How do you know that there is no *a priori* desire? I submit that there is within each man the desire to know the truth. As a scientist, you are already committed to it. This being a corollary of the human state, then one accepts the fact that desire has fallen into a state of encystment, encrusted, as it were, by material preoccupations. I do not now make jokes when I say that the crust is removed very simply. *Desire* desire! Desire to know with your whole being, with your mind, your heart, and your soul. Then you will begin to know. Then you become a pilgrim on the road of eternal knowledge."

"This will be most difficult for me, Signor Petrus. I have been too trained in the scientific method."

"Do not abandon it. It will become a tool in your ascension. You will not now accept what I tell you, but it will happen. As the strength of your desire grows, as you begin to seek to make compatible the forces of the material world with the higher, unseen forces of nature, there will arise within you a compulsion to cross new boundaries. You will strain to do so, not always with success, and in your failure to reach beyond the material you will begin to pray, not verbally, not with the name prayer given to it, but with a psychic desire so strong as to come to the outer limits of prayer. And ultimately you will name it for what it is: prayer, profound and real, consuming and selfless. Then, for the first time, you will recognize Being and give it the name God."

"You begin to overcome me, Signore, not so much with what we would call logic, but with the very fervor of your belief."

"Perhaps it is intellectual intuition awakening. Listen to its voice. There have been others before you who found the way. Your own countryman, Alexis Carrel, discovered this very secret, but it began with the *desire* to know Him whom others called God, Him who had no place in the observable world of science.

"There is much I do not know about science," Sicola continued, "hence it boggles the mind to see the child on the grass as having sprung from a procession of parents who ultimately trace their heredity to a unicellular organism. Indeed, it boggles the mind, but it is, in itself, of little importance. Importance lies only in the determination of the origin of such a process as being subject to accident or authorship. Out of accident no such ordered, functional complexity could arise, it would seem. And if there is authorship — on whose grounds there are other proofs — then we are faced with Being, a Being so omnipotent as to have planted the seeds of His existence, proof of His Being deep within the consciousness of every man. Therefore, you have not only *a priori* desire but *a priori* knowledge, and no such knowledge could exist without a desire to perpetuate itself in knowing Him more."

Bouchard turned his head away from Sicola, not entirely certain that he could grasp the concepts that the older man had been discussing, yet disturbed at the threat they posed to his comfort, haunted by the promise of the possibilities for investigation he had not considered, suddenly uncertain of himself because these possibilities hinted at the incompleteness of his dedication. For the moment, it was too much for him. These were ideas he would have to turn over in his mind at another time, a time set aside for private thought. Now it was important to divert the conversation to other things. "The boy finds great pleasure in the puppy. In many ways they are so alike, full of frivolity, mischief, and unconcern for larger matters."

Sicola agreed. "But in one way, at least, they are very different. It is in the soul possessed by one and not the other." Then he turned his attention to the youngster on his knees, his head buried in his arms, which were folded under him as he burrowed into the grass. The dog yipped and tried to lick at the boy's shielded face, first trying one side, then the other, and in failing finally decided that the positive act of using his nose as a lance would penetrate through the fold of the child's arms. The boy giggled as the sniffing puppy tickled his ear. Then he rose half way to his knees and held his arm out in front of him, inviting the dog to sit. At length, he commanded the dog, "Speak!" and the animal cocked his head from side to side and let out a soprano bark. "Speak!" the boy repeated. "Say, 'Hello, Riccardo!' " The puppy barked again. Then, with annoyance, the child looked at the two men sitting on the bench and asked, "Why can't dogs talk like us?"

Bouchard laughed. "Because dogs are animals, and people are human."

"That's all?" the boy pouted, dissatisfied with Bouchard's answer. "You don't know very much."

"That's true," Bouchard agreed.

"I'm gonna teach him to talk, I betcha."

"Betcha!"

"Heck!" the child said in disgust, "What do you know?"

The scientist grinned. "So we come to that again, and again I agree that I do not know very much."

"My father says God knows everything. If God knows everything, how come He doesn't share it with us? How come He won't show me how to make the dog talk?"

"Because, my boy, then we would know everything and there would no longer be any pleasure to learn. God is God, and we are we, and we cannot be God. We cannot even pretend to be God, because if we did we would not always do things His way, and we would become very comical, like a clown pretending to be king." He turned to Sicola and smiled as if Sicola knew he was role-playing.

"Do you know God?" the boy asked.

"No," Bouchard answered.

"How come?"

Bouchard hesitated. "Because, dear child, I never tried to know Him."

"How come?"

"Because I was too busy."

"You're not busy now."

"Yes. I'm not very busy now. But where shall I find Him?"

"In church, I guess."

"Perhaps that is where I shall start, then."

The child threw the stick and screamed to the puppy to fetch it.

Bouchard and Sicola were alone again. The scientist scraped the sole of his shoe along the gravel beneath him and was silent as Sicola straightened on the bench and breathed in the clear air of spring, his pulse quickening in joy over the providential leadership of a child. Then Bouchard arose from his seat and extended his hand to Sicola. "Great journeys have begun with smaller starts," he said.

"I hope," Sicola smiled, "that we will meet again — at the end of your journey."

Come All Ye Faithful

Sicola got out of his Fiat to look back at the city from his hillside vantage point and, awed by the spectacular sight, sucked the cold December night through his teeth. The lights of Rome crept into the skies and cast a warm aura above the city, as if the light had been airbrushed on the dark mantle of night. Rome seemed on fire, while here where he stood Nature had drawn a curtain over herself. He pulled his collar tightly around his neck and fluffed the fur piece up around his ears. The silence, the cold, the darkness offered stark contrast to the glow of civilization in the distance.

Civilization. It was a beacon in the sky that signaled the fact that people gathered there in a common purpose, united in commerce, needing the sight and touch of other people about them. It was the joining in community of people to share with one another and to gather security from others' presence — a security so singularly ignored after a time as each one became inured to it, and in this habituation it was as if one had become blind to his own neighbor. Proximity, the too-familiar touch of humanity, seemed only to jade one to the needs of others, and the cry of the human heart was unheard because the ears no longer heard what the eyes no longer saw. Poor Rome. You become fat with your graces, and you believe they are your right. You are aware of the crime about you, of the lust, the poverty, but because there is larceny in you also, depravity in your own soul, poverty in your own spirit, you are indifferent — which is the greater sin.

It was Christmas Eve, and Rome was celebrating. The merchants had dramatized love and peace on earth with the music of carillons piped from their store windows, and it had drawn the people off the streets and into their stores in unprecedented numbers. The harmony of love had come to them on the wings of music, while in the aisles they rushed pell-mell, brushed irritably against each other, and used their charge accounts resentfully, knowing that January would present the price. The season had trapped them. Christmas was a bankrupting set of obligations to be met, and it got costlier each year. But the merchants, unerringly aware, prospered while they mouthed the platitudes of the economists, who spoke of the salutary effect of such an orgy of buying on the nation's economy.

In the teeming aisles there would be the predators of Christmas, those sorry ones who also had become swept up in the theme of giving even when there would be no money to pay for the gifts. So they would steal, perhaps out of some misguided love for a child or a wife who would go without unless misappropriation were applied, or perhaps because crowds made capture all the more difficult and they would realize the profit in another system, which would feature bargains without question of source, and there would be a ready market.

There would be parties and toasts and kisses and errant hands probing bodily recesses in drunkenness.

Office girls would submit in the name of Christmas love, or in the name of love in general, and the season would lend their suitors an air of degeneracy without shame, of conquest without contest, accepted also in the name of Christmas.

To the churches they would come in droves. The truly devout, the regular attenders, would be there without seats or denied entry entirely because Christmas Eve Mass was a function for those who were irregular but who came this once because, again, it was the custom. And their coming was like the green patina on a bronze statue, all outward, never penetrating beyond the surface. The pageantry would be edifying to the aesthetic sense, or perhaps the charitable view would describe it as a momentary awakening of buried spirituality, but it was certain that few would enter into the profound drama that would unfold before them. Few would sense the gift of Incarnation, God's very gift to them, and fewer still would feel compelled to give to Him in return out of the depths of their souls. The tragedy of it, Sicola thought, lay in their view of this as a spectacle, eliciting no response from their hearts to the drama of Incarnation that would lead so inevitably to expiation. It had all begun with the joy of birth, and had ended with the greater joy of rebirth, and in between there was pain, suffering and death, but they would not see it or feel it. For most, it would be another sensate pleasure, a charming spectacle.

This was Christmas Eve for Sicola, the first in his pontificate when he had been absent from the Vatican, when he would not celebrate Midnight Mass at St. Peter's. Tommaso had understood and had made excuses, long since having become accustomed to Sicola's ways. "I must," Sicola had told Tommaso, "find the soul of Christmas among the souls of the Church. Beyond Rome, out in the country, there are those who call out to heaven in their misery, and perhaps they believe that heaven has no ears for them. I can at least give them the Mass."

He had heard of a small village, ahead just a few miles, which counted its population at a hundred souls, more or less — less in those lean times when husbands took off for Rome to make a living, which was more and more impossible to do from the effete land around their village. They were his mission this night, a blighted people on a blighted land, ignored in their eyes by God and ignored in everyone's eyes by the Church. There was no priest assigned to them, essentially because there were fewer priests to serve in these days, and those who remained must of necessity be assigned to larger population centers. But tonight they would at least know Christmas.

Sicola looked up at the ceiling of the night. The atmosphere was clean and crisp, and he searched for Orion and muttered to no one, "The Belt of Orion. It seems even now to grow tighter about the waist as we come closer to the poverty of the forsaken." And far to the north was the bright one, Polaris, and he wondered whether it was this star, having somehow moved eastward, or another, that had hung over Bethlehem on that night when eternity was born for man. He fixed his eyes on it and walked in its direction as the light snow under his feet crunched from his weight. The Fiat would have to be left behind, for there was only a trail ahead.

This was not like the approach to Rome, whose lambent lights cast a glow in the skies. The lights of the village were muted, yet visible. There was warmth in them, but it was a warmth too weak for radiance.

They welcomed him nonetheless, and his pace quickened as he hurried toward them.

He arrived at the edge of the cluster of houses,
scarred, unpainted, windows patched with cardboard
or stuffed with rags. And as his steps left a trail in the
pristine snow and signalled his coming with the soft
padding of packing snow, a man, leaning against the
house, called out to him, "You walk alone on a cold
night, stranger, and no one comes to our village. Perhaps you are lost?" He pulled a tattered windbreaker
up around his face, knocked his hot pipe out on the
corner of the house and walked toward Sicola.

"Hallo," Sicola greeted him. "No, my friend, I
am not lost. I have come to your village to offer
Christmas Mass tonight."

There was a catch in the man's throat, as if a gust
of cold wind had shoved part of a word back into his
throat. "My God! You are a priest?"

"Yes, Signore," Sicola answered.

"Then I am twice blessed tonight. My wife, Gio-
vannina . . . Jenny . . . is in the house. Tonight —
sometime tonight — she will give me a child. And
now this. It is as if God tells me, 'No, Gasparo, I have
not forgotten you. See! I come to bless this new life.'
Come, Father. Come into the house and warm yourself. There is time yet before midnight."

Sicola followed him into the house, which was
warm and bright. There was not, he noticed quickly,
the smell of the usual Italian house with the sweet,
tangy odor of cheese and sauce. Instead there was the
faint but undeniable smell of barnyard. And over in
the corner of the bare living room, Sicola observed a
cow munching at hay in a box.

As if sensing Sicola's question, the man waved at
the cow and said, "On a night like this, the cow must

be kept warm. No cow, no milk. Come, let me introduce you to my Jenny. The pains have been closer, but suddenly she seemed to tire and dozed. It was then that I decided to go outside for a moment or two."

"You do not have a doctor or a midwife?" Sicola asked with some alarm.

"No, Father. We are too poor for doctors, and the midwife moved to Rome with her husband and children. Besides, men have assisted at births in our village from necessity. We have been forced to deliver our calves along with our children."

"*Mannaggia!*" Sicola blurted out. "I did not realize that children still came into the world without some help from science."

"It would be better if science were here to help us, Father. But since it is not, we must make do. All we have is our old ways — and our trust in God. And sometimes trust becomes most difficult, but we keep it all the same." He stuck his head through the doorway of the bedroom, and Jenny smiled back at him, reaching for his hand.

"I heard voices, Gasparo. Who is with you?" she asked her husband.

"You will never guess, never in a million years, *bambina mia*. It is a priest, come to say Midnight Mass in the old church. And it was providential that you slipped off to sleep so that I could go outside, for if I had not, he might have passed our house, but now he is here and will bless you and baptize the baby, perhaps."

The woman's pale face brightened, and there was in her voice, also, that catch, only here there was no wind. "Gasparo, Gasparo, please ask him to come in."

The man beckoned to Sicola, who had taken off his coat and boots, and now the unmistakable sign of his ministry, the Roman collar, gave Gasparo a surge of joy, and his eyes glistened as a boyish exuberance overcame him. "Come, Father, come. We are so happy. So happy. Come."

Sicola stepped into the tiny alcove of a room to greet the young woman and took her hand in both of his own burly hands. He paused to look softly into her young face, too young, he thought, to have known so much pain, yet it was there staring out at him in her wanness. There seemed also to be a peasant beauty made greater by the strife and contests of marginal living, stoically beautiful, with a grandeur of defiant strength. Her long, black hair accented a pale, tired face whose lips, cracked but full, testified to a sensuous, robust beauty, and her eyes, black and sparkling, were the mirror of a profound soul, the depths of which were beyond seeing.

"Father . . . Father . . . Father," she murmured as she raised his hands to her smooth white cheek, "how proud we are to have you with us, tonight of all nights. Between my pains I spoke to the Holy Mother to be with me tonight, to give me only a small sign — even if it was merely the peace of her touch — that she was by my side. Never did I expect that she would reward me so. I love her so, always I have loved her. But tonight I know what it is like to be kissed by her."

Sicola knelt by the bed, and as he did so, he became aware of a dog lying on the floor at the bedside, and over in the corner of the room a chicken clucked a muffled cluck, as if in its sleep. Then he turned back to Jenny and said gently, "Such a love for the Mother of God, my child, does not go unnoticed either by her or by God Himself. As for me, you can be assured that your child will be baptized, and that this visit is fortuitous for me also."

Gasparo touched Sicola's shoulder. "Father, I will go to the next house to tell them of your coming so that they can send their son to tell the whole village to make ready for Mass this very night. They will clean the altar, and we still have the vestments from other days when there was a priest here. Someone will also ring the bell, which has not sounded in this valley for such a long, long time." He paused a moment, his face still bathed in joy. "Father . . . Father . . . how can I find the words?" Then he left quickly.

As the husband left the house, Jenny was seized by a contraction, and she cried out, "Gasparo!" Her forehead glistened from the sheen of perspiration that oozed through her pores, and she raised her head and shoulders in a reflex action.

Sicola became tense and fearful. Nothing in his priesthood had dealt with the sudden delivery of a child when no more professional help was available. He could only give her what he was qualified best to give, comfort, encouragement, and prayer. He let her grasp his hand, and there was a strength in her grip that whitened Sicola's knuckles. He wiped her forehead with the cloth at her bedside and whispered, "Patience . . . patience, my child. All in good time." She tried to smile at him, but the pain turned her lips downward instead. Then the contraction stopped, and she sagged, wet and limp, back into the bed.

Mannaggia, he thought, what will I do to help her? What if the baby comes before Gasparo returns? And even if he is here to help with the delivery, are not these conditions so unsterile as to create other problems? He knelt beside the woman, now sapped of strength, her eyes closed and divided by the tense vertical cleft at the bridge of her nose. Silently he prayed: "Remember, O most gracious Virgin Mary, that never was it known that any one who fled to thy protection, implored thy help and sought thy intercession was left unaided. Inspired with this confidence, I fly unto thee, O Virgin of Virgins, my Mother. To thee I come; before thee I stand, sinful and sorrowful. Oh Mother of the Word Incarnate, despise not my petitions, but in thy mercy, hear and answer me. Amen."

Sicola placed his head on the edge of the bed and continued to pray, "Christe Eleison . . . Christe Eleison . . . Christe Eleison." How long he·remained in prayer he did not know, but it was as if he had been awakened from a dream when he heard a knock at the door. He arose, wondering why it was so necessary for Gasparo to knock at the door of his own house. When he opened the door, he met two men, their heads protected with parkas.

One of the men spoke. "Father, do you have a telephone in the house? Our plane developed engine trouble some distance from here, and we were forced to land in an open field. We saw the lights of the village, and we would appreciate it if we might be permitted to call Rome for assistance. We will, of course, reverse the charges."

Sicola stood for a moment, unsure of himself when he saw that it was not Gasparo, then he recovered with embarrassment. "Come in, come in." He explained that he too was a visitor, that it was most unlikely that there would be a telephone in the entire village, but if they would wait until Gasparo returned, he would be certain to know. "Meanwhile," he continued, "there are other matters of prior importance. Jenny . . . that is, Gasparo's wife . . . is about to deliver her first child and there is no medical help in this God-forsaken village. I am most apprehensive."

"We were hoping to get back to Rome to spend

Christmas Eve with our families, Father, but since we are detained here through no one's fault, perhaps I can be of assistance. Please, Father. Direct me to the woman and proceed to provide all of the hot water that the pots in this miserable hovel will contain. I am a doctor."

"Son of a gun! She works fast!" Sicola smiled as he looked up at the ceiling of the house. "*Grazie, Madre mia! Grazie!*"

What? Oh, the woman, you mean? Let's see how far along she is."

He followed Sicola into the narrow bedroom and gasped with displeasure at the sight of the dog and the chicken. "Get these animals out of here!" he burst out angrily.

"*Momentino!*" Sicola grinned with pleasure at the turn of events. "First it would be well to announce you. Jenny, my child, good fortune smiles. This is a doctor, the man of science Gasparo had hoped could help in your delivery. Do not ask how he comes to be here. All that is certain is that he . . . that he comes from above . . . from heaven in an airplane, no less. I leave you now. I have other work to do." He swooped up the chicken in his arm, but the dog was part mule, he discovered, for he would not leave the side of his mistress.

"Never mind, never mind," the doctor said, "just get the chicken out of here, and work on the water, and tell Aldo to get my knapsack."

Sicola left quickly and began opening closet doors in search of pots and pans; then he remembered the other man, and he said, "Aldo, Signore Dottore would like his sack. Which one is his?" The man handed the bag to Sicola, who scurried off to the bedroom.

When he returned, Sicola checked the pots, then took a seat opposite the doctor's companion. "I am very sorry, Signore. With all the excitement, it would appear that you are the forgotten one of the house. Perhaps you could break a leg, or something not quite so traumatic, maybe just a finger, and we could put Signor Dottore to work at both ends of the house."

"No, thank you, Father," he laughed. "It would appear that at this moment he would be forced to leave me with the pain, and I am such a coward."

"You are a coward?" Sicola smiled. "You should have seen me but a moment before you arrived. I was fearful that I would hereafter be known among the flock as Padre Midwife. A most frightening thought, I assure you."

"I am sure, Father."

"But it worked out well. Now Jenny will have proper care at the birth of her child. You have children, Signore?"

"Yes, Father. Four. Two boys and two girls, though they are all quite grown now. I thought to myself, while you were busying yourself with the water, that the conditions of this birth are not unlike those that surrounded the birth of Umberto, our first-born. We were both young, Anna and I, and we were uncertain where the coal would come from to heat our tiny apartment, and where the food would come from to nourish Anna enough to provide milk for Umberto. I did not want the child, at least not at that time, for I had plans, and my plans allowed for a proper time for all things, including the birth of a child. Somehow, Father, the plans did not wish to materialize, and I went from one failure in life to another, and as the failures mounted, the greater the delay in having our first child. But I continued to ex-

ercise great caution, I assure you. Our life, our condition of poverty, did not allow for the entrance of new
life into such squalor. But somehow it happened anyway."

"But you seem a prosperous man now. You fly
about in your own airplane. It is apparent that the
squalor did not remain." Sicola studied the man carefully for the first time. Handsome, fully masculine,
with graying temples and silver wing-like streaks at
the sides. The face was ruddy and pleasantly lined,
especially at the corners of his eyes where four frown
lines arched downward nearly to his cheeks, as if he
had peered into a strong sun frequently. His nose was
sharp and patrician, and his lips broad and full. A
man with zest, Sicola thought.

"Yes, Father. Money is no longer a problem. But
he was the beginning. Umberto, that is. It was as if
when he came he brought not only his own bread but
mine also. Anna and I were in love, but now it was
different. We were a family, and with the recognition
of this new status there was also a new view of other
matters as well. It was as if good fortune had been a
symbol of my need to prove to Anna that she had
married the right man, and the more I tried and
failed, the more I read into her mind thoughts that
were never there. But now, with Umberto, there was a
joy and a desire to succeed so suddenly new to me
that I gave it no thought, as I do now. I simply felt.
And with feeling, attitudes changed, and yes, success
came also. But I shall never forget that he was an un-
wanted child."

"I think, Signore, that you are a good man, that
you have always been a good man. Perhaps . . ." The
door burst open and Gasparo came in breathless and
shivering. He saw the stranger sitting across from Si-

cola. "Father, when I saw the fresh tracks in the snow outside the house, I was unable to account for them. First you, now two other sets. Have the three wise men come to my house tonight?" He smiled, but through the smile the question remained in his eyes.

Sicola told him of the forced landing and of the arrival of the doctor and his friend. "The doctor is with Jenny now. Why don't you see if he needs your help. The water should be coming to a boil soon."

Gasparo excused himself and disappeared into the alcove bedroom.

"You were about to say something, Father," the man said to Sicola.

"It seems that I am always about to say something, Signore, but I am at an age where I forget very easily what it was."

"How do Gasparo and the villagers provide for themselves, Father? I have never seen such poverty, and so close to Rome. I was not even aware of the existence of such a village until tonight."

"They are farmers here, farmers who refuse to give up belief in the earth, which has long ago given up on them."

"They know nothing else?"

"I am sure they do, or they must, but they are so poor that they do not have the capital to invest in alternate occupations and the equipment they would entail."

The visitor grew silent, and Sicola left him to his thoughts. He could hear Jenny, and her pains seemed to be coming with greater frequency. Her cries were muffled, as if she were biting something to keep herself from screaming. Gasparo had been making quick, nervous trips to the hot water, and now he was gone again into the room. Occasionally, he could be heard to comfort his wife, but Sicola was uncertain of which one of them suffered more.

At length, Sicola's companion spoke, as if coming slowly out of a reverie that was so far away, one in which he had been lost so as to be oblivious to Gasparo's movement in the room and Jenny's struggle with the new life that surged forward in the denouement of birth.

"Father, I am a religious man at heart. I have always believed it to be so, at any rate. But in late years I must admit to having less time for these thoughts. It is not so much that I did not believe, nor that I did not care. It was simply that one gets swept up by currents at times, and there is such a force and a direction to these currents that he spends all his time fighting them, and in this preoccupation he forgets other matters, as I have forgotten — no, put aside — God.

"The doctor and I are very good friends. He has even invested in my business. Together, we decided to make a trip in search of a new location to build an assembly plant for the automobiles I manufacture. This is how we happen to have strayed off course and were forced to land here.

"Do you suppose, Father, that it was no accident?"

"How can one say with certainty, my friend? All that one can say is that it would be like Him to do such a thing. We must not see the hand of God in all things, but we can see the permissive will of God in all things that happen. There is a subtle difference, which I will allow you to contemplate."

The man grew silent once again. He would be lost in his own thoughts, Sicola knew. Perhaps it was just as well. So much had happened since he crossed the threshold of the small home that he had not had sufficient time himself to reflect on these events. He was, he thought, not altogether unfamiliar with poverty. It had marked his own childhood. If one were to believe some of the sociologists, poverty was an important determinant in the growth of crime, and he would not dispute these men. But were they not missing something? Why, for example, did many priests and nuns, doctors and engineers, prime ministers and presidents, even sociologists themselves come from poor homes? And what of the saints? Many there were who were members of the king's court, but far greater the numbers whose diet was insufficient, whose sleeping accommodations were crowded, whose very menial existence made them unclean in the view of those better off. What then was truly the determinant? The secret voice of God in their hidden hearts? Or perhaps the single love of one person, lost in the multitude of the indifferent, who truly cared, truly loved, truly saw in the depth of the heart the reflection of Christ. Assuredly, but there was something else, also. Of one thing Sicola was certain: poverty in and of itself was no more a determinant of crime than wealth in and of itself was a determinant of selfishness. Yet one had to face certain questions at the same time. How much buffeting by nature would Gasparo and his family tolerate before he became embittered and turned upon God by turning upon society to take his needs? And Aldo. As his empire continued to grow, each success spawning new successes, how long would it be before he would consider that he was so completely the captain of his own fate as to require no help from the supernatural? How long before Gasparo, on the other hand, would become similarly entrapped by affluence, should it bless his valley? They were imponderable questions to Sicola at that particular moment, but something Aldo had said came back to him: that he was truly a religious man but he simply became too busy, too swept up in his own problems to maintain that vital liaison with God. Hence the inevitability of drift. Was this, then, after all, the determinant? Given a devout family in which a strong prayer life exists, given the continuity of this prayer life, how was it possible for Gasparo to become embittered by the buffeting of nature, how possible for Aldo to become lost from the touch of God? For was it not in this ever-present, daily touch that the lifeline to Him existed? And insofar as this vital line of communication was maintained, it would be impossible, absolutely impossible, to see poverty or wealth as anything less than the springboard to sanctity.

It would seem that the culprit was pain, then. Bitter pain? Or glorious pain? Jenny lay on her bed at that particular moment suffering the intense scourge of pain; yet in her heart was such a great love of her who was and is the prototype of motherhood and maternal pain that she now used her pain. Her pain would not use Jenny and leave her spent. Jenny would use the pain, drawing from it the very juices of strength, for she was in love with God, and she would momentarily become a partner with Him in the creation of immortality. The pain, this particular pain at least, would soon be over, and she would look at the child in her arms and know, as only a mother can know, that life is a miracle. She would know that it was her pain and her conquest of pain that had brought her into the vortex, the very ecstasy of His love. She would know all these things because she had maintained the line with Him for these many years.

Now she could only trust, and love all the more Him whom she loved so deeply.

Sicola thought back at the course his mind had followed, and it seemed to be summed up in so few words: pain and prayer, love and trust.

He looked up at Aldo, and it seemed that Aldo had come through his own meditations, reaching whatever conclusions, at the same time as Sicola.

"Father, we will locate our plant here in this valley. It is close enough to Rome for convenience, and remote enough to give us the space we need. This will bring with it not only jobs but medical facilities, and until the plant is finished I promise you that one day a week there will be a doctor here to attend to these people. And you, Father, will arrange to send a priest here!"

"Your business judgment is good, Aldo. But how do you presume to say that I will arrange to send a priest here? Who do you think I am?"

"Do not play the clown with me. One in my position either gets to know personally those worth knowing or is in their presence on so many occasions that he would know them elsewhere, even when they do not wear white . . . Holiness."

"It is as you say, my friend. There will be a priest here soon."

As he spoke, there was the choking scream of newborn life and the sound of laughter in the alcove. "A boy!" the doctor said with a laugh. Sicola knelt at the door of the room, and Aldo joined him. The infant's crying subsided, and Gasparo and the doctor joined the other two men on their knees as Jenny held the child close to her warm body. Now her face was restful, unlined, radiantly happy. She looked into the child's face with only the trace of a smile as if her mind had turned elsewhere to express her silent gratitude for this incomparable gift.

Sicola prayed silently, rose to his feet and kissed Jenny on the forehead. The men stood crammed into the tiny room, and for the first time the dog moved and let out a bark. Then Sicola baptized the child.

"Now let us go to Mass," he said. "You, Gasparo, will want to stay with Jenny."

"No, Father. I will be all right. All of you go. Gasparo has special reason to go tonight, do you not?"

"I do, *bambina mia*, I do."

He opened the door for Sicola, and all of them were astonished at the sight that met them outside. The entire village waited outside Gasparo's door, each man, woman and child holding a lighted candle. They formed a human tunnel, and as Sicola walked between the lines, he blessed them. He took his place at the front of the line with Gasparo, and the procession headed toward the tiny church.

The bells chimed in celebration and the villagers sang *Adeste Fideles* as they filed through the front door and down the apse of the church.

Sicola thought of the carillons piped from Rome's store windows, of the jostling crowds, of some of the vacuous faces in the pews at church, of the expensive presents that would be distributed. There would not be one person in Rome who would know more joy than the least of these people. To those who measured the joy of Christmas by the abundance of their gifts, and to those who measured the sadness of Christmas by the paucity of gifts, there is a common sadness, measured by the total loss of the presence of Christ on His own day.

In this village there was a spiritual richness that

rose like a mighty flame from the cold, bleak earth. Tomorrow the villagers may know again the gnawing fear of poverty, the bone-chilling pain of unprotected bodies lashed by the frigid breath of winter, but tonight all that mattered was the Mass, that living reminder that Christ had come for them, not unaware of their suffering as they had supposed, but so fully aware of it as to give them this sign that they were treasured, special, most beloved in His heart.

And who is the richer, Sicola wondered, these or the Romans? "The first shall be last and the last shall be first," he thought. Then the Mass began, and there were present three men wiser than before, and they were equal among the peasants of the field. Outside the animals were tethered, and above them blinking as it seemed to descend to the spire of the church was Polaris. Or perhaps it was just unusually bright on this particular night when the air was so clear and crisp. Twice in two thousand years, it was not — really — too much to expect, so why should one doubt it?

Amoebic Dysentery

Sicola had always been impressed with stories of people who were able to reduce the Lord's Prayer to a microscopic dimension so that it could be engraved in Latin on the head of a straight pin. It was impressive, he had thought, because it illustrated man's fixation with life at the other end of the microscope. It was all jolly good fun, but it really meant nothing unless someone first looked at it carefully and then translated it properly, and that had already been done before the useless exercise in reduction. He may very well have read, instead, the last will and testament of the inscriber's father who had gone to his rest forgiving his debtors. In short, what one saw in miniature did not of necessity implant such an image on the brain as to disclose universal truths writ large.

On the other hand, if it was one's intention, as it was Aristotle's, to form an intelligible universe by discovering the universal in the particulars, well and good, but in the assembling of the particulars into a whole there was a serious question of defective judgment. For truth, indeed, has always been hidden in the minutiae of life, and because man had been accustomed to deduce from what he saw, the problem arose of either not having seen what he thought he had seen or of having its image distorted in his brain by the very process of enlargement and deduction.

Men had still to learn how to look truth in the face and transfer its material image into a metaphysical implication. Like beauty, truth was to them in the eye of the beholder. And that, it seemed to Sicola, was patently ridiculous. For such a view of truth was, in itself, a contradiction of truth. Truth is one, consistent, incontrovertible, eternal, impervious to myopia, and a chameleon only to the situation ethicist. For that which is, remains, though the viewer may see a cat while others aver that what is seen is a skunk. Hence the question remains: what was truly seen, and what was its meaning in the context of universal truth?

The Vatican may have stood these many centuries as a monolithic testament to the spiritual obligation it held so high, but this did not mean that it had not waded into the realm of science. There were those only too concious of this usurpation, testifying at the shabby treatment the Church had extended to its faithful soul Galileo. Sicola himself winced at his recollection of history, and while pitying the defender of Copernican astronomy, he was quick to point out that this was a quarrel between churchmen and science and that both Pope Paul V and Urban VIII had taken great care never to declare themselves *ex cathedra*, a cop-out to modern thinkers perhaps but certainly an indication of the regard of the Church for the long-implicit doctrine of infallibility.

So Sicola, eager to know more of science, entered the Vatican laboratory as man, theologian, scholar, intellect, even Bishop, but not as Pope. If the time called for it, if his knowledge were such as to see perdition in the espousal of a particular theory of science, he would act as Pope. Now he was interested only in the search for truth. Perhaps he would find it today, perhaps tomorrow, perhaps it would be for some future Pope. For of one thing he was certain: the strides of science were now becoming so great as one day to go arm in arm with theology or, on the contrary, become the Deus Maximus of the new times. He must, therefore, know more to rule better.

He sat before the microscope on the workbench and reached for the slide nearest to him. It was labeled "Amoeba." He placed it into the microscope and lowered his head to the eyepiece as he began to bring the single cell of life into sharp focus. It had been many years since he had studied biology at the seminary, but he recognized the irregularly shaped protozoan before him, looking ever so much like an egg that had dropped and broken open on a hot pavement. Rounded lobes like indefinite arms spilled out from the center of the blob and the nucleus stared up at him like a one-eyed monster. Floating below the nucleus the open mouthed vacuole seemed to move and change its shape as if it were pursing its lips and saying "Oh-h-h-h" to Sicola at having been discovered. He watched as the amoeba moved, changed its shape, contracting its lobes and shooting them out in other directions.

"You move quickly, little fella," he muttered.

Then Sicola was startled. The vacuole opened and closed in a rage and the eye-like nucleus arched disdainfully. A muffled sound came from under the glass. Sicola listened carefully, unbelieving at first at what he had heard. "You ain't seen nothin' yet, *amico!*"

"Ah," Sicola smiled, "so you are a talking amoeba?"

"Si," the amoeba answered.

"And Italian, too?"

"What else, stupido! I was picked up in an Italian gutter."

"You calla me stupido again, and I squash you like a cockaroach."

"You thinka you are the big stuff, no? Joosta because you are the Pope. Already you want to excommunicate me. Holda you water, wise a guy. Remember, as the oak comes from the acorn, even popes come for the amoeba. We are *compagni!*"

"But, my little blob, why you say that? We do not look alike."

"But I have it from good authority."

"Si? And who issa you authority?"

"You never heard of Chuck?"

"Chuck-a-who?"

"You know, Chuckie baby. Chuck Darwin."

"I amma no familiar witha you friend Chuck."

"Thatsa joosta what I would expecta from a Cattolico," the amoeba said. "All of you are alike. You blind yourself to science. It was Signor Darwin who discovered that all life starts with the amoeba. But, no, it pleases you to believe the hocus-pocus you preach about God waving His hand and presto, there is the man."

"Ah, so. It is *that* Darwin you speak of. Yes, my little forbear, him I know," Sicola said, suddenly understanding. "Let us speak of him more. Since you know so much, perhaps you can a tell me what it is you wish to be when you grow up, a chicken, a cow, a horse, a man, perhaps even a theologian?"

"Let me out of here, you clown, and I will be Pope."

"You could do worse."

"Some of a my brothers have a no ambition.

That is a why they become fish. Something inside of them says that it is fun to swim and play in the water. They have no great ambition, so they become what their ambition is, simply fish. Others see themselves swinging from the trees and they become monkeys, but what you do not understand is that it takes many centuries for the ambition of the fish to evolve into the ambition of the monkey. As the fish plays in the sea, he begins to realize that there are other things on the lands, and soon the ambition of the fish to be more becomes passed on to his children and the ambition grows and grows with each succeeding generation until one day the fish finds that he is a reptile. He can now breathe the same air that humans breathe, but still he must crawl. And the process continues until finally one day he is an ape, but this takes many eons also. So the chimpanzees and the orangutans you see today in your zoos are also harboring secret ambitions, and as their offspring are born they will be born more developed than their parents. Then there will be the day when they will become men. It is automatic. Life evolves. Accept it."

"*Mannaggia,* Amoeba. This is such a grandiose picture you present to me. Tella me. How do you know this to be true?"

"I read a book once."

"So, my little egg splat, you read a book. And you accept what you read? Joosta like that?"

"Certainly! The sources are great men; why should I not believe them?"

"The answer is most simple. Because you are but an amoeba, you cannot reason. There are many people — *homo sapiens*, we call them — who are like that. Amoebas all. They react to stimuli, and they do not reason. So, if it gives you peace, you have already achieved your ambition. You are like men who do not reason."

"But why," the amoeba asked, "is it so necessary? That is what the intellects are for, to do my reasoning. You are not much different. You take creation on faith."

"You know," Sicola said, "how to hurt a guy. But let us develop this thought for some distance, Signor One-eye. Consider the ground rules of science, which tell us that there are certain qualifications before a theory — which is what the *theory* of evolution is — can be considered a *scientific* theory. There must be events, processes, or properties *which can be observed,* and the theory must be subject to laboratory experimentation subjecting the original predictions to the test. Even when falsifying evidence is introduced, the results will be predictable. In other words, 'Vas you dere, Charley?' and 'Putta you money where you mouth is.' "

The amoeba's vacuole pouted, and it retorted, "Just so much rhetoric. You cannot put creationism to the same test as you wish to put evolutionism, Signor Know-it-all. But the evidence for evolutionism is so remarkable that only a boob like you could not see it."

"Let us reason as friends, or remember what I said about the cockaroach," Sicola said testily. "I submit that on scientific grounds, you are correct. Both evolutionism and creationism are unproven and unprovable according to the requirements of establishing a scientific theory. But admit to me that they are both accepted as acts of faith and I will tell you that it takes a far greater faith to accept evolutionism than creationism."

"Oh, pooh!" the amoeba said scornfully.

"And pooh onna you, too, mister. Now looka here. One of the most popular theories concerning the origin of the universe would have it that up there in the sky was a bigga ball that contained electrons, neutrons, and protons. They do notta tell how the ball gotta there in the firsta place, but they say joosta believe that all the energy and the matter of the universe was first in this bigga ball. Then one day, BOOM, and we have the universe, and here we are several billion years later with a three-pound brain composed of 12 billion neurons in a most complex and complicated arrangement. To believe this does not require a superb act of faith?"

"Do not confuse me with facts. As an amoeba, I still claim to be the father of all living life."

"If I could only make of you a Catholic!" Sicola blurted out. "With such a faith as you have, I could promise you more than Darwin. For was it not he who convinced you that out of the single cell came different species. Can you tella me what properties are so unique to you that you can divide and become a horse, a fish, a bird, a crocodile, a man, and all under the parenthood of a single cell called an amoeba? I find it easier to believe that God created the universe, populating it with different species, each of which would know variations and mutants, but all remaining under the one family name of its species. Your theory strains credulity. It is little more than a hundred years old. When it survives the centuries that the Genesis story has survived, the world will make room for it with bearded loyalty. Until then, shut uppa you face."

"Did anyone ever tell you you gotta big mouth?" the amoeba asked petulantly. "I tell you that the history of the world proves that as civilization has evolved, so has nature, so has man, so *will* man."

"You do not even know the history! *Mannaggia*, history itself should tella you that life goes from the complex to the simple, for each moment of life is a moment of deterioration, each breath a breath toward death. Where is the growth in all of this? Yet you wish me to see the amoeba growing and evolving to a higher state, when all the while it contradicts the vital force of life itself. You were born to die, my friend."

"Words, words, words! Prove it, you donkey!"

"Okay. I prove!" Sicola pressed the glass slides together and watched the amoeba in the microscope, its vacuole gagging, and its lobes flailing in the throes of death. "*Requiescat in pace!*" he said mournfully. "Whatever you are, whatever you hope to be. Skidoo! You ain't a gonna do it inna my house!"

As the amoeba began to drown and gurgle in its own juice, it could be heard to shriek, "Chuckie-ba-a-by . . . whe-e-e-re are you-u-u? He-l-l-l-p!"

Back to Nature

Sicola and Tommaso were, for one day at least, ruminants in another world. "Let us get away for a brief period," he had said to his secretary, "and meditate away from the Vatican. Let us chew the cud, so to speak, and perhaps, in the chewing of morsels already ingested, a new flavor will come to old thoughts."

"A very good idea, Holiness," Tommaso replied.

It seemed natural, therefore, to go to nature in the raw, and what better place than the zoo, speaking of chewing the cud. There one would find nature reduced to its animal level, for did not the anthropologists, in the search for the meaning of man, revert to those vestiges of primordial man extant in today's world? So he would go beyond even the anthropologists.

The two men strolled along the broad promenade of the zoo, Sicola munching peanuts and Tommaso coping, what else, with the spun angel hair of sugar in a paper cone. They arrived at the fenced-in monkey island and were drawn to it simultaneously. Monkeys chattered and leaped from mound to mound, while others swung from vines. Caves speckled the man-made cliffs in a replica of the native habitat of all monkeys. Nothing was overlooked in making their lives happy and natural. Was this not microcosm enough? Sicola thought.

"Let us observe Darwin's friends," Sicola motioned to Tommaso. "See how happy they are. They have everything they want. Nothing is denied them. They are fed, their medical needs are taken care of, and they procreate — at random, it is true, but that is the way of the animal kingdom."

"Of the animal kingdom only?" Tommaso asked.

"Wise a guy!" Sicola answered with a nudge to Tommaso's ribs. "Look, Tommaso! There is the keeper. Would not our study be more informed with his assistance?"

Tommaso signalled to the keeper, clad in gray cotton work clothes, and he came to the two men with a smile. "Si, Signori?" he asked.

"You know all about the monkeys, my friend?" Sicola questioned.

"Si, Signore, I attend to their needs."

"How do you attend to their needs?"

"By seeing that they remain healthy and enjoy the good life to the fullest, Signore."

"Ah, I see. They are the cute rascals, almost like children, no?"

"Do not be fooled, Signore. They look like children, and they act like children in their mischief, but by monkey standards, many are very mature in years."

Sicola paused a moment to look about the enormous pen. "There is a group off to the side, my keeper friend. Two of them are together and one strokes the other so gently. They are capable of love?"

"Oh, si, si, most definitely. They love very much."

"But, poor child, one of them is afflicted with the limp wrist. He has no doubt injured his left hand that he holds it so, yet he keeps stroking his partner and protruding his lips to the lips of his a girl friend. Why you not fix the wrist?"

The keeper smiled. "There is nothing wrong with the wrist, Signore."

"But there must be. See how he stands. First the hand is on his hip, somewhat misshapen and bent so unusually at the wrist, then he holds it up and the hand bends forward in such a soft, loose gesture. There is no pain?"

"No pain, Signore."

"How can you be so sure?"

"Because, Signore, he and his friend, they are both males."

"So?"

"You are naive, Signore?"

"Naive? How you mean? Oh-h-h! *Mannaggia*, I begin to getta you point."

Sicola whispered to Tommaso. Tommaso listened, his eyes becoming enlarged as he burst out, "WH-A-A-T? They have them, too? Holy smokes!"

The keeper laughed at the reaction of the two men. "There is something very interesting about Bruce, my friends. That's his name . . . Bruce. He was just like the other boy monkeys until just a short time ago."

"What happened?" Sicola asked.

"Who knows? He just could not help himself; he would tell me if he could talk."

"Wan way theessa minoote . . . then like that the next?" Sicola asked the keeper.

"Si, Signore. You are surprised. You have read, I am certain, of similar metamorphoses in the human condition. One becomes distinguished for bravery in the war, a most masculine climate you will agree, then according to the newspaper reports, he says 'I would never have chosen this life. But I do not have the choice.' So it is with Bruce, I suppose."

"Tell me, my friend, of all the monkeys in this commune, how many are like Bruce?"

"Very few, very few. It is known, of course, that Nature has made a few mistakes, but statistically they are so very few as to be unworthy of notation in the arithmetic. Certainly those accidents of Nature do not approximate the numbers manifested by their unusual behavior. They seem to increase recently — among the young, especially — because they seek to imitate Bruce. But on the other hand, some do not take to it and return to the old ways."

"Howza come?"

"Please to look at Theo, who now joins Bruce and his friend. See how he embraces both of them."

"He is one, too?" Sicola asked.

"Si. But take note. See how he places his hand first on the head of Bruce, then on the head of his friend. Meanwhile, he bows his own head."

"I have noted. So-o-o-o?"

"He is the minister. His special province is with the monkeys like Bruce. Always he walks about with his eyes cast upward. The Holy One, we call him. Then he gives comfort to his flock. How they love him."

"But why do some return to the old ways. What has this to do with the minister, the Holy One?"

"Continue to observe. See, another approaches. He has the stick in his hand, and he brings it down on the head of the minister. Now he chatters to the other two. But they stick their tongues out at him. He loses this one. Him we call the Pope."

"The Pope!"

"Si, the Pope!"

"Tella me, does the Pope win very often?"

"Not often, but sometimes. But he is like il Diavolo with the minister."

"*Mannaggia,* so he should be," Sicola said with wonder.

The one known as the Pope bit the knuckles of his right index finger and extended a disparaging flip of his right hand toward the minister as he walked away. Then, as he trudged on, downcast, he picked up a log and lifted it over his shoulder, bending over with the weight of it. He came to a tree and flung his back to it, his arms outspread on the log laid over two lower branches. His head slumped down on his chest, askew, and he wailed as if in pain.

The Holy One watched thoughtfully, picked up a bamboo pole near him and approached the Pope, who leaned in mock crucifixion against the tree trunk. The Holy One poked the pole into the right side of the Pope's chest.

Bruce approached the Holy One, tapped him on the shoulder, and waved his right index finger in a sideways wagging motion, shaking his head from side to side.

Sicola turned to the keeper and muttered, "Perhaps there is hope for Bruce yet, my friend, and even for the Pope."

"Do not count on it, Signore. It would appear that the Pope has won a battle, but the war remains to be won. And he is aware of it. See how he puts his arm on Bruce's shoulder, all the while pointing to his cave. But Bruce stamps his foot in a feminine gesture of rejection, and his tongue flaps in a sign of the raspberry. He turns to his love and kisses him, while the Pope cries in his anguish."

"Poor Pope!" Sicola said sadly.

"Si, my friend. But he will not give up. He will come back and try again. He is much like our present Pope, you see."

Sicola brightened. "A good man, our present Pope."

"I suppose. But . . . how do the children say it? . . . 'spaced out.' He is like the famous bull in a Florentine shop."

Tommaso finally found his voice and snickered behind his hand as he said, "Tell us more of your views on the Pope." Sicola glared at him, and Tommaso sobered, recalling life in a poor country parish.

"He is a good Pope, Signori. Unlike any other in the history of the Church, you must admit. You know the expression . . . he goes 'where angels fear to tread.' "

"I believe, my friend," Sicola interrupted dryly, "the full expression is that 'fools rush in where angels fear to tread.' "

"This one is no fool. He is, how you say, bullish. But he will get the job done."

"I think so, too," Sicola added laconically. "But look, you were right. He comes back."

"So he does," the keeper grinned, "but I knew he would. See, he carries a bucket of water with him and he dips into the water with the large pine cone on a branch, and sprinkles it at the group. As he does so, they fall back, as if in fear, but he proceeds into their midst, continuing to scatter water about him. Bruce falls to his knees and brings his hands together. This, gentlemen, I have never seen before. I am at a loss to explain.

"Look, now the Pope adjourns to the small rock and sits upon it. He crosses his legs and leans his elbow on the rock, resting his head in the palm of his hand. He does not look at the group, but see now, Bruce approaches and kneels at his side. The Pope nods his head. Bruce continues to chatter into the Pope's ear. Son of a gun, the others form in a line as if they await their turn. The Pope, he puts his hand on Bruce's head . . . it remains . . . it is still there. Now Bruce arises and walks to the Pope's cave, and another takes his place by the side of the rock. He, too, goes to the cave. I believe, Signori, that they will all cross the line soon. This is a most interesting spectacle. But look, the minister is the only one remaining. He stands alone. The Pope rises and speaks to him, but the minister shakes his head. Now the Pope shoves him. Holy Mother, he falls into the pond as the Pope walks away from him, back to his cave. Meraviglioso! Bravo! Bravo! Bravo! This I must report. Goodbye, my friends."

The keeper vanished in a scamper of agitation.

Sicola stared at Tommaso. "Vincenzo Scully he is not, but *mannaggia,* I don't think that his superiors will believe him. Life in the booby hatch will be not much of a change, however.

"It has been a good day. Let's return to the Vatican."

The two men walked away, arm in arm. Suddenly, Sicola drew up sharply, pulled himself from Tommaso and said, "Watcha that, buddy!"

Tomasso smiled, "We must check the holy water when we return, Holiness."

"Yes," Sicola answered wryly, "and let us be certain to remove all reminders of effeminism from the Vatican, also."

"Like what, Holiness?"

"Gay's Anatomy!"

"That is *Gray's Anatomy,* Holiness."

"Then let it stay."

Miracolo!

Sicola had been here before as Pope. He had addressed the assembled thousands as an affirmation by the Church of the miracle that had taken place here nearly seven decades before. The Church, dubious, skeptical, reserved, had long withheld any approbation of the startling event of a pinwheel sun, which had seemed to plummet toward the earth bringing fear to the hearts of the faithful and the curious who had witnessed it. Ever cautious, she had not — in the face of so shocking an exhibition of the supernatural — wished to deviate from her long-standing policy of protecting her souls from the unsubstantiated claims of hysterical, overzealous religious fanatics. Even when she, in her secret heart of hearts, had known that no human hand could have brought about so spectacular a manifestation which suspended the laws of nature, still she had withheld even the remotest acknowledgment of this "miracle," until she could no longer deny it. There was no natural explanation for such thaumaturgy as dislodging the sun from its fixed position, an event, confided to three innocent, guileless children long before it had occurred. The evidence of divine intervention abounded.

But now he was here as one of the pilgrims, one who wished to go unnoticed in his reverence for the

Mother of God herself, hoping additionally to sense the mood of those others who came.

The devout came humbly to pray that Mary would stay the hand of her Son from the disaster toward which all humanity seemed to be catapulting itself. Their hearts, pure and simple, had no difficulty in accepting what they had not themselves witnessed. And they were filled with so great a love of God that they felt His pain as He continued to be ignored, much as the followers of Aaron had ignored Him. There was bestiality and hedonism now as there had been then. There was a golden calf now as there had been then. And they prayed that God would no longer be offended, for those closest to Him still feel as He feels, suffer as He suffers, and weep as He weeps. But they prayed also because one could not truly love Him without loving the souls He had created in His image, even when those souls had sullied the image. And it was in their love even for sinners that they prayed that the recalcitrant could know the serenity of loving God and being loved in return. They prayed as if they resented the very gift of free will, seeming almost to demand that God, by celestial fiat, instill only one will in His prodigals — His Will, beneficently transforming them into myopic creatures with a vision only of the Sacred Heart of Him who existed by reflection in all things. He was to them transcendent rather than immanent, and immanent only to the extent that each person, each thing, was a mirror that reflected His image. It was this kind of myopia for which they prayed, that the sense of the eternal, the awareness of the Almighty, the vision of infinite love could be seen to the exclusion of all else and fix itself so firmly on the retina of the soul as to transfuse His Oneness, which mattered more than the otherness that made them move and act to deny Him.

And there were here also the casual pilgrims, those students who came to enjoy the architecture of the great basilica and the curious who had heard of this monument to Catholic superstition. There were the self-centered who searched for an elusive faith they so sorely needed and desired, but a faith sought through the special attention of God to them alone in the form of some personal miracle. For them it was not enough to know that their salvation lay in the objective study of magisterial truths proclaimed by the Church. They looked instead for some recognition of themselves as singularly chosen, and they would recognize the miracle in some supernatural manifestation centering on themselves, or at least on the awakening of an emotion within themselves. For this, to them, was God — a feeling, a binge of romanticized born-againness, which would be destined to pass because no emotion lasts forever and feelings are built on moving sand. And when it passed, they would again deny God under the pretext that He had denied them, abandoned them to their own aridity. They were the same as those to whom Thomas à Kempis had alluded when he wrote:

> "Jesus has many lovers of His heavenly kingdom, but few ready to accept tribulation. He finds many companions at His table, but few when He is fasting. All desire to rejoice with Him; few are willing to suffer anything for Him.
> "Many follow Jesus as far as the breaking of bread, but few to the drinking of the chalice of His passion. Many reverence His miracles, but few follow the scandal of His cross. Many love Jesus as long as they meet with no adversity;

many praise and bless Him as long as they receive some consolations from Him. But if Jesus
hides Himself and leaves them for a little while,
they fall either into complaining or into dejec-
tion."

And among the multitude there were those outwardly indifferent souls, mere sightseers of the spectacle of worship strange to them but interesting for its
evidence of the magnetic appeal of Roman Catholicism. To them, skeptical to be sure, this was an excur-
sion into strange lands and customs much like the ad-
ventures of anthropologists whose academic interest
is to maintain detachment while observing the sacred
rites of pagan cultures. They would film the proceedings in Ecktachrome slides and movies, and upon
their return their lectures to friends and acquaint-
ances would attest only to their good fortune in re-
cording another strange cult. Some would remain on
the fringe of this spectacle, never attempting to gain
more than the untouched knowledge of the academi-
cian, but others would find in it a haunting call for
them to slake the hidden thirst so long denied and dis-
guised in their skeptical hearts.

And as for Catholics whose faith is based only on
the desire for emotion, these would find that God
touches some with a surging heart, an airy lightness, a
throbbing in the veins, only to draw them close
enough for their minds to take over. And these, being
rational people, would recognize that their love was
indeed an emotion rising from attraction and ending
in knowledge of and oneness with the Object loved.
This was the gift of faith, meant for all men, realized
by few — the few who permitted an open window in
the soul for the ingress of God.

Sicola walked about the plaza of the great basilica, looking into the faces of these pilgrims, searching for some clue to the impact of the shrine on their minds and hearts and souls. He listened to them as many prayed the rosary aloud and others talked of events at home. It was difficult to know for certain who would leave the shrine changed even in a small way, but perhaps, he thought, this was only as it should be, for whatever small miracles would transpire should be private matters between God and His chosen ones.

Then he was startled as he turned absentmindedly and felt the thrust of another shoulder into his. "*Scusa!*" he apologized as he looked into the face of the man who, recovering, spoke something in French. Then as recognition came to the man, his expression changed and he said with delight, "Father Simon . . . Simon Petrus, is it not?"

"Si," Sicola answered, "but how do you know me? Ah-h-h, it is you, my friend from the park in Rome. Bouchard. Jean-Paul Bouchard. It is some kind of a miracle, indeed, that I should meet you, here of all places. I have thought of you many times. *Miracolo!*"

"*Miracolo*, indeed," the scientist laughed. "It begins to sound as though we take up almost where we left off in the park many months ago. I do not believe in such things, but come, let us sit and talk."

The two men walked arm in arm to the edge of the plaza where they found a bench. "It was on a similar bench that we talked the first time," Bouchard said. "The coincidence is striking. One wonders whether or not all of our meetings will be on benches."

"Yes, very interesting indeed. Perhaps one bench

even will be in a church some day," Sicola smiled.

"Ah, yes, my friend. Do you remember the small child who replied, 'in church,' when I asked where I would find God? It was as if the simple faith of a babe had awakened in me memories of my own tender youth with the inexpressible awe of the mystery of a Presence felt but never seen when I was in the church of St. Michel. Somehow I had grown away from it, and I envied the boy for what I had lost. So I did try to find it again in church, and I will admit to a return of a quiet comfort not known to me for many years, but always the scientist in me seemed to keep me on the boundary of faith, never daring, perhaps not really wishing to cross the line. Since then it is as if I have been on a voyage whose port is unknown to me yet I am compelled to maintain the pilgrimage, and always there is this inner gnawing of skepticism for the Christian claims, which seem to go alongside a growing sense of knowing, and an inordinate thirst to pursue beyond this ephemeral veil of knowing that seems to settle about me. There is that ambivalence, which reminds me at times of the American entertainer who would sing in his rasping, grating voice, 'Did you ever have the feeling that you wanted to go, and still you had the feeling that you wanted to stay?' It is most perplexing. It is as if I have been driven by a voice to penetrate your mysteries while another voice speaks to stay my interest with the most rational objections to the incredibility of those things so credible to you."

"It was ever thus," Sicola replied. "The devil does not wish to part with his own, and by his own I do not imply that all of those under his aegis are libertines, murderers, thieves. Many of those captive to him are captive by indifference, doubt, or that intellectual scruple that passes for atheism. These may be highly ethical people, but their weakness is not so much in their actions as in their passivity to the divine plea, 'Come to Me.' Still what you experience is very promising also, for it speaks of struggle; it speaks of the inner joust that wages between God and Satan. That you persist on the pilgrimage is noteworthy, for it signifies that the 'Hound of Heaven' will persist in your defense as long as you persist in the voyage."

"You make it sound so simple, my friend, but it is not. I see, but I do not believe. For example, I am here because I have heard of the great miracle that is supposed to have occurred here many years ago. Your people cling to it tenaciously. They persist in their prayers, even though it would seem that the cause is already lost. They pray on the basis of a mass hallucination in which I cannot believe because it is contradictory to nature. The sun spins, and it seems to dash toward the earth! This is rubbish! Against all the laws of nature."

"So it seems, my friend," Sicola smiled, "that Mr. C. S. Lewis was correct. I recommend you read him. Here we are, the two of us: one a naturalist, the other a supernaturalist. For you, any discussion of the possibility of miracles must be preceded by the philosophical view of their possibility, for the evidence will add up to nothing for the man who admits that no such things as miracles are possible in the first place. Lewis demonstrates this thesis by citing the case of the Bible scholar who, in attempting to date the Fourth Gospel, fixed the date of its writing *after* the execution of Peter because in the Gospel Christ predicts the death of Peter. 'A book,' observes the scholar, 'cannot be written *before* events it refers to.' If there are no such things as miracles, the scholar was correct. If miracles do indeed occur, the scholar has only succeeded in demonstrating his unbelief, but he proves nothing. So, we return to the philosophical view of the *possibility* of miracles as that which really separates us, indeed, separates you from the full union you seek.

Bouchard hesitated for a moment, the skin folded like a quotation mark between his eyes. "Father Simon, how do you define a miracle?"

"St. Thomas," Sicola answered, "defines a miracle as 'that which is done by God outside the order of all created nature.' And Mr. Lewis, anxious not to use the word 'God' too early in his argument says that a miracle is 'an interference with Nature by a supernatural power.' Hence, unless there is something beyond nature there can be no such thing as miracles.

"But to become philosophical on the possibility of miracles, there is a further prerequisite. One must admit to the existence of a supernature — God — and one must accept in the existence of God the fact that it is He who created and who creates. The naturalist believes that only Nature exists. By implication he sees Nature as a self-existent, self-perpetuating, and *self-creating* body of heterogeneous forces, or as Lewis says, 'the whole show . . . going on its own accord.' He says that everything that happens happens because it was stimulated by a prior action. Therefore no naturalist can possibly perceive the notion of free will, for free will connotes independent action, and to the naturalist natural and spontaneous are one and the same thing.

"Now, my friend, we also believe that something exists in its own right, but before it could exist it had to derive its existence from something that *preexisted* it. And this being true, then it follows that all things are traceable to one Thing that preexisted all things, a

Thing that causes other things to begin to exist, to cease to exist, or to be altered, because all things are dependent on this higher Thing for their existence. And that one self-existent Thing is God."

"It seems to me, Father, that you impute a kind of remorseless godlessness to scientists, which is not altogether true. Many do, indeed, profess a belief in God, as you very well know. Others find their concept of God somewhat altered from the view you present."

"Those among you who profess a belief in God," Sicola interrupted, "see Him as residing within things, perhaps indeed being the thing itself, but they do not capitulate to the notion that God stands outside Nature and made it. At least this is true of a very large segment of your group, and I speak only of those who are confirmed naturalists. They see only a great 'process' or a 'becoming' arising from a Nature that exists on its own in space and time, and nothing else exists. The supernaturalist does not deny Nature as the naturalist denies God. On the contrary, he sees, as Lewis says, 'one Thing as existing on its own and producing the framework of space and time and the procession of systematically connected events which fill them. This framework and this filling he calls Nature.'

"There are some naturalists who try to remain naturalists and yet entertain a belief in God. To them God is a 'cosmic consciousness,' an *emergent* God, and many people are more comfortable with this view of the God within us rather than the transcendent God. God emerges from the mass of swirling atoms within us, and hence is, in effect, created by *us*. Now we have a universal consciousness that has thoughts, but these thoughts are but the product of irrational causes. This cosmic mind, like our own, would be the product of a mindless nature. So we have not solved the problem, for we can expect to receive no help from this cosmic mind unless we place it at the beginning, if we assume it not to be a 'product of the total system, but the basic, original, self-existent Fact which exists in its own right. But to admit *that* sort of cosmic mind is to admit a God outside Nature, a transcendent and supernatural God.' Therefore we are back where we started.

"Assuming a God outside of Nature does not admit that this God created Nature, so some assume that God coexists with Nature, but this, too, is not rational, for Nature is not thought, and Nature had to be brought into existence by thought. So again we return to the beginning, the Creation. And, my friend, there is no way of avoiding the hypothesis that God created the universe if once you accept the *existence* of God.

"We are concerned with the observable," Bouchard commented dryly.

"Then observe, my friend, observe, for there are contradictions in the position of the naturalist. It was held by science that all matter consisted of small particles that moved about according to a strict pattern of movement, interlocked with the whole system of Nature. Then science learned that this was not true, that these particles moved randomly and without organization, yet mathematically it was possible to predict these indeterminate actions according to the probabilities applying to the tossing of a coin. Hence if the thing itself is without rigid control and may at the same time have a certain predictability about it, there would seem to be some credibility to the notion that a force greater than the thing itself controls it. And as Lewis says, this is hardly proof of the supernatural but some indication of the subnatural, and this being so, if there is a back door leading to the subnatural there may also be a front door opening on the supernatural, 'and events might be fed into her at that door, too.'

"The contradiction lies, further, in a system of thought that denies the validity of rational thought. Every theory of the universe that makes the mind a result of irrational causes is an inconsistency. As Mr. Lewis quoted J. B. S. Haldane, 'If my mental processes are determined wholly by the motions of atoms in my brain, I have no reason to suppose that my beliefs are true . . . and hence I have no reason for supposing that my brain is composed of atoms.'

"Therefore, if nature is to go its own way, on its own accord, there is an incompatibility with reason, for reason is that which acts upon nature to give it order and direction. When Nature seeks to impose itself on rational thoughts, 'she only succeeds in killing them,' Lewis tells us. But reason can invade Nature and make her captive, for every act of your consciousness attests to it, even the fact that you are attending these very words, for if Nature had her way all thoughts would ramble and all attention to them would also ramble. And this may, indeed, occur under emotional stress. Emotion uncontrolled is Nature at its face value, and emotions rather than being a justification of Nature serve only to interfere and suspend reason, rather than to set up a variety of natural reason.

"But it is Pure Reason to which we trace all other reason, and that Pure Reason is God. It is God who not only preexisted all things but all thinking, and that which existed first and gave life and meaning to what is brought into being by its efforts not only exists on its own but exists incessantly. Lewis tells us, as did Aquinas, that the human mind comes into Nature from Supernature and it has its source in an eternal, self-existent, rational Being, whom we call God."

Bouchard looked intently into the quietly reasoning face of Sicola, and he showed understanding at times, disbelief at other times. Now he asked quizzically, as if he had read Lewis: "If God is at the beginning of all reason and infuses the mind with His thought, how do we reach the wrong conclusions with the right thoughts?"

"Lewis would reply that human thought is not so much God's thought as 'God-kindled,' for, my friend, how would free will exist if all reasoning photocopied the perfection of Pure Reason? There would then be no need for this very discussion. What?"

"You continue, like the last time, to get the better of me, Father Simon, and you do it not so much with the force of your own words, but with those of others. But you will admit, my friend, that your sources are biased. You use Catholic thinkers to defeat me as if Catholic thought is supreme."

"C. S. Lewis, Signore, was not a Catholic, but there was little that separated him from Catholic thought. We are pleased to number him among the members of the Invisible Church, and equally pleased to gainsay that he presently occupies a high place among the saints."

"Let us grant, for the sake of argument, the validity of all that you have said, but are you not missing what was to have been the point of our talk? You started out by discussing the possibility of miracles, but it served only to lecture me on the existence of God."

"Is that not really the basis of any belief in miracles, Signor Bouchard? Once you have accepted the existence of a transcendent God, the author and creator of all thought and being, and of Nature itself, is it so difficult to accept the fact that He who creates Nature can first suspend Nature and secondly work through Nature?" Then he paused and looked steadily into the eyes of the scientist for a long moment and said finally, "Since I owe so much to the late Mr. Lewis, it is only proper that I should reply to you further with his observation that '. . . in Christianity, the more we understand what God it is who is said to be present and the purpose for which He is said to have appeared, the more credible miracles become. This is why we seldom find the Christian miracles denied except by those who have abandoned some part of the Christian doctrine. The mind that asks for a non-miraculous Christianity is a mind in process of relapsing from Christianity into mere "religion." ' "

"You have a way," Bouchard intervened, "of making a point that does not avoid personal implications. I am sure you intended that last remark as a summary of my own spiritual condition."

"Not at all, my friend. It was a general observation which just happened to be appropriate to your previous condition."

"My previous condition?"

"Si, Signor Bouchard. Are you so blind as not to see the miracle transpiring in your own life?"

"Miracle? What miracle?"

"Here is the fault of all who ponder miracles from the outside. They see only the spectacular and call it a miracle. There are many kinds of miracles. One is the kind that surpasses the power of the forces of nature, as in the resurrection of the flesh or affecting instantaneous cures, or the spinning of the sun,

but there are other miracles intended by God to draw
men of good will to His very heart. These are personal, quiet, even natural. He may do so by some extraordinary manifestation to prove a truth of faith,
but more commonly He will use the seemingly natural
course of human events such as suffering, either physical or mental, during the course of which the favored
one will grasp a truth so commanding as to feel himself drawn ever so gradually into His very arms."

"And you think that this latter kind of miracle is
taking place within my own life?"

"Si."

"But why, good Father?"

"Because He loves you, because you are a good
man, and because He whispered to you through the
voice of a little child, '*Sursum Corda*,' and you have
felt ever since the call to lift up your heart, a call
which brought you 'coincidentally' to this place, and
'coincidentally' to renew an acquaintanceship with
me, which — on its surface — was not renewable
when first we met. Do you believe this?"

"I do not believe, Father, but I *begin* to believe."

"*Miracolo!*"

The two men walked into the basilica, and only
Sicola heard the choir of angels and smelled the gentle, sweet aroma of roses wafting about the two of
them.

And Bouchard? He would never be the same
man again, for there is a miracle in the loving kiss of
God, even when the kiss is so tender that men are unaware of it.

The Women

They were the most militant of all of the women's groups, and Sicola moaned as he realized that he was to meet with them in the audience room at two o'clock. There it was on his schedule, "2 p.m., Audience, 100 Members, Women Involved For Emancipation." If he could get through this, he thought to himself, heaven would be a certainty.

He turned to Tommaso and said, "Tommaso, it is now fifteen minutes to the hour when I am to meet with the razor tongues; please to turn on the closed-circuit monitor so that I can have some intelligence on the mood of the enemy."

Tommaso grinned and remarked as he flicked the switch, "Holiness, you sound like you are what one might call a Ms. Anthrope."

Sicola glowered at him. "Tommaso, sometimes you look like a hyena. I am in no mood for the jokes! *Mamma mia*, but look at them, they wear pants! Let us listen to the kittens for a time. Do they purr, or do they screech? *Mannaggia*! Hear them. They screech, but it is not so much that sound that disturbs me. Some of them seem also to hiss."

"Perhaps, Holiness, it remains for you to hiss also. Then it can be said that you met with them and you hissed and made up."

"Tommaso, so helpa me, I will assign you to a small parish in Venice, under the water. Be still, I must listen."

In the great audience room one hundred women chattered like the sound of wet concrete sliding down a metal chute. At length, one who seemed to be their leader stepped up on her chair and clapped her hands for attention. The rumble subsided and all of the ladies took their seats.

"Girls," she began, "the Pope will be arriving soon, so let us conduct ourselves with decorum and courtesy, but at all times, remember, he's just a man. He puts his pants on each morning just as we do, one foot at a time." The ladies giggled, and one of them shouted, "Right on!"

Sicola listened, brought his eyebrows together and muttered, "Ahma gonna git you, but buono!"

"What is more," the chairperson continued, "I want to see none of this ring-kissing. His office permits no such distinctions according to our code."

"Keessa my foot, signora," Sicola mumbled.

"Now, let us go over the agenda," the woman continued. "I intend, in your behalf, to tell him that with him or without him, women will not be denied. Naturally his espousal of our beliefs would help in getting public opinion on our side, but we've got enough clout without him. As Helen Reddy has told us, 'If I have to, I can do anything. I am strong. I am invincible. I am woman.' First of all, we want women priests, and who knows, one day even a woman pope. Also, this big push on the part of the Vatican for motherhood has got to go, but go. And none of this Virgin Mother baloney! We don't need images created from fairy tales. Now, we must make it clear, however, that we are God-loving and God-fearing persons, but we happen to believe that God is not a male chauvinist. God is a woman, I tell you, *She is a woman*! Why? Because only women are creative, and if all of this was created, then it had to have been by a woman.

"Then we plan to move into the area of contraception and abortion. The Church must change its stand on these very vital issues of our time. Why, we even have priests and bishops on our side, do we not? Even they agree that every woman has the right, complete and total, over her own body. We all know that sex is here to stay, and for those of you who enjoy it, let it be understood that you can have fun without putting a penalty on it. Right?"

Her audience applauded her, and as Sicola sat in his chair near the monitor, his elbows on his knees, his hands cupped under his chin, he belched. "I think, Tommaso, now is the time for our fun, too. Get them from the dressing room and release them one at a time. I will sit here and watch."

Tommaso did as he was directed, and Sicola turned down the sound of the monitor, and watched the women in pantomime, which seemed to him all the more hilarious.

A bell sounded off the audience room, and Sicola watched as the women rose in a gesture of greeting. The door on the far side of the room opened. The women turned in that direction and waited, but no one immediately entered the room. Then Sicola saw them gasp, and he turned up the sound, for coming through the door was a large chimpanzee dressed as a dowdy woman, padded and bosomy. The chimpanzee held a baby chimp in her arms and fed it from a bottle as she walked toward the papal throne. Trailing behind in what seemed like a never-ending procession were ten very small chimps, each clad only in diapers. The small chimps clustered at the base of the throne and looked up adoringly at their mother, who promptly laid aside the nippled bottle and reached under her wide-skirted dress for a large, illustrated edition of *Grimm's Fairy Tales.* She proceeded to chatter in gibberish to the assembled chimps, occasionally looking up to pull the skin back from her lips in a mock laugh.

The women sat in shock, then they broke the air with an explosion of acrimony. "This is contemptible. An insult. A sacrilegious affront to women," they shouted.

Sicola rolled on the floor and held his sides as he laughed with a hysteria that brought tears to his eyes.

Shortly, Tommaso came bustling into the audience room, feigned consternation and anxiety on his face. "Have you seen them? Have you seen them?" he shouted to the babbling women. "Oh, you rascals, there you are! However did you come to be here?" Then he turned to the women, apologetically, "A thousand pardons, ladies, how they got loose is a mystery, to be sure. We hope that the animals did not frighten you." Then he gathered up the mother chimp, and the others followed him dutifully through the door. As if it had been an afterthought, he turned, poked his head through the doorway and shouted, "His Holiness will be with you in a moment. Please! Please be seated." Then he vanished, a baby chimp in one arm and its mother in his other arm pulling at his cassock.

After a few moments, the door opened again, and Tommaso, wiping his brow, ushered in the Pope. A woman in the back of the room expelled a hissing sound, which Sicola seemed to ignore. He stood before the huge chair in the center of the room as the chairperson approached him and extended her hand limply.

"Sir," she addressed him, "we are happy that, through this audience, you have given recognition to Women Involved For Emancipation, which is a further evidence of your interest in the cause of women everywhere.

"There are, however, certain matters we feel should be brought to your attention, matters on which you have expressed yourself in public, and which are counter to the thrust of our organization. These subjects include . . ."

Sicola held up his right hand to interrupt her. "Signora, let us save some time for you. You wish to discuss with us, for the purpose of reversing the stand of the Church, such subjects as the ordination of women to the priesthood . . . a deemphasizing of the importance of motherhood and the symbolism of Mary, the perfect Mother . . . and last, butta not least, you would like us to say it is hokee-dokee to enjoy the play withouta the pay. Si?"

The chairperson looked incredulously at Sicola, then out at the audience. "Good God!" she exploded, "we've been bugged!"

Sicola turned to Tommaso, his palms up and his shoulders hunched in a questioning gesture, "Bugged . . . bugged? Tommaso, what is this bugged?" Tommaso merely returned the gesture.

"Your Holi . . . that is, Sir, are you saying that you did not have bugs planted in this room?"

Sicola met her glare with calmness. "Madame," he asked, "do you see any bugs? Ladies, please to look under your chairs. Do you see cockaroaches, beetles, ants, any kind of bugs?"

While it was true that he hadn't given her a direct answer, the chairperson took this nonetheless as a denial. "If you do not have bugs in here, then how, sir, were you able to repeat our agenda, in the precise order — if not in the same words — as we discussed them before your arrival?"

Sicola folded his hands before his stomach and cast his eyes to the ceiling, a most angelic and humble expression on his face. "You ask a very interesting question," he said, as if he, too, had no idea of how such a miracle could have taken place.

The women grew restless and began whispering among themselves. Out of the hubbub, Sicola heard one word repeated several times, "Eerie!"

Sensing that Sicola had somehow gotten for himself a strategic advantage, and fearful of its effect on the membership, the chairperson turned to Sicola and said, "Well, it's neither here nor there. It doesn't change a thing, so let's get to the point."

"Si!" Sicola agreed, then parried, "Anybody ever tella you, you are a very pretty woman?"

She flushed with some pleasure, then recovering her composure, she said, "Thank you, but address yourself, if you do not mind, to these points, Sir."

Sicola began, "You are of the belief that God is a woman . . ."

A hundred women sucked air in a gasp that threatened to suck Sicola up. "He's done it again!" he heard them say. "He's done it again!"

"Eh?" The Pope raised his hands in a questioning gesture. "What have I said?"

"Let it pass, Sir," the chairperson whispered uncertainly.

"Why you want to make God a woman? You crazy! Make a Him a man. If a you want to getta God to play ball with a you, make a Him a man. I tell you why: He's a sucker for a woman, a good woman! You don't believe me? Reada you Scriptures. What's it say? Mary, the Holy Mother, Maddalena, Mary and Martha of Bethany, Mary Cleopas, the women on the way to Golgotha. All . . . all, I tell you, His special friends. He woulda do *anything* for them. Anything that was good. Would you want it any other way? You would not want to do what is bad if God said it wassa bad. But ask Him for what is good, flutter the eyelids iffa you want. He will be putty in the hands.

"You, Madama Chair, you married?"

"Yes, sir."

"You husband, he love a you?"

"I think so."

"Okay. You go to him with a fire in the eye and you say, 'Hey, Wallyo! Give me a hundred dollars for a new dress!' He give you one bigga fight. BUT! You say to him, "Sweetsheart, I love you ve-r-r-r-y much. I wanna look nice a for you.' POW! *You got it!*"

The women giggled. Off to one side a woman was heard to say, "Why do the handsome ones always become priests? What a man!"

"I tella you what's you trouble," Sicola continued. "You anda you husband want to play house, butta you want to change positions. *Mannagia!* You never had it so good! Shoo, he's a somnagun if a he makes you his slave. Tella him Sicola says it is okay if you give him one bigga shot in the eye. You are not his slave. You are his wife. You work by his side, not three feet behind him.

"You come a see me as if the Church is the adversary of women, and I say to you that the Church has always been your friend; the Church teaches the equality of man and woman. It was our illustrious

predecessor Paul VI who said, 'Men and women are
equal before God, equal as persons, equal as children
of God, equal in dignity and also in their rights.' But
there was more teaching, not only from Paul VI but
others, including the angelic John XXIII, who said,
'Nevertheless, although the rightly proclaimed equality of rights must be acknowledged in all that pertains
to her human person and dignity, in no way does it
imply similarity of function.

" 'The Creator has given women talents, inclina-
tions and natural dispositions which are proper to
her, and differ from those He has given to man; this
means that He has also assigned to her a particular
function.

" 'If we did not clearly recognize the diversity of
the respective functions of man and woman and the
way in which they inevitably complement each other,
we should be working against nature, and we should
end by humiliating the woman and depriving her of
the true freedom of her dignity.' "

Sicola had grown serious now, as if he were
reaching out to the women in audience to grasp each
by the hand and to reaffirm in them the depth of the
Church's love for them. The chairwoman sensed this
and some of her hostility seemed to dissipate before
Sicola's warmth. There was a new tone in her voice,
hardly conciliatory but more one of rapprochement,
of wishing to discuss openly the cure of a sore which
had festered in the hearts of women for centuries.

"Your Holiness," she began, "I am not unmindful of your good intentions. Perhaps it is for that
reason that we are here, to enlist your help in establishing women in their new role, for we have been
victimized by men in and outside the Church for too
long, and women are now becoming aware that we

have surrendered too much of ourselves to the male interpretation of our function, with all respect to your good Pope John. Let me give you an example of what I mean if I may quote from Luke 11:27-28. 'A woman in the crowd raised her voice and said to Him, Blessed is the womb that bore you, and the breasts you sucked. But he said, Blessed rather are those who hear the word of God and keep it.' From this it is obvious to us that Jesus clearly felt it necessary to reject this baby-machine image of women and insist again on the personhood, the intellectual and moral faculties, being primary for all."

"Madame," Sicola commented, "We did not disagree with this theology when it was first expressed by the theologian Leonard Swidler of Temple University, but we would point out that the meaning is more profound even than you would have it. For it is well known that Jesus honored Mary, His mother, above all women, and His answer to the woman was intended neither to demean Mary, motherhood, nor the just pride of a mother, but was rather Jesus' way of emphasizing the superiority of the spiritual relationship with God's word or kingdom over a purely human relationship with Christ Himself, as another biblical scholar has pointed out.

"Biblical historians have cited that women during the time of Christ were subjected to a secondary role as well as subjugated by a male-dominated society, and this was, indeed, the case, but those women who followed Christ were liberated in the truest sense of the word, for no longer did they see themselves as part of a caste system that denigrated them in spirit and position, but instead they were so filled with the essence of love, which is God, that this permitted them to view men as husband, brother, partner under the divine and protective love of one Father, one Lord, and one system. And under this selfless system each recognized his or her peculiar *function* as a complement to the other, not in competitive contradistinction to the other. The poet John Donne has expressed it, 'If they be two, they are so/ As stiffe twin compasses are two,/ The soul, the fixt foot, makes no show/ To move, but doth, if the other doe.' "

"But, your Holiness, through the centuries since the time of Christ, men have so dominated the social, political, and religious hierarchies as ultimately to see woman only as a whore, a wife, or a virgin."

"You seem to have covered the choices so well as to lead one to ask: what else is left? In terms of the *moral* order, are not these the only real options for a woman? But while two of the three are noble, the seeds of sanctity lie in all three. For it is sanctity and sanctity alone that should concern you, and once it does, you will find liberation, as the women of Christ's time found it."

"We seem to be getting nowhere at all, Sir. You have ready answers, it seems, which beg the question. So you return to your only answer, which is that we should strive for sanctity."

"Is there any other answer? For you or for me? For women or for men?"

"But there are women who wish to do precisely that, and they wish to do it in the priesthood, but they are denied this. In reply to the request of these women, you reply that Jesus chose only male disciples."

"No, Signora, we do not say that Jesus chose only male disciples, for numbered among the disciples were many women indeed. What we have said is that

Jesus chose only male *apostles,* and there is a difference."

"But, Sir, you yourself alluded to the fact that Jesus was born and raised in a Jewish culture that extended few rights to women. And one of your own nuns has said, 'Consequently, every attention to women by Jesus as recorded in the gospel must seem as a challenge to the status quo.' And she makes the point that God *asked* Mary to bear the Son of God. It was Anna who was one of the first persons to proclaim Jesus' mission. 'Women sinners,' Sister reminds us, 'had as much access to Him and equal mercy from Him as men sinners. Jesus broke the code also by talking to a Samaritan woman, and then He let her become an apostle of His message to her people.' Does this not imply that Jesus was willing to extend high privileges to women, even the priesthood, but was restrained by the mores of His times?"

"If, my dear lady, Jesus was willing to break the code by speaking to the Samaritan woman, why did He stop there? You do believe that He was God incarnate? Hence why should God be fearful of breaking man's code when He came to establish His own? Why did He not say to Martha or Mary, 'You will be among my apostles? Why did He not say it to His own Mother? In the very quintessential act of the priesthood, the consecration of bread and wine into His very body and blood, in this memorial to His victimhood — the Mass — there was no woman present to be commissioned to 'do this in memory of me.' Was it because He loved women less? Of course not! He loved some of them even more, if the flattering truth is what you seek. It comes again to the matter of inherent *functions,* and it was in His view the function of man to be priest and the function of woman to attract others to this priesthood, and to perform those ancillary duties which inhere within the singularly devoted hearts of women."

"You speak of Martha and Mary, your Holiness, and in this we see a further justification of the fact that Jesus was addressing Himself to women in the call to ordination. I do not have to quote Scripture to you, but simply to establish the background: you will recall that Martha was performing the chores of a servant, preparing the house for Jesus' comfort and cooking the meal they were about to eat while Mary sat at His feet to listen to Him. Martha became petulant and asked Jesus to reprimand her, but His answer was, 'Mary has chosen the better way, which shall not be taken from her.' Doesn't this imply to you that Jesus was calling for women to choose this other alternative of serving Him in the priesthood?"

"You have said yourself," Sicola interposed, "that Mary sat at His feet *to listen.* All that this implies to the Church — and it applies equally for men — is that there is within the contemplative life an opportunity for sanctity that can oftentimes become lost in the very movement of active religiosity. It was Christ's way of saying, 'Come to Me. Listen to Me. Let My presence overcome you like a flood of love that courses through your very being. Pray. Before all else, pray.'"

"You insist, Holiness, on maintaining a sexist view of religion."

"And you insist, dear lady, on hearing the aberrant voice of Dr. Mary Daly who pleads for the 'castration' of sexist religion, who harangues that it is 'women who are in a position to experience the demonic destructiveness of the super-phallic society in our own being.' It is not the function of the Church to deny you. It is the function of the Church, however, not to deny God, who speaks to her (and you see we reverence you even by imputing a feminine gender to the Church) — who speaks to her through the Holy Spirit."

The woman shrugged her shoulders in a gesture of despair, which was as if to say, "He will not listen. I cannot convince him." She turned to her group and cast her eyes upward in a mock signal of resignation. But then she seemed to remember again the lines, "I am invincible. I am woman." And she went off in another direction, hoping still to make Sicola concede. "It seems to me, Sir, that the Church is a totalitarian state which has determined that another totalitarian state, namely Russia, propagates a way of life that enslaves all humankind. Yet in Russia women are more liberated than in the Church. Let me quote to you from the Soviet Constitution: 'Women in the USSR are accorded equal rights with men in all spheres of economic, state, cultural, public, and political life.' What have to you say to that?"

Sicola smiled. "How do your American motion pictures say it? 'He speaks with forked tongue.' So does the Soviet Constitution. There are 19 million more women than men in the Soviet Union, yet not one of the 11 members of the Politburo is a woman. You have women in Congress, and the Church has women in positions of leadership in the Church. But there are no women even in the party secretariat.

"In industry half the workers are women, but nine of every ten plant managers are men, and only 12 percent of factory supervisors are women. The official newspaper of the Young Communist League decries this and points to the fact that women's average wage is significantly lower than that of men.

"In education three of every four schoolteachers are women, but three of every four high school principals are men. In science only 10 percent of Doctors of Science are women. In the field of public health 90 percent of Soviet medical personnel are women, but nearly half of all chief physicians and heads of hospitals are men.

"Among the work force, not only are women paid salaries far lower than men, but they are forced to take on backbreaking heavy labor, which American women would not choose to do nor be forced to do. So here equality seems to prevail to the detriment of women. A Soviet journalist wrote, 'A girl doesn't realize that the years given over to a male occupation can rob her of the main thing: her happiness as a woman, the joy of motherhood.' Should I continue, or is the myth of feminine equality in Russia sufficiently destroyed?"

The chairwoman smiled weakly at Sicola. "You seem to have been ready for us, Holiness, for you have done your homework exceedingly well. I was not aware of the statistics you quote, but something within me cries out at the statement you just read about the joy of motherhood. First, it is not all joy, and secondly why do you insist upon creating a mystique of motherhood as if it were a prerequisite for canonization?"

"Si, Signora, it is not all joy, as being Pope is not all joy, as being an artist is not all joy, as being a husband who pursues his vocation is not all joy. Joy is the result of conquest over meniality, over repetition, over boredom, over frustration, over denial of small successes. Joy is the fulfillment of pain overcome. And motherhood gives no *carte blanche* to holiness, for holiness is achieved equally, and sometimes more fully, in singleness and in virginity, but to her whose role is the married state the *via crucis* exists no more nor less than for her whose decision is virginity or in a marriage relationship that bears no children.

"But to seek a world in which women assert independence, primacy and total separateness from the love of a good man is a neuroticism. Mary Wollstonecraft in her militant *Vindication of Women's Rights* was to take this position. George Sand was to pick up the torch and carry it high. But significantly these extreme feminists, and many others today, were women of broken homes, homes dominated by cruel fathers and suffering mothers who were martyrs to the overpowering male, mothers who refused to cry out as their daughters were to do. And modern psychology has traced the life histories of the Mary Wollstonecrafts and the George Sands to draw a clinical picture of neuroticism, which found its outlet and expression in free sex morals, in promiscuity. And as Alexander Magoun has said, 'promiscuity and the inability to love go together.' And therein lies the paradox. For in expressing a hatred for man on the one hand, in clamoring to be like him in every way, in shouting for the abolition of marriage as a sacred institution, there is in these very women an inherent desire for the proximity of man, the protection of man, the love of man. And in the act of sex there would be no way to reverse their roles, male and female. Mary Wollstonecraft herself was to reach that time when she would beg for legal marriage and the true love of a man. All too late perhaps she was to learn the wisdom of a latter-day sociologist, Jacques Leclerq, who would say that 'physical love is the token of total intimacy. It is the sign that the lovers have nothing to refuse each other; that they belong wholly to each other.' The sex act can yield no more than is brought to it, physically or emotionally. In cases where the sex act has become a mere gratification of senses, where there is no love to impel it toward a spiritual end, the satiated male rolls over and goes to sleep, as if he had just enjoyed a meal that left him lethargic, and cathartic. But intercourse as a love act is the full expression of a love that does not end with orgasm. If it does, it is mere passion, and passion is a butterfly that flits in transitory pleasures from flower to flower.

"Marriage, too, has a nature. It is within its nature to make as one man and woman, the fruit of which union are children created in love and nurtured in love thereafter. Where love is missing from this union, children become the product of an animal passion only, and they in turn develop their own neuroticism in a direction more nearly animal than human, except for the intervention of the grace of God. Now you have a scientist who would make you more fully machine and less woman, for he says that a world in which men are virtually unnecessary is now possible. Dr. Earle Hackett of Australia has said that the human species could now be maintained with only a small bank of men as a source of semen, since men are little needed in today's industrial society. This is an affront to your very femininity. And if this is the symbol of the Utopia of the vanquished man, you will be the worse for it.

"Take care, dear ladies, for Rosemary Haughton has said, 'The early feminists wanted only legal justice, but the present women's liberation movement questions all that seems the basis of a stable society. When the lighthouses of custom were taken down, the familiar ways of thinking about marriage and love suffered shipwreck. . . . Women who choose married life must choose it not for protection, not for fulfillment, or in a romantic search for an impossible paradise for two, but in order to grow in love for God and man, with the one she marries and with her children. With this sense of direction in life, she can become the core of a new Christian community. . . . The revolt of women often leads not to freedom but to wild experiment, and the pathetic attempt to convince oneself that new sexual partners are better than the old.' I would remind you that this lady has spoken up in your behalf on many of the issues that beset you. In this instance, listen to her as the voice of moderation, as the voice of one who wishes to entwine your cause with the cause of God."

"You do not seem to deny that women have certain rights, your Holiness," the chairwoman mused softly. "You preach only that we avoid extremes, is that correct?"

"Madame, I am against hate, and I am for love. I am for love when it is especially centered on God. I merely request that you be the self that God created."

"But each of us has a different notion of that self, Holiness. Some of us see ourselves as totally free, and that all exercises of that freedom are but manifestations of the flowering of our true selves."

"Some freedoms are the freedom of Satan; others are the freedom of God. In the one there is no restraint, and in the other there is self-control. The one is animal, the other human. Be rather like the Image from which you were created; hear one voice, the voice of God, and in hearing Him you will become more like Him."

"Some of us would like to do that very much, Holiness. We have been trying for centuries to know who we really are and what is truly expected of us."

"You spoke a moment ago of coming to flower. It is within the nature of a rose to be a rose. It cannot transfer its essence to be anything other than a rose in its specific nature, and a flower in its general nature. It cannot become a peony, nor a gladiola, nor a marigold. It is a rose, and in fulfilling its nature it becomes a more perfect rose. Neither can it become another species outside the nature of a flower. It cannot become an aphid in order to protect itself from an aphid. So it is with a woman. She asks, who am I? and her answer is to be found in nature just as the identity of the rose is found in nature. For she is, indeed, a rose in the human garden, made in perfection, blooming in the fullness of God's love, reflecting this love in the beauty of her immortal soul. But like the rose she, too, can wither and fail to bloom because the pests of nature attack her and stifle her abundant potential. The crime against the rose is committed by the parasite, which inhibits the nature of the rose. The crime against woman is in the denial of her womanhood, by herself or by others.

"The trap of Satan is set when a woman seeks to be like her enemy rather than to become more fully woman, hence more fully feminine. He who seeks to diminish you needs to be overcome as the aphid must be overcome. But we are all at the mercy of the gardener, for it is the gardener who is solicitous of the rose, and it is the gardener who attends the rose with devotion that brings its magnificent beauty and aroma as an enchantment.

"It was said by a poet that a tree lifts her leafy arms to pray. Who can deny the prayer in the fully ripened bloom of a velvet rose? If there is the aroma of sanctity, as it has been described, is it not like the fragrance of the rose? A rose which, in truly fulfilling its nature, has come to full bloom?

"Woman, become more woman and more perfect in that which you are. If you are demeaned, if your strength is sapped by the male parasite who would deny your fruitfulness, strive always for the bloom, and in the striving know that God, the ubiquitous Gardener, loves her — or him — who most seeks to grow in the nobility of His design. For it is not so much that you are attacked, but that you come to flower. It is not so much that you are cut from the stem as a bud, but that you come to full flower after the cutting, and rest in the vase of eternity as that which bloomed in radiant color when it was picked by God Himself. This, dear ladies, is sanctity. Cultivate it. Pray!"

The chairwoman, swept along by Sicola's quiet intensity, tried to assert herself once more, then, looking out at her kneeling membership, she dropped also to her knees.

"O my God," Sicola prayed. "Bless these women so that they may look upon their uniqueness, their power to save the world, their ability to share in the creation and delivery of souls to you. Let them see their uniqueness not as a challenge to men but as supportive where it needs to be supportive, dominant where it needs to be dominant, but always submissive to You, their Father, for what You want is their perfection in the spirit and their ultimate worthiness to be with You for all eternity.

"And let them behold the matrix of Woman who was Your mother, who said, 'let it be done to me as you say,' and in this was shown to the world the summit rather than the nadir of submission, not to men, not to things, but to You. So that they may not see

Mary as fainthearted and so subdued as to be without a positive nature, let them give witness to her strength in its very subtlety. See how she called upon Your love with a firmness so gentle in her implacable knowledge that You could not refuse her. She said simply at Cana, 'They have no wine.' And though it was not yet Your time You were moved by her love for You and Yours for her. And there was wine. Let them invoke her intercessory power also for them, yet let them turn to her not as God, for there is but one God, but as the woman who is the model of all women, as the woman who most understands their inmost natures, as the woman who would lead her kind to guide with love the arm and the tongue of impetuous man. *Salve, salve, salve Regina!"*

Sicola took the crucifix from Tommaso and raised it over their heads, tracing a cruciform pattern in the air above them. He gave them the Papal Blessing and said to them, "Go, my children, go with the love of God and His Church."

The women filed out quietly and as they reached the Square, they saw the mother chimpanzee parading in front of St. Peter's her diapered babies trailing behind her, and in her right hand — held high above her head — was a placard on a pole. It read: "I am a W.I.F.E."

The chairwoman smiled and said, "Isn't she darling?"

It was said, however, that when the Associated Press released the picture and the story of the audience to its member newspapers throughout the world, the sound of women vomiting was heard everywhere.

Sicola knew that he couldn't win them all. "But perhaps in time . . ." he said wistfully to Tommaso.

A Possible Fantasy

Sicola sat at his desk and studied the man sitting across from him. He was tall and lean, and there was a hollowness under his cheeks, but the tiny broken blood vessels on his cheekbones softened the ascetic appearance with a rosy tinge of color. The man's white hair, so straight and neatly in place, showed streaks of yellow along the sides, marking him as a blond in his youth. But the eyes, Sicola thought, were most remarkable — blue but not cold, rather warm and generous and twinkling with humor. He wore a Roman collar, but unlike that of most Catholic priests, his suit was gray.

"The ecumenical movement has come a very long way since the days of Pope John, my friend."

"Ah, yes, indeed, your Holiness. I can remember a time when such a meeting as this would not have taken place."

"Si! But here we are now, good friends, enjoying our commonness as brothers, yet without despising each other for our small differences."

"Some would say, Holiness, that our differences are not so small, that Rome is being most obstinate in relinquishing its hold on those few areas that still divide us."

"Yes, my friend, I am aware of this. Some of

146

your scholars have great integrity, and their beliefs — like ours — are very strong. Others remain the prisoners of their youthful environments, which instilled into them vehement hatred of the Church. We love them both, and we long for unity because it is the will of God that we become one."

"Do you suppose it will ever happen?"

"Of course, Reverend, it will happen. But it will not happen easily, and it will not happen because we sit at a table and discuss our differences. Discussion removes trivia. Major obstacles must be removed by God Himself through the graces He sends and with which He touches the heart in the deepest and most hidden corners of understanding. It is the head that unravels, but it is the heart that understands."

"Well put, Holiness. But I would assume that it is *our* hearts you feel must be touched, and not yours. Is that correct?"

"The human institution that is the Church has made many errors, has blundered abominably in its intercourse with our separated brothers, good friend — and we know it. But that *divine* institution which is the Church, which is established by *divine* laws outside of human invention, does not err — no thanks to weaklings like me, simply because God does not allow it. And those things that separate us are inviolable. We cannot arbitrate, for the law of God is so intractable as to be subject to no arbitration. To you these laws are recondite, for you view them through a history conceived in rebellion and perpetuated in prejudice, and old notions do not die easily, but it is hoped that one day they will as the General said, fade away."

"I think I understand. Perhaps, like many of my associates, I do not concede, but I *do* understand, if I might say so. That is, if one puts himself in another's place, it becomes easier to see as he does, and we then recognize the honesty that brings him to such a position. And I believe you are doing somewhat the same thing with us.

"But you must admit that even in this area progress has been made. For example, there are still many of my Protestant persuasion who deny that Christ is truly present, body and blood, under the different species of the host. But that number is lessening. So you see, it is possible through dialogue to build a bridge between us."

"Ah, yes. You are right. But dialogue only builds the bridge; it is God who makes you cross it."

"Perhaps intercommunion would tend to get us across the bridge."

"We cannot allow it, for it would hold the Eucharist up to display as a meaningless symbol only. And man cannot receive into his heart and soul what he rejects in his mind. If it is bread he accepts, it is bread he will receive. But we will not be guilty of calling it only bread.

"Already, in our eagerness to win you back, we have — in the eyes of many — protestantized the Church. In an effort not to offend you, some in the Church — knowing of your indifference to the cult of Mary — have sung Mary's tune *sotto voce,* and others have refused to let it be heard at all. But that will change and is now changing, for she will not be suppressed.

"We have simplified our liturgy to make it more meaningful to you. We have done many, many things to make you aware that the door remains open to you. But so far is enough. We cannot tamper with transubstantiation, and we cannot surrender Scripture and tradition to you."

"Yes, I know to what you allude," the minister smiled. "What you are saying is that perhaps the chief stumbling block to our unity is the maintenance of the idea of your sovereignty."

"No, Reverend, not my sovereignty but papal sovereignty. Papal infallibility, if you will."

"But we do not understand how you can take scriptural passages like 'whatever you bind on earth shall be bound in heaven' as divine fiat that Peter and all of his successors would enjoy the same privilege."

"Need I tell you of all people, my friend, that every word spoken by Christ was a word directed to the world, not only of His times but of the times to follow until the very end of time. How can you not see that the words spoken to the beggar, the leper, the centurion were words spoken to us today and not recognize the significance of 'upon this Rock I will build my Church, and the gates of hell will not prevail against it'? He has entrusted to Peter, of whom I am but the successor, the 'keys of the kingdom.' The keys open only the doors to heaven, hence we are concerned only with eternity and cannot abrogate so divine a contract.

"It is not merely important but critical that we come to see as one, not many. Come, follow me to the garden that I may illustrate."

The two men walked through the wide open doors of Sicola's chambers to a terrace above his garden. The minister towered over Sicola's six-foot frame, and he threw an arm over the Pope's shoulder in a gesture that warmed Sicola. As they walked down the flagstone steps to the edge of the garden, the minister said, "It is the foyer to heaven, good friend, where we will meet again one day."

"I am convinced of it," Sicola smiled. "Now

observe, please. Over here, the gardener has planted these trees. Note how close they are and how many are growing, but they grow into one another, and their height will be limited. Each is sucking the nutrients of the soil and denying to the other what it needs for full growth, and each is vying for its glimpse of the sun. Now observe over here, the gardener planted but one tree at the same time as these others, yet take note of how full and tall it is; note also its symmetry, its perfect shape. Nothing crowds it from reaching up to heaven."

"There is great sense in your observation of nature, Holiness, but I hope that you do not imply that our competition disturbs monopoly."

"Competition? No, my friend. God is pleased that each tree competes to be better than the other in ascending to the heights of heaven. What dismays Him is that such a competition diminishes potential, or prohibits the actualization of potential, and each soul has the potential to become holy. Yet how can some do so when the true riches of His graces are denied a return to Him.

"To the large tree the sun is like the Eucharist, which nurtures it and yet continues to make it hunger. To the small trees there is no Eucharist, because neither will allow the other to receive it. For the spirit to be denied the Eucharist is of greater moment than if the body were denied food. But there is one sun, one Church, one Eucharist, and one body. It is not merely important; it is crucial to the world that we become one."

"Amen, your Holiness."

The two friends walked back to the terrace, and Sicola took no note of the fact that he had left his walking stick pushed into the soft, moist soil around the small trees. As he remembered, he turned with the minister to recover it. The small trees were gone, and in their place stood a broad and full tree. The crook of Sicola's walking stick hung curled around the lowest limb of the tree, dangling like a small child calling for attention.

The minister, astonished, turned to Sicola and said with a quaver, "Holiness, I know that legerdemain is not among your accomplishments. But how in the name of God . . .?"

Sicola paused for a time, similarly astounded, then whistled and said, "Good grief, Charlie Brown!"

All in the Family

There was a high sky, and Sicola felt a sense of exhilaration as his lungs swelled with air that came to him clean and pure off the mountains. He studied the purple mountain, a monolithic symbol of the grandeur of God Himself, and observed how the snow sat comfortably on the head of the mountain like a regal crown and on its shoulders like an ermine stole. In the infinity of the horizon it stood outlined in sharp definition, a silent statement of Nature undefiled. Infinity? No camera could capture true infinity, he thought, as he set the old Leica and raised it to his eye. But he had to admit this came very close. It was magnificent, incredibly breathtaking. And it had been there, going unnoticed by those men who walked with heads down, seeing only the effete gravel under foot and the ant mounds that formed on the footpaths. Only those who walked looking toward infinity would ever see the majesty of God, and Sicola was filled with the view of it, and the very implication of it.

This was his day in the country, his opportunity to get away and meditate. His only company consisted of his gnarled walking stick and the singing voice of Nature, whose melodies Sicola knew so well because he was attuned to the subtle winds that breathed as they talked in a gentle whisper. He was attuned also to the semaphores of vegetation that waved to him as prince of joy, friend of the infinite, reader of the forces that brought verdancy and beauty. He was the patron of the arts of Nature, recognizing the genius that painted the awesome beauty that lay before him, blending, mixing, daubing, all with a harmony and order, so brilliant, yet so soft.

This was Almighty God kissing the earth. Only here would he find that solution so fundamental, so central to the problem of that other world writhing with the agony, the passion, the aimless flailing of its own misery. Here God would show it to him in all its pristine simplicity. Of this he was confident. And as he walked, there was the spring of youth in his steps, and he sang with a praise that must have reached heaven itself, for there was no restraint of inhibition to muffle the praise of God who created this, this superb composition of beauty with purpose.

As he walked, the crunching earth and gravel giving way beneath him, he swung his knapsack off his back and reached inside for the bread and cheese, which would have a taste he had not noticed in Rome. Even as plain a fare as this came to him sharp and rich and so delectably sweet. Only the Italians, he thought, could make such a cheese as this, and then only the simple ones, the uncomplicated inhabitants of a social order in the midst of nature.

Sicola reached a high point in the road, and before him there lay a valley through which a narrow river snaked and curled. Squares of varying shades of green marked the patchwork of farms in his view. And there, nestled about the river, a small village snoozed in the warm noonday sun. Rising above the

mélange of small plastered huts, white and clean, rose
the spire of a tiny church that extended above the
valley like an exclamation point proclaiming
"Peace!"

He stabbed the earth with his walking stick and
made for the quiet hamlet. As he approached, a small
stucco house came to view. It sat perhaps a mile from
the community of houses ahead, alone and even more
remote than the village itself. As he neared the house,
Sicola observed that no fence kept the life of the town
away. It sat on a knoll above the townsfolk, visible to
them and, certainly, Sicola thought, accessible for
local ceremonials. They must have come often for pic-
nics in the shade of the magnificent tree that grew in
front of the house. Near the roadside, a child sat.
Perhaps he was twelve, maybe thirteen, Sicola
thought. He had skin as pure and stark as the small
white house, and golden highlights warmed his chest-
nut hair, which fell softly around his ears. There was a
delicate pink translucence about his lips, and his
brown eyes were placid and thoughtful as he sat on
the small carpenter's bench beneath the tree. He studied the broken chair before him, fitting rungs into the
dowel holes in the legs.

"Hallo," Sicola sang out to the boy.

"Good morning, Signore," the boy smiled as he
became suddenly aware of Sicola walking toward
him.

"Do you have water for the parched throat of a
wayfarer in this glorious country?" he asked the boy.

"Oh, yes," the boy replied, "come with me to the
back of the house." The boy took Sicola by the hand,
and his face was animated with the excitement of an
alien in his yard. He pulled at the tall man's arm as if
he were impatient to lead the visitor to the well be-

hind the house, and there also to his father, who
worked in the shop a few paces from the well.

Sicola tried to understand the new awareness of
pleasure at the touch of the boy's hand, but reason
eluded him. All he could vouch for was the feeling,
which gave him a sense of belonging in his new environment.

"Babbo, Babbo," the boy shouted as they turned
the corner behind the house. "We have a visitor! We
have a visitor!" Then he let go of Sicola's hand and
ran to his father, who emerged from the shack, wiping
his hands on a worn work apron. "Look at him,
Babbo. He is a giant! Is he not?"

"Slowly, my son," the father smiled amiably.
"He looks like all men, except perhaps just a little bit
larger."

He walked out to meet Sicola, extending his
rough hand. As they shook hands, he said, "The eyes
of a child see all men as giants, do they not? How can
I be of service to you, my friend?"

"I had been spending the day in climbing your
hills and admiring the beauty of your countryside
when I came upon your home. The throat begins to
become tight and dry from so edifying and breathtaking a view as you are blessed with. I thought perhaps
you could let me drink from your well."

"But of course," the man said with such concerned fervor as to bring a smile to Sicola's face. The
warmth of the child was the warmth of the father, he
thought.

The man pumped water into a ladle and handed
it to his visitor. Sicola finished it off without hesitat-
ing to take a breath. "Ah-h-h," his voice grated with
pleasure, "it is only water that truly satisfies thirst.
And such pure water at that. I thank you, sir; now I

must not impose further upon your hospitality. I will be on my way."

"No . . . no," the father objected sympathetically, "you must sit for a time. Rest. It will give you new energy for walking."

"If it is no trouble, Signore. Perhaps I could just sit for a few moments. But do not let me interrupt. Please . . . go on with your work."

"It can wait, I assure you. It is not often that we see strangers in our valley. Come! Let us go into the house." He would not accept Sicola's reluctance to disturb the routine of the man and his family, and soon, with the boy running ahead, they entered the rear door of the house to the kitchen, where the wife stood smiling and ready also to make him welcome. The man pointed to a chair at the table while his wife brought out the glasses and began to pour wine for the two men.

"I am Giuseppe," he introduced himself.

"That is a very happy coincidence, Signore." Sicola said as he shook hands again. "My name, too, is Giuseppe." They laughed happily at their commonness.

"And this, my traveling friend, is my beautiful wife, Maria." She touched his hand, and as she did so, Sicola was struck with the triteness of words to describe her beauty. She was, indeed, a beautiful woman, but it was not so much the features that marked her loveliness as a serenity, the same serenity he had seen in the boy. From all three this quality exuded, but in the woman there was a unique placidity that seemed to say that she could find comfort in all things and, having received it so bountifully, could impart it to the entire world simply by her manner. One could not feel turmoil in her presence, he was convinced, for to do so one would have to be a devil, who alone would resent the source from which her serenity derived.

She had that color of the northern Italian, fair of hair and skin, and in this the boy resembled her. But the boy took his brown eyes from the father, for hers were blue, bluer even than the blue he had seen behind the snow of the mountains. And her hair, what a golden, molasses sheen, as if she had spent her morning in combing and brushing it. It fell below her shoulders in gentle waves, framing her face as if by a radiance of golden light. Her mouth, too, was like the boy's, with that trace of light red wine, moistened and tender. But that tranquility! Sicola came back to it. It was as if it were born of an understanding — deep and loving — of all things and all people, and in the fullness of its understanding it lent sympathy, strength, and charity to all of creation.

Giuseppe was, indeed, much like her. How could one live with such a one, Sicola wondered, and not become affected by such peace? Her husband worried not the least about tomorrow, for he knew that as the birds and the lilies of the field were provided for, so would he, who was greater than the birds and the lilies, find the comforting embrace of God even amid the prickles of life. He was strong, muscular, and only a little shorter than Sicola. There was about him the pleasant odor of sawdust, which lay in the cuffs of his trousers and sprinkled across the burly hair of his arms. His hair was black and curly, and his brown eyes were open and gentle, set amid a lined olive complexion. But where Maria's serenity was quiet, Giuseppe's was cordial and outgoing.

These were people who perhaps, even in Rome or London or New York, would remain the same,

Sicola observed, for they seemed not so much a product of the tranquil valley as progenitors of peace, by whom the valley's citizens themselves must have become affected.

"And you, my son," Sicola turned to the boy, "what is your name?"

"Emanuele, Signore."

"Ah, that is good. Giuseppe! Maria! Emanuele! I am very pleased to make your acquaintance. I drink to your continued graces."

"That, Signore," Giuseppe said happily, "I will drink to."

What had been a simple stop for water on his day's outing became a more protracted stay for Sicola. There was a commonness beyond first names, more felt than understood. And as Sicola was reluctant to leave them, they too were opposed to his going from them. They had spent more than an hour about the table simply in conversation, that lost art of western culture. For here there was no television, no radio, no distractions to the joy of familial oneness. All life had its meaning in the family, and this was not to imply that the child of such a family would become an appendage of the home, thus to remain even in adulthood so that he would never leave. One day Emanuele would leave for other parts, but he would take with him — and give to civilization — what the family had given to him in the form of love and selflessness, even of privation and its concommitant, which is called courage by those who become nourished by it.

They urged him to remain, and he did. For three days.

They sat at the plain kitchen table, draped with a red checkered cloth, and sipped the wine that Giuseppe himself had made. Strangers did not often come to their valley and Sicola's host was anxious to know all about him. Who was he? What brought him here? Did he have to return quickly?

"I am a priest, Giuseppe, who looks for the hidden secrets of God so that I can deal with the flock with greater understanding. One becomes so occupied with the business of salvation at times that his very activity impedes the growth of the spiritual mission, which is his primary duty. And the spiritual message lies in the heart, hence one needs to find that time of solitude wherein he can plumb the depths of his heart, where God speaks most intimately to him who listens. But sometimes, as you pour water into the pump of your well to make the well perform more quickly, one must also contemplate God amid His glory. The message lies in Nature, and you have it in abundance here."

"So," Giuseppe drawled, "you are the priest. Then it is to be 'Padre,' not 'Signore.'"

"Whatever pleases you, my friend."

"And have you thus far found in our mountains the answers you seek?" Giuseppe asked him.

"What I have found, I have always had. But it was as if it were reborn, this overwhelming sense of creation, so vast, so ordered, so grand, and so incomprehensibly beautiful. In this, no, there were no answers for me, but answers are the flowers from the seed. As awareness is the seed, understanding is the flower. And one begins first with so tremendous a sense of awareness, so encompassing an awareness of his own humility at his place among the minutiae of infinity, that he becomes all the more awed by the loving genius of creation. This is the ultimate awareness, and from it springs ultimate knowledge. At this moment I am aware, most humbly aware, of the immensity of God, of transcendence made immanent, of the littleness of this priest. This your mountains have given me. Perhaps you can give me more."

"I, Father?" Giuseppe asked. "What can you learn from me?"

"This I do not know. But as I entered the area of your home, even before crossing the threshold, I was filled with the notion that here was that for which I had searched. Here was the atmosphere that needed most to be brought to my world."

"But here, Father, there is just Maria and me and Emanuele. I build or repair furniture, and sometimes my Emanuele helps me. Maria tends to the house . . . ah, no, Maria does more than tend to the house. It is she who holds it together with her love. For our amusement, I make some wine, Maria sews, and Emanuele, he plays with Ignazio, his friend, the lamb. What can you find here?"

"Much," Sicola answered.

Maria had remained silent as the two men spoke. Occasionally she would smile at Giuseppe, or reach over to thread through Emanuele's hair with her fingers. But, for the most part, she studied Sicola's face, her own face showing that mood of restfulness that pervaded the home. Now there was a pause when Giuseppe simply smiled at the priest and said nothing.

"I think," she began, "that our new friend will find what he seeks, for God leads him who already carries God in his heart."

Sicola turned to her now. "Signora, you have God in your heart, in your face, and even in the very tips of your fingers."

"I am a serving maid of the Lord. Be it done to me according to His will," she replied.

Sicola remained with the family for three days, each of them peaceful and happy, and he began to know more and more what he had first only sensed. Through his observations and his conversations with them he noted that here, as in few families of the modern world, God was not simply a concept of catechism, not merely a vengeful deity who hovered over them keeping daily score of their minor transgressions — though Sicola saw even more of these — but a being integrated into the very breathing, eating and sleeping of the family. It was true that their prayer life was external, manifested in unison, and profound, but there was also an interior prayer life that was timed to the beats of their hearts, rhythmic, constant and ofttimes unconscious. When Sicola asked Giuseppe if he prayed always, Giuseppe replied that Maria had taught him the "Jesus prayer," a short, simple ejaculation which he repeated over and over so that it became so habituated that when he awoke in the morning he found his mind turning over the words, "Lord, Jesus Christ, Son of God, have mercy on me." It was as if they had been repeated in his brain even in sleep with the steady beating of his heart. And throughout the day, at his work bench, in times of play, at mealtimes, the words repeated themselves again and again. It was in this way, he said, that one day he experienced a sense of merging, of unison, of integration with the very heart of Christ. He questioned it not. He was at one with God through Christ.

And Maria, too, would sit under the large tree in the yard, peeling and slicing potatoes for the meal, and her face expressed a kind of quiet rapture that told Sicola that her mind was floating through space and time and found its rest in the mind of a generous Benefactor who aligned the simple act of peeling a potato to the handiwork of God. Sicola could not take his eyes from her. He was the Pope, the spiritual head of a great Church, and here she was, a simple house-wife, so rapt in the ineffable love of God that she could teach him theology, uncomplicated and total and true. It allowed for no condescensions to modern thought, to situation ethics or evolving morality, be-cause there is a truth so simple when it is born in the totality of one's love for God that it sees it as timeless and unchanging as God Himself.

And Emanuele was like a pool over which Maria and Giuseppe stood, and in him was the reflection of his parents, mirrored in his face, the depths of his heart and his soul. It was Emanuele who would leap from his cot in the morning and go directly to Sicola. Then he would kneel before the priest and say, "Fa-ther, bless me, please." As they recited grace before and after meals, it was Emanuele who would turn to Sicola when it was over and say, "And bless the Church, dear Lord." Sicola, touched, would kiss his brow and say, "Some day you will make a good Pope."

Then the strange thing happened. It was on Sico-la's third night with the family. They sat about the fire and talked. Sicola told them of what was happening in that world far beyond their mountains, of the wor-ship of sex as a sacrament unto itself in the new order instituted by Satan, of the rise in crime, of the seeking for mind expansion in drugs, of the submergence of marriage as a contract before God, of the alienation of children from their parents through legislation, of the murder of life conceived but unborn, of the rebel-lion of women prone to a grandeur beyond their natu-ral grandeur, and then he spoke of the defections in the Church, and his face grayed, his shoulders sagged, his voice cracked. These, he said, were those chosen ones who could have pointed the way to blessed eternity if they but had a portion of the prayerful communion of Giuseppe, Maria and Emanuele.

He turned to Maria and said, "Oh, Maria, you who have such a way with Christ, pray that this bitter cup be taken from the Church, and then it will be lifted also from the whole world. You, who are a mother, must know of the pain of Holy Mother Church when the least of her children suffers a prodigality so great as to cut forever the ties that bind one to heaven. Ask Christ to give us a sign of what it will take to restore to a troubled world the peace of God."

They sat in the dimness about the fireplace, as flames licked hungrily at the stones, throwing flashes of mottled light on the faces of the four. Sicola looked at Maria, and he saw her bathed not in the flickering light of the fire but in a radiance so bright that it caused him to blink and watch with his eyes only partially opened. The serenity remained, but somehow it was tinged now with a sadness, and from her eye there slipped a tear that coursed beside her nose and remained in the crevice of her cheek. She did not speak. Then she placed her right hand into the pocket of her blue apron and brought out her rosary. She stood. And the others knelt as they prayed the rosary.

Sicola had said the rosary every day since his youth, and all fifteen decades since his seminary days, but he had no recollection of every having prayed with such infused devotion. Always he had meditated upon the mysteries, but his meditation had been through the process of his own will. Now the mysteries lay before his mind as if projected by a force beyond him. There was a new reality to the Agony in the Garden. Sicola not only saw the sweat of Christ pouring as blood from the pores, but he seemed to share in the suffering, tasting the salt as the blood trickled into his mouth, joining in that divine awareness of the ultimate, the necessary, the incontrovertible need of expiation. And searing through his brain was the burning question, "How many times must you suffer, dear Lord? Even today?" And his compassion grew so great that he wished only to take the place of the suffering Jesus who knelt at the rock in the garden, and say, "Rest a moment. Let it happen to me instead."

But it was not to be. For soon they came and took Him, shackled His stripped body to the post and flogged Him, flogged Him with no mere leather whip, but with that multi-stranded device of torture on whose tips were tied the sharp pieces of metal to make the pain all the more unbearable and the gashes all the deeper. And in the very flagellation of the Son of God, the bestiality of men seemed to give the lie to the dictum that man was made in His image. "Was this also necessary, Father?" Sicola found himself asking as he winced and found his shoulders hunching from the expectant pain of the next slashing cut across the back of Christ. "Oh, my God, the pain! That man should endure it is heinous indeed," Sicola shouted within himself, "but that God incarnate should be so treated is the mystery of all." This was a part of the great salvific mystery that still eluded him.

Pain. Suffering. Indescribable agony. But was it so necessary to add humiliation, dear Lord? To crown with thorns, mocking the claim of kingship, satisfied the mockers, but what did it do to You, Lord? You looked out into the crowd and saw the faces of men who only yesterday followed You, hung on Your words, and now they joined in the jeering. I could not have endured it, Lord. But You did. In silence. Animals, animals, all of you are animals! Sicola's throat moved with the words, but no sound came from his lips.

Now You are weakened. There is not much strength left in Your body. Hardly enough left to stand. And yet the cross is placed upon Your shoulders and You are told to carry it. The weight of it is the weight of all of the sins of history, of Sodom and Gomorrah, of Moses' legions in the desert, of Dachau, of the pogroms of Russia, of the incredible denial of God in our own times, of the pornography, the licentiousness, the violence, and of the slow but growing disintegration of autocracy in the family, in government, in education. No scale could measure the weight of a single sin in the ponderous weight of the cross. All of the sins made the cross so heavy that You fell three times, that mysterious number three again, as if — even in this despicable humiliation — there was a foreshadowing of the three days that would follow your death. As there were three falls to earth on the way to the great Gift, there would be three days of waiting before the greater Gift of the Resurrection. And as the Cyrenean is shoved into the road, he is told to take up the cross in Your stead and is repelled by it, but finally he carries it unwillingly. Sicola's agony now was the agony of shame as he heard himself say with a sob, "Lord! Lord! There am I. I am the Cyrenean, fearful of the cross."

It is said by many, Lord, that the Crucifixion was the climax of the drama, and perhaps it is so, but yet was it not also the denouement? Was this not the unraveling of all that had transpired with its implications of what was to be? Was this not a time when it would seem that no greater pain could be suffered than You had already endured, yet who among us could endure the piercing of the flesh with nails? Who could tolerate the slow death of asphyxiation, as the weight of Your body, suspended upon the cross, pushes downward on your lungs. Then You press with Your remaining strength at the nails in Your feet in order to raise the chest for just a short gasp of air, and the nails tear away at the wound, and soon You cannot raise Yourself any more. It is consummated! Sicola's head dropped to his chest. Then he raised it slowly and the thought came to him: This was the denouement: It was expedient. It was for me. Now I am free to follow Him where He has gone.

When they had completed the *Salve Regina,* Sicola turned to the family about him. Maria looked sadly into his eyes, and in the glance there was a silent plea to lift the Son's burden. Giuseppe now sat before the dying embers of the fireplace, his folded hands between his knees. He was silent and lost in the stillness that followed the recitation of the divine tragedy. Emanuele still knelt, his face turned upward, and Sicola felt a compulsion to pick the child up in his arms as one takes a lamb, feels the warmth of its body and the softness of its wool, and draws it ever closer to himself. Emanuele, Emanuele, he thought, what a road you will be forced to take in the years ahead! But here you have found all that you need, all that you will ever need, to follow the road as it leads to the very arms of God. For here is the cell of life, which was so perfectly formed in its prototype, the Holy Family. On your pilgrimage, my child, remember always to turn to the people of your time with the injunction: "Behold your Mother."

Part II

TALKS TO UNIVERSITY STUDENTS

The Fountain

We sit under this bowering tree, my students, and we contemplate the mysteries of nature and of the universe, and how unfathomable they seem to us. At least this is so for those of you with the mark of humility on your brow. You are struck by the giantism of the world around you, the infinitude of the depths of the pool that is knowledge, the insignificance of the place your own soul has in this wondrous magnitude.

I also look out among you and see certain of you whose expressions reflect the surety of the mighty, the elite, who will vanquish their world with their own certitudes. And I feel sorrow, my young friends. How is it said among you? Yes, "the world is your oyster!"

To both of you, I say: go to the fountain to drink, with thirst that is unquenchable, but once you have quaffed the waters, know that you will be thirsty again, and that successive journeys to the fountain will not raise the level within you beyond its momentary potential, but it will permit you to be filled with the juices of endurance, plaguing you to return again and again with unfulfilled thirst. Know also that the fountain belongs to each of you in equal measure, and know that the pool is limitless, but that the capacity to drink at any one time is limited.

Does this not fill you with both joy and humility?

The superb joy lies in knowing that the water is there for all, a munificent gift of nature; humility must arise in your minds for the restriction on the design of your being that makes it possible to become surfeited only for the moment.

All of you I would warn lest these small sips from the fountain fill you with a kind of drunkenness, which overcomes all good sense and leads you to that state of euphoria that becomes so centered on your knowledge as to consider the mere act of drinking sufficient to place you above the centuries of mankind that preceded you. It is the tendency, my students, for man — no matter at what point in life — to view himself from the standpoint of his own uniqueness, and this is, at times, good. But when he views his knowledge as solely acquired, it gives rise to vanity. For remember that you are but an increment in time, while your knowledge is an aggregate of all of time. Let him who stands before the intricate architecture of a magnificent bridge be not so vain as to view it with the silent or expressed thought: "How great am I, for I designed that mighty bridge." No, my dear friends, he did not. He is responsible only for the degree of his incremental knowledge and his infused imagination, which capitalized upon the centuries of successes and failures of noble creatures preceding him. The centuries became reposited in the book of knowledge that comes to you today, but what you do not read is the sweat and the blood, the fatigue and the failure, the hope and the discouragement. Knowledge comes to you purely, even with its footnotes. It is for others to supply the marginal notes.

Knowledge is without selfhood. It cares not to whom it imparts itself. Knowledge only has selfhood when it reaches you; then it becomes no longer "it," but you. It is you who identify it with the mark of your own individual thinking and purpose. As knowledge gave itself to you, it is for you to pass it to others, much as the baton is passed.

But whence comes this knowledge? When you say to me, from the great books written by the great men out of all of history, you are correct, though lacking in perception if this is, to you, the only source of knowledge. For there is still another book of knowledge whose treasures are beyond the pages of all of the books in all of the libraries of the world. It is as vast as Nature itself. For it is Nature.

The printed book of knowledge is facts, and facts are not to be decried, for facts are like lineaments, like flesh and bones and sinew, a part of the outer man. In Nature lies the hidden story of the soul of man. Probe it deeply.

If the end of knowledge is for your glory, then you must be content with facts, but if the end of knowledge is the perpetuity of the soul of man, then all knowledge must be entwined with the correlative purposes of Nature. You say, my young friends, Nature is without a mind, so how can it have a purpose? The answer to your question comes from the very pages of the printed book of knowledge, and it comes from the great minds of history, minds that saw the absolute necessity of looking into the natural order for its answers.

Aristotle spoke to you of his "Unmoved Mover" and his "First Cause," tracing motion and matter to their sources. It was he, moreover, who was to give us the first halting steps in a thought process involving Nature as being both actual and potential, all at one time. Ergo, my young minds, if all of Nature is an actuality with potentialities, and all of Nature is traceable to a Universal Mind that is its first cause, then man and Nature share a oneness in their actuality, their potential, and in their creation. Is it too far a jump in rhetoric to expect you, then, to see a purpose in Nature?

As the book of knowledge is incomplete, my young friends, so, too, is the book of Nature incomplete. Each is complete only in the Universal Mind, but to you they remain as chapters only. Subsequent chapters will be written, and you will write them. You who write them best will try your newfound knowledge in the court of Nature. It will be for you to ask, "What is the fundamental nature of man? What is the fundamental nature of that which serves man? What is the fundamental nature of that which man must serve?" Do all relate to the Universal Mind? Can actuality be linked with potential to equal the perpetuity of the universal soul of man? Ah, my friends, I see that I have lost you because I speak in the language of the philosopher, but it is not my function to lose you, so I will explain in your words, and I will do so without shame, though I may offend some of you.

It is apparent to you when I speak of the Universal Mind that I do not believe so complex, so vitally interrelated a cosmos was the result of accident, pure and simple. The Unmoved Mover, the First Cause of Aristotle, the Universal Mind of whom I speak is the God of man, of beasts, of plants, of the strata and substrata of our world. There is a fundamental nature even in God, my students, and reason tells me that even though He created all of nature out of nothing, He did not create nature without a purpose, for then He would be capricious, and it is against the nature of God to be capricious. The rock has the actuality of its nature to be a rock, but it was for man to learn that the rock has swirling within it molecules and atoms that gave it the potential for energy. Man is the actuality of his tissue, and swirling within him are the molecules and atoms that provide igneous energy. The energy of the rock can be joined to the energy in the mind of man to produce only a great explosive force, which is destructive and incapacitating, or it can bring warmth into his home, effect cures in the bodies of the sick, or move man from one place to another. I ask you to consider once more, what is the fundamental nature of the rock? What is the fundamental nature of man? Are they joined together to serve the fundamental nature of God?

It is for you to decide. One way is the richness in the printed book of knowledge. Learn it well, for then your greatest competition in life will be Univac. It may give you joy to be so compared to the computer with its vast lore. It may even place you above your fellows, for your acquisitiveness will give you treasures unequalled by Midas himself.

Or you can go beyond the book of knowledge and delve into the book of Nature. That way lies wisdom. And who knows, my bright, eager young people, perhaps even sanctity. Does that frighten you?

We will talk again. Go now.

The Fountainhead

The day is a glorious one, my young friends. We sit beneath the tree as the sun strikes its perforated canopy and prints upon your faces the mottled design of light and shade, warmth and coolness, knowledge and un-knowledge.

Even in the patterns of the sun there are symbols that have meaning, for where there is light there is shadow. Thomas à Kempis says to us, "Every perfection in this life has some imperfection mixed with it, and no learning of ours is without some darkness." It is for us to pursue perfection, and in its pursuit we come ever closer, ever bridging the gap, for only God is true perfection.

Does it disturb you that I speak of God? You who occupy the oyster, do you look upon what I say as subversive to the objective study of reality? Indeed, you do. It is written on your countenance that I bring to you the opiate concocted by man to make palatable something not wholly understood? That I assert divine order to what you proclaim is the admirable accident of the ordered universe? That I bring to you "legend" when you are occupied with that which is measurable?

Does it give you comfort to know that you stand with the legions who, like you, remain skeptical, pragmatic, attuned to the now-ness of our times? Then be comforted, for now.

I ask only that you give acceptance to a fundamental corollary of scholarship: that you do not deny what you do not understand, that you admit the possibility of truth in what you do not believe, that you come to the fountain willing to drink. For it is only in this way that true knowledge is attained. The pursuit of evidence requires it.

Let me give you examples out of history. Closed minds have ruled much of that history; it was for minds that were open to bring light where there was darkness. The satanic was at one time imputed to the study of hypnotism, and indeed it is a paradox that openness of mind was a mark of those who were most diabolical. Hence came the Svengalis of history who placed the stamp of Satan on that which would seem consigned forever to the dungeons of black magic. Even out of evil, God brings good. For is it not true that hypnotism is today accepted by men of science? Would it be so if a scientist had *not* said, "What if there is truth in this notion that one can plumb the mysteries of the trance-induced mind?"

Within this very century it was proclaimed to be against Newton's own law for men to fly and cavort in the skies. What if those daring pioneers of aeronautics had not said, "Suppose that it is true that man can fly?" Every preeminent development in the growth of knowledge has begun with a positive assumption.

Does it not strike you as unscientific when a scientist who is granted the coveted Nobel Prize for his discovery of the molecular structure of DNA, who was, in effect, able to break the genetic code of life, proclaims (with the same certitude that marks your faces) that there is no ultimate spiritual reality, no Creator of the ordered complexity to which he is exposed in his microscope?

Does this not remind you of your choice once again? Is it the quest for knowledge and the Univac for which you strive, or is it the desire for wisdom and serenity of soul that impels you?

Can you, therefore, not begin the study of God with the same presupposition? Suppose that it is true? Then let us see where the merest inkling of affirmation will take you. For in Him is the greatest wisdom, and from Him will flow to you all the wisdom you seek.

I say to you, my bright young men, that God exists and it is self-evident that He exists, and for these proofs I am indebted to history itself. It was other minds who built this ladder to the unknowable, and it is in synthesis that it comes to you through me.

Aquinas — the forgotten man of today — tells us that something is self-evident in two ways. It is evident in itself, though not to us; truth inherent, yet undiscovered. Or it is evident in itself and to us. When it is self-evident in itself and to us, it is because we are familiar with the truth in its very essence. But because we do not know the essence of God, He is not self-evident to us, hence He must be demonstrated by His effects. We may have some vague notion of His existence implanted in us by nature, but this is not to know *absolutely* that God exists. To hear footsteps on the walk outside your door is only to know that someone approaches. It is not to know with certainty that your friend or your beloved approaches. As yet there is no identity, only an awareness. And is is more than awareness you are seeking. It is the identity you will embrace, not the sound of footsteps.

There are those pitiable souls who will deny that the existence of God is a matter of rational proofs. But this is so because they have permitted themselves to become afflicted with philosophical myopia, a condition of environment. In each of us, at birth, there was that *a priori* voice of conscience that spoke within us a sense of joy when our acts were good acts and conversely nagged and gnawed at our wills when we performed an act that was bad.

This has been demonstrated in our own times in the study of aboriginal tribes dedicated to the wanton killing of their kind. Murder became their religion, and their gods smiled upon him who showed bravery in the commission of this violence. The confirmation ceremony of the adolescent was most simply a test of his skill and courage in the commission of murder. But the sociologists point out that he approaches the ceremony of killing for the first time with fear, and it requires a supreme act of will to take the life of his brother. Because it is expected of him, he does so, and his mood initially is without exhilaration. He is charged with a sense of awe and fright, and in many cases, he retreats to the forest in nausea. His vomiting is the symbol of the release of his inhibitions, and he returns to his tribe for their accolades. In pride, he becomes a man. He is now one of them.

I say to you that the first consideration in our ascent to the acceptance of God lies in the admission that He gave us life with this vague knowledge of Him, which we call conscience, it remained for His will to submerge it. Conscience may be encrusted by our wills, but it remains.

But God gives us other evidences of His existence. The Apostle Paul says, ". . . His invisible attributes are clearly seen . . . being understood through the things that are made" (Rom 1, 20). And Aquinas reaffirms the apostle in telling us that God can be known by His effects.

It is acceptable that all of life, all of the universe is a most spectacularly ordered unity, complex yet interrelated in ways not completely known, but of its order we are certain. Now I suggest to you, my eager minds, that there is no order without design. You submit to my judgment a paper that defines and elaborates your thesis, and without *order* it is merely a jumble, a hodgepodge, leading us nowhere and ending without conclusions. But you *design* your thesis carefully, structuring it, supporting it, and you give it substance, order. But it was design that made it so, was it not? And all design requires *authorship*, does it not?

Who then, I ask you, was the Author of so magnificent an order as that which we study in the cosmos, in the world, in man, in the animal, in the plant, in the rock? Only a Universal Mind could design so grand a complex as the universe itself.

Or let us take the matter of the ball dropped from the roof. Gravity, you say, makes it fall. But whence comes gravity, my friends? As all motion requires a mover, who was the First Mover? Put another way, is there not a cause for every effect? And if the cause of the birth of a child is union of man and woman, do we not accept that the birth of the man and woman had a prior cause in the birth of their progenitors? Men of science give credence to this, and in doing so some go even beyond the coming together of the first man and the first woman to the single cell. But even in granting the unproved assumption of all of life commencing from the single cell, is there not inherent in all of this a chain of causes that presupposes a First Cause?

Now let us consider the nature of accident. Even in accident there is a cause. The young man trips over the hidden mine and dies. Accident? No cause? Ridiculous! The mine was placed there for that effect. The young man drives the highways on a winter night when the road is covered with a film of ice. He grows careless, and his rate of travel is greater than safety permits. The car strikes a tree, and he is injured. Sad, it is true. But accident, in the sense you would have me believe of the accident of creation, is patent ignorance of cause and effect.

Again I look at some of you and I see the words written across your minds: you build a logical case, my teacher, but ultimately it is faith that brings you to your position. Yes, I say to you, it is faith in this sense: let it be known that the existence of God can be known by natural reason, but that faith presupposes natural knowledge, as grace presupposes nature and perfection the perfectible.

The light shines in some of your eyes as the ideas I have given you begin to take root. To others of you the eyes show the glint of steel, defying the entry of that which you choose not to accept. To all of you I say that this one belief in the existence of God is the fulcrum upon which all other arguments in our lectures will be balanced. Meditate on these thoughts at your leisure; may you meditations become like the salt that brings a greater thirst. Slake your thirst in the waters of the fountain springing from the subterranean stream of wisdom.

We will talk again. Go now.

Of Falling Leaves

A leaf falls from the tree and undulates through the unseen particles of air about us. It is a lazy journey, but inevitably it comes to rest by our sides. The leaf has served its purpose to the tree; now it moves on. By dying to itself, it can now serve the earth, passing on to it the nourishment it contains, but for a little while it will serve also as a blanket on the soil, protecting it from the elements, making certain that the moisture from the earth is not sucked from it too quickly by the sun. Then it will make its own unique contribution to a form of new life.

Pick it up, my young scholars. Perceive its shape, its color, its intricate network of veins. Those minute passageways are the conductors of nutrients that provide shape, size, and color to it. This is order, my young friends.

And I repeat from our last seminar: nothing is ordered without a prior design, and there is no design without an author.

The dog gambols on the green off in the distance. Unlike the leaf, in the dog there is a form of intelligence. He will respond to commands; he will avoid pain when experience has taught him to do so, and he will give affection. Yes, my friends, and he will also show anger. He, too, is ordered magnificently.

180

Food is ingested, digested, converted to energy, and he continues to live as his heart beats with the pulsating need to be cared for.

Are these not the same characteristics that mark you and me? Yet he is a dog, and you are a man, so wherein lies the difference? You say, he cannot count. He cannot perform the intricate mathematical assignments you are capable of doing. He cannot conceptualize. He cannot learn of Shakespeare, Molière, and Ibsen. He does not have within himself the ability to know the essence of things, of matter and spirit, of time and eternity. He cannot drink from the fountain as it is your power to do.

Yet there is a divine order in the leaf, in the dog, in human life. There is a sameness in design and in authorship, but there is a difference, is there not?

Ah, my bright young minds, you seem to know precisely where I am taking you. The thoughts of the teacher are transparent to you. Yes, my students, that which is common to us and to no other form of life is, indeed, the soul.

It is not an invention of modern times that each man is composed of body and soul. Dionysius alluded to "spiritual matter," and Aristotle and Plato took more definite stands on the separateness of the spirit or soul. As is the tendency of all thought, all knowledge, it was for later students and philosophers to bring growth to early knowledge. Here you see the quest of man for the essence of life.

My old and holy friend, the Forgotten Philosopher of our times, tells us that the soul is the first principle of life. The first principle of life! . . . Does it not tell you that the Universal Mind worked from that principle first, that He created the soul first of all because it took precedence in His world. For His world is a world of the spirit, and out of His own environment He created that which was of His environment and was to return ultimately to that environment.

And the mystery of it all still prevails. That He is able to create so many souls, each with its own uniqueness, no two alike, each created with a love so singular and so complete as to make one wonder, in this age of production, how He could invest the same limitless love for each. And because He made each soul with the limitlessness of divine love, He made each one perfect and incorruptible.

You question me, my friends? You say where lies the perfection of the mongoloid? Where lies the incorruptibility of the murderer, the rapist, the embezzler?

You see through your eyes, my students. I ask you to see from the depths of your wisdom. Only the body and the mind of the mongoloid are marked with imperfection, as the itinerant traveler's clothes are marked with the patches and holes of imperfect garments. But the soul was made perfect, for God does not make that which is imperfect. The corruptibility of man is but the corruptibility of the physical man, for disease corrupts the body, but the soul endures. Death corrupts the body with the inevitable decomposition of all matter, just as the leaf fell to earth to fall into decay. But the soul of man is incorruptible; having been created in eternity, it will return to eternity. That the soul may become stained does not require it to be corruptible. That it may languish in hell does not mean that it dies.

That the soul is spirit we know. It is not mind, as some would have it, for the dog has a mind. It is not simply more developed mind than the minds of animals, because there is no potential for animal minds to be more. The soul of man is spirit for it is that which animates the mind in thinking, feeling, growing, acting, in knowing the essence of things, unlike the most developed animal in all of creation. The animal has found its completion in the completion of its potential. Man finds his completion as man in his soul, whose potential is without limit. Yet it is also true that the completeness of the soul requires the body to make it so, for the human body cannot exist without the soul. When the soul departs the body, the body returns to nothingness. As man finds his completion in the soul, so too does the soul continue its spiritual existence awaiting the return of the body for its ultimate completeness outside of time. Its completeness awaits that point in the design of the Universal Mind when all souls will once again reside in their corporeal habitat, their beings restored to the fullness of their pristine uniqueness.

Does this not speak to the issues of life that surround us today? Incumbent upon this understanding of the soul, should there not be a better understanding of new life, of procreation, of the destiny of the human species?

Consider! If procreation is an animal act and that is all, with no Grand Design, then life begins at the first flailing arm and choking scream outside the mother's body. If procreation is the vital life force, the prerequisite of the "first principle" of life, then the moment of creation is the moment of conception. *For the creation of a soul is the creation of spirit, and spirit is in the mind of God, whose will suffers no delay between the thought and the act.*

We hear much of viability, which is defined as that point in the development of our species wherein human life can sustain itself independent of its mother, that is to say, outside the womb. I submit to you, my young people, that viability is a false concept, created to serve a convenience, though it may be under the subterfuge of noble societal concerns. These concerns may vary: what is conceived to be an over-multiplication of the human species, the right of a woman over her own body, the economic difficulty of providing for new life, the pleasure of profligacy without responsibility, birth as a result of rape or incest, or the use of unsterile and illegal methods of terminating life.

The arguments brought to bear against the deliberate termination of fetal life gain in strength, hopeful of small victories that will grow into ultimate and total victory. This is the hope that will — it would seem — continue to savor only small conquests until man comes to accept that fact of life which is the soul. For as all matter consists in an actuality that has inherent potentiality within it, so also does the inseminated egg have within it the actuality of the soul with the potentiality of intelligent life. Once begun, all other stages that follow are merely the stages in a continuum, and for whatever seemingly humane reasons, there can be no termination by man in what God has set into motion, unless man is willing to face the consequences of a wrath which can only show itself in dire consequences to society in the present, the future, and in eternity.

Then, my leaders of tomorrow's world, if there is a uniqueness of the soul by virtue of its divine origin, its fullness of divine love, does this not suggest to you a consistency in the view of all of life? Is the developing life more or less precious than life in its terminal stages? Is the soul of the murderer less precious to the Designer because of the heinous crimes he has committed? Is life taken on the battlefield justifiable, even in the guise of freedom?

These questions must be answered *sub specie aeternitatus,* from the light of eternity, for the convenience of a human rationale leads only to very human solutions, does it not? But to him who lays bare his soul to God in humble adoration come all answers, because in the mystical communion of the soul of man with the heart of Christ can only come commonness of purpose.

But let us reason at this time like men, God-centered but outside the aura of mystical contemplation. Let us assume that you, my intent young friend, still live while your son has reached the age of eighty-five. The possibility is most remote, you will agree, but since we are making mere assumptions, let us continue to suppose. At his advanced age, your son lies in a hospital bed, his bladder incontinent, his body weak, his voice a whisper, but life goes on. His heart is strong, his mind is alert. Still he suffers, and inwardly he questions his Maker concerning his useful function on this planet.

You sit by his side and you remember holding him in your arms as an infant; you remember the touch of your lips against the softness of his cheek; you remember the pride he gave to you in his success, small and large. You remember his vigor and energy, his enthusiasm and determination, now gone forever. And you know that you love him.

You love him so much that you are torn between your desire for his recovery and your hope that his suffering will cease in peaceful death. At that moment, the physician enters, speaks gently to the old man, then draws you aside with convincing detachment, medically oriented discernment, and says, "It would be so easy for me to end it all for him. A simple injection and he would be gone." And he would be correct; it would be so simple. "He will die with dignity," you are told.

You ponder the choices as you pray. There is an awareness within you that you were co-creator, with God, of the soul that still lives and will continue to live, regardless of the fact that it is reposited within a shell of wrinkled skin. And you ask: can I destroy that which I created? If, indeed, I was a partner in the creation, can I do so without the permission of the Senior Partner? Do I not abrogate my partnership forever if I do not act in concert with Him? It occurs to you, further, that your partnership is not even an equal partnership, for it was He who created you, hence there are not two equal votes having the value of fifty percent each. His vote, then, counts for more.

You are saddened by your decision because it is your wish for him to reach peace, but you must say, "It is not mine, not yours, to take what we do not fully possess."

So the vigil continues, and finally you know that the end is near, and you let him go peacefully, without the supportive systems of medicine. The vote was cast, and there was no ballot box. He who made, took. He who possessed, repossessed.

For all, there is a time to live and a time to die. That is our certainty. Our uncertainty lies only in . . . when!

Is all of this less true for the criminal guilty of a capital crime? I do not think so. Let Him who made, take; Him who possessed, repossess. What is of importance is your responsibility to the criminal as well as to the crime. It is no less to the offended, which is society, and the loved ones of the victim. But what is common to each is that which is common to all, the soul. It is the all and everything that matters to God. This strikes you as severe, but you will recall that I asked you to judge all things in the light of eternity. You say, should the murderer be permitted to live with impunity, should there be no punishment? I say to you that society must punish, just as a father who loves the son must punish, but ever in the process of dispensing punishment is the undercurrent of salvage, just as in His Being is the undercurrent of salvation. The strides of salvage will seem small, and the end far, but it is within each to provide the increment of his times, for as Pasteur learned of microbes, it was for Salk to deal the blow to poliomyelitis. In between these two giants of science stood the many increments of learning which were a part of other times. And so it can be in the process of salvage.

What I have said is only slightly less true of war, which is the ultimate outrage in the settlement of international disputes. History is replete with this stupidity, and it would seem that history must continue to repeat itself, but must it? Perhaps you will have a say in this matter. I ask you to conciliate, arbitrate, compromise — try all means short of committing your nation to the wanton destruction of human life, but keep before you always the sacredness of your own life and your obligation to maintain it. If a man holds a gun to your temple and it is within your power to put an end to his threat, you must do so, even if the cost of it is his life. If a man — driven by Satan — is determined to subject your children to slavery, to deny their God and their right to worship their God, go to their rescue by whatever means is necessary to reinstate their freedom to be and their freedom to worship. This is what it comes to, but I beseech you: do not impute to all wars a holy crusade when they are, in fact, serving another motive.

So the shadows of our day begin to lengthen, perhaps even as the shadows of our times grow long. As one signifies the nearing end of day, the other may carry within it the implication of the nearing end of our opportunities to enhance the human condition. I ask that you remember that the human condition — as important as it is — is of insignificant proportion to the condition of the human soul.

Other leaves have fallen to the ground, each a tribute to the fullness of their beauty, the enrichment of our sense of the beautiful in life. One day soon the tree will be bare.

We will talk again. Go now.

Under a Bowering Tree

The tree spreads its limbs over us like Goliath with a hundred arms. Behold the breadth of this bower, with all the limbs, like arteries, coming from the stoic trunk. Its grandeur cries out to us for attention. It is like a rock with a hidden life force that impels it to verdant vegetation. It is magnificent.

Whence comes its power? How does it achieve such beauty? From what hidden source is its purpose enriched?

You say, my young friends, that its nutrition comes from what is not visible to us, from its root system which feeds it as the tributaries supply the great river. Who can quarrel with you? — for you are correct, and, moreover, to be commended. Now you begin to look for your answers in the things you cannot see with the eye. But we shall not congratulate you excessively, for all of us were aware of the importance of these roots, these underground siphons of the soil. Is there not more? Indeed, there is more, you tell me. For the tree would not be so great a symbol of authority without taking sustenance from the air, the sun, and the rain, all elements of a higher realm than earth.

Like other figures of authority, the tree exudes a monolithic, rocklike strength that is not without benevolence. Its durability is unquestioned, for it has survived ravages from without and within, so we know it to have strength. Its benevolence is also without question, for are we not comfortable in its lap as we sit and ponder eternal questions while it stands as a protector between us and the heat of the day?

There is, indeed, authority in the tree, but it is authority derived, authority entrusted, authority governed. For God governs all things by His providence.

That I have used the tree as a device is by now apparent to you, for it is with higher realms that we occupy ourselves. It is for us to make known to you from the obvious that which is not always obvious to eyes that do not see beyond surfaces, moments, immediacy. That was the task of the Forgotten Philosopher, or the Angelic Doctor, as he is also known. It was he who left to us the vast critique of Nature which saw within it the hand of God in an ordered universe, who saw that God, indeed, governs the tree and all things by His providence.

We have learned that we know of the existence of God by His effects, and having witnessed these effects, it was for us to find the source which we know to be God. We stated, moreover, that God is not a capricious God, hence all of His effects are ordered to one end — Him. There could be no other purpose, for it is against the nature of God to create that which is good and desire it to serve an end less than the highest end, which again is God.

If God is the end of all things, then by His providence He governs or rules all things, for things that are ordered to a certain end are subject to the end. Because all things are directed to the end of divine goodness, it must follow that He is the governor of that which belongs to Him, that which He desires most. Rulership stands above the subject, but the subject chooses the course because there is benevolence in authority. In love He attracts; with indifference we deny. He governs with the consent of the governed.

That He directs is a fact of His governance, however. God is the first Unmoved Mover, and all things that are moved are moved to an end. Therefore, God moves each being to its end, even as it has no knowledge of that end. Now, I submit that it is not possible to move toward an end in an orderly fashion without having knowledge of that end, unless that knowledge is held by a Universal Mind that has knowledge of that end. The arrow does not have knowledge of the target, but it reaches its mark by the knowledge of the bowman.

Therefore, the whole of nature must be directed by a greater knowledge, for it is a principle that the smaller takes its direction from the larger. The disciple is not above his master. And the order of Nature consists in smaller parts having direction imparted to them by their larger parts. God, who is the progenitor of all, is the Whole containing and directing all the parts, large and small, near and far.

Consider the hidden beauty of all of this, my students. The nearer a thing is to its cause, the greater share it has in the effect, which is illustrated best by the observation that things are hotter as they are nearer the fire. If this is true of all of nature, of which man is a part, consider the need of man, then, to become closer to the Cause. Only then does he become more like the Cause and have a greater share in the effects. This is the challenge He leaves with you. The challenge, however, is not without a caution: as the leaf is not greater than the tree, do not assume that your ever-closer proximity to the First Cause permits a pride that usurps him whose greater nearness was ordained by God.

For God is pure intellect, pure will, pure spirit. His is pure goodness, supreme and self-contained. And His intellect bestows goodness on things in the measure required to reveal His own goodness. But it is intrinsic in the divine order that all things partake of divine goodness by way of likeness, by assuming the goodness of the Giver. That which is most like Him is closest to Him, and that which He wills chiefly is the good consisting in the order of things. And as things are more enhanced, more enriched, the divine order is more ennobled, giving authenticity to the fact that God governs all by His divine intellect and through a hierarchical dimension.

He instills in man the need for perfection, which urges him ever and always to higher plateaus. Perfection is thus made possible, for every created thing attains its ultimate perfection by its proper operation, and perfection is more assured as things come closer to their ultimate end. The end is the equivalent of the source.

Of what am I speaking? Do I deal in conundrums? You say, the old man never speaks of things unless there are other meanings. But he speaks in such riddles that we cannot relate his words to his motive. Are these but the symbols of other messages?

He who has ears, let him hear. There is message enough, even for him whose ears hear only what is audible. To him whose ears are attuned to the infinite, whose eyes perceive the spirit, there is more.

It is not enough to know that God exists. To exist may be passive, indifferent, even capricious, but we know that God exists actively because He governs. Moreover, we know that those who are closer to God, *by fiat,* share a greater degree of divinity than those who are farther away. By fiat also they are charged with the benign — though oftentimes strict — governance of those for whom they are responsible.

To Him who governs, obeisance is due. But to this obeisance we must give consent, else it is like a curtsy from the knees while the mind is in rebellion. And to him who is chosen by fiat similar willing obeisance must be given. "He who is not with me is against me; and he who does not gather with me scatters" (Luke 11, 23).

The tree — like the rock — is but a symbol. When moles attack the roots of the tree, the body dies. When the rock becomes subject to the winds there is erosion. And there is sadness in heaven for the demise or the diminution of what is held highly. Still, the moles have no souls, even as this symbolic tree has no soul. The rock has no soul even as the elements have no souls. Hence there is no accountability. Only the Tree of which we speak consists of a soul, being at one with the Soul of God. And the moles and winds that attack it similarly have souls, free to love or to attack that Tree which is the Church.

Yet the Tree will stand for all of time. It may weaken. It may even bend, as it has on other occasions, in other times, but there is regrowth, and it flourishes with a grandeur and a beauty surpassing its prior health.

Standing over the Tree, working through it, is the ever-present light of God. Because it is closest to the Sun, it has within itself the heat which is most like the Sun and, therefore, has a greater share in its effect. Because He loves, it loves. Because He governs, it governs. Because He draws us closer to Him, it draws us closer, also. As He seeks our perfection, so does that which is closest to Him.

There is an anarchism in Nature that does not have its center in God, and that which does not have its center in God must be bent to God's purpose, or being bent to its own, it will destroy itself. Because the Tree is beneficent in its gifts, loving in its protection, it suffers the onslaughts of the moles in patience, all the while extending its arms both to heaven and to earth. And as its limbs become burdened and arch downward to touch the earth, it offers its attackers a bridge, the grace of entry to its highest boughs — by way of its embracing arms. One may hear it crying softly in the winds for those unwilling to take passage in its hold. For, like God Himself, the Tree has one concern: the souls of the earthbound.

> "We have in our day no prince, no prophet, or leader, no holocaust, sacrifice, oblation, or incense, no place to offer first fruits, to find favor with you. But with contrite hearts and humble spirits let us be received; as though it were holocausts of rams and bullocks, or thousands of fat lambs, so let our sacrifice be in your presence today as we follow you unreservedly; for those who trust in you cannot be put to shame" (Daniel 3:38-41).

I ask you to take these thoughts with you. Meditate on them. When you have meditated sufficiently, you will know that each of you is drawn by an inner voice, without identity to some of you. You know only that you seek a better way than the way you know. What you do not know is the means by which you may attain it. Some of you will seek the love of your fellows and will be known by your secular deeds. You will be called humanitarian. Others will tread the earth, but your eyes will seek to penetrate the haze above you. Therein lies the effulgence of heaven.

Hear the Tree crying softly in the winds?

We will talk again. Go now.

To Know the Sun

What do you know of the sun, my young friends?

You know that it gives life to living things. We would not seek shelter under the tree were it not for the sun, for it could provide no shelter if it could not grow and have rebirth according to the season. Verdancy is the gift of the sun. The sun gives to our world light and life, heat and feeling, growth and maturity. It gives its beneficence without discrimination to those who respect its power, those who are willing to bask in its luxurious warmth, those who convert its rays to the fostering of new life. That which is indifferent to the sun becomes a desert, a wasteland, a barrenness.

There is beauty in the sun, but there is no other beauty in the observable universe that will not permit you to look directly at it. To behold it directly is to become blinded. We know it only by looking at it through filters, never to know it completely. I can savor all other things of beauty in their fullness. I can look unashamedly into their faces without fear. And as I look more deeply, I begin to know more deeply, and thence to love more deeply as well.

The sun is the enigma of God. As science seeks to know more of the sun, theology seeks to know more about God. The enigma endures, but the search goes on. As new filters are designed, more becomes known of the sun and of God. Always we are impelled to know, to know, to know. It is to man's credit that he does not heed the words of Sirach (3:20-21), who spoke rightly about so much else: "What is too sublime for you, seek not; into things beyond your strength search not. What is committed to you, attend to; for what is hidden is not your concern."

It is within the nature of man to take steps, however, feeble, to know the unknowable, for in doing so he does not know all, merely more. But, my students, why this drive to know more about the sun, more about the planets, more about disease, more about science and engineering — and yet no more about God than simply that He exists? Why does a man give willingly ten years, twelve years of study to become a doctor or an architect, and show unwillingness to spend his life to know about God, with whom the man will spend — or fail to spend — time without end? If knowledge of the things of life have such importance to us, why not the things of eternity? Why only a knowledge of the pea and not of the pod?

As a child you were asked, "Why did God make you?"

And in your simplicity you returned the words of your book learned by rote, "God made me to *know* Him, to *love* Him, to *serve* Him, *and to be happy with Him in eternity*." Then you left it and went on to other things.

Note the order of the infinitives. They are not unplanned, not without order or logic. It is a testament to the wisdom of the Church that it recognizes this fundamental fact of love, namely that it must be preceded by knowledge. One must know before one can love. How can you tell me that you love literature if you do not know literature? Perhaps you mean, then, that you love the idea of literature, and if this is true it falls to the fortunate that they will truly love literature when they have become immersed in it, for then it was by some coincidence that their idea of literature coincided with their subsequent knowledge of literature. Or let us consider love as it is seen in drama. Is it love when boy meets girl and at the moment their eyes encompass each other's being they become aware, incontrovertibly aware, of their deep and undying desire for each other? Perhaps so, but would it not be better to call it attraction, while love remains yet to be established?

The attraction to God inheres in each of us. That it has failed to become love lies in the imperfection of will, and it is the will, my friends, that guides us to know so that we may truly love. God created you as an act of His Will, and it is the will within you which must activate the intellect so that you may return to the source of your existence. The will pushes. The intellect probes. The will is driven by attraction. The intellect is driven by the will. But the end is to know God . . . within the limits of your potential to do so.

This is not to say that only the learned can arrive at salvation merely through their gifts of intellect, for all manner of error is perpetrated in the name of intellect. There are those whose ignorance is so great as to place them at the lowest level of intellect, yet they have what the learned long to possess: a faith so confident, so luminous, so fervent as to give them a *mystical* knowledge of God. As God is pure Spirit, He transmits Himself in the form of knowledge that arrives to them on the wings of spirit. Essentially their knowledge of God consists in thinking about and longing for God, and in His mercy He permits them to know more fully the Object of their thoughts. These gifted souls *do* know God; therefore, they love Him all the more through their greater knowledge.

Perhaps this can be expressed best in the words of the theologian Frank Sheed, who has said: "If we love God, we shall ultimately get God: we shall be saved. If we love self in preference to God then we shall get self apart from God: we shall be damned. But though in our relationship to God the intellect does not matter as much as will . . . it does matter . . . for we can never attain a maximum love of God with only a minimum knowledge of God."

Therein lies the key, my scholars, to attain a maximum love of God. Given, then, the strength of our wills, the preexisting attraction to God developed by a kind of baptism of desire, the spirit hungering for God's love and aching within itself to give in return, there remains with us that fundamental challenge to embrace God fully because we fully know Him. Let us not be misled by the words, "fully know Him," as if they imply that we can know God fully. We cannot. Let me illustrate much in the manner illustrated in the Autobiography of St. Thérèse. In the one hand we hold a water glass, and in the other a wine glass. Now we direct that you take the decanter containing water and pour into each glass enough fluid to reach the very brim of each. One glass is smaller than the other, but, my friends, which glass is *more full?* You answer that they are equally full, neither can be more full than it already is because each has the potential for fullness circumscribed by its volume. It is in this manner, also that we can know God fully, not in the fullness of His being, but in the fullness of our own.

"And you shall love the Lord your God with your whole heart, and with your whole soul, and with your whole mind, and with your whole strength" (Mark 12:30).

Note well, my young friends, that it is with the wholeness of *you*. You cannot love God with the whole mind of Fulton Sheen, or Thomas Merton, or Francis of Assisi. Perhaps their minds can help you to plumb the depths of your own mind, but as each of them has been accountable for the fullness of his potential so also will you be. "To whom much has been given, much is expected." But to whom little has been given, all of it is expected.

To those of you already marked with the gift of love, there is little I can tell you that you do not now know about the path to fuller knowledge of God. We have already discussed the road map, which is Nature. It speaks to you clearly of the existence of God as it does of His love for you. It is the path of the philosophers and the theologians, but there is room on the path for us also.

But so as not to leave us bereft of other signs, He gives us His revealed Word. For . . . "In the beginning was the Word, and the Word was with God; and the Word was God." So to him who cannot see God in a leaf, let him not be disturbed. This way is not for all. But to all is the Word.

In the Word lies saving grace; in the revealed words lie the path to the Word.

This is to say, my students, that in the Scriptures He speaks now and for all time. To read them is more than to be swept up in a literary form unique among all literature. It is more than a study of divine law. It is a mood, a milieu of sanctity, an aura of divinity, an osmotic penetration of the soul that drenches it with the mystery and glory of salvation. For while there is the risk of reading Scripture from differing points of view, there remains always the totality of its effect upon the soul who approaches his reading with openness and humility. It is this that makes saints and near-saints. In Scripture are the words that prime the pump of the mystics.

Merton tells us something of this:

"The basic claim made by the Bible for the word of God is not so much that it is to be blindly accepted because of God's authority, but that it is recognized by its transforming and liberating power. The word of God does something to anyone who really hears it: it transforms his entire existence. The word of God penetrating our inmost being is more than a communication of light: it is a new birth, the beginning of a new being."

I submit to you, my students, that knowledge of God has as its prerequisite this very element of "new birth, the beginning of a new being." It is then from this point that the mystical power inherent in each of us begins to establish that union in spirit with God which is the beginning of knowledge.

But even in this, care must be taken that we do not begin to impute to our new birth such direct communication as to make void the surest source of all knowledge . . . the Church, which is the surrogate authority of God on earth. She who is called Mother Church is guilty of all kinds of imperfections related to men, but she has ever been, remains, and ever will be perfect in the surrogate responsibility of directing the souls of men. God incarnate thus ordained that He would be with her until the end of time, and that to her keeping was committed the keys of the Kingdom.

Through twenty centuries since the first ordinations in the Cenacle, the Church has been ruled by frail humans, some libertine, some stupid, some self-seeking, but throughout the Papacy the vilest of its leaders have been powerless to do other than treasure the keys. And let it not be known by these few, for out of its ranks in history have come legions whose charisms have marked them among the elect. Saints and sinners, all have spoken for God, and God through them.

To those then who seek the fullness of knowledge, go to her. Now she weeps. Now she is bent from the flagellation of her own children, but ever does she love, and deep is her wisdom. And if you would continue to grow, pay no heed to the weeds that have grown in her garden, but instead look at her finest flowers, those great men and women who were heroes for God while carrying her banner. If you find the language of Augustine archaic, turn to Newman; if it is modern language you seek, turn to Sheed or Sheen or early Merton. But since Peter, the parade of saints seems without end. It is to them that the Church owes its glory. It is to them you should turn for your ascent to God.

Their yoke was easy, their burden light. This is not to say that on the path of the Church there are palliatives to suffering like the bonbons of the material world. Indeed, the Church's way calls for heroes rather than cowards, for it is no easy way against the temptations of our society. It is easier to sleep than to pray. It is easier to be carnal than to be pure. It is easier to deny life than to give life. It is easier to take than to give. It is easier to live sumptuously than to deny yourself. It is easier to preach social justice than to live it in prayer, mindless activism rather than contemplation. It is easier to titillate the senses than to avoid the occasions of sin. It is easier to lose the sense of sin than to admit the presence of sin. It is easier to take a new wife than to take on celibacy. It is easier to equate animal passion with Nature than controlled love with Nature. These are the norms of the world that give the lie to the Good News.

But for a moment, become like the Little Flower and you will see that when your soul is entrusted to God, when your will is given in holy abandonment to His will, it becomes a greater joy to receive the bread of the Eucharist than the bread of the world. It is sweeter to deny your lust than to find the emptiness of satiated senses. It is sweeter to transcend than to descend. It is sweeter to love than to hate. It is sweeter to be embraced by God than praised by men. It is sweeter to be in heaven than to languish in hell.

Once all things are viewed in the light of eternity, the choices become fewer, and the few that remain are no longer choices but certitudes. Then truly is His yoke easy, His burden light.

Heroism is the conquest in small things that are the susceptibilities of cowards. Heroism lies in the recognition of God, and many times in the ostracism of men. Heroism is the Way of the Cross. Cowardice is the refusal of the Cross. Heroism makes the Cross as a feather. Cowardice multiplies its weight.

This is the message of Christ; therefore it is the message of the Church. How will you take the message? Will you see in it the need for personal identity, for relevance, for evolutionary morality? Or will you see that you have no identity detached from Christ, that you are in Him, He in you, and that the you in you no longer matters? Will you look upon His law as changing by virtue of a changing society, or will you see His law as immanent, monolithic, unchanging?

Will you ask, "What is Truth?" Or will you say that Truth is God in the Church, and that what was true yesterday is true today and tomorrow because Truth can have no error in it, else it would not be Truth?

Will you assume to yourself infallibility because the Spirit kissed your brow in a moment of luminous love? Or will you say, "Indeed, I have received a charism, which I accept humbly, for I receive it through no merit of my own."

Recall, that which is closer to the flame has within it the greater share in the heat and light that comes from the flame; that which is farther from the flame has a lesser share by lesser proximity. Does your pride, indeed, place you closest to the flame, or does your knowledge of God's hierarchy speak to you of His governance through His Church? Are we to have one church for each soul, headed by that soul in the *guise* of the Holy Spirit? Or is it in the Nature of God to create one Church for all souls — as there is one God — under the *mandate* of the Holy Spirit?

You will admit that in the heavens proximate to our earth there are not many suns. There is but one sun. All human life is subject to its gentle warmth or its withering heat. This is to know something of the Nature of God. Now, we have men of science seeking to capture the heat of the sun, store it in great solar warehouses, then distribute it beneficently to mankind. This is the Church.

Yes, my dear young friends, God indeed made you to *know* Him, and the ways are multiform: in Nature, in His Word, and in His Church. And I submit to you that not the least of these is His Church, for it speaks the universal language of love, which is God.

We will talk again. Go now.

To Love the Sun

It is the apt conceit of the poet to see God in the sun, to recognize that the sun suspends itself above the earth as an object of awe, and to affirm that man's servitude embraces the servitude of love. For as the tree loves the sun "and lifts her leafy arms to pray," so does man rise to the grandeur of his full flower as the noblest design of God and lift his arms in the servitude of love. Not all men reach or attempt to reach so mystical a pinnacle, to be sure, but to them who seek will come knowledge, and to them who know will come love. Then they are captive. Then there is blessed servitude.

As it was love that nourished the tree, it was love that gave you life. Love is marked by constancy. It is not fickle, for it is with you always, even when the loved suffers, and even more in the midst of the lover's suffering. This is the way of God who offers surcease from the world, urging you to drink of the fountain that shall also become a fountain within you . . . "leaping up to provide eternal life."

Without love, my students, all that lives would die. As the desert represents the barrenness of love, the forest is the richness of love. Where no springs exist, where no fountains burst forth, there remains aridity, unflowered potential, undelivered seeds, emptiness and death of the spirit. But you who receive love openly, submissively, trustingly, you will send it out from your hearts in the gentle, cooling sprays of new baptisms. As the fountain from which it comes is limitless, undiminished, inexhaustible, so is the fountain within you.

All of this is prologue in speaking of the nature of love, but we are concerned here with the two essential aspects of love. Let us consider God's love for us, then our love for God.

Seek not what you already have, my young friends. There are among you those whose scrupulosity leads them to search for ways to be noticed and loved by God, as a child would say to his mother, "See what a good boy I am!" thus courting the approval he so anxiously seeks. Flesh of her flesh, bone of her bone, born of her love, why need he seek for what was his from the moment of her first awareness of him? So it is with God.

The very fact of your creation and existence is the sole fact of His love. Would God create what He does not love? Did we not say that God is not capricious? Then He does not create baubles for His amusement. For He needs none. On the contrary, it was an evidence of His supreme love that He created you in His image and likeness, only a little less than the angels. Just as the artist expresses that which is himself, so does God reflect Himself in us. For you who seek graces, this indeed was the first grace: that you *are*!

Hence creation was an act of love by God. It is, moreover, a further act of His love that we continue to exist. For God does not abandon that which He creates. Man may abandon God, but to the end He remains steadfast, proffering hand and heart in a mystical lifeline to Him. You doubt this for you see the waifs of humanity and you say they are abandoned by God. I submit to you that they are waifs of humanity because they have been abandoned by humanity, not by God. For should God truly abandon, there can be only nothing where there was something. The eminent lay theologian Frank Sheed puts it in this manner:

> "There is an emptiness at the very center of the being of all created things, which only God can fill; not an emptiness merely in the sense that it cannot be happy without God; but in the sense that it cannot *be* at all without Him. God does not simply make us and leave us. . . . The carpenter . . . can make a table and leave it and the table will continue, none the worse for his absence. But that . . . is because of the material he used, namely wood. Similarly, if God, having made the universe, left it, the universe would have to rely for its continuance in existence upon the material it was made of: namely nothing."

And, my friends, I tell you that those most abandoned by men are most loved by God, who treasures them "more than the lilies in the field." Of suffering we will speak another time, but you know that you do not love your child less because his body becomes wasted by cancer. You love him more, so much more that you cry out to God to let you take his place on his bed of annihilation. And was this not what Christ did? You who are "abandoned": have you forgotten so soon? You read the morning newspaper and your heart is torn by the immolation of the bystander who rescues another only to lose his own life in an oblation of dispassionate love. Where are your tears for the nails as they pierce His hands and feet? Where are your tears for the blood that trickles into His mouth from the thorns that crown His head in mockery and pain? Where are your tears as He pushes His weight on the nails in His feet to raise His body only enough to let His lungs suck in the air that will keep Him alive long enough to permit more suffering and to fulfill the prophecies? "Greater love has no man than he give up his life for a friend." And greater love no man has ever had than that he suffer and die in humiliation not merely for one man but for all men. Of this great love Fulton J. Sheen remarked, "Giving takes on some value because there was once Divine Giving which, across the debt of sin, wrote: 'Paid in full.' "

Do not, then, question God's love for you; rather, question your love for God!

From the most humble, unlettered souls to the intellectual giants of the Church, the way of loving God is open. There are no mysteries to the peasant, whose theology is simple and direct. The mystery of the theologian is but the mystery of his language. The way that is common to both is in the ineffable consolation of prayer.

God is reached essentially through the prayer life of those who find that the emptiness at the core of man can be filled only by God — by loving Him without restraint, even without petition, except to ask for greater love. Dostoyevsky reminds us: "Be not forgetful of prayer. Every time you pray, if your prayer is sincere, there will be a new feeling and new meaning in it, which will give you fresh courage, and you will understand that prayer is an education."

"Prayer is an education," indeed, for one finds in

the release of the mind to supernal flights that there is lost to us all sense of personal identity in a flowing, moving, merging with the Oneness of Love. No longer are we bound to earth, by earth, but instead the consciousness that is below consciousness gives us a kinship with genius, no matter how mundane our lives, and it becomes part of the Universal Consciousness, which is God.

Prayer — whether articulated or mental — presupposes total concentration, total surrender, total openness. No longer are distractions the plague of prayer, impeding abandonment. I do not speak of a *technique* to reach God, my students, as if the mystical employs tools of its trade. I speak only of mood, desire, reaching, hunger, consecration. I speak of the release of clutter in the mind, the creation of emptiness in the mind and spirit that is, in itself, an invitation to enter. That He will enter is certain. That He will choose *when* to enter is equally certain, for frequently one's greatest awareness of His presence will be preceded by many days of aridity, which creates only a greater thirst.

Then He comes.

It is at this moment when great saints received the locutions that have become a part of the literature of the Church. Because we do not take rank with them, our communication may be less verbalized, more in the sense impressions painted upon the mind by God. Impressions may come slowly. There may be but one thought, but it will be that kind of thought which is an awakening, an awareness of a truth so simple, yet so beautiful, as to create within us a bliss heretofore unknown. Now you begin to know. You are at the beginning of the beginning. Ahead lies greater knowledge, greater love, and an intense heightening of the need for the Eucharist — daily.

So, my students, the ascent to God, the love of God, starts as an act of the will, which establishes the mood of desire. And to desire strongly implies total submission of the will to the one desired. It is in this sense a holy abandonment, which is so consuming as to be reckless in the pursuit of human love, but which is the only acceptable totality in loving God. In its all-embracing totality we recoil at the thought of offending our Love, mortally or venially. At its highest point, which is experienced only by a few, there is the desire to suffer in complete imitation of Christ. One wishes then to imitate, as completely as He will allow, the poverty, humiliation and Cross of Christ. This kind of love curdles the juices in the stomachs of the uncommitted, for it is truly a hard road, but therein lies the only imitation of Christ because it attempts to make the lover more completely like the Loved.

But let us not be so concerned with the end when we have yet to know the beginning. That you cannot — at this time — bring yourselves to accept suffering, I will concede. That you cannot pray, makes me weep for you. But perhaps prayer becomes more possible to him who contemplates nature and therein reflects on the complex orderliness that presupposes authorship.

Who is to say whether a man comes to prayer from the logic imposed by Nature or turns to Nature as a manifestation of the mystical within him, which seeks to be concretized, documented, and testified to by the very hand of God in the world? It matters little, except that there is both assent and ascent, all at one.

It is in nature that communion may also occur.

One needs no Walden Pond to find the mirror of God in the leaf of a rose bush, not to speak of the rose itself. Each man becomes his own Thoreau in his own garden. Consider that the seed is planted in the warm, moist humus of earth, and soon tiny tendrils peep above the soil, weak and dependent, needing shelter and nurture. This is radiant birth from matter that measures less than a sixteenth of an inch, and already it bursts to a size dwarfing its beginning, soon to grow into a marvel of beauty. Soon it unfolds to us, tender pink, or velvet red, or pristine white. We know little of botany, but the miracle of it all is never explained fully, only the science of it all. We know that photosynthesis results from the blessing of the sun and the soil, and that — somehow — from the roots to the flower there are hundreds, thousands, of freeways delivering cargoes of nutrients that feed the bloom and the green. Inhibiting growth and beauty are the Lucifers of nature, the aphids, mites, spiders and all that would keep the kiss of God off the rose.

So it is in the generation of human life. From the implantation of a seed invisible to the human eye comes life. And in the seed is all the potential to write the *Divine Comedy*, to build the Panama Canal, to sculpt the *Pietà,* to be a pope, a president, or a rake. Complexity with order marks the study of man. If there is doubt of this, study the ear, learn how sound passes through it to the brain. See the delicacy, the miniscule parts, the precise functions of each of the parts, all encompassed within an inch of the temple. Every organ testifies to the miracle of existence, and every function to the love of God. But man, too, has his Lucifers of sub-nature, which strike the heart and sully the soul.

Behold the leaf. Behold the rose. Behold the ear.

Behold the fingernail of man. Then behold man, and know that such a magnificent accident is preposterous. What is more preposterous is he obuseness of men *who fail to see in all of this a Creator who must be adored.* We are worms by comparison, but the capability to reason should tell us, as it told Fulton J. Sheen: "As the smallest light beam is but a reflection of the light and heat that are the sun, so all truth and all love have their origin in God."

So it would seem that the dissection of loving God thus far consists in prayer and total abandonment of the spirit, in reflecting on the contingencies of Nature that speak of a First Cause, and finding love on a rational basis through an admission of humble fealty to Him whose authorship deserves no less than total love.

But, my bright young people, still there is something missing, and great care must be given to this missing element so as to see its importance in the proper order of love. This is the love of one another. It is expressed in Mark 12:29 in the following manner: "Hear, O Israel! The Lord our God is one God; and you shall love the Lord your God with your whole heart, and your whole soul, and with your whole mind, and with your whole strength! This is the first commandment. And the second is like it, 'You shalt love your neighbor as yourself.' "

It has been said that our times are apocalyptic, but I would suggest to you that our times are also sociological, secular, and humanistic. It is this milieu which is so earthborne and earth-ridden that it seeks to make human love itself a god. Even in the Church there is dissension over love, when it is true love that waives dissension. It is the contention of some biblical scholars that the two commandments — love of God and love of neighbor — are coequal. This is to ignore all theology and bend Scripture, for let it be called to your attention that, in the very priority of the two loves in the scriptural statement, there is given precedence to loving God as the *first* commandment. That the *second* is like the first is still to maintain the priority of the first. The two loves, however, are adjunctive to the extent that eternity is not grasped through the pursuit of one love to the exclusion of the other. This is testified to by John in his first letter (5:1-3) when he says, "Everyone who believes that Jesus is Christ is born of God. And everyone who loves him who begot, loves also the one begotten of him. In this we know that we love the children of God, when we love God and do his commandments." Note the emphasis on "when we love God and do his commandments" as the primal force of love of neighbor.

To him who reaches for the stars *only* through his humanity, let him realize that this will be the full extent of his reach. The stars. To him who embraces his neighbor and all of humanity as the result of an avid prayer life, a profound contemplative life, will come the Beatific Vision. Like the fountain, the love of God is directed vertically in a showering spire that casts its cascade on the children of God. To seek God horizontally will bring back to you the love of humanity. To seek God vertically is to find agapè, that perfect love that sees Christ in all men because it sees Christ first.

Secular love without God is an earthbound love, which makes nice people but not saints. Christian love is the personification of Christ in the waif, the beggar, the criminal, the sinner, the leper, the neighbor who is both richer than you and poorer than you. Secular humanism sees love in the legalization of abortion, in the drug culture, in the sex culture, in the riots and revolutions of our times. Christian humanism is an outpouring of the heart for the crucified Christ linked to the crucified humanity.

There is no good without God. That which seeks to portray goodness as an amoral or unmoral function of society builds with good intentions, but it is a truism of our times that the road to hell is paved with them. Writing in *L'Osservatore Romano*, Bishop Cahal B. Daly says:

> "It is not possible to love God without thinking of men and including men in that love — for God made men out of love and loved them so much as to send Jesus Christ, His Son, to die for them; and all human sonship and sonly relationship with God must include a sharing in Christ's love for men.

> "But it is possible to love men without thinking of God; and this attitude could be the modern version of Antichrist."

The whole value question is inherent in Christ's demands that His disciples owed Him greater love than they would give to their very families. "He who loves father or mother more than me is not worthy of me. And he who does not take up his cross and follow me is not worthy of me" (Mt. 10:37-39).

Because love has a spiritual dimension, it has a circuitry that requires it to be directed to God, whence it flows with electric directness to those whom God loves. But again, recall to your minds, my friends, that all of this cerebrating tends to discuss the problem of techniques, and God requires only one technique, which takes us back to the very start of our lecture, namely, that true love of God consists not so much in loving Him, but in allowing ourselves to become a receptacle of *His* love, for only then can we respond to what He initiates. With such openness, we arrive at agapè.

Go now . . . and truly love.

Part III
IN AMERICA

High Flight

Sicola understood one thing. He knew that the secret to being incognito was to be completely oneself . . . but out of uniform. He knew that if he chose to travel as a priest he would be guilty only of the slightest dissembling, for he was, after all, a priest. Still, he knew he would be unrecognized because context is an important part of recognition. For example, many Americans recognize Steve Garvey in a Dodger uniform, but he could be faceless in a crowded subway in New York City in his civilian clothes. Similarly, if one were to see Paul Newman walking down the street, there would be the shadow of recognition, but one's impulse would be to remark, "How he resembles Paul Newman!" One's mind has already accepted the fact that he could not possibly be Paul Newman because somehow this strolling figure was out of place in this particular setting. We recognize people in the setting in which they have become identified, like the nurse who attends a patient in a hospital and goes unrecognized by the same patient in the supermarket.

So as to scramble all of the elements of context, uniform and setting, Sicola had Tommaso drive him in the Fiat to a mountain resort in the Italian Alps. From there he took a train to Paris, all the while being highly visible in his Roman collar but wearing a black suit appropriately dishabille. No one gave him a second glance.

At Paris, he took a taxi to Orly Airport and boarded a transatlantic flight to America. It had already been established with Tommaso that the Pope was on retreat. He wished to think and to pray, and his whereabouts, though known, could not be revealed in order to assure his privacy and to protect him from the peeping lenses of telephoto photography. Tommaso knew his itinerary in America and he would be in regular contact with him. Should there be any unplanned events to change the appointed time and place for receiving Tommaso's calls, Sicola had arranged for the installation of a special telephone in Tommaso's quarters with a number known only to each of them.

He sat back in his seat and watched the other boarding passengers with interest. There was the volatile Frenchman in a beret who gesticulated and chattered to his female companion, wife or whatever, who trailed behind him. "Claude," she said in French, "slow down. You drag me as I were one of your harlots. *Mon ami*, America will not move while the aéroplane is still on the ground." Following the French couple was a retinue of men wearing turbans, and Sicola imagined that they must be part of a U.N. delegation. They paraded through the aisle like silent toy soldiers, implacable and unperturbed. A small child with the eyes of a Hummel figurine floated ethereally to her seat, awed by the frenetic passengers perhaps, but obviously impressed with the huge plane that would soon defy gravity. "Does it really fly?" she asked her heavy-ladened father.

Behind the child and her parents a man looked from left to right studying the numbers on each seat.

When he spied his number beside Sicola's seat, he glanced at the itinerant Pope, and Sicola sensed just a trace of annoyance on the new passenger's face. It was as if to say, "Good Lord, a priest, of all people!" He slipped into the seat beside Sicola and nodded perfunctorily.

He was tall and blond, and the tan plastic-rimmed glasses threw out white reflections that did not hide the pale blue eyes behind them. His forehead was wide and furrowed and there was a tinge of pink on his gaunt face, as if he were flushed with the boarding mania of the moment. The lips, Sicola noticed, were thin and precise as if only precise words came from them. A scholar perhaps. One could read much from lips. They spoke of reserve or of passion, of contemplation or of impetuosity, of grace or abandon. Coupled with the crisp blue eyes, they made Sicola see him as a man of reason, even single-minded reason.

Perhaps, Sicola considered, it would be best to allow conversation to find its own hole in the barrier he sensed between him and his new neighbor. Not that he was opposed to forcing communication. Forcing traffic with the human species was his addiction. But for now, it would be better to wait.

He took up his breviary and tugged at the ribbon to open to his place. The man on his right seemed to notice and crossed his left leg over his right, shifting his weight to his right buttock and giving Sicola the greater portion of his back. Sicola stole a glance at the passenger's hands, folded together, his thumbs beating each other nervously. The man reached into his traveling bag and drew out a magazine. Sicola had not once read a word from his breviary, so fixed was his sidelong gaze at the man beside him. His companion placed the magazine on his lap as he cleaned the lenses of his spectacles, and now Sicola tipped his head to read the name — *Philadelphia Studies*, a magazine Sicola recognized as an American journal for Catholic priests and theologians. He began to feel proud that he had so accurately labeled the man as a scholar, but this was even more than he had hoped for. Perhaps he was a lay professor of theology. They would have much to discuss.

His new neighbor stood to remove his jacket, and the magazine fell to the floor. Sicola moved as if cunning were a reflex action, and he grasped the periodical with such alacrity that his head struck a glancing blow off the man's knee.

"*Mannaggia*," Sicola blurted, "Your knees are made of steel."

"Sorry," the man apologized. "Are you hurt?"

"No, no, Signore. I am called *testa dura*, hard head, for a good reason." He leafed through the magazine before he returned it, musing with feigned surprise, "So, you have an interest in theology? I know this journal. You are perhaps a professor?"

"Yes, Father. I teach at a Catholic university in Washington."

"That is good my friend. There was a time when there were few lay theologians, the subject having been thought to be the province of priests."

"I am also a priest, Father."

"Ah, so-o-o? I am Father Simon. And what are you called?"

"Curare. Father Charles E. Curare."

"You are THAT one? The one who argues with the encyclicals, who preaches of another magisterium parallel to the Church?"

"How do you mean, THAT one, Father?"

"It is only that the name Curare is known far and wide as one of the disputants in the cause of theological dissent."

"Do you deny theology the right to dissent, Father?"

"No, my friend, not if it is complementary dissent. But contradictory dissent, that is quite another thing."

"A theologian can love the Church and still contradict its teachings when the Church is patently wrong. Don't you agree?"

"One must guard against this notion. When one truly chooses the Church he is indeed a theologian. But when a scholar sees the hand of God through the eyes of humanity, he should more properly be called a 'homo-logian.' This is what some of your confreres are doing. You must choose, then, to be theologian or homologian, and if it is to be the latter you deny the absolute mandate of the Church."

"I am wary, Father Simon, of this absolute you speak of. It was Lord Acton who said of the Church that 'absolute power corrupts absolutely.' The new openness of the Church obviates the possibility of absolute corruption as long as theologians accept their call to be watchdogs of the Church."

"Watchdogs? The first syllable of your name becomes appropriate," Sicola said angrily. Almost immediately he knew that he had given in to an emotion that would make future argument all the more difficult.

Curare studied Sicola coolly. "Father, there is not much point in discussing it further. Invective is a poor substitute for argument."

"I apologize," Sicola recovered himself, "for losing control for the moment. The points each of us have to make are too important for name-calling."

"If you are willing to concede that much, then perhaps you will be willing also to listen to reason. The call for dialogue presumes the historical pilgrim identity of the Church, which does not pretend to have all the answers but is open in its quest for truth. The call for a developing dialogue and an ongoing quest for truth differs sharply from the traditional absolute concept of morality."

"I have already admitted the need for dialogue with theologians," Sicola interrupted, "but you assume that it is the magisterium which must bend to your theology, and dialogue to you is but another name for apostasy."

"On the other hand," Curare pointed out, "you wish to cloak every magisterial statement with infallibility. There is no such thing as an infallible magisterium on particular moral questions; the essence of specific moral decisions would forbid anyone, in my opinion, to pronounce an infallible judgment on them. The hierarchical magisterium has taught in the field of particular moral matters with what would seem an authentic, authoritative but noninfallible voice. The word 'noninfallible,' no matter how you approach it, still means that this magisterium is fallible."

"Your glossary of terms needs amending, Father Curare," Sicola answered. "The term 'noninfallible' does not mean 'fallible,' nor does it even imply the possibility of error. A father says to his son, 'My son, your driving habits have been erratic. You may not have the automobile tonight, especially in view of the weather conditions that prevail. I would not wish to send you to the emergency ward of the hospital by permitting you to do what has potential for harm.'

The father does not say with infallibility that the son will be injured in an accident. The order is therefore noninfallible, but we must not construe, either, that it is fallible. The basis of his judgment is seated in wisdom, a wisdom that assesses very distinct possibilities. You could more readily impute fallibility if he permitted the son to drive and gave him assurances that no danger would befall him. What is more, by this time the son should have recognized two things: that the wisdom of the father is greater than his son's, and that to be a member of his father's household requires his assent to his father's authority. It was Paul VI who said, 'No one is entitled to accept a label without its contents. This would not be honest. To be a Catholic means to be attached to the Church, a sincere and total profession of the faith of which she has the deposit and, therefore, a joyful acceptance of the living magisterium which Christ has conferred on her.' "

The two men had become so engrossed in their conversation that they had been hardly aware that the plane had taxied to the runway. They buckled their seat belts and sat back in silence while the giant airplane scurried down the runway like a bird with divided loyalties — a part loyal to the earth and its sustenance, a part to the heavens, its natural habitat, but boding an uncertain future for the chick whose mother offers gentle assurances. Sicola knew about true freedom, the ecstasy of freedom, the utter and absolute detachment of freedom that was a condition of his parish among the stars, beacons to the earthbound.

The late sunlight brushed the tops of the high clouds with a pink blush, and between its puffs Sicola could see the speckled blue and green of the coast of

France where the sea lapped at its beaches, but now the earth was unreality and the only reality was the heavens, momentarily bright in the waning sunset, presaging the night with its bright sentinels, the stars, already rubbing their eyes for the night vigil. Now they were his hope. It would be they in whom the pilot would place his trust, they toward which he would look for direction. All else was earth, covered by clouds and approaching night, untrustworthy, even impertinent in its promise which could no longer be fulfilled. Now there was only heaven and its occupants. Nothing else had meaning.

Curare's appetite had been honed by Sicola, and he was eager to demolish the unlettered parish priest who was his new companion.

"Papal pronouncements in the future," he said to the contemplative Sicola, "must be made after more complete consultation and collegiality with the entire Church so that popes may speak more authoritatively for the entire Church, but not even collegial pronouncements on particular moral questions will ever be made in absolute certainty. The Church must speak out on specific problems facing the modern world and its people with an awareness that her voice has no absolute authority but that she puts forth what she considers the best possible teaching for Christians, understanding that she might be wrong.

"There must be some kind of check against the powers residing in certain institutions of our society. This will demand certain reforms democratizing institutions like the Roman Catholic Church; but I do not expect such safeguards for the individual to do away with the papal and hierarchical offices in the Church — if these are put in perspective. The revolt of the theologians against the papal encyclical on artificial contraception demonstrates the use of power to counteract a possible abuse of power.

"Co-responsibility demands that the Church as an institution surrender the power to order and guide the lives of the members of the Church as a society. Laws and organization can no longer guide all the activities of society and the individuals it comprises. . . ."

Sicola had listened attentively to Curare's words even as he stared out the window at the increasing blackness of the sky. It was as if the plane were steering a course directly into a Stygian vapor so enveloping as to touch off fears that there would be no light ever, only this enfeebling torpor and errancy in the midst of uncharted darkness. But above him there broke through the malignant murkiness a blinking effulgence that seemed as close as the wing light on the airplane, except that it was above it. If it was a star it was the brightest he had ever seen, but certainly the altitude of the plane could not have made so great a difference as to make it this much brighter. Whatever it was, star or celestial body of another sort, it broke through the blackness, tearing through it, not so much to bathe the plane in light but more as a signal that every inky, enshrouding night carries the navigator's hope of a straight course, a certain port. In it was certitude, the very certitude Curare had rejected. His church was the church of murk and muck, of uncertainty and pilgrim aimlessness. His church was a church so circumscribed by homologians as to have lost forever the Theos of all certitude, the Father of night and day, who aimed His shaft from His kingdom to Sicola's with the simple answer, "Who follows you, follows Me. Who hears you, hears Me." Certitude. Uncompromising. Intractable. Absolute.

Sicola turned to Curare at length, and the theologian sucked in his breath at the transfigured expression on the face of the masquerading Pope. His eyes had caught the beam from the distant light, and they shot out spears of cold fire, the fire of blue diamonds. His skin had lost its warmth and its tan, and there was an alabaster translucence to his face. The radiance was frightening to Curare, not so much because there was ugliness, but because it lent to Sicola a serenity and a beauty that had occurred so suddenly.

Then Sicola spoke, softly and kindly.

"My son, you are called, 'Father,' but you are a father without certitudes. How can you lead your children when you are so uncertain of the way yourself? How can you bring them to me unless you have come to me first and therefore know the way? And how can you come to me unless you seek me first in the spirit, as a child?"

Curare was perplexed at the use of phrases like "come to me," and "seek me." Who was this idiot that he spoke as if he were Christ? And how did he bring about this eerie transfiguration? Was he a priest or a sorcerer? At length, he reasoned that the best defensive measure was a confident offense. "You misunderstand my use of the word certitude. I do not lack certitude, Father Simon. My certitude lies in the fact that I know because I do not know. And so it is with the Church as an institution. She cannot know all things. She can only guess at what is correct, and the circumstances affect the correctness of any given situation. Morality is no longer fixed, but changes according to the times and the needs of the people."

Sicola listened to Curare, and the cold diamond fires that issued from his eyes livened and burned their heat into Curare's brain. Curare felt a numbness attack his mind and his body, but Sicola's words were clear enough to him. "God is Absolute, my Son. And from God all absolutes flow. The Law is absolute. If it is tempered it is tempered only by the absolute mercy of God. It is not yours to dispense. Only mine. For it is such a mercy that forgives without condoning. It is such a mercy that is tendered to the Mystical Body, which is the Church, the only leniency. It lies in the statement, 'Whatever you loose on earth shall be loosed in heaven.' This power belongs neither to you nor to the theologians. Only to the Church.

"You impute to yourself a separate magisterium, and in this is the sin of pride, for while the Holy Spirit comes to all men with a sure hand, He does not compel men to grasp His hand. And when they do, it is His purpose to lead into the Church, not away from it. It is bestowed not to the theologians whose charisma is their fatuous intelligence, but to the Church whose guiding spirits were fisherman, tax collectors, shepherds, the dross of life, quickened by the fire of the Holy Spirit to direct and guide the intellects and the wills of men of learning whose humility bends the knee to this everlasting presence of Christ on earth, which is His Church. Such an example was the Angelic Doctor, St. Thomas Aquinas, whose divergences with the magisterium were known, but whose contributions were enormous. Even he embraced this humility when, before his death, he said: 'I have taught and written much . . . according to my faith in Christ, and in the holy Roman Church, to whose judgment I submit all my teaching." But the commonness of Aquinas with all holy men was the commonness of prayer. When, my Son, did you last make a holy hour? Speak to the world of theology when habitually, day in and day out, you have knelt before the Real Presence. Only then is it trustworthy."

Curare felt the numbness dissipate, but he was not cleansed of doubt, not washed of vacillation, not cured of the malaise of ego. That there was a diminution of the confidence of his position he knew, but the heart of the rebel beat a kind of "*Dubito ergo sum*" through his being. Perhaps he had been chastened, but not altogether vanquished. He turned his eyes from Sicola, whose expression was relaxed and gentle, his tan having been restored, his eyes once more normal. Then, as if to take up the argument anew, he blurted, "But . . ."

In that moment of doubt, he felt the plane turn its nose downward, and he was propelled forward, his shoulders and head striking the cushioned seat in front of him. He pushed himself back and placed his feet against the forward seat to keep himself from lurching ahead again. As he strapped his seat belt he noted that Sicola had not moved, but instead sat comfortably in his seat studying Curare. The theologian looked out the window near Sicola, and the blackness gave him no frame of reference, but the tilt of his body, the screams of the passengers, the fright in his heart told him that the airplane was in a sharp descent. It would crash soon unless the pilot could lift the nose of the plane.

Then he found his voice and screamed an impassioned plea to the pilot, who would be unable to hear him, "Pull up your nose!" he cried. "Lift us, lift us. My God in heaven, lift us!"

Sicola sat implacable and unperturbed, all the while not moving his eyes from Curare. Tenderly, he touched Curare's arm. "Amen," he whispered. "*Sursum corda.*"

In the years ahead, Sicola would receive reports on Curare's lectures. One of his favorites would be the one Curare delivered before the American Society of Theologians. It was titled simply: "Pull Up Your Nose."

A Beachhead

There was simply no keeping tab on where Sicola would turn up next. To be Pope, he had often said, one must be in touch with people, and virtue and sin, with the "smarts" and the ignorant. He must ride the surf of life, skim the froth, slip into the trough and use the pull of the current to raise himself back to the crest.

This was no mere analogy, for Sicola, even at fifty-nine, was inordinately strong and supple. He had an elasticity at the knees, a sure sense of balance, and a stomach that was lean and taut. It was the physique of an exceptionally healthy man whose life had been a romance with the sea.

To have him turn up at the beach at Monte Carlo would have caused, just the same, no small ripple of excitement. But imagine the headlines if one were to see him riding the surf off Newport Beach, California! Incredible? Indeed, preposterous! But there would be no headlines, for Sicola turned up in odd places like the Invisible Man. When he wasn't being called, "The Clown," they called him the "Invisible One" because of his penchant for appearing incognito even when, or especially when, visiting foreign nations.

There was a hurricane off the tip of Baja California, whose only concern to the sun lovers of Newport Beach was in the ten- to fifteen-foot swells that it created for their resort. The heat in Los Angeles and its suburbs this August day drew whole hordes of bathers to loll on the sands or ride the waves. It was no day for swimmers, but it was a frothy, saline picnic for the adventurers in wet suits. As one stood on the beach and looked out at the mountainous whitecaps, spilling over themselves like foamy beer, the black-suited surfers dotted the sea as if a school of porpoises were bobbing in the suds. Sandpipers scurried stiffly on soda-straw legs and jabbed their long noses into the shuffling sands in a foray for marine life along the water's edge.

Sicola had been tiptoeing on the spilling ten-foot waves since early morning, and as the sun reached midpoint in the sky, he slithered over the angry sediment at the edge of the beach, picked up his board, and wearily trudged a few feet in the dry sand, then finally sprawled out in exhaustion. At length, he stripped off his wet suit and enjoyed the delicious warmth of the sun on his body. He lay there for half an hour and then, propped up on his elbows behind him, he surveyed the beach scene.

Before him, wherever he looked, was cleavage undisguised, unadorned, front and rear. A plump woman walked toward the water, her back to him, flesh folding over her bikini, buttocks bouncing, and above the low-slung bikini there was revealed the top third of nature's own rear-guard incision. Sicola shuddered at the sight and thought it quaint that calories could be so singularly reposited in one place as if joined together in a family picnic. "Pull uppa you pants," Sicola shouted without thinking, but the wind threw the words back at him, and the only sound that reached the woman's ears was the roaring gurgle and hiss of the dashing waves.

A few feet from him a young sea nymph of a girl tossed a Frisbee at a tanned, athletic boy. They laughed and giggled at her ineptness with the disc as she leaped for it and fell into the sand. She wore a tiny V of green fluorescent cloth between her legs, and her full breasts seeped out of the skimpy matching wedges that were a visual euphemism for a halter. Sicola watched as the young couple eventually threw themselves on a blanket — she on her back, he on his stomach beside her. She handed the smiling boy her suntan lotion and patted her bare stomach in a coquettish sign to lavish oil on her skin. Sicola pitied her helplessness, her seeming inability to reach her own tiny navel. The bronzed face smiled, and white teeth gleamed in the sun. He craned his neck and bent down to kiss her lips, all the while applying the lotion in a swirling motion unrestricted to the original area of application. She pushed him away teasingly and giggled, then she lay back again and Sicola saw her patting her chest. Obediently, the young man followed her instructions, and his hands began to ply the lotion to her chest, ultimately to creep amidst the cleavage. Then the embrace.

"Where do we go from here?" Sicola wondered.

"Sicola's fatigue left him, and he sprang to his feet. The warm sand spurted up through his toes, and he plodded heavily toward the young lovers. He looked down at them, waiting for them to unfold. Startled, the girl looked up at him with a petulant, "Want something?" The boy glared sullenly.

Sicola smiled at them and asked, "Whatsa the time, please?"

"Time to bug off," the frustrated boy muttered under his breath.

The girl hunted through her oversized beach bag, finally spilling its contents on the blanket, and reached for the wristwatch which poured out along with the chewing gum, lipstick, sun tan oil, and facial tissues. In a pique, she said, "Half past twelve."

"Holy smokes!" Sicola said. "Time a to eat. Whatsamatta, you no hungry?"

"Who wants to eat?" the boy growled.

Sicola looked at the girl, then back at the boy, and grinned, "I'm a see a you point."

He thanked them and returned to his spot on the beach. There was a serenity and a gentle warmth to the beach, but Sicola fumbled with the chest beside his surfboard and worried about the boy and the girl. He foraged through the chest for his food, then cast a long look at the other occupants of the beach and knew that he felt a sadness for them, too. There was a glory in creation symbolized by the sun, which had been placed in the heavens by God, but there seemed to be a worship of that which was created rather than of Him who created, and in the transfer there was an irreparable loss.

"Whatta to do?" Sicola mused to himself. "Whatta to do?" There was a sense of helplessness like being caught in a riptide and knowing that the only way out was to go along with it, offering no resistance but finding a way out by swimming parallel to the shore.

He lifted the bread, broke it, then prayed over it. The simple act of saying grace before his meal filled him with an awareness of providence. As God had provided this meal, as he accepted it as one of God's own graces, he knew that the only resource in a time run amok was prayer. Just prayer. Then trust — deep, confident and abiding.

The boy and the girl watched him and were suddenly filled with a hunger that had not been there before. It was midday, and the beach was at its warmest, but the girl felt a chill, and her shoulders hunched in from the cold. She watched Sicola as the chill passed. Then she reached for her beach robe and threw it over her head, slipping it down over her body.

The boy said, "Golly, I feel funny. Sort of hungry."

"Me, too," the girl said quietly.

Sicola broke off another piece of bread and sipped the wine he held in a simple plastic cup. He looked at the boy and girl and saw them watching him with tenderness and hungry desire.

In his left hand he held out the bread, and in his right the wine, both outstretched to them.

His eyes softened. Then he smiled and said simply, "Come!"

Joy, According to St. Matthew's

St. Matthew's Church was a swinging church, Sicola had heard. They were "with it," if one could judge by the crowds in attendance at Sunday Mass. Moreover, it was truly ecumenical, in the spirit of Vatican II, Sicola was told. When he asked his informant what he meant by "in the spirit of Vatican II," he was apprised of the fact that first of all the liturgy was "relevant," and, secondly, the body of Christ was not reserved for the so-called "elect" but for all, sinners and saints, Catholic, Protestant, Jew, Moslem, any and all.

Sicola had but one comment: "Deez I gotta see!"

So it was this off-handed conversation that led him to the rectory of the new, modern St. Matthew's Church to introduce himself to Father Conlon, its pastor, and to ask permission to concelebrate Sunday Mass, since he was a foreigner visiting America and without a parish affiliation. Smiling, affable, and friendly, Father Conlon hesitated for not a moment. "Of course, Father, all are welcome at St. Matthew's, even Eye-talians! You may not be familiar with our liturgy, but that needn't concern you. I'll cue you in as we go along."

"Why you gotta cue me, Father? Is there not but one liturgy for the Roman Church?"

"Oh, the essentials are there," he grinned broadly, "but we feel that to make the liturgy truly meaningful, it should spring from our hearts and show what joy we feel to be invited and to participate in this feast, this banquet."

"Ah, I see," Sicola glowered. "Then you are not so much the priest but the Master of Ceremonies. You are, so to speak, a kind of Jessel and Hyde."

"That's very good wit, Father, for an Eye-talian. I am surprised that you have heard of our George Jessel."

"He calls me every year for a contribution to the United Jewish Welfare Fund. And I give."

Sicola thought to himself, "A bishop he will never be, for there would be no way to make a mitre to fit such a head, but maybe, joosta maybe there would be a chance, if I could perhaps shave the hair."

Then he said aloud to Father Conlon, "My friend, this is a poor parish, no doubt. The collections are very small?"

"*Au contraire*, Father. Our people are most generous. The church is paid for, and we have money in the bank — that is, mind you, we have some money in the bank that the Bishop doesn't quite know about. Why do you ask?"

"Mebbe you can dip into the treasury to get a haircut, no?"

The pastor slapped his thigh and threw his head back as he laughed at what he construed was another Eye-talian witticism. "Father, my priesthood requires me to identify with the young people of the parish. How else would I get them to church? This makes me one of them."

"But you are not one of them, Father, and I do notta think that the identity is to be with them, but witha Christ."

"Well, didn't He have long hair?" Father Conlon asked with a leer.

"There was not a barber on every corner of Nazareth, Father. But," he interrupted, "what time you wanta me here Sunday?"

"Why don't we plan on concelebrating the ten o'clock Mass?"

"Si. Hokay. See you later, alligator."

At half past nine on Sunday, Sicola was in the vestry of St. Matthew's Church. In an attempt to be helpful and to get things ready for Father Conlon, he searched through closets, then looked out at the altar in order to find the Roman Missal and the Lectionary and set them up for the prayers and readings of the Mass of the day. There was no Missal or Lectionary to be found anywhere, so he went out to the kneelers in the sanctuary and prayed until Father Conlon arrived.

Father Conlon was a short man with a ruddy complexion and a bulbous nose. He wore his sideburns in the fashion of what were at one time called mutton chops, and his black hair was almost shoulder length and frizzed out on top and at the sides as if he had been electrocuted. He was muscular, and his flared trousers were tight at the thighs and in the seat, emphasizing not only his musculature, but a fundament that was round, divided, and protruding.

He breezed into the vestry, his ever-present grin showing white enamel against a red backdrop. "Hi, Father," he sang out cheerily. "Tell you what I think we ought to do. See, we start out our Mass here with a procession from the back of the church to the altar, and because you are not familiar with our methods, I think it would be a good idea if I lead the procession and you remain at the altar to greet us as we arrive. Right?"

"Right." Sicola agreed. "But where is your Missal?"

"Don't give it a thought, Father. The Holy Spirit is our Missal. All you have to do is observe and come in anytime the Spirit moves you. Hang loose, ol' buddy."

Sicola was beginning to feel a strong revulsion for Conlon, and at the words, "Hang loose," he was tempted to mutter that he would like to hang one on that red light he wore for a nose. Instead he said, "Si, this is what I am here to do — observe."

Father Conlon, dressed in his Mass vestments, scurried out the door of the vestry and headed for the front door of the church. Sicola waited in the vestry for the signal to stand before the bare table that served as an altar. He was waiting for the gentle tinkle of a bell, when upon his ears burst the raucus tones of a saxophone, tambourines, and guitars, all shaking the walls of the church and Sicola's eardrums with a rock beat, loud, repetitious, and cacophonous.

He walked out to the sanctuary and took his place before the altar, and as he did so, the two doors at the center aisle came open with the crashing sounds of unorchestrated bedlam, but what he saw left him more shaken than what he heard. Leading the procession were three young girls in their late teens dressed in filmy, gauze-like costumes that revealed naked legs and midriffs. Transparent scarves streamed and fluttered about them as they danced to the rock beat. They swooped down low with their arms outspread in a modern version of ballet, and their hips jerked and swayed in a bouncy rhythm. As they danced toward the altar, they shed the scarves in a seeming imitation of the Dance of the Seven Veils until ultimately they revealed themselves in a costume only slightly less revealing than contemporary beach wear. Following on their heels was Father Conlon dancing to the same beat, an incongruous sight in his priestly vestments. And at the top of his voice he gargled out a song without words, a song which simply repeated over and over again, "Oh, jolly joy . . . joy . . . joy! Hallelujah. Joy . . . joy . . . joy!" Then followed, for lack of a more descriptive word, that which passed as an orchestra.

Sicola stood at center stage, his jaw limp and his mouth open. There was unbelief in his eyes. He finally found the fluid force required to move his frozen legs and took his place behind the altar awaiting the jazzed-up Conlon.

Father Conlon, perspiring, redder than ever, joined Sicola behind the altar to a thundering ovation as the musicians stopped playing and the dancing girls took their places at the side of the sanctuary.

Then the Mass began.

"The good, the merciful, the loving God be with you cats," he shouted at them, beaming and smiling, as a color wheel in the choir loft threw tints and shades of the spectrum at him.

There were various answers to the opening greeting. Some shouted, "Yeah, man!" Others sang out "Cool, man, cool. And that goes for you, too. In spades."

Sicola wasn't certain he could go through with the rest of the Mass if what followed took this opening as its guide. But he was there and he knew that he had to see it through, even though "concelebration" did not mean to Father Conlon what it meant to the Church, for Sicola's role seemed more confined to that of a spectator than a participant. And as the Mass progressed this was to become more and more the case. No one was going to upstage Conlon. If anything, it was Conlon who would upstage God Himself.

It soon became apparent to Sicola why Father Conlon required no Missal. Everything seemed extemporized. The Penitential Rite lacked even the remotest sense of contrition, and in fact Conlon introduced that section of the Mass by saying, "Now, folks, let's get in the mood to dig this banquet by remembering that God wants us to do our thing, to be true to the nature He gave us, and to find joy . . . joy . . . joy in each other, and if we have offended each other, let's turn around and say, 'Sorry about that, friend.'"

To say that the Gloria had even the remotest resemblance to that orthodox paean of praise would be testing even small truth. It was a revelry of emotional holy rollerism that left the congregation limp, but quiet enough to sit back and hear the readings from the poetry of Rod McKuen. There was no Gospel reading because the intent was to show that the Gospel was written indelibly in one's heart, already inscribed there at our birth because of Christ's salvific immolation on the cross. Mankind was forever forgiven his sins and the miraculous nature of salvation implanted the Word in the hearts of all men. Instead, Father Conlon spoke extemporaneously, one was led to believe, on the forces within men which, when stifled, brought a whole legion of bodily ailments. Was this not God's own way of telling us that there need be no psychosomatic illnesses if we could be but true to the central driving forces within us? Did God create us to become cripples, he asked, or did He want for each of us to find perfect fulfillment on earth? — so that when we passed through the veil that separates the world of the living from the world of the hereafter, we would go completely purged, because fulfillment meant purgation at the same time.

Sicola listened and watched with mounting fury and fear. Fury at heresy run amok, and fear of its consequences to the soul of man. He was, he thought, watching animality turned loose, appetite unrestrained, Satan in total and absolute control. He began to think ahead in the Mass. What would Conlon do with the Consecration; how would he handle the Communion? And a dread filled his heart as he recalled violations in other communities, which had already been recorded as nothing compared to this, their extension when left unchastised and undisciplined. He would not let it happen, he vowed. Somehow, he would put a stop to it. But how . . . how . . . how?

In disgust, Sicola left the sanctuary and, still clothed in his vestments, went through the door of the vestry and stepped into the open yard behind the church. He took long, oversized rosary beads from his pocket and began to pray aloud, first reciting the Apostles' Creed, that fulcrum of Catholic belief and doctrine. As he prayed, his voice grew louder and more furious, as if he were trying to penetrate the very clouds above him with a petition to heaven. There followed the Pater Noster and the three Aves for faith, hope and charity, and the futility of it all became pervading — what faith? what hope? what charity? — and brought a quaver to his voice and a glaze to his eyes.

"The first Glorious Mystery," he prayed, "the Resurrection of Jesus Christ." The joy of Easter. The risen Christ. The triumphant Savior. He had fulfilled His promise to rise in three days. Would He who created man as a symbol of His love allow all this — suffering, humiliation, death, resurrection — to come tumbling down as a mockery to Him? Or was the resurrection a foretoken of His ultimate triumph? Sicola meditated the first mystery as he repeated over and over again, "Hail Mary, full of grace, the Lord is with thee. Blessed art thou among women, and blessed is the fruit of thy womb, Jesus . . ." The Magnificat, glorious in its recognition of her, ever more glorious in its promise for mankind. "She," he thought, "whom He loved, so at one with Him, could but look at Him more than any other, and He would accede to her. What an incomparable relationship! What a monument, what a meaning this gives to the very idea of divine love!"

As he prayed Sicola was unaware that his steps were taking him, fully vested in the robes of the Church, away from St. Matthew's Church and into the neighborhood of neat, quiet suburban homes surrounding it. He prayed aloud, but his thoughts centered on his meditation of the mysteries, and as he was lost in his thoughts there began to trail behind him the neighborhood dogs, mongrels, purebreds and all, with not so much as a whimper to distract him. The parade of animals grew large and followed for more than a block, while Sicola, unaware, continued to intone the words of the Aves. Then, as the residents of the neighborhood peered out their windows or watched as they watered their gardens, they too began to follow the procession with the dogs in the vanguard.

By the time Sicola had come to the Salve Regina, he was back at the massive double doors of St. Matthew's Church. "Hail, holy Queen, Mother of Mercy, our life, our sweetness and our hope," he prayed as he entered the church through the front doors.

Father Conlon had, by this time, come to the Consecration of the Mass, and Sicola's skin crawled with disgust as he saw at the altar what he had come to know as a "submarine sandwich," except that this was the largest loaf he had ever seen, extending to three quarters the size of the altar. Inside the bread, which was cut horizontally, there were pieces of sandwich meats that overlapped the bread and protruded through the incision.

Conlon held it near each end and raised it high above his head in a gesture of communal offering and sacerdotal consecration.

". . . to thee we cry, poor banished children of Eve, to thee do we send up our sighs, mourning and weeping in this valley of tears. Turn, then, most gracious advocate, thine eyes of mercy toward us, and after this our exile show unto us the blessed fruit of thy womb, Jesus. O clement, O loving, O sweet Virgin Mary . . ."

Sicola was now at the foot of the altar. Conlon looked aghast at the entourage that followed the visiting priest. He stood frozen, still holding the gigantic loaf of bread above his head. The congregation, too, suddenly sobered as if they had been given an antidote to a drug that coursed through their veins and clouded their minds.

At the close of Sicola's prayer, as he murmured tenderly, "Oh sweet Virgin Mary," it was as if the dogs had received a signal to break ranks.

Suddenly they were all over the altar, pouncing on Father Conlon and tearing the gargantuan sandwich from him. They gorged themselves, some yelping in their eagerness, others snarling at any that would compete for a share in the prize.

Sicola seemed as amazed as Conlon, for with the

milling, surging force of the animals at his knees, he was roused from his meditation and looked about him at the large assemblage of animals and people, some still carrying their garden tools.

Conlon surveyed the mass of snarling animals, then shouted, "Someone get these damned beasts out of here."

As if he in particular had been addressed, a St. Bernard lumbered toward Conlon, stood on his hind legs and embraced the small priest with his front paws thrust lovingly around Conlon's neck. In fear and panic, Conlon darted from the church, and for whatever reason (it remains unknown), the pack of animals chased him all the way to the rectory, where ultimately he found refuge.

The neighborhood residents were soon followed by the newly subdued congregation in cleaning the debris from the altar and the aisles of the church.

Sicola went to his car, which was parked behind the church, and brought back into the vestry the requirements for beginning the Mass anew. He washed his hands, then sounded a small bell as he was to enter the sanctuary.

The congregation rose, and Sicola noted that a man wearing shorts and a sweatshirt had taken his position at the side of the altar as server.

"The grace of our Lord Jesus Christ and the love of God and the fellowship of the Holy Spirit be with you all."

"And also with you," the congregation returned.

Some distance away from the church, there was the long throaty baying of a hound, and Sicola smiled inwardly as he addressed the people of God: "My brothers and sisters, to prepare ourselves to celebrate the sacred mysteries, let us call to mind our sins."

As the people recited the act of contrition, Sicola turned his eyes to the high domed ceiling of the church and muttered, "Sonofagun!"

Only a Fraction

Sicola's tour of the United States was masterful in its deception. According to the press releases he was at Castel Gondolfo, his summer residence. Periodically, bulletins were issued and quoted in the secular and religious press concerning this or that observation on our times.

Aside from Tommaso, everyone thought that he was there, including those occupants of the summer home itself. No one saw him, but they had been told that the Pope was in seclusion following the spiritual exercises of St. Ignatius. No one questioned; all understood.

At appointed times, Tommaso was instructed to telephone Sicola, one time in Los Angeles, another in Chicago, at small and large cities throughout the vastness of America. Sometimes he traveled as a simple priest, but many times more he would wear the clothing of a laborer or farmer, a vacationer or business executive. All that set him apart was his accent, and in America, this land of the melting pot, no thought was given to accents.

Each morning Sicola would awaken at five, wash, dress, and read his breviary. Then he would go to his closet and remove the small rectangular case that contained his chalice, the Roman Missal, a supply of hosts, and altar wine. On his dresser he prepared a simple altar, where he said Mass and remembered the intentions, expressed and unexpressed, of the people he had met in this vibrant, teeming nation of people so given to the enjoyment of their senses. As he raised the Host at the Consecration and said, ". . . this is my body which will be given up for you," he would feel a searing tear at his chest as if it had been lanced, and he would remember the recent experience. . . .

She was a most beautiful woman, he thought to himself, but was it not strange that great beauties had the faces of the nuns of times past, and he could almost frame her countenance in the nun's habit with the whiteness of a wimple and the embracing cover of a veil leaving visible only the stark, simple beauty of her face. It even seemed tranquil. One could not tell much about faces, he concluded.

Here she sat in her magnificent nineteen-room apartment, a *marchesa*, it was said. Above the divan where she sat was a huge surrealistic painting that exuded an eerie quality, unreal, lonely and frightening. The painting, she explained, was of her, her two children, her husband . . . and her lover, all in the same picture and all a representation of her very open and current life-style. She and her husband stood in a windswept desert with sand nearly to their waists, he looking away from the viewer, with the heads of their young daughters painted on his torso. Lurking over the shoulder of her husband was her lover. The marchesa held her hands across her breasts in what seemed to be her self-concept of demure morality. Her red hair billowed away from her head like flaming tongues, and her eyes were solemn, dark-ringed in a physiological prelude of death. Behind the figures were high, craggy rocks in mauve and brown, licked and spat upon by the raging sands. This painting was her great and cherished prize, but Sicola wondered if the artist had not seen and commented more than the Marchesa had noted in the picture. It gave him the feeling of the joylessness of purgatory.

Sicola had gone to her New York apartment in the company of a new friend, a reporter for the largest news service in the country. The reporter had suggested it as a way for Sicola to get to see the hidden corners of America, "sort of off the tourist trail, you know."

"Why," she complained to the reporter, "are people only interested in my sex life? Sex is only a fraction of my life. Yet the attention of the press seems so centered on that small part of my life."

She had raised money for hospitals in Laos and Mali, orphanages in Pakistan; she had sponsored a Vietnamese family and was now supporting nineteen foster children. But all anyone was interested in was her "unconventional" married life.

She was, she said, married to a prominent diplomat and was at the same time sharing her bed with a romantic Frenchman. "But that is the way of life today. My husband has a girl friend. No one is jealous, and on the contrary we are all ecstatically happy. We would have had an awful lot of conflicts in our life otherwise. I adore my husband. He's shrewd, gifted, creative and exciting. But Pierre is wonderful, too. If I were to describe them I would say that my husband has a zest for life and Pierre has the knack of living.

"We would never consider divorce," she said as if the idea were revolting and immoral. "Family integrity is important, and we have an excellent working relationship. We three are extremely good for one another."

Then she pouted, and her green eyes showed the hurt as she complained of the lack of understanding, the ostracism of some of her charities, whose leaders had asked that her name be removed from their committee lists. "It's too bad when your name prompts knowing grins," she remarked with a petulant toss of her long red hair. "I think the difference between me and other women is that most merely dream what I have realized. If they had the opportunity, I think they'd do as I do too.

"I consider myself very moral," she emphasized. "Why, this summer on Ibiza I was the only woman at the beach with her bikini on."

That was the essence of the news service story as it appeared in the next day's newspapers. Unwritten was the strange event that took place after the Marchesa had assumed a moral posture based on her conduct on Ibiza.

Sicola felt that searing tear at the right side of his rib cage and raised his hands in an involuntary gesture of pain. The Marchesa turned to him as a soft murmur of pain came to his lips. Then she noticed the bleeding in the palms of his hands, and she gasped, "Oh, my dear man! You have somehow cut your hands. However could you have done it?"

Sicola sat transfixed, his eyes unseeing and directed toward the ceiling. At the corners of his eyes little globules formed and slowly trickled down the valleys of his cheeks. It was as if he were in shock, and the Marchesa became frightened. She moved toward him quickly and held his hands, wiping the blood from his palms with a tiny lace handkerchief.

As she daubed at the wounds a scent of roses came from the wounds and enveloped her, and she was filled with a sorrow so encompassing as to make her weep, all the while lamenting, "You poor man . . . you poor man."

Sicola then looked at her with tenderness and gratitude. The wound stopped its bleeding, and he said to her kindly, "Grazie, Maddalena!"

The Marchesa looked with vague apprehensiveness into Sicola's eyes, then questioningly at the healed hands. At length, she studied his face and, almost in a whisper, she said, "Maddalena? . . . Sir, who are you?"

Sicola picked up the camera he had used to photograph the Marchesa beneath her painting, and he started to leave the apartment with the reporter. At the door, he turned to her and said, "One who would be your friend." Then he left.

". . . Take this, all of you, and drink from it: this is the cup of my blood, the blood of the new and everlasting covenant. It will be shed for you and for all men, so that sins may be forgiven. Do this in memory of me."

Sicola placed the chalice on the white altar cloth on his dresser, and the image of the Marchesa seemed to shimmer in the soft, creamy wine in the cup, her flaming hair blending with the gold interior highlights of the chalice.

As Sicola recited the Memorial Acclamation, rising from the wine and echoing within the chalice was the voice of a woman who joined him in this memorial of what was and was yet to be. "When we eat this bread and drink this cup, we proclaim your death, Lord Jesus, until you come in glory."

To Father Daniel

There was a time, my son, when the Church so prospered that many of the leading lights among our separated brethren returned in great numbers to the arms of Holy Mother Church, while at the same time there were some few defections from the Church, and these few left with trumpets blaring. It was said among our people with amazing lack of charity that "we have taken their finest flower, while we have given them our weeds."

Then in more recent times a most influential newspaper on your western shores gave great space to "the celibacy crisis" within the Church, and again the cry was heard among our people. "They show the world our weeds, but nothing is said of our finest flower, those who remain in the priesthood."

My son, let it be known that these are the words of our soldiers, loyal to the Church perhaps, but impetuous in their loyalty, for the Church does not see souls — any souls — as weeds. All are potential flowers, with weeds in their midst sucking the nutrients of the earth around them so as to limit their potential for beauty. The weeds are the agents of Satan who would inhibit all that is good and all that is beautiful in the creation of the Father.

But let us now speak more specifically to you,

our beloved apostle. While we do not see weeds among our souls, it must be recognized that the association is rhetorical and not without its point. It is offered by way of contrast so that proper recognition can be given to those stalwart souls who give credit to creation by their example of piety and action. Such a one were you.

You, Daniel, have been among our finest flowers. And I am grieved.

I am grieved much like the little child in your American folklore who turned to his hero, a gentleman I am told, called "Shoeless Joe Jackson," and said to him most tearfully, "Say it ain't so, Joe!" I am your Pope, yet I am at this moment like the small child, dismayed, grieved, and crushed by the loss of one so great.

I am told that you seek laicization although you have filed no such petition yet. I know that I must accede to your wishes if this is truly the desire of your whole mind and your whole heart. But, my son, my own mind and heart suffer too, and it is about this suffering that I wish to speak.

It has been said that the loss of our priests has been most marked among our liberal sons; that those more conservative, even orthodox, such as you, do not leave. Yet you wish to leave. Does this not tell us that defections are not the result of Vatican II and its alleged divisive effects? Nor is the turning from one's priestly commitment related in any sense to the labels attached to our priests, liberal or progressive, conservative or reactionary, priest or bishop, democrat or republican. All are human, therefore susceptible.

No, my son, there lies beneath the enigma a cause so basic as to be common to all, and the cause is most insidious because its effects occur before one is completely aware of what has happened. So surreptitiously does the cause-and-effect relationship take place that, once it has run its course, it becomes difficult for some, impossible for others, to become disentangled.

With energetic zeal the young man goes forth after his ordination. He is at first selfless, imbued with the sense of his mission, committed totally to Christ. *Ora et labora*. He prays and he works. Then success comes to him, and his name is recognized. He works harder, all in the name of God, but he does not have so much time left in the day to pray. Gone is the breviary, gone is the holy hour, gone the rosary, gone is the victimhood of the priesthood, as our son, Fulton Sheen has said.

"But it was all for You, Lord!" he says one day when he has realized that he has been on a treadmill of activism. And over him Christ sorrows, and He says to His beloved, "Did I not tell you that Mary's way was the better way?"

This is not to imply, my son, that you no longer pray, that you have not been aware of the miracle of the Mass, that Christ has passed completely from your thoughts. It is only to suggest that one's commitment to correcting the inequities of the world may tend at times to dilute prayer and to make it become less frequent, even at that time when it is most required of us. That there is need for laborers in the vineyard is without question, but God has greater need of your spirituality and the example it provides to those who will follow you. Let those who respond to your piety become the laborers, for it is more in keeping with their lives and their involvement with the world.

We can ill afford your loss at any time, but especially in these trying times. There will be another to take your place in the days ahead if it remains your purpose to turn from your vocation, but he will have a uniqueness different from yours. Your loss will be measured large, but this too shall pass.

It is good that you have taken time to meditate on your decision. I would ask that you do so daily before the Blessed Sacrament, that fountainhead of theology, that wellspring of divine love, that ocean of wisdom. It is only there that — in holy abandonment, complete and trusting — one begins to sense slipping from him all sense of selfhood, gradually and ultimately in fullness, to be replaced by a kind of mystical transfer that knows and accepts Christ, only Christ. You become, like Him, a victim committed to the Father with such overwhelming passion as to seek the immolation of all self.

Listen as he says to you, "Come to Me!"

May He hear my prayer as I call out, "Come back, my brother!"

Your friend in Christ,
Sicola

Joost a Little Miracle

It was a warm Sunday morning in September, and Sicola had gone to hear Mass at the nearby church. Even at seven-thirty in the morning there was a bleached look about everything as the sun burned through with a warning of oppressiveness yet to come. The men wore their sport shirts loosely, draped rather than tucked into their trousers. The women wore sleeveless dresses of light cotton, either in white or in pastels, and the effect was to give at best the illusion of coolness.

At least the church was air-conditioned, a far cry, he thought, from the old churches where one sweltered. Somehow, even with the heat and the smell of everyone's perspiration, the churches were filled in those times, and not for one Mass only but for as many as five and six each Sunday. But on this day the Church of St. Louise de Marillac had been barely one-third full.

The Mass having ended, he walked toward his rented automobile outside the church, remembering the fervent sermon by the white-haired Father Walsh, who must have shared the loneliness of Christ when he said, "And where are the other ninety-nine?" Even in his fervor there was a sense of hopelessness as he spoke of the obligation of Jesus' Mass, of the debt of

257

love we owed to Him for the sacrifice He had made for us. There was no ranting, no hellfire and brimstone, but he spoke rapidly, excitedly, a man caught up in his own love for Christ and trying desperately to infuse the whole world with a similar zeal. But when he was through, tired, saddened, frustrated, he was forced to recognize the fact that he had been addressing the wrong people, for these were the people who came regularly each Sunday, some even daily. Where were "the other ninety-nine"?

Where were they, he thought, the people who would deny Him this tribute for one hour? "Could you not watch and wait with me for one hour?" What was of such pressing importance? The beach? The mountains? The bed? He gave them a new manna of affluence, and as with the old manna, they were surfeited and then brought complaints against Him. They wanted more of Him but gave less of themselves. They sought that which titillated them and soothed their senses while He stood alone, unattended, even ignored.

"Damn . . . Damn . . . Damn!" he exploded. "I will find you and drag you if I must, but find you I will. This time I will go as a priest."

He was within an hour's drive of the beach or the mountains, and a flip of the coin is all it took to decide upon the mountains. He would try Lake Arrowhead.

The mountain community was jammed with people who ascended above the smog and the heat of the lower valleys to enjoy a weekend of relaxation. The town brought back to him a remote memory of his own earlier vacations in the alpine villages of Switzerland. It was quaint, and there was a scrupulous cultivation of old-world charm so inconsistent with the sensate new-world appetites of its inhabitants. In the square the vacationers milled about the shops, while some, tired from their pilgrimage through the retail outlets, sat on benches and munched at ice cream cones.

At length he took a seat on one of the benches beside a young man and woman. They sat cooing at their young daughter perhaps only a year from First Communion age. There was a dab of chocolate ice cream on her nose, and her mouth was smeared with a brown crescent giving it the appearance of turning upward in a happy, syrupy grin.

Sicola smiled as he sat next to the young mother. "Nice a day," he commented cheerfully.

"Oh, yes, Father. Isn't it lovely?"

"You like a the cioccolata, bambina?" he asked the child.

"Mm-m-m!"

They were a handsome family, he thought, both in their late twenties, not yet completely settled but beginning to have that first awareness of a more mature life, evidenced perhaps in the sureness with which she accepted motherhood and the relaxed, almost vague way in which he allowed her to be maternal while he assumed a position just above it all.

"Careful, Sharon. Don't get ice cream on your new dress," the woman said, while her husband assumed a mock expression of authority, as if to back up his wife's admonition with the strength of aloofness.

"All children can think of is how best to gorge themselves," she said to Sicola with a smile.

"That, my child, issa one observation you canna make about lottsa grown-ups, too."

"Right you are, Father," she chuckled.

As long as the stranger was going to get philo-sophical, it seemed proper to fall within the realm of man-talk, a cue for the young husband to become in-volved in the conversation. Besides, this was a priest, and it would be good to impress the priest with his sense of good and evil, right and wrong, moral and immoral.

"A perfect case in point, Father, is the scene around us. Look at that fat lady over there. She wad-dles about from shop to shop, one time feeding her face with a hamburger, now with popcorn, and every-body spending money like it's going out of style. They don't need all the things they're buying any more than the fat lady needs all the calories she's stuffing into herself."

"Ah . . . si!" Sicola muttered. "It is the way of the world. What can one do?"

"I'll tell you what we can do, Father. We can have another depression. Then they'll soon find out what it's like."

"Ah . . . so-o-o? You know about the depres-sion? You do not somehow seema so old."

The young man flushed, then recovered. "Well, my dad has told me about it. Has he ever! Told me how they were happy to have a bowl of soup to eat in those days."

"They were very trying times, my son," Sicola mused. "But you speak of the need for another de-pression. The woman you speak of . . . the fat one . . . she is of an age to remember the depression, yet she seems to learn nothing from it. Surely, there must be something more that is needed. No?"

"Well, then Father — no offense meant — may-be you fellas are not doing your jobs. Maybe you got to get to them and tell 'em that they're acting like pigs."

"Ah, my friend, we come a to that, eh? Tella me, my son. You go to church today?"

"Well, we — that is, no. You see, we had to get an early start so we could enjoy the day and get Sharon out of the smog."

"You go a last Sunday?"

"I think you've missed my point, Father. That is, I don't think I have made myself very clear. You see, Father, I believe in God, and I want you to know that my wife, Eloise, and I are very religious persons. And we *do* go to church on occasion. It's just that I don't feel — now I'm speaking for myself, mind you — that a person has to go to church to be religious. God is in my heart, and I can pray just as well at home as I can in church. But I suspect that those people who go to church every Sunday are the ones who go right out and live it up as if they have no comprehension of what's happening in the world today. Know what I mean?"

"Si. I know. Tella me something. You Cattolico?"

"How's that again?"

"Are you a Catholic?" Sicola repeated, this time paying special attention to his speech.

Eloise, too long out of things and anxious to give testimony, blurted out with enthusiasm and pride, "Oh, yes, Father. Both of us. Parochial school, and the whole works."

"Tella me, then, issa the Blessed Sacrament inna you home?"

"Of course not, Father," the husband interjected.

"Onna Sunday, whenna you say you have God inna you heart, do you have a Him totally — in body and in spirit? Canna you receive the Eucharist, the body and the blood of Christ, inna you bedroom, or inna you Chevrolet onna the way to Lake Arrowhead?"

"Of course not, Father. But don't you think He knows that we try to live our lives without hurting other people, by loving others and believing that He exists?"

"My son. He loves you as you are . . . according to the limit of your ability to know and to love Him . . . but He asks that you become perfect as He is perfect."

"Aw, c'mon, Father!"

"Tella me this: whatsa you business?"

"I'm an architect."

"Whatsa you ambition?"

"To be the best architect I can become."

"How this going to happen?"

"By work, and study, and experience — by throwing myself completely into my work."

"How long you think it willa take you to be the best?"

"All my life, I suppose. Becoming good, really good, at what you do is a never-ending proposition, and there's always more to learn, something you missed. It makes you humble when you think of how much there is yet to know."

"But you are a willing to spend your life inna the pursuit, no?"

"Yes."

"How longa you gonna live?"

The young man burst into laughter. "If I knew that, Father, I'd wait until the last month to buy my life insurance instead of carrying it now. But — with luck — to my seventies or eighties. Why do you ask?"

"It will be clear to you. Tella me. How longa is eternity?"

"Forever, Father. Time without end. Everyone knows that."

"Thenna why you give such dedication to some-a-thing that will last maybe fifty more years — iffa you lucky — and so little to whatta will be forever?"

The young man was silent. Sicola's logic made him uncomfortable. He had been maneuvered and he knew it, but there was no escaping the man's conclusion. The priest had made his point, and there was egg on the young man's face.

"Father . . . you make a very good point. I can't quarrel with it, but there is one difference. I know architecture, and because of it I love it. God is somehow unreal, a person or an idea I have heard about. I do not know Him. So how can I love what I do not know?"

"Willa you come with me. For joost a few min-ootes?"

Sicola had passed a Catholic church on his way to the shopping square, and when the young couple nodded their agreement, he drove them to the church. It was vacant and cool as they walked down the aisle toward the tabernacle. "Now talk to Him, my children. Tell Him a what is inna you hearts. Then let you mind become open, and He will enter. Tomorrow tell Him again, anda the next day, anda the next."

Sicola raised his right hand over the kneeling family and blessed them, and as he did so the sanctuary light winked briefly. Then he was gone, leaving them alone with their thoughts.

Quietly he walked up the aisle and took a place in the last pew at the rear of the church. He knelt, then placed his head in his hands, which rested on the back of the seat in front of him.

"Miracles," he said as he prayed, "I have never

asked for. One's faith does not require them. Witness, for example, dear Lord, those miracles You performed, and still man turns from You. But sometimes perhaps joost a small miracle would help me inna my work. So, Lord, I know You are all wise, all knowing, while I am nothing. But iffa what I ask makes a good sense to You — maybe joost a little one? Eh?"

Sicola looked up, and his eyes went to the young couple who knelt before the tabernacle. Then he blanched as he began to see forming above the tabernacle and just below the crucifix a tableau taking shape in a wispy haze of gray-white moisture. The figure of Christ seemed to come off the cross, and He stood there suspended in the vapor, the crown of thorns around His head, His face bleeding and weary. Then He stretched out His arms with a burden to the young parents, who sat transfixed. In His arms He carried a child, their child, limp and asleep. The apparition grew larger as it came nearer to the stunned and frozen couple. Then Christ bent His head to kiss the brow of the child and passed her over the rim of the pew to the parents. His voice was deep and gentle and soft, and He spoke only one sentence.

"Return her to me in the same way you received her." Then the wisp of vapor disappeared.

Sicola bent his head and whispered, "My God, my God! I love You!"

He walked out of the church, and in his ear he heard, "I will be with you until the end of the world."

Monday Night Football

It was time for Monday Night Football, and in every home in the United States all activity came to a halt. At least in the East and Midwest, families had already finished dinner and the dishes were washed. On the West Coast portable television sets were moved into the kitchen so that, during dinner, no one would be deprived of seeing the kickoff. Even grace before meals was dispensed with, at least in those few homes where it was still practiced.

When Sicola had noticed that grace before the meal was either not an observed form or was temporarily in suspension at the Weaver house, he bowed his head and silently prayed, "Bless us, O Lord, and these thy gifts. . . ." No one noticed.

Howard Cosell droned through the preliminaries, giving verbose sketches of leading gladiators in the night's contest. Sicola, anxious to be proficient in the English language, carried a dictionary with him everywhere, but soon he found it was useless in following Cosell. Cosell would yet vindicate himself, however.

Tommy Weaver was sixteen and on the Jayvee football team in high school. He sat to Sicola's right, and Sicola watched him raise the fork to his mouth robot-like, unaware of what he was eating and equally unconcerned with its taste.

George Weaver, Tommy's father, sipped at a can of beer and grunted, "Cosell, you got a big mouth."

Tommy, his mouth full of potatoes, agreed in a mushy voice, "Yeah, Dad. He sure uses big words, don't he?"

"Doesn't he, Tommy," Eleanor Weaver corrected. Long ago Mrs. Weaver had decided that on Monday nights you either joined the men in the family or you spent the evening in solitude, a solitude wasted in contemplation because of the jarring crowd noises from the TV set, the intermittent wrangling between Howie and Don, and the above-it-all commentary by Frank, not to mention George's sudden explosions, like, "Gawd, what a catch . . . what a catch!"

The Rams had kicked off to the Redskins, and Sicola watched the set as the camera followed the course of the ovate ball, and then he cringed as a horde of men threw themselves at the return specialist. The runner had taken five or six leaping steps into the crowd of red jerseys when he was struck first by one man with what seemed like the force of a truck, right in the stomach. Sicola had swallowed his steak at that moment, and it stuck in his chest tearing at his alimentary canal as if it were the very size of the football itself. He choked and reached for the glass of water in front of his plate.

At length, Sicola smiled and said to anyone who would listen, "Why he so mad at the man with the ball?"

Tommy laughed, and said, "He ain't mad at him, Father. Boy! What a stick!"

"He used a stick, Tommaso?"

"No, Father," George intervened, "that is what they call a good hard tackle."

"Oh," Sicola mused, "I see." But he didn't.

Time and again, the quarterback would hand off to a runner, but the front four of the Rams held and Frank Gifford would repeat, "And again, he was barely able to get to the line of scrimmage."

"What is this line of spinach?" Sicola asked.

"Scrimmage, Father. Scrimmage!" Tommy said with disgust. That's where the players are lined up against each other, and the ball carrier hasn't been able to penetrate the defensive line."

"Uh-huh. *Capisco*." He turned to Eleanor and shrugged his shoulders. She smiled back at him with an expression that said, "Me too." Then Eleanor, with her quiet wisdom, said to Sicola, "Father, why don't we let the little boys watch their game, while we grown-ups — you and I — go into the living room and chat. We'll save dessert until later, and I'll get the dishes when we're finished."

Eleanor pointed to the comfortable lounge chair, and Sicola sank back in its surrounding softness. In the background they could hear the chatter of the three football announcers as it mingled and tried to rise above the din of the crowd.

Sicola smiled at his hostess and said, "George and Tommaso. They are good friends, more than father and son?"

"Yes, Father. Buddies. Fishing, football games, baseball games, movies. Everything together. They're great friends."

"This is good, you believe?"

"Well, I don't know how good it is, but I will admit that it gets a little lonely for me at times. I look around and they're gone, either in the workshop building a birdhouse, or they've taken a trip someplace where the fishing is supposed to be out of this world. And even when they're in the same house, they're in front of the TV set looking at a game or Wide World of Sports or whatever."

"What does thissa do to Tommaso's discipline?"

"Discipline? What discipline? Father, George is so chicken-hearted, he wouldn't deny that boy a thing. I have to do it all. And you know, Father, it isn't the same. It just isn't the same. I keep telling George, it's great that he loves the boy so much, and I love him for it, but love comes in all kinds of packages and sizes. A father is a father, and a buddy is a buddy, and you've got to be careful that never the twain shall meet."

"I know of what you speak," Sicola said thoughtfully.

"That's a little hard to believe, Father. You? A priest? How could you?"

"Ah, yes. I know," Sicola said slowly. "A priest, you say. Is not a priest called Father? Is not the Pope himself called Il Papa — The Father?"

"Yes, but you have no experience in raising a family."

"Si. But I have never given birth to the lamb, yet I know about raising the sheep."

"That's an interesting comparison."

"It is not mine alone."

A player had been hurt on the field. The game was delayed while he was being examined, and discussions proceeded concerning his removal from the field in a stretcher. Besides, the Rams had intercepted a pass before that and were ahead seven to nothing, so George poked his head into the room sheepishly and said, "Hey, what are you two up to? Good game! Come on in. What do you say, Father? I'll explain it to you."

"That's okay, George. We'll just sit and talk," Eleanor said with a smile.

"Heck, no!" George grinned with a sense of guilt. "That's no fair. Father's our guest." Then he walked into the living room, popping the top off a fresh can of beer. "Watcha talkin about?"

"Raising sheep," Eleanor laughed.

"Oh. Sounds interesting."

"It was a mere figure of speech, George," Sicola said. "I wassa saying thatta the priesthood is like fatherhood, the Churcha like the family. And the Pope is the beega Papa who musta raise his sheep so that they remaina close to him, who is also the shepherd."

"Sounds tougher than raising one kid, Father." George slurped out the words as he sipped his beer. "I know a guy with ten kids — would you believe it? ten kids! Don't envy him a bit. One's all I can handle."

"The Pope hassa no choice, and if he did he would choose to be the father of millions, notta the father of a few."

"How's that, Father?"

"Because, my son, if there are only a few, then he can lead only a few into heaven. When there are many, then more can enter. Because he stands *in loco Dei*, his responsibility becomes greater, but so, too, does his love. For it becomes more like God's love, which is not divisible by the parts over which it is to be distributed. There is as much for one as for all. And so the Pope loves also."

"Yeah, man. But now you're talking about an army. How do you keep 'em in line? Somehow I can't recall McArthur saying, 'I'm gonna love you G.I.'s so much you'll do everything I tell you.' "

"To spank is not to love, George?"

"Well, I'm sure you can love a kid and still paddle him. I haven't had to do it, though."

"Perhaps you do not love Tommaso as you think."

George flushed at what he thought was an insult by a guest who knew little of his relationship with his son. "I love him a great deal, Father," he said tersely.

"I am sure of it, my friend. I amma saying that you do not love him as you think, if you find it painful to putta the hand to the bottom before the head gets so strong that he saysa to you, 'You have a no right to act like a father, for you are my friend only.' The time will come when you are disturbed over a transgression so important that you must intervene. Then because the shepherd's crook was not applied early enough and often enough, the sheep moves out of the sight of the shepherd."

"Generalizations, Father. Sheep and people are different."

"George, my good American friend, it was notta so long ago that the Church had a Pope who was a very holy man. Love filled himma so much that the watchwords of his reign were charity . . . reconciliation. I know of no miracles he performed, but that he is in heaven, I amma convinced. But there are faults even in the saints, and his fault was that he loved as you conceive love.

"He said, 'I will share my office, my responsibilities witha you,' and when his sheep believed him they told him that they knew more than he. They threw away the uniforms, they disobeyed all that was holy, and they said to their people, 'Do what you like because the Pope does not know what life is all about.' And one of them said, 'The Pope issa fallible. He can make the mistake, only the people are infallible.'

"But soon it was almost too late. You see they were right. The Pope can make a some mistakes, but these are the mistakes of the discipline. In the knowledge of what is right, of what is God's law, he cannot err, not because he is not human — oh, how human he is — but because God is divine, without error, and works through Il Papa.

"Now . . . when this Pope said, 'Come back,' he would always add 'iffa you please.' And they did not come back."

George listened intently, beginning to see the broader picture, beginning also to hear Eleanor's voice when she would say, "George, for heaven's sake, will you please speak to Tommy about taking out the trash? He just ignores me." And instead George would do it. Everything the priest said was sensible, but somehow he was expecting George to go against his nature. And he just couldn't do that.

Tommy came into the living room, and George greeted him cheerily, "Hi, Tommy."

"End of the first quarter, Dad. Aren't you gonna watch anymore?"

"Tommy," Eleanor said, "during the break, please take out the trash."

"I'll do it after the game, Mom."

"You say that every time, Tommy; then you end up putzing around, and you go to bed without doing it. I'd really appreciate it if you did it immediately."

"Oh, Mom!"

"TOMMY!" George raised his voice. "Do as your mother says."

The boy looked at his father in surprise and started to complain.

"*Now*, Tommy!" George said firmly and quietly.

His son stood looking at his father, and there

was the slightest glistening in his eyes. Then he turned and went out the door, obediently.

"I feel awful," George said.

"I'm sure you do, dear," Eleanor comforted him. "But it needed to be done."

He flicked the television set on in the living room with impatience and irritability, and the picture brightened as Cosell's voice droned on, "What a marvelous tribute this team is to coaching. Here's a man who, as a player, had learned that self-discipline was the only way to perfection in athletics. Now as a coach he demands the same spirit of self-sacrifice and dedication from each of his players. They call him tough, some people do, but I'll tell you something: his players love him and would, if necessity importuned, make the supreme sacrifice for him. He will not win all of his games, but he'll always be a winner, on the field or in the hearts of his men. Take it away, Giffer."

Sicola looked at George, who sat by the set in disbelief. It was as if Cosell had been listening to them and decided to give his own wrap-up.

"I thought," Sicola said, "that football was only a game. This Cosell? Is he perhaps a Catholic?"

Symbolism Under the Elm Tree

Sicola sat in the cool shade of the elm tree on St. Bernard's Seminary campus. He leaned back on his elbows and looked into its leafy lacework as the sun filtered through and left mottled patches of gold on the rich, weedless grass. The grandeur of the tree spread over him like a protective giant. There was no way, he thought, of calculating its age, but it seemed to him to be a hundred years old, a mute testimony of the strength and beauty of the past offering itself to the present.

He began to open the book he carried with him to read in moments like this, quiet, serene and contemplative. Over his right shoulder he heard the voice of a young man, vibrant and cheerful, "Hi, Father!"

Sicola turned to look up at the youthful seminarian gazing down at him. His blond hair was long, but neatly coiffed about his ears and just above the nape of his neck. It was a happy face, made more radiant by the beauty of the day and the glint of the sun on his white, even teeth. It was the face of a boy alive and energetic with a newly awakened urge to manhood.

" 'Allo," Sicola said to the student with a warm smile. "The beauty of your campus is distracting, no? How you study with such glory surrounding you?"

273

"I guess you get to take it for granted after a time and don't give it a thought."

"That is the way with the truly good things of life, my son. It becomes easy to look at them without perceiving them."

"Right you are, Father. Say, now, I didn't mean to interrupt your reading. I just wondered if you were new on the faculty this term, and I wanted to say hello." He threw himself down beside Sicola without an invitation and he reminded Sicola of effervescent soda sending its bubbles up to the brim and popping softly at the air around it.

"No, my son, I am joost a visitor for the day."

"You are a teacher, though, aren't you, Father?"

"Yes, I am a teacher."

"I knew it . . . I knew it. I can always spot teachers, even in a crowd. Something sets them apart. I don't know exactly how I do it; it's just a sense."

"I hope you are well known for your good sense, my young friend," Sicola laughed at his own *double entendre*.

"I hope so, too, Father. What's your field? Philosophy, sociology, psychology?" He paused after each word, and his voice lifted on the last syllable with that same refreshing exuberance coming through even when he asked a question.

"My field is the Church."

"Oh, a historian!"

"In a way, si."

"History is being written in the Church today, Father. I think that the changes are good. The Church was too long in becoming modernized, don't you think?"

"In some things, si; in others, no."

"But isn't it good to see so much of the meaningless symbolism being stripped away? The people didn't understand it, anyway, and now we can reach them more quickly by our directness, by getting rid of the trappings of religion that we call symbols."

Sicola sobered and reflected for a moment. Then, as if he had not heard or, having heard, wished to change the subject, he said to the seminarian, "I am Padre Simon. What issa you name?"

"Oh," the young man said with tasteful embarrassment. "I'm Larry Stone." He extended his hand and gripped Sicola's warmly and firmly.

"Why you do that?" Sicola wanted to know.

"Do what, Father?" he asked, perplexed.

"Why you shake my hand?"

Young Stone laughed, genuinely amused, without a trace of annoyance. "Isn't it a custom in your country, Father. I thought it was a universal gesture of friendship all over the world."

"You say 'custom,' then 'gesture.' Would you also say 'symbol,' my son? Is not the shaking of hands a symbol of goodwill and affection that exists, or should exist, between men? And is this not a symbol that comes to us from the past? You would not discard it, certainly?"

"I see your point, Father, but you'll have to admit that young people today are not interested in symbols, and if they thought about it, they would probably get rid of the handshake as well."

"And they would, my young friend, soon replace it with another symbol. Man cannot live without symbols, and if he does not have them, he will create them, sometimes even unconsciously. They who would destroy all symbolism were very quick to adopt the peace sign. Many have even used it to replace the crucifix, thinking in their shallowness that it was as one with the Cross.

"Your people have taken to the wearing of beards and long hair. Is this not a symbol of their wish to be without conformity to the prevailing standards? Yet is it not interesting that they turn to the past for their symbol, for was this not the style a hundred years ago? And in their nonconformity, are they not conformists more bound to their peer group than the true rebel would wish? Yet the symbol is treasured because it is like a badge, a uniform that symbolizes their membership.

"Even the demonstration becomes for many only a symbol. Some would lose their lives for the cause if called upon to do so, but they would die in the pride of their symbolism. Others would turn and run at the first threat to their skins, but they, too, would flaunt their demonstration as a symbol of their justified fury, or their witless neuroticism, as the case may be."

"I begin to see, Father, why you are the teacher and I the seminarian." Stone was not toally convinced by this priest's views, but there began to gnaw at his stomach a sense of uneasiness that comes from notions being toppled, from humility in the face of wisdom, and from a hunger to fill the void he felt within himself. This is a strange man, he thought. Worldly one moment, yet otherworldly the next. Padre Simon's earthiness made him comfortable, while his air of aloof holiness made him feel distant.

He had always heard of the priesthood as a vocation, and often he had questioned the use of the word, for carpentry was a vocation, as was medicine, the law, and teaching. But the priesthood. Wasn't that something more? Wasn't it involved with the realm of spirituality, which concerned itself with life and living not as a mundane "vocation" but as a voyage to eternity? There was in Simon this touch of eternity, this passive expression of sanctity, which exuded a tenderness and a gentleness that seemed part of another world.

Stone brought himself back to the priest, who studied the young man's face kindly, and there was an expression that seemed to say, "Let us talk more. What have you to say in reply to these things?"

"But what has this to do with the Church, Father?" Stone finally blurted out. "You seem saddened by the turn from symbolism in society, but what is it that disturbs you in the Church?"

"My young friend," the other began genially, "I could count ways in which the leadership has been guilty, ways in which the people, too, have shared in this guilt. I could say that when the Church obligated the priest no longer to use his canonical fingers at Mass for touching only the consecrated Host, she began to presage this current trend away from the sublimity of symbolism. When men designed churches stripped bare of all ties with the past, all reminders of reverence, all inducement to holiness, it opened the chasm still more. Then the statues went, and even Mary, the Mother of God, was consigned to a basement where her face is veiled with the mesh of spiders, and her image in the hearts of men became more blurred as the statues were hidden. Then the votive lights disappeared, and along with them the prayer of petition before the altar of God. Soon women came dressed immodestly as the veils and headdresses disappeared. And now it is rare even to see genuflection.

"That the Church should modify the nun's habit was perhaps good, but do you suppose that there was ever a thought given that this gesture of ecclesial love would lead to the near total abrogation of the habit itself, which stood for centuries as a symbol of the nun's loss of selfhood in the embrace of Christ? Only one identity mattered. His!

"But, my son, the loss of all of these symbols and more is summed up in the act of moving the tabernacle to the side altar and in some cases to no altar at all — merely aside, somewhere in the sanctuary. Where is the symbolism of Christ in the center of the church? And where is the symbol of Christ at the side altar? The altar upon which Christ's victimhood is celebrated is in the center of the church. And the crucified and risen Christ can no more be separated from the Blessed Sacrament than the fact that what you are cannot be separated from your thoughts. I tell you, my son, if we are to believe that Christ is to be the center of our lives, why, then, is He not in the center of our churches? Mere symbolism, you say? Symbolism, but hardly 'mere,' for as the sickness of the mind manifests itself on the body, so does the weakness and the sin of our times manifest itself on the body of the Church."

The boy began to feel a chill even as the warmth of the sun found its way through the network of leafy boughs above them. It was true that Stone had felt something edifyingly holy and learned about this man, but somehow his words began to make him depressed. Joyousness had characterized the young seminarian, perhaps because joy had been his diet to the exclusion of any pain, any concept of suffering, any relationship, even, between suffering and joy. All he knew now was that Father Simon had put a pall over the gaiety of salvation by attacking near the heart of his beliefs.

"But, Father Simon," he said, a wrinkled frown

on his face, "is it all hopeless, will there be no solution, is the Church destined only for suffering?"

"No, my son, the Church is not destined only for suffering. She will suffer greatly, but as with the woman who must suffer before she brings her child into the world, there will follow great joy, made all the greater by suffering. And even as with that ineluctable ecstasy which is childbirth, she will know anxiety as the child passes through its many stages to maturity. But she will know alternately pain and joy, and one day even pride in the knowledge that she has created a candidate for heaven.

"So it has been with the Church for two thousand years, and so it will be with the Church to the end of time, for do you need a greater assurance than that 'I will be with you until the end of time'?

"But if it is clues you seek, let me assure you that there are indeed such foretokenings as to give one great joy and solace. Look, my son, to art for the moment. Read the signs.

"It is said that the artist sees, or senses, the times ahead of him. Thus we saw in our century the rise and ultimately the prevalence of abstract art in its most drastic extreme, foreshadowing society's break with the romantic, with the studied detail of the verities of realism. The paintings of Jackson Pollock in your country — and a host of artists in Europe — turned from form, from the secure realism of art as we knew it, to art without apparent discipline, without reality and, to all but the avant garde, without meaning.

"Poetry became unmetered, unrhymed, undisciplined also. Your Walt Whitman began the break with *Leaves of Grass*, but the break was not so severe as it was to become by the later poets who treated restraint as anathema to the free spirit of art.

"And the music of a whole new school of composers introduced discordance nearing cacophony, as if music also sensed and returned the beat of revolt that was in the air long before it was pressed into the heartbeat of humanity.

"We saw the squareness and the straight lines of architecture, emphasizing the useful, the functional, the pragmatic, again in revolt against the baroque, the gothic, the Victorian.

"All of this was as if to vomit the past from the collective bellies of our creative seers. But was this not, also, symbolism?

"You will ask, my young friend, 'Where is the hope you promised me in all of this? Where are the signs?'

"Look at the paintings that now are being purchased, look at the broader representation of art taste in your galleries and you will see, my friend, the slow but certain resurgence of realism. A major American periodical quotes a leading gallery owner as saying that 'the pendulum has swung.' According to this publication, people are returning to John Singleton Copley, Charles Wilson Peale, Thomas Eakins and Winslow Homer, and turning away from Jackson Pollock and Mark Rothko, and the other esoteric, abstract artists.

"We go to the extreme pulse and we look at what is called the Rock music, and while it still assaults the eardrums, there is a marked sign of softening here also. Romance begins to sweeten the air and the ear.

"Architecture remains severe, but not so severe as formerly. Curves begin to break and give grace to the utility of straight lines. Warm woods begin to replace chrome and black.

"Yes, my son, the signs are here. And soon, it will be discovered, man will find that he wants more than nakedness, more than confusion, more than discord, more than dissent. He will clothe his nakedness with meaning and create new symbols and revive old ones. Within his soul God cries out to him, and he will hear and create symbols that relate to the fundamental meaning of life, which is God. And as the artist foretold our present generation with its emphasis on sensate utility, the artist will rise again to portray the new era, which will find its central concern in the parousia, the return of Christ to the world, and he will do so in terms that will emphasize the need to be ready, to be open and, once again, to seek that which is most pure and elevating to the spirit.

"And I say to you, my young friend, that this leads back to the Church. For art is but the foretokening; art is the occult seer, but it is the Church which is the one true, indestructible and eternal reality.

"You will be a part of this reality. Thus is it not important that you see man from the eyes of the Church rather than from the eyes of man? Is it not important that the richness of the Church was born in antiquity, and out of antiquity has come not only 'Good News for Modern Man,' but the wisdom of tradition, the unerring intellect of the holy Doctors, Aquinas, Augustine, Teresa, Chrysostom, Irenaeus. Name them. They are legion. They preserved the deposit of truth. They and the Church have given the symbols their meaning. Do not destroy them."

Lawrence Terence Stone sat beneath the umbrella elm on the campus at St. Bernard's Seminary. The cheery smile was gone, but so also was the prickling, stifling depression of moments ago. His face was sober and earnest. He looked at the stranger for a very long time without speaking. Finally he whispered with veneration and pride, "Father, you ought to be Pope!"

Sicola smiled, then blessed him.

Out, Brief Candle

An Italian wake is an experience containing equal parts of grief and alcohol, the women gathered together in the viewing room, somber and commiserating, the men in an anteroom or kitchen swilling down whiskey and raising their voices in argument, banter, or general conviviality. It is a phenomenon cultivated through the centuries, traditional in its self-flagellation on the one hand and impiously disrespectful in its lack of solemnity on the other.

As for the grieving women, the pulling of hair and the copious tears most frequently are the manifest histrionics of those most remote from the real pain of death. They are the friends and neighbors who neither entertained a second thought for the deceased while he lived nor — in some cases — knew him at all. It is the function of those attending a wake to wear faces painted by El Greco in the belief that such a posture conveys to the immediate family their great sympathy, real or feigned.

Sicola would often wonder about it. Unconscionable as it was, perhaps the men's behavior came closer to honesty than the women's. If there was hypocrisy in the viewing room, there certainly was none in the kitchen, where the ample spread of cold cuts and liquor was an occasion of feasting and camaraderie. Yet, he wondered, in either room was there real honesty? Was there any small degree of contemplation on the meaning of death? Were its implications lost to all alike in their good intentions, and in their sense of their own immortality?

In America it was not much different from his native Italy. He had been asked to attend the wake for a young boy barely into his teens, a mere fifteen when he had died. He went as a priest, and as he entered the viewing room he noticed that folding chairs bordered the room in a square along the walls. Women in black sat, some wailing, some red-eyed and sober, others staring blankly as if their mere presence was an obligation sooner dispensed with.

He nodded to the man who met him at the arched entryway, shook his hand and strode to the kneeler beside the casket where he knelt in prayer. He studied the boy's youthful face, waxen, unreal, puffed in artificial repose, and he thought, "To remember this is unreal for the parents. What about the vitality of him who lived? Was that not a memory more to be treasured than this memento of the taxidermist's art? Why this meaningless custom of open caskets to haunt forever on earth the minds of those who gave him life, prayed with him and played with him?"

Then he prayed. "Almighty God, it is indeed true that this boy, Lorenzo, had reached the age of reason and therefore was capable of sin. But what sin, dear Father? In fifteen years he remained a mere infant in the normal span of life, which tends to sully the soul as one lives longer. He had not the time to become so sullied. Was not his soul, dear Lord, close to its pristine purity at birth? Take him into your arms, then, as one of your favored ones, and in the warmth of your embrace, encompass also those who loved him and taught him to love You, that they may endure this sadness and see in it the means of their own sanctification." He made a sign of the cross over the dead child and rose to his feet.

The boy's father approached him. "Thank you, Father, for coming. Come, let us join my wife and we can talk." The father's eyes were bloodshot, his face drawn and gray, and he fought the catch in his throat. His wife took Sicola's hand in both of hers and squeezed tenderly, graciously. Her face, Sicola thought, was tranquil and stoic, but the eyes did not smile along with the lips, and it was the eyes that mirrored one's true feelings. The trio moved to a divan in a corner of the room away from the others.

"Some day, Father," the husband said, "we will realize that all of this is pagan. Despite all of my revulsion, I find — as all others must — that we are trapped by conventions, by the wishes of older members of the family more oriented to this tradition. And we accede, though in our hearts we wish there was another way, a way that commemorates the passing of the soul without consideration to the body, which is now vacant of the soul. Why can't it be, Father? Why can't one die only with the prayers of the Mass and the rosary while the body is enclosed in its casket ready for burial but no longer visible, a statue having no resemblance to the boy we knew. They can all say, 'How peaceful, how beautiful he looks.' But to us he is dead! That is an irreversible fact, and we have visions of his life that seem so disrupted, so maligned by this . . . this . . . cadaver. God, Father, when will be put a halt to it?"

The man bent his head so that his chin touched his chest, and he shook as the tears flowed within him while his will held them back. He was silent for a long time. His wife took his hand, and Sicola tried to comfort him with words he knew were inadequate to assuage this grief, this loneliness, this abject resignation to a power so great as to deny even prayer for an erasure of the inerasable fact of death.

"My son," Sicola said kindly, "this is the moment when you are alone with God, who is closest to you in your grief. I have no power to give you strength, but He does. My inadequacies are most emphasized at such times as these. But consolation comes to you. This I know. It comes to him who seeks it, one who becomes so aware of his nothingness as to throw himself into the arms of God in total abandonment."

"This I know too, Father," the man answered. "I have found that one may control his actions, even his destiny, but there are times when he cannot control all things, when all that is most precious is taken from him. I suppose most fathers cannot help shaking a fist at heaven and asking, 'Why? Why him? Why not me? He had not begun to live,' as if living were all that mattered. I must confess, Father, that I did not do this.

"After his death," the boy's father went on, "instead I went immediately to the Blessed Sacrament. It was as if in my heart I knew that He was all that remained to me, all that my heart craved. I could not find the words to pray, however. I just sat there numb and stupified by this terrible emptiness. If there was any prayer it was in the *desire* to pray. At such moments, Father, I am sure that you would agree that it is the Real Presence that matters, so I found myself sharing my thoughts with Him, and I suppose that this was a kind of prayer.

"My mind began to retrace my son's lifespan

from that very moment when he was being born. It was all telescoped in that hour before the Blessed Sacrament. I remembered writing a letter to God at the very hour of Lorenzo's birth, though I was not aware at the time that Maria was giving birth. I have the letter with me for I have carried it since that recollection before the altar. Listen to what I wrote, Father, for in it you will see that the boy was given to us for a short space, though he fulfilled a long time.

" 'Most merciful Creator, who joined with my wife and me in making this human life, I pray for Your Hand in the work that follows.

" 'Bring Maria through this day with that feeling of sublime ecstasy and joy which must accompany doing Your Will. Give her pain, my God, only that she might taste the full sweetness of holding Your Hand in her pain.

" 'And, most loving Maker, show us both the way throughout this child's life. Sleep with us in our home, dine at our table, play with us in our gaiety, work with us in our labor. Be with us always. For with You — and through You — we can accomplish all . . . all that is good and holy, all that we want with our lives.

" 'Make this child pure of mind, of body, and of soul. For from You this gift came to us. To You we would like to dedicate it.

" 'We love You. Teach us to love You more.' "

The man paused and his hand trembled as he held the yellowed paper. "That was the letter, Father. And as I knelt before the altar I remembered that I had acknowledged before God that Lorenzo was His, a gift to us, and to Him the child's life would be dedicated in return. Indeed, I had no rights of ownership, only gratitude for the sharing.

"And as I thought more about Lorenzo I began to see that never was there anything but love that came from him. No impertinence. No rebellion. Just gentle submissiveness and demonstrated love, much like the child Jesus Himself. The impressions began to build, and with them a conviction that the child was given to us purely and remained in purity. And when he died he was still totally pure.

"One looks at his children with a frightening sense of responsibility, as we look at the rest of ours, faced with the charge to return them to heaven. How difficult this becomes as they grow older and are subject to other environments, other influences. But in Lorenzo, I had no reason to fear, for he achieved what he was meant to from birth, only sooner. How fortunate!

"This became a fact so stunning in its impact upon me that I began to long with all my being for a holiness that would permit me to be with Lorenzo in eternity one day. But as the thought occurred to me, Father, it was as if I had been slapped — gently, to be sure, but hard enough to recognize that God calls all men to Him, and the truly holy man seeks Him because he has learned to love Him, not what He created. For Lorenzo to become a bridge was His plan, but it was important to cross the bridge to Him and Him alone.

"Let no one tell me that God does not speak to him if he has need of Him, if he will go to Him and listen.

"It was as this realization came to me — before the very altar of Christ, Father — that I wrote again. It seemed fitting that as I wrote when he was entering life, I should write as he left. This was, for me, his requiem:

"Out, Brief Candle

Your flame,
Like a luminescent teardrop,
Flickered,
Struggled,
Then died.

Out, brief candle,
Unused,
Wasted,
Unfulfilled.

We knew your warmth,
Your brightness
Briefly.

Still there is the beam
Dancing joyfully
In our mind,
Yet searing harshly
In our heart . . .
To light up again and again . . .

As if God, holding our candle,
Kissed it with His breath,
Not to extinguish the flame,
But to renew it
In our heart . . . and His.

We loved you!

Is it to lose you
Because He loved you more?
Or is it to live on in Him?

Sanctus! Sanctus! Sanctus!"

Sicola had been watching the man intently. It was as if all the agony, all the mystical communion of this shattering experience had been building layer on layer within him, and now the very sight of the Roman collar had touched that hidden lever of reverential respect for the priesthood so that it came spilling out of him, confession-like, in his ventilative need. Perhaps, Sicola thought, these were the words he had wanted to share with Maria, but there was this constraint, this holding back from her out of respect for her own sorrow, out of fear that she would either not understand or, understanding, become all the more grief-stricken.

Maria held her husband's face in her hands and kissed him. "I did not know, Salvatore. I did not know about the letter, nor about your thoughts. It explains much. It explains the blessing of our love in the midst of misfortunes that have torn other marriages apart. It explains the blessings of eight beautiful children, all of whom remain close to each other, to us, and to the Church. It explains how we can see the death of Lorenzo as the bond that unites us to each other and both to God, and in this bond, through whatever else may befall us, we remain one in Him."

Sicola turned his head from the man and his wife in this deepest moment of their union. His eyes moved from one person to another along the walls, ultimately to rest on an old woman in a rocker. She was a hulking woman, stooped, her jaw set with a matriarchal defiance as if she defied life to hurt her more than it had already. She rocked, one hand grasping the arm of the rocker, the other the crook of her cane, planted firmly on the floor. Her white hair was pulled back in a bun, and it called all the more attention to her face, furrowed between the eyes, showing experience with pain, tragedy, birth, death, frugal living, and above all, determination. She rocked as if she counted the moments before she too would be called, and she looked at the boy in the casket with a kind of fierce sorrow. She was ready, but unfathomably it was the child who was taken.

Then he turned to watch Maria consoling her husband, and it was as if the image of the woman in the rocker remained, for in Maria he saw also the old woman, battered by the winds of life, but rocking staunchly, her weatherbeaten face a testimony to her ability to integrate suffering into her being, to convert it to an adamant resistance against its pain, so that her heart would be preserved as a reservoir of comfort and sustenance to those she most deeply loved.

Sicola shook hands and left, mystified at the buoyancy of his step, joyful in the knowledge that there was some measure of victory for people — even in the face of death.

The Golden Dome

Sicola pedalled his bicycle through one of the communities that merged with the life of Los Angeles but kept its own identity in the vast suburban sprawl along the Pacific Coast. It was one of those towns just a few miles inland from the beach communities, and had it not been for the signs it would have been difficult for him to know for certain where one ended and the next began. It really did not matter to him because he enjoyed the warmth of the sun, though it stayed in the low seventies as the cool sea breezes kept the thermometer from reaching the more torrid heights of the valleys inland. The climate was so similar to certain coastal cities in Italy, except that in Italy there was not this teeming homogeneity, and when he left a village he was made aware of it by the open countryside.

But this was pleasant all the same. There was just enough sway to the tall palm trees that lined the streets to confirm the breeze, and the air was clean. There was no mist, and visibility was perfect. Off in the distance he could see the golden dome of the chapel at the Catholic college, which nestled on a rise of ground above the boulevards and the neat houses along Sicola's course.

There was a peace within him, even as the automobiles honked and swished by him, a siren screamed in the distance, and a jackhammer rat-tatted on the asphalt at the intersection. One thing about Americans, he thought: they liked to dig holes in their streets. These were all signs of life, vibrant and active, all a symbol of this part of the United States that was bursting its britches like an adolescent growing too fast. There were other parts of America offering contrast to this brash, ebullient coastal energy, areas where the pace was more subdued and the attitudes more intractable. He loved them both, but he was here now, and at this particular moment he loved this town, these sounds, this movement, these people. Was that not, he thought, the nature of papal love? Even as the children of the Church were diverse in their cultures, in the degree of their animation, in the scope of their opinions and ideas, they were still his children, and he loved them equally. If some of them were errant, he loved them as deeply as the inerrant, though his pain might be increased by their peccancy.

He headed for the golden dome, and he remembered that this Jesuit stronghold of education had been at one time the rock-like bastion of Catholicism, standing strong and intransigent against the winds that licked and whipped at it with the will to change it. But no more. Uncompromising once. Steadfast against the currents. Guardian of the magisterial truths. But no more. Now diversity was proclaimed in the name of the health of the Church, and it was said that one had not really seen diversity until one had visited its campus. Others had said, diversity hell! Protestant up to its nostrils! Where the truth lay, Sicola intended to find out, but nothing would disrupt him this day when all was well with the world, when peace and tranquility found their true definitions in his soul. Paternity required patience in popes no less than in natural fathers. Nothing would change this. He would maintain equanimity at all times.

When Sicola arrived at the campus he noted the signs announcing "Charismatic Prayer Meeting" pointing to the large gymnasium. He would be interested in this meeting, he thought. The Church had been watching the movement with a careful scrutiny, for in it were the seeds of personal holiness if they were nurtured with care. He recalled how Joshua had complained to Moses that Eldad and Medad had been prophesying apart from the select seventy on whom the Spirit had also descended. Joshua had said, "Moses, my lord, stop them." But Moses' surprising reply had been, "Are you jealous for my sake? Would that all the people of the Lord were prophets! Would that the Lord might bestow his spirit on them all" (Numbers 11:25-29). And there was a further instance in the Gospel of Mark in which "John said to Jesus, 'Teacher, we saw a man using your name to expel demons and we tried to stop him because he is not of our company.' Jesus said in reply: 'Do not try to stop him. No man who performs a miracle using my name can at once speak ill of me. Anyone who is not against us is with us' " (Mark 9:38-43). It had been clear to Sicola that the Holy Spirit comes to those who are open to Him, but in this condescension lay the need of humility, for the Spirit encourages least the notion of elitism or separation from the body of the Church, in whom the Spirit has always resided and ever will reside in primacy.

He followed the arrows but learned it was a meaningless exercise, since all that was necessary was to follow the sound of clapping and singing. When he had arrived at the double-doored entry to the large hall, a polite man apologized that there were no more seats but said he would be free to watch from the door, which would be kept open.

At length the man spotted a single vacancy among the rows on rows of folding chairs set up in an inverted U, whose mouth was so narrow as to be a mere slit in the teeming crowd. He pointed it out to Sicola, who slowly threaded his way through the babble of excited people. Once seated, he became more attentive to individual sounds and voices. All about him were exclamations of "Praise the Lord," and there was an animation that made him uncomfortable and wary.

He turned to the man at his left, who had been speaking with enthusiasm of the guest prayer leader, a man of apparent renown in this new and spreading movement.

"Who is this man you speak of? What is his background, this Jimmy Hull?"

"Oh, this is your first time! Praise the Lord! Welcome! We love you."

"*Grazie*," Sicola answered him with a long questioning look.

"Jimmy Hull," the man went on, "is a great leader in the charismatic movement. He has memorized the entire Bible, word for word, and he has been truly chosen by the Holy Spirit. His prophecies for the world are frightening, but this is the way of the Holy Spirit. He wants us to change our ways."

"This is a Catholic college, Signore. Is this a Jimmy Hull a Catholic?"

"No, my friend."

"Ah, I see. Then the facilities of the college are merely made available to others. This is a non-denominational meeting. *Corretto*?"

"I suppose you might say that but you don't seem to understand. You see the Holy Spirit Himself is nondenominational. All those old notions and barriers are falling down in the wake of what is going on today. The Holy Spirit wants us all to be one. No more structures that isolate us and make us different. All religions are the same to the Holy Spirit."

"I see," Sicola mumbled. The fervor of the man blended in with the gaiety of the others in the room, and it made hearing difficult.

He felt a tap on his shoulder and turned to a woman seated at his right. Her face beamed with expectant joy, and she murmured sweetly, "Do you have the Holy Spirit, Sir?"

He remembered suddenly that some years ago a charismatic had posed the same question to Mother Teresa of Calcutta, whose sanctity on earth seemed without question. Her reply had been, very simply, "I hope so."

Sicola found himself answering, "I hope so."

"Ah, but you are not sure! That means, of course, that He has not chosen you. If He had you would know it by the way you *feel.*"

"By the way I *feel?*" Sicola asked. "That is how you know? By the *feel?*"

"Oh, yes, indeed!" she gushed. "And when you feel it there simply is no denying it. You know that He has chosen you. And the feeling is with you every moment."

"*Mannaggia!*" Sicola burst forth. "What a sinner am I. For I confess that I do not have such a feeling with me at all times. If the truth were to be known, Signorina, I must admit that I have it only rarely."

"We will change all of that for you today. You must begin, of course, by desiring to have Him."

"I do . . . I do . . . I do!"

"Then don't worry. Everything will fall into place."

"You say," he questioned, misunderstanding her, "that everyone will fall on his face?"

She giggled. "Just be patient. You'll see."

The prayer meeting seemed about ready to begin as a nun carrying a guitar filed into the hall along with an entourage of other musicians and singers. She led the group in several songs, and everyone joined in with great gusto and excitement. Then she spoke demurely into the microphone, "By this time you must know that you are all saints of the Holy Spirit. He has chosen you from the world to lead His crusade."

The woman beside Sicola murmured, "Oh, Jesus. Thank you, Jesus. Praise the Lord. Hallelujah. Oh, Jee-e-e-sus!"

Then came the inevitable. The nun announced, "So let's all sing 'When the Saints Go Marchin' In.' "

Pandemonium erupted. The congregation sang with a frenzy. Arms were outstretched to heaven as if to open hearts to the entry of the Holy Spirit. Others clapped to the beat of the music. It was a tent show revival meeting in every sense.

Sicola looked, unbelieving, at the woman beside him, then at the ecstatic faces about him, and a vague fear began to set in.

"Their bladders will soon open up and the new Noah will float away if there is no control," he thought.

The singing completed, Jimmy Hull took the microphone and addressed the fevered congregation. "The Holy Spirit is now with you," he shouted.

"Oh Jee-e-e-sus," the woman screamed in an orgasmic delirium. "Hallelujah! I love you, Jesus. Jesus, Jesus. I love you. Praise the Lord."

Behind Sicola a woman was munching on an ear of corn, all the while muttering, "Praise the Lord. Hallelujah!" Her companion, a woman of some discernment, complained, "Sally . . . Sally . . . for God's sakes, you're getting corn in the gentleman's hair, you're so close. Sit back."

Sicola brushed the back of his head and picked out a kernel of corn. "It suits the occasion," he groaned.

Suddenly Jimmy Hull's microphone went dead, and the congregation strained to hear.

"Holy Spirit, you goofed!" Sicola found himself saying aloud.

Some men fiddled with the wires, and finally the booming voice of Hull rang out in the hall amid resounding applause.

The woman beside Sicola, her eyes closed as if in a trance, whispered, "Thank you, Holy Spirit, thank You. Thank You. Thank You. Now get rid of the skeptics in our midst."

Sicola turned to her and said, "Shoo, and where'sa you love now?"

She seemed to ignore him.

"Now," Jimmy Hull continued, "everybody turn to your neighbor, grasp him by the hands and tell him you love him in the name of the Holy Spirit."

The man on the other side of him embraced him. "I love you in the name of the Holy Spirit."

Sicola said, "*Grazie . . . Grazie . . .* Thatsa nice."

A quiet settled over the auditorium. It was finally broken by what seemed a foreign language coming from a woman in front of Sicola. Her arms were outstretched, and strange words were sung in a melodious chant like the intonations of a cantor in a synagogue. "Ah-lo-ol-a-mo-gi-bi-gi-na- Is-ray-el. Channa-do-fro-me-Is-may-el." The strange words continued for nearly a minute while the audience was hushed, many with their eyes closed and their arms raised.

When she was finished a man several rows away picked up the chant, while Sicola watched in amazement and incredulity.

He turned to his left to hide a smile and saw beside him a new face, not at all the same man who had been there when he looked a moment earlier, yet he had seen no movement by the previous occupant of the chair. There was a radiant handsomeness about the man, and his head was bowed in prayer. He remained in meditation for several minutes as Sicola studied him and searched his memory for the time and place where they may have met in the past. There was a haunting familiarity about him that was unsettling to Sicola.

At length the man raised his head, turned to Sicola and smiled, and as he did so Sicola was filled with a rapture that transfixed him and made him powerless to move. Words turned over in his brain, questions like, "Why do I know you?" "Why are you so like men in appearance and yet so unlike them, all at the same time?" "Why do you smile so, as if we are known to each other, yet you do not tell me who you are?" While the questions were framed in his mind, they never reached his lips.

But the stranger seemed aware of them all the same.

"Giuseppe, have no fear. I am Michael, and I am visible only to you."

"Not THE Michael?" Sicola blurted out finally.

The woman at his right turned to him as she heard what seemed to be glossolalia and nudged her companion. "How quickly the Lord works!" she said. "Praise the Lord. Listen. He speaks in tongues."

"Nonsense," Michael smiled at Sicola. "Pay her no heed. The language she refers to is no language at all, understood neither by men nor angels, by saints nor God. The gurglings in your throat are merely the sounds of awe. Have no fear, Giuseppe. I am the messenger of the Lord, and I come to be your guide through the alien land of Pentecostalism."

Sicola felt the constriction that bound his throat suddenly relaxed, and he said with great humility and piety, "St. Michael, the Archangel!" As he uttered the name of heaven's greatest warrior, he spoke in a voice that carried through the hall, and heads turned in his direction.

The girl at his right complained, "He is hallucinating! If he had the gift, he would be speaking only to the Holy Spirit, as we do, but he addresses himself to St. Michael. I am sitting beside a madman. I thought there was something strange about him when he sat beside me. Someone call a doctor. He belongs in a hospital, not with us, for this is certainly the work of the devil, who comes to disrupt the work of God."

"This," the Angel said, "is what happens, Giuseppe, when you allowed the prayer to St. Michael to be removed from the end of the Mass." Then he drew from beneath his coat the sword of Michael and it seemed to Sicola to gleam like a shaft of light, dazzling and diffuse. He pushed Sicola aside gently and extended his sword toward the girl's southerly region, then jabbed, ever so slightly but with sureness and full intent.

The girl leaped to her feet with a startled gasp,

then took her seat once again, confused and uncertain about the source of her pain. She remained quiet as her companion studied her with some concern.

"These, be assured, are good people, Giuseppe," the Angel continued. "There is potential for good in their fervor, but there is danger also, for it is but a short step from fervor to fever, and some of them become so fevered that it is time for you to speak up more commandingly."

"What would you have me do, my director?" Sicola asked.

"You will know what to do at the proper time, Vicar of Christ, but for now merely consider their errors. You have before you an assemblage of popes in their own right, for they have belief that what comes to them in their fervor is the voice of God speaking singularly to them in contradistinction to the Church. They impute to themselves an infallibility not even inherent in the idea of papal infallibility, for yours is circumscribed while theirs knows no bounds.

"They speak in a language unrecognizable to heaven itself, coming from a delirium that has its genesis in the hunger for God but is manifest in a religious neurosis that separates reason from theology, understanding from worship, and leaves only emotion, which is rampant when it is separated from the will. This is hysteria, and in this hysteria there is great danger to the mind. The path to the Holy Spirit lies in reason not in such a neurosis. Picture the Church without the reason of Aquinas, and there remains Holy Rollerism only. This is not from God.

"They find their comfort from the Apostle Paul, by citing his comments in Scripture, 'I would that you all spoke with tongues . . .' but they forget the rest of his words to suit their purpose, for he continued to say, 'but rather that you prophesy [which is to say, preach]; for greater is he who prophesies than he who speaks in tongues.' They have this gift of isolating the words of Scripture as they do when they quote Paul further, 'I thank God I speak with tongues more than you all,' and again they neglect to complete the thought, which goes on, 'yet in the Church I had rather speak five words with my understanding, that by my voice I might teach others also, than ten thousand words in an unknown tongue.'

"Certainly, Giuseppe, I do not have to recall Scripture to you, for you are most aware of the fact that no single person in the history of the world was more filled with the Holy Spirit than Our Blessed Lord, yet He never spoke in an unknown tongue, for God is not the author of confusion. When Jesus wished to speak, He spoke directly, and when He wished to pray, he prayed in the very words of His time, words that have been given to us in Holy Writ. Yet these people among you would have you to understand that unless you speak in tongues you are outside the pale of God's community of the elite.

"It is most interesting to note that the saints never spoke in tongues, yet history is replete with the claim of heretics who proclaimed that they spoke in tongues, a characteristic that marked the Montanists, the Albigensians, and the Protestant Pentecostals of modern times. There is wonder in heaven that no charismatic seems willing, while he quotes St. Paul, to remember that he also pointed out that 'the one who speaks in tongues edifies himself; while the one who prophesies (that is, preaches) edifies the Church. . . . Now brothers, if I come to you speaking in tongues: how does that help you, unless I speak to you with revelation or knowledge or prophecy or in doctrine?'

"Your own G. K. Chesterton served notice of these dangers when he wrote in his *Orthodoxy*:

" 'Of all conceivable forms of enlightenment the worst is what these people call the Inner Light. Of all horrible religions the most horrible is the worship of the god within. Anyone who knows anybody knows how it would work; anyone who knows anyone from the Higher Thought Centre knows how it does work. That Jones who worships the god within him turns out ultimately to mean that Jones shall worship Jones. Let Jones worship the sun or the moon — or anything rather than the Inner Spirit; let Jones worship cats or crocodiles, if he can find any in his street, but not the god within. Christianity came into the world, firstly, in order to assert with violence that a man had not only to look inwards, but to look outwards, to behold with astonishment and enthusiasm a divine company and a divine captain. The only fun in being a Christian was that a man was not left alone with the Inner Light, but definitely recognized an outer Light, as far as the sun, clear as the moon, terrible as an army of banners.'

"Giuseppe, let them imitate Mary. Was anyone more possessed of the Holy Spirit than she? John Cardinal Wright has said of her in this regard that she possessed the Holy Spirit in silence:

" 'Mary walked . . . by faith, not vision, real or pretended. She knew fear; she suffered from limited understanding and every human misgiving consistent with her sinless nature. She was what each of us must be if we are truly servants and agents of the Holy Spirit. It is in her constant "yes" to God's will and to the promptings of the

Holy Spirit that we are called to imitate her, not with holy histrionics but with the silence that reigned as the angels softly sang at Bethlehem and in the entire life of Mary from the valleys of Nazareth to the hill of Calvary. Next to docility and closely related to it, the greatest gift of the Holy Spirit to Mary seems to have been patience. . . . Of all her examples to us of how we should be the servants and agents of the Holy Spirit, this is Mary's most timely and opportune lesson in this age of aimless activism, spiritual restlessness, noisy, agitated and polarized religiosity.' "

The girl next to Sicola watched him intently. She was annoyed by his sudden appearance of mysticism. There was little color in his masklike face, and his skin seemed to have a brittle transparency about it. His eyes were fixed and staring outward at someone or something beyond the walls of the auditorium itself. Occasionally he spoke, and his words were clear and intelligible, but they made no sense because they were responses only and their meaning was lost unless there could be some knowledge of what he was responding to.

At one time she tried to shake Sicola without success, and the congregation — which had now gathered around his seat — urged her to stay away from him lest she, too, become afflicted by the evil malady that had risen from the nether world. He seemed unaware of what was being said about him.

A rustle passed through the congregation. Father Burns, a priest in attendance, heard the commotion and made his way through the throng to where Sicola sat in trance.

"Perhaps," he commented, "the man is epileptic. Has anyone telephoned a doctor?"

"No, Father," one man replied. "It's not possible. I've never known an epileptic to talk during a seizure. This man is either catatonic or in the midst of a religious experience."

"That's hardly possible," the girl next to Sicola snorted. "He's not one of us. I talked to him just before it happened, and I got the impression that he was a visitor, that this was somehow strange to him. It simply does not make any sense whatsoever that the Holy Spirit would come to one uninitiated. No . . . this is satanic. I'm convinced of it."

The priest gave her a long, wry look and muttered, "Come on, now, don't be so quick to judge." He pondered for a moment, then he continued, "There's one way to deal with evil, if that's what it is, and it may help even if he's afflicted with a mental disorder. I would like to adjure Satan to leave him by sprinkling holy water on his brow and blessing him."

Shortly, someone returned with holy water and a crucifix, and the priest sprinkled the water lighly on Sicola's head and raised the crucifix over him in the sign of the cross.

Suddenly it seemed that Sicola was awakening, for he began to stir, but then there was a gasp from the congregation as they saw before them, not merely the man who had occupied the seat moments before, but one now vested fully with miter, cloak, and crozier, and standing defiantly beside him was Michael in that universally recognized image, winged, a sword in one hand and scales in the other.

Sicola, still garbed in his papal vestments, and St. Michael the Archangel then began to ascend above the crowd and float toward an altar where they remained suspended for many moments, a tableau against the backdrop of the large crucifix on the wall.

It was as if the crucified Christ behind the altar had come out to meet them and taken a position between the Archangel and the Pope. Then the tableau evaporated and disappeared.

The congregation remained in the hall for an hour after their experience, and for forty-five minutes there was no sound, not a cough nor a sneeze, nor a whisper nor a song. Just silence.

Then someone led the group in the rosary. As they came near the end of the Apostles' Creed there seemed to be a new emphasis on the words, "I believe in the Holy Spirit, the Holy Catholic Church, the communion of saints, the forgiveness of sins, the resurrection of the body and life everlasting. Amen."

Sicola was aware that he was pedaling on the boulevard and he looked back at the golden dome of the college chapel. "It was my intention to visit the campus," he mused, "but the day is a delightful one, and I do not wish to become embroiled in controversy on such a day. Perhaps another time."

Ereh Ecnah Con!

Sicola climbed the grassy hill leading toward the abbey that stood in monolithic majesty over the valley below. America being a very young country, the abbey did not compare in hoary antiquity to the monasteries of Europe, some of which predated the Middle Ages. But this was the home of the solitary monk who had made such an imprint on the pages of religious literature. This was the place where in silent contemplation one very holy man had grasped eternal truths through sheer mystical piety, where in his solitude and single-minded contemplation of God he had found the key to expanding the mind so as nearly to embrace infinity.

He arrived at the great door of the monastery and was greeted by the extern monk, who knew immediately of his appointment. It had taken much doing for Sicola to arrange this visit to Father Bede (the "mystic of the mountain," as he was called), for he did not go as Pope, as he had seldom revealed his identity during his visit to America. But he had arranged for Tommaso to write a letter to the Abbot requesting an audience for a visiting Italian priest named Father Simon, and the Abbot had acceded readily at the mere sight of the papal letterhead.

And now he was at the Abbey. The extern apolo-

gized that Father Bede did not live in the main building of the monastery with the other priests and Brothers, preferring, like Charles de Foucauld, a more aus-
tere hovel for his ascetic prayer life. So he led Sicola
away from the main building through manicured gardens, into the briars and weeds of an open field, until
they could see a knoll on which was the weatherbeaten shack that was the home of Bede. The monk
pointed out the shack from a distance and left Sicola
in the middle of the field to go the rest of the way
alone.

Sicola noticed the rocks and weeds and thorns
that marked his path to the hill, and he expected to
find a similar barrenness around the shack, but he
was surprised and pleased to see small patches of
earth — tilled and black with nature's nutrients — in
which there grew roses of such perfection that he
wondered how it could be possible for no weed seeds
to blow into the beds or no aphids to feast on the
succulent leaves. And as he reached the summit of the
hill he sensed a spirit of such tranquil holiness as to
make even weeds and aphids respectful. There was an
aroma in the air, sweet and heady and calming, and
though the shack was constructed of rough-hewn
boards with gaps between them, it was as if he were
knocking on the door of God's very own mansion.

Father Bede answered Sicola's gentle tap and
said with warmth, "Ah, yes, you must be Father
Simon. Come in, please."

The room was bright and cheery even in its barrenness, but it was barrenness without sterility for it
seemed to Sicola that the very air of the room teemed
with unseen life, gay and expectant, praising God
molecule by molecule.

"I have been waiting to hear something of Italy

and His Holiness. I met him, you know, a very long time ago. He was a mere curate then, and I was traveling through Europe with a youth hostel. We were both very young, and no doubt he has changed, perhaps even grown portly, but as a young man he was most athletic and most holy."

He reminds one of St. Ignatius in his animation and St. Francis in his passivism, Sicola thought, for both qualities seemed to express themselves in Bede's way of speaking and in his bearing. There was a lilting excitement in his voice as he spoke, and yet the lean but vital face had a serenity that was luminous and holy. It was as if self-denial and frugality had been a unique food on which he had seemed to thrive. He was not, Sicola thought, a holy-card portrait of the ascetic saint, sad to the point of eliciting sadness, pained to the extent of picturing sanctity as a tasteless adventure in self-torture. No, this was a good and pious man whose commitment to physical life was only to its barest, most basic needs, but in his spiritual and intellectual life he was indeed epicurean, for everything about him exuded this fact that unremitting commitment to those matters of the soul were indeed the bread of his life. It was as if love — not as defined by men of the world, but as experienced by the true mystic — had a totality and a dimension and a direction so complete, so full, and so direct that it found its end in its very source, and in it there was an overflowing so magnificently profuse as to engulf him with the very electricity of life.

"The Pope," Sicola said, "is well, and he remains at his same weight, perhaps because he comes from mountain people, perhaps because he has never allowed his limbs to fall into disuse."

"You know, Father," the hermit said, "he was

most kind to me, providing me with food for my journey, hearing my confession, and then giving me the Eucharist, truly the bread I needed for my pilgrimage."

Sicola searched his memory, but no image of a past meeting with the man came to him. But that was not unusual, he thought; it was such a very long time ago when he was a parish curate.

"When you return to Rome perhaps you would take with you an account of a most extraordinary vision which keeps recurring," Father Bede continued. "It is most remarkable because two angels appear to me, one speaking in my own tongue and most comprehensible to me, while the other speaks only a few words and these are in a language strange to my ears. One appears in a radiance of light which bathes his white tunic, while the other lurks in the shadows and is only barely visible to the eye, but more than a little audible to my ear, though he seems only to punctuate the words of the White Angel with exclamatory remarks which I do not yet understand."

"What is your vision?" Sicola asked.

"It seems to be a modern version of Thomas More's *Utopia*, wherein the world as we know it somehow has righted itself, and there is a peace among men so as to make it seem almost a heaven on earth. It is as if this place has become the fulfillment of Jeremiah's prophecy that 'I will place my law within them, and write it upon their hearts; I will be their God, and they shall be my people. No longer will they have to teach their kinsmen how to know the Lord, for I will forgive their evildoing and remember their sins no more.' The White Angel seems to transport me about this new society describing its wonders to me. And — occasionally — there is the comment from the Dark Angel in a kind of glossolalia.

"In this land there is a president, but there is no legislature, no lawmaking body of any kind, for no laws are necessary beyond the Ten Rules that govern the people, and these Ten are so inscribed in the hearts and understanding of the people that even the subdivisions of these laws come as naturally deduced, for the Natural Law seems ultimately to have found its place, there being no quarrel with it. And because there is no need of the vast machinery of government, there are no taxes imposed by the government, but there is a benefaction imposed voluntarily by each member of this society upon himself.

"First, let me treat of its history, and then I will give you examples of how it works by showing comparisons with facets of modern life."

Father Bede, in recalling the vision, seemed instead to be falling into a new ecstasy, unmindful of Sicola's presence.

"In the shambles of human civilization, man has somehow rediscovered the work ethic of a long-lost time, a time in which the distinction between the artist and craftsman was a distinction only in form. For the craftsman was indeed an artist, and the artist shared the craftsman's zeal for the perfection of his talent. It was a time when men knew the greatest happiness in work, which comes when each man's work, like a properly tailored suit, fits him perfectly, drapes properly on his frame, and enhances his stature with a raiment that is the awareness of his dignity. Men did not look at the clocks in their workroom to determine the time of starting and the time of ending their work, but only to the quiet spirit within their souls, a spirit that cried out for each man to make the thing being made a creative, prideful, conscientious expression of himself, yea, an expression even of his soul. He started his work early, for eagerness and excitement were the offspring of his desire, and he worked late only because the surging force within him bore no relationship to time and leisure, that myth which has come to mean lassitude.

"But in this strange land all work is preceded and ends with a prayer, and in between, work itself becomes a prayer. For in the prayer to 'prosper the work of my hands,' they ask God, in effect, to 'make the work of my hands perfect that it may be returned to You in the fullness of its perfection.' All else then is secondary, for in seeking first the Kingdom of God, men have an assurance that all else will be provided according to their needs. There are no machines here, not because machines in themselves are evil but because from history it was learned that the worship of machines was the worship of utility and in the worship of utility men also became like the machine, unthinking, robot-like, a vehicle to be measured only by its productivity rather than its creative capabilities, its sensitivities, its soul.

"The natural creativity in the soul of man stands alone, and it cannot be tied to material gain, for when it does it serves other ends that become 'induced needs,' and these needs grow into greater needs until in the end the need draws the rein on the creative spirit, making it the very servant of an expanding need. Need for more of that which provides transitory contentments then becomes the unappeasable and voracious consumer of that joy which was the sole reason for work, perfectly conceived, perfectly performed, and perfectly given as the true gift of the soul from which it sprang. And all gifts have at their base that perfection which is service, service to God. 'The service of God,' Eric Gill tells us, 'is perfect freedom

— perfect freedom is to be bound to himself — he can be and love nothing but himself. And we are free when we are his, of him and bound to him.'

"And because work is a circumference with God as its center, all radii lead from the circumference to God, and all that is tangential to the circle is tangential to work, and work, having its genesis and completion in God, allows for no tangents alien to God. Hence, greed, a natural tangent of work having no central focus but itself, is repelled. And thus the Profit Motive — the Tangent God of modern times — is now but an ancillary function of service.

"I see a new society of communalism without peer in the history of the world, but there is an abhorrence of socialism, of statism of any kind, and communism has been turned out. Oddly, however, this new society seems to have grown out of the very communism that is now anathema to its citizens. And this is interesting, for man's noblest dream of democracy failed because it had within it a pluralism that gave honor to individuality on the one hand and destroyed individuality through counterproductive forces on the other hand. In the course of the great democratic experiment there was found venality and self-aggrandizement, and the needs of the people became submerged in an ethic that worshipped Horatio Alger as the creator of a dream of vast wealth if one merely lifted himself by his own bootstrap. Now this was good in its deference to human initiative and diligence, but because its end was totally material and self-oriented, other selves became lost in the principle of the survival of the fittest. So democracy, designed by noble men with noble dreams, suffered ultimately from a surfeit of itself, of its own selfhood. In the midst of affluence and prosperity there existed poverty and disease and exploitation of misery. And man, looking for a better answer, turned to the state to rescue him and in so doing surrendered the very liberties planned into democracy by its fathers. For now the state began to provide services that destroyed initiative, putting to rest the very work ethic so central to it in former times, and many of its citizens saw work as a pointless exercise in competition with the largesse of government. All things would be free: food, clothing, shelter, health care, communication, transportation, even education. Chimera of chimeras is the word 'free,' for governments, no less than persons, cannot spend from purses that fill themselves automatically. And soon there was dissent from those with ambition and enterprise for the burden they were forced to carry in taxes, and there was dissent from the recipients of the state who demanded more. And in the shout for more, more, more there was an escalation in the cost of goods and services that was to place them out of the reach of many.

"So amid the dissent there grew a kind of populism not unlike the rabble-centered hysteria that followed the French Revolution. Power to the people, a euphoric dream, was the militant cry of radicals. Too much government was the complaint of the mercantile establishment. And in between was the mindless, apathetic middle group, which complained in silence, exercising no thrust in any direction and following the ebb and flow of tides in which they were captive merely because of their own failure to swim.

"Now the time was ripe. For in the apathy of the largest, most powerful group lay impotence, and from their impotence an assertive minority triumphs by default. Bloodlessly, but not without pain, Antichrist encircled the world without a contest, and there followed the loss of all freedom, all choice, all self-determination. Generation followed generation, and misery followed misery as each generation saw a loss of more of the selfhood that had marked democracy. The right to worship God fell before the overwhelming force of a red wave that engulfed persons, governments and institutions. Even the Church — outwardly — was destroyed, for many of its priests and nuns and bishops, in the name of liberation theology, had served in its physical destruction. The Pope remained true, but his words lacked power as he issued encyclicals that were ignored or translated into meaningless and diluted documents by a Church press in the hands of heedless editors. The Holy Father was a general without legions, for legions require commanders, and there were none.

"But it is in this very destitute state of the world's soul that the voice of God is heard most. Has it not been true in all of history that man has turned his eyes and his voice to heaven in the anguish of his pain? And from the essence of totalitarian travail there sprang new seeds, which were given life by divine waterings. And there came into being a theocracy, which could never have been born from democracy but only from totalitarian despotism. For man — even in the sunniest days of the democratic state, even in his very denial of authority — craved a surrogate father. His elected officials were required to transmit this image when free elections existed. And when he lost his freedom it was because, even then, he sought this surrogate father in the commissar. And through his captivity, he began to learn once more to pray, now praying for deliverance by the Father who had always been and who would ever be, not a surrogate but the only real Father. Though the doors of churches were closed, though the Church had been silenced, the Church reigned in the hidden thoughts of its children, and they prayed in the last freedom that remains to men, in the one freedom that could never be lost in the death of all others.

"And God answered. He answered with enlightenment, and enlightenment came after the cataclysm that leveled the earth by leveling — and making truly level — all men. In this new theocracy men carry within their beings the image of the divine, which is a mirror in which every man sees himself and his brother too. Here love has the only meaning it was intended to have, a complete and encompassing love of God so great as to shower humanity itself with its excess."

Then a strange voice, deeper and raspier than Bede's, seemed to shout through the hermit, "YENO-LAB! EREH ECNAH CON!" It was apparent to Sicola that the holy priest was the vehicle for that other angel whose pejorative tones lent the sound of disapproval if not the language.

Father Bede seemed to shrug off the interruption as he continued. "Here there is the true welfare state. No man goes without his basic need, yet there is no federal or state-sponsored welfare programs, not even life insurance companies, health or casualty insurance companies. Moreover, everyone receives education to a degree suited to his aspirations and abilities. And these benefits without taxes on the people. Strangely, there is still money and goods remaining in their vast silo to provide for the needs of India, Africa, and certain countries of South America and Asia. I have seen it, and it does indeed work."

"Preposterous," Sicola muttered. "How can it be possible?"

The priest continued his narrative as if he heard

Sicola, when in fact he had not. "This is possible," he went on, "because, through the choice of individuals themselves, there are no millionaires — only brains and inventiveness and enterprising dedication, which have the worth of millions, nay billions. Even usury is unknown in this society, for it has no place here. Every man is a Francis, every woman a Teresa of Calcutta, every child a Little Flower, for all are consumed only with the love of God; all seek the perfection of themselves in the pursuit of prayer and work, and all work has as its ultimate end the ennobling of society and the grandeur of God in man."

"YENOLAB! EREH ECNA CON!" the voice interrupted.

"Just as in the society of yesterday, there are captains of industry, scientists of great creative genius, healers of incomparable ability, artists that seem to be a reincarnation of Michelangelo, and Beethoven, and Virgil, and Dostoyevsky. Aquinas and Aristotle live again, as does Plato, for ideas that were primitive now take their shape in a receptive man governed by a transcendent God. It is indeed true that His law is placed within them and written on their hearts, for the youngest child knows the truths of antiquity in the new light of eternity, and all — young and old alike — have a power to discern the immutable laws of nature as the testament of the living God.

"The coin of the realm exists, and it is paid for the efforts of men, but now man sees in this coin a new use, a new end; he takes from his purse what is needful to sustain himself, and all else is returned to the coffers of men to be used to enhance the dignity of man before God. No law mandates this but the law written in the heart, for long ago it was learned that such imposition, unwillingly made, gave rise to oppressive taxation born in selfishness and greed and leading only to greater poverty. But when it was learned that true happiness is found in the spirit, voluntarism became the watchword of the new society. Each man, indeed, is his brother's keeper, and his brotherhood extends even to the unnamed, unseen alien in another land, for is he not also the child of God, and is there not a common progenitor for all men?"

"YENOLAB! EREH ECNAH CON!"

"Before the Great Fall no part of society escaped from the cancer of avarice, and microcosmic of all society was the field of entertainment, and more specifically that of sports. There was a time when the salaries paid to entertainment figures — motion pictures, television and sports — constituted a kind of obscenity. Let us isolate, for example, the matter of professionalism in sports, though the pattern fits other areas as well. Before the new spirit came to men, sports figures had reached an economic stature that placed them on a level much higher than those whose contributions to their society were greater. The athlete was paid in a manner that exceeded the limit of his true worth, his true contribution, and once he had achieved this summit, there still remained within him the hollowness of his victory, the emptiness of his material fortune. It was possible for such a person of unique muscular coordination and strength to command an income greater than the rulers of nations, the healers of the body, the presidents of corporations, the teachers of the young, and many other contributors to the community, though even many of these knew wealth beyond their needs. Moreover, because of the admitted shortness of their careers, it was their goal to receive recompense not only for the few years when they could perform with agility, but in their retirement years to receive incomes of which diligent people in other occupations would receive but the merest fraction after having served forty or more years in conscientious employment. You do not call this an obscenity?

"Men had striven for a leisure state for centuries, that state of existence which would permit time to be free only to the extent that it would foster the creative spirit of men to reach heights of worthwhile pleasure, that state that separates idleness from personal fulfillment, boredom from the attainment of the heretofore unsatisfied realization of potentials centering on the perfection of the human soul through the perfection of human skills. And when man arrived at his leisure world, he found as the Hindu philosopher observed, that it was not leisure in the sense of 'working with ease,' but only an idleness that Plato termed 'living in sport.' And in this idleness, in this living in sport, men spawned the new greed of Sport, the athlete made idol and the idol cast in plastic, a synthetic product of man's own imagination like the calf at Horeb.

"And feeding this 'living in sport' was the promoter of the gladiator's skill. In his corporate zeal he feigned the spirit of boyhood, dedicated to perpetuating playground ideals, but in the board room consideration was given only to the economic trade in human flesh, the reverence for packed stadia — packed even in the face of national hard times — the revenue of food and parking facilities, and lastly the politics of pressure, which when applied to a community's jugular vein brought it to its knees in the surrender of free stadia in which larger fortunes could be made without an investment in physical plants. Some even asked for and received the mineral rights under the playing field and the air rights above it.

"During this period of ever-escalating greed, it was found that athletes and promoters slowly but most certainly were slaying the very goose that had laid their golden eggs, first because internecine wars began to engender apathy on the one hand and antagonism on the other from the very sources of their revenue, namely those known by the sobriquet 'fans,' and secondly because the source of talent began to resemble a dry hole spewing up greater and greater mediocrity. And mediocrity was inevitable, because wealth was the passion of athletes and promoters — or corporate heads and workers if you wish — no longer the love of perfection. Because a ready source of talent had been customarily supplied through what was called a farm system, there was in those long-ago years a continuous source of talent sharply honed as it moved ever upward to the Big Plateau, at the same time providing entertainment in the lower plateaus for many millions of people. The participants were, for the most part, men whose object was to unite muscle, love, and delight with intelligence and the heightening of their skill. And they drove themselves to that degree of perfection that would satisfy their only ambition, to play on the Big Plateau regardless of the amount of financial reward.

"This structure one day passed into oblivion, for this was the age of utility through technology. The farm system was no more because there came the Cyclops of the Airwaves, which was able in its panoramic gaze to drink in the drama on the field and to transmit this view to all corners of the nation. This was called Progress, and progress is always measured in terms of wealth. Cyclops brought more wealth than the promoters dreamed was possible. No longer were the lower plateaus able to endure, for who would watch the apprentice when he could behold the artist, and seemingly without cost or effort on the part of the viewer. So the lower plateaus became known as El Foldo.

"But whence would come the talent provided by the lower plateaus? 'Ah-h-h,' said the promoters, 'from the colleges and universities,' little dreaming that the merest education would bring with it the ability to perform arithmetical feats, such feats dwelling essentially on currency. And so it was. The colleges and the universities became the new lower plateaus. So where once education was the thrust of these institutions, now added to their function was the training of those who could fling a seamed sphere or to strike it resoundingly with a stick. Or there was that game whose emphasis was on the acquisition of real estate, a mere hundred yards of it. One man would tuck an ovate ball under his arm and employ the technique of gradualism in squatter's rights, moving ever down the field with the object of possessing all hundred yards. This was not so simple, for he had to face the denial of such acquisitiveness from eleven men determined to make the ball edible by the carrier and thus halt his march as he felt the solidity of the ball pushed seemingly into his intestines, or lower.

"Oh glory of glories! There was the game of bounce ball, once played by average men of average size, but now dominated by men whose glandular elephantiasis made a travesty of skill with a maneuver known as the 'slam dunk,' which elicited squeals of ecstasy from the small minds who worshiped giantism. The object of such a game was to toss, with uncanny accuracy, a sphere into a hoop, but as the athletes grew taller the height of the hoop seemed to grow less. To cry, 'where is the skill?' would subject one to the abrasive insults of the adherents of such a travesty.

"Viewers and commentators began to be engorged to their molars with the state of athletics, but sports continued to thrive until the Great Calamity, surviving even the period of the Antichrist, during which time incomes were confiscated but athletes and entertainers still enjoyed a kind of deference which set them above their peers.

"But after the Great Calamity it was as if the clouds had been seeded with a catalyst that released a fine mist of tranquility, as if the very ozone were permeated with a cleansing antitoxin which began to settle over the earth and fill its inhabitants with some miraculous grace that inspired them to see the nobility in work, the good in effort, the joy in dedication to a selfhood beyond self. It was as if man suddenly heard Plato, who had averred centuries before Christ that 'when thou art rid of self, then thou art self-controlled, and self-controlled art self-possessed, and self-possessed, possessed of God and all that He has ever made.'

"And in this new spirit, men came together and reasoned as men that the intrinsic worth of a man is to be acknowledged and rewarded, but that there was an intrinsic worth to all men which needed rewarding. And even the indolent spawned by socialist ideals became alive to the joys of a new work ethic, which had as its credo (1) to love with all one's heart, all one's mind, all one's soul this eternal Self, (2) to love with every fiber that occupation through which he would seek to become as nearly perfect as his love and his talent would permit, and (3) that while this would essentially be its own reward there also were needs of food, clothing and shelter which must be sustained and provided for. This was the rule that would be applicable to participants and promoters alike, whether they were in the fields of entertainment or teaching or government or industry.

"Continuing with the example of sports, however, in this new age there are contingent benefits to 'fans,' also called consumers. They have found that there is a reduction in the cost of their attendance at these spectacles, just as there is a reduction of costs throughout the marketplace as a whole, this being a reflection of more judicious disbursements at the pay windows of the participants and promoters. More people are permitted therein to share vicariously in the drama of the arena, just as more are able to share in the material goods of the market, and — astonishingly — great sums are still realized at the turnstiles. When it was learned that economic inflation had its root in greed, it was possible for all gross income to be divided into fair profit, cost of talent, and cost of operation, all of which were now reduced. And that portion allocated to fair profit in sports contained within it a portion earmarked for the colleges and universities which would maintain the flow of talent to all fields of endeavor and hence provide the means of keeping open the doors of academia for the nourishment of the nation's gross intellectual product. Small and large business establishments similarly marked a portion of their profits to specific social needs. There was no national edict calling for it, just as there was no mandate on individuals to apportion a part of their incomes to benefactions for the public good. The command was in the air that men breathed."

"YENOLAB! EREH ECNAH CON!" screamed the voice of the Dark Angel. "Hah, hah, hah . . . EREH ECNAH CON!"

"Be not misled," Father Bede continued with no notice of the Dark Angel. "The description of the transcendence of sports from a gluttonous occupation to one of total service is but an example in miniature of the conversion that came over the entire world, in whatever field. The 'fan' certainly was the same person who, in the marketplace is called the consumer. The athletes were not different from that breed of men who passed through the halls of knowledge without ever brushing against the walls and from matriculation to graduation were filled singularly with the notion that at the end there lay riches simply for having made the journey. And once graduating, their puling cry to the captains of industry was, 'Pay me well, pay me more, though I will give you no more in return. Unlike my father's father I will not be concerned with apprenticeship, mastering my occupation, accepting small wages while I learn in order to become proficient. I am ready now to lead. This scroll asserts it.' And in the vast labor market there were those similarly infected, both educated and uneducated, who shouted, 'I will band together with my brothers for a greater share of your profits — perhaps even ultimate and total ownership of your business — unless you grant our demands and those which will follow year after year without end. We will, if necessary, cause you to cease operation and to lose everything, as we have with some corporations and certainly many newspapers. And do not ask for more than shoddy work in return. Even if we are unemployed as a result, even if the consumer must be burdened with this cost, we will destroy you for not recognizing the sovereignty of the employed over the employer.' They had only learned too well the lesson taught by the promoters themselves.

"And were the promoters of sports so different from the giants of industry and commerce whose surveys and charts dwelt on ever increasing shares of the market, whether by dissembling in representing the benfit of their products or by the use of conglomerate entities to reduce competition in the name of lower costs to consumers, oftentimes ephemeral and short-lived? Have they not also been guilty of peonage, that offshoot of industrialism that makes men and women an extension of the machines they operate in grimness, with boredom, with a soulless lack of intellection or inventiveness — more expendable than the machines they operate? Was the trading of flesh in sports so different? Where profit is the only motive of a business, there you will find greed and exploitation.

"But all this is gone, descending to its grave along with the Dow-Jones average, for in former times there was the theory that income was derived from two sources, a man at work, or money at work, and the theory worked well for its time and its economy, but now all income is derived solely from the effort of noble work, each man fulfilling to his very limit the power of creativity, inventiveness, and concentration. He worries no longer about tomorrow, for tomorrow will be filled with that same brotherhood, in which all men are truly one with one another . . . and with God, whose beneficence is not so much ladled as available for each. They seek and they receive."

"YENOLAB! EREH ECNAH CON!" chortled the Dark Angel.

"This new spirit," Sicola asked in disbelief, "did

it merely descend upon the people without warning, as if one day the world was dominated by evil and the next by the good? Surely, you do not expect me to believe in such a prophecy that allows for enlightenment without light, without even a dawning?"

"All of this came about not with such a suddenness as one would believe from this *précis* of a vision. For again it was Jeremiah who foresaw, 'I will pronounce my sentence against them for all their wickedness in forsaking me, and in burning incense to strange gods and adoring their own handiwork.' For too long men had followed a star that was not the star of Bethlehem but a descending asteroid, blood red in its center and in its contrails, leading ever downward to its own destruction. It was as if there were emanating from this star such false auras as to lead men to believe in the neuter pronoun 'it,' rather than the personal pronoun 'you.' And as they worshipped the principle of 'getting with IT,' the 'IT' lost its T, as that of the Cross was lost, and there was left only 'I.' The accursed 'I' began every thought, and every thought centered on Individuality, for was it not proper for this word also to begin with the letter 'I,' which was so worshipped?

"The 'I' asserted itself in rights which man took upon himself in usurpation of the rights of God. 'I have the right to death with dignity,' man said, or a woman would say, 'I have the right of full freedom and choice over my body, whether it be for promiscuous and unlawful pleasure or in the termination of the other life I carry.' And this was — in God's view — patent nonsense that could not long endure without the reminder that He was the author of all life, hence all prior rights resided in Him.

"And even in the convents and seminaries this

doctrine became widespread as the religious life became no longer one of reparation, of self-abnegation,
of imitation and identity with the crucified Christ.
Now it was self-fulfillment, self-identity, and a kind
of self-abuse ensued, for in this glorification of their
selfhood they brought harm to themselves and to
their goal of happiness and fulfillment, forgetting that
it was Paul who pointed out that 'I live, yet not I, but
Christ in me.' For harm comes, indeed, to him who
separates the individual self from that unity which is
the everlasting Self.

"And there were other manifestations of the influence of this falling star, manifestations most apparent in the loss of reverence for family life. Now children, rootless, loveless and aimless, found no solace
among parents, faithless, careless, and Godless. And
as children were permitted a new freedom, they followed this freedom into the false tranquility of sensate pleasure that again denied the Cross, for had not
their parents denied it before them? Where there is no
Cross there is no Christ, no redemption, and society
found itself unable to redeem itself, heedless of the
fact that the redemptive process continues for each of
us in the carrying of our own cross. Instead they rested in the blissful assumption that the redemption by
Christ was in itself a *carte blanche*, hence there was no
need to repeat the example of His expiation, His purgation in the salvific process. There was no recollection of His telling any who would be His to 'take up
his cross and follow Me.'

Then it came. With frightening ferocity. An
economy based on false growth, spiraling ever upward, imitated the law of physics illustrated most
aptly in the too-steep ascent of an airplane whose
power cannot match the steepness of its climb, and it

finds itself falling into a spin as it hurtles toward the earth and its own destruction. Oppressive taxation, unusually high and usurious costs for the use of money, rampant increases in wages and the cost of goods followed the dictum of the physical law, and soon there was collapse, total and complete, as first cities became bankrupt, then families, then the nation itself. There were those who said, 'It will pass!' But it did not. It was then that men became the captive of the Antichrist, dressed as a Red Bear, the Antichrist who had patiently watched the greed in democracy rise to so great a level as to make it ready for capitulation. It was then that the seed of man repeated itself generation upon generation in the world of oppression that denied liberty and worship. And when man was reeling first from the blows to his economy, then from his subjugation to the Bear, he was struck by natural calamities, quakes, fire, pestilence and death.

Then man, having endured this for too long — in his own measure of time — fell to his knees and sought death with David, 'How long, Lord? How long? Rescue me from my enemy.' And heeding this prayer, death came instead to the enemy. The clouds opened. The earth closed its gaping seams. The sun shone again, sending its warmth through clean air, purified by prayer. And a blanket of serenity settled over the earth."

"What a delightful fantasy!" Sicola mused more to himself than to Father Bede. "I was prepared," he thought, "to hear of some prophecy, some great spiritual insight, some message for our times, but instead I hear only a fairy tale. I am convinced that this man has lived alone too long, that he needs the company of other men, that the life of a contemplative so separates him from reality that he mistakes fancy for mysticism."

Father Bede turned to Sicola, hearing the unspoken words of his mind, "You *have* heard prophecy . . . spiritual insight . . . a message for our time. Why, your Holiness," he asked acknowledging the papal presence for the first time, "does the world see the truth in *1984* and call the prophecy of 2084 a patent fantasy? Certainly that Orwell masterpiece elicited in its time the same disbelief, but as it comes to pass more and more in our day, the author is honored for his insights. Why, for that matter, does the world gasp at every utterance of Jeane Dixon and yet ignore the Mother of God at Fatima? Is it so strange, indeed, that one day her words will also come true, that the Rock will rise above the infirmities of the soul and prevail in the fullness of its own divine glory?

"Since Mr. Orwell prophesied 1984, is it a strain on credulity to accept also the Millennium?"

Then again Sicola heard the voice of the Dark Angel, this time slipping into English in his excitement, "Millennium? Millennium, you say? Wheeeew! I thought you were talking of *this* time, *this* place, *now*! WON ECNAH CON!"

"It would seem so," Father Bede answered the Dark Angel, finally understanding his backward speech. It would certainly seem so."

"AIGANNAM!" Sicola whispered. "How I long to see the day!"

Part IV
AND TO ROME AGAIN

The Dove

Mannaggia! It was only a bird. Why should its death so shatter Sicola as to leave him feeling emptiness and a fury all at the same time?

But to him, it was more than a bird. It was life. It was trust. It was tenderness. It was dependence. It was beauty. And he sorely missed this bird, as he sorely missed the qualities it represented.

This bird was a dove, and it had swooped into Sicola's life uninvited, at first only as an interesting experience, then to remain as a friend much like the entry of other friends in life whose coming was accidental only in the sense that their appearance was beyond their power or ours to plan or predict. But one wonders, all the same, about such "accidents" in their catalysis to evoke hidden love and joyful communion. "We were friends, my dove and I," Sicola mused, "and how much our friendship owes to the supernatural force that brings animals and people together, or people and people, I have no way of knowing. All I feel certain of is that there is a spirituality in all love, not necessarily in romantic love, which has its origin in a higher love that is man's momentary glimpse of divinity."

The dove was softly tan with a black, narrow collar about its neck, the mark of a mourning dove. It flew one noonday into the Vatican Gardens and alighted on the arm of one of the patio chairs, ultimately hopping down to the concrete where it seemed to waddle in unconcerned at-oneness with Sicola's life. It made no move to fly away as he approached it, but simply danced ungracefully and scudded under the chair. As the delighted Pope reached for it, it moved from his outstretched hand as if it were uncertain of his intentions, seeming also to have a kind of ambivalent trust which called it to stay, even with reservations.

At length, Sicola's hand closed over its wings, and it *let* him capture it. There was not even a flutter of its wings to offer protest.

Temporarily, Sicola placed it in a large corrugated cardboard box while Tommaso searched for the cage he had used for a parakeet of other times. Then Sicola poured parakeet seed in a saucer, placed it on the floor of the cage and introduced the dove to this token of his friendship. The dove ate with omnivorous abandon as the seeds scattered about the floor of the cage in its eagerness to attack the meal. Once surfeited, it slumped, Buddha-like, into an ovate fluff and closed its eyes to doze.

Uncertain what to do with it, ultimately Sicola listened to the wisdom of Tommaso who averred courteously that the dove was meant for freedom, to live in nature, which was its true habitat. The two men kept the bird in the cage overnight. The dove showed its anger at this imprisonment by fluttering wildly, and Sicola knew that Tommaso was right. So in the morning he fed the bird again and then opened the door of the cage. The dove flapped to the doorsill, looked at Sicola as if for permission, then flew away. Even with so short a friendship, Sicola was saddened by the bird's departure, but certain that he had done what was proper.

Throughout the day the Pontiff would look for the dove and wonder where it had gone. He thought of St. Francis almost as if the very thought were a prayer to bring the dove back. At around five o'clock that afternoon, by now having resigned himself to the fact that each had been a mere episode in the life of the other, just a pleasant interlude, Sicola was weeding in a patch of new lawn when he heard the flap and flutter of wings within inches of his face. The dove drifted past him and swirled in an inverted U to land about three feet from where he knelt. He picked up the bird, and again it did not struggle. In his cage his head bobbed and his beak pecked as the parakeet seed swirled about his new home. Sicola would send Tommaso out to purchase pigeon mash, he thought, as soon as he was certain that the bird was going to remain with them.

But, even though the dove lived with Sicola for about two weeks, he did not have Tommaso buy the mash. He wondered later whether this was not the flaw in man that inhibited him from immediate commitment, a flaw readily apparent to the higher force that created interludes and moments with the potential for permanence. At any rate, the dove had seemed perfectly happy with the parakeet seed. And the friendship between the man and his bird had progressed to the point that Sicola no longer kept the dove in the cage overnight. Now he would pour the food into the dish, and the dove would come to Sicola and eat from it as he held it in his hand. Then the dove would fly up into the large pine tree in the garden and remain there, occasionally looking down at Sicola as he went out to talk to the dove almost as if it were human. For the most part the dove remained in the tree, occasionally flying away and out of sight for brief periods. But it always returned, and it no longer seemed to treat Sicola with guarded affection. Now they were true friends.

Then in the early morning hours one day before rising, the Pope heard a thumping patter on the roof over his apartment, a sound he had heard so many times before as his cat had scurried to chase other cats, or perhaps even birds. And there was a foreboding in his heart, a gnawing fear as he thought, "*Mannaggia*! I hope the dove is not on the roof."

But it had been. And when Sicola dressed and went out to the back lawn an hour later, he saw the disembowelled carcass of the dove, mangled, its head askew, feathers scattered over the lawn, and he did the manly thing by not weeping. But his stomach wept, his brain wept, and the weakness in his limbs was a form of weeping.

Then the anger swelled, and he turned to the cat curled on the quilted patio chair in somnolent content after the feast. And he hated her, hated her so that he wanted to avenge the bird by smashing the head of the cat, which also had learned to trust him. He wanted to, but he did not.

Instead, he was filled with a sorrow. "*Absolvo te.* I have lost a friend," he said sadly. "I have lost him to the so-called balance of nature, which is ruthless and unfeeling, because nature is soulless. Let no man justify the most brutal of human conduct to me as 'natural,' for men are above nature and come to know it only through those laws in it which reflect divinity. Nature is without a soul and answers to itself. But humanity is endowed with that element of spirit which is Supernature, that thing called the soul, which forever separates man from Nature because it is transcendent in its union with the soul of Supernature, which is God."

He could not hope for the return of the dove, but he could hope that that unity between the dove and him — which is the reflection of God in nature — would be better understood by men in a world that seemed to take its pleasure in imitating nature rather than finding in it words writ large by God.

The Rebel

Introibo ad altare Dei. . . .

"I will go to the altar of God, to God who gladdens my youth." How Sicola had loved the mellifluous grace of the old Latin Mass, how he had pondered over the precision of its doctrine, how he had revered it as the Mass of all times, modified only slightly but never changed in its essentials since the Council of Trent from which it derived its name, the Tridentine Mass.

It was gone now. Replaced by the *Novus Ordo*. Forever? Who was to say? Forever is a long time.

Still, the fact remained that when the Tridentine Mass was in full flower, so also was the Church. Did the loss of the Mass as it had remained since Pius V bring about near anarchy in the Church, the rootlessness of the once faithful?

Sicola tossed under the covers on his small cot in the Papal Chambers. The question had haunted him not only as a cardinal but as Pope as well. And now it had come to this. Archbishop René Desfeux, once his treasured friend, a man for whom he had had only the greatest admiration, had brought the Church to the brink of schism. His knowledge of both Church history and theology was incontrovertible. His logic was sound. He had even had Sicola with him most of the way. But this recent move! This was an act of open rebellion, which testified to the fact that Desfeux shared the same pride, the same exclusivity of thought as the heinous Kugelfinger, who was far more to the left of the Church, far less holy than Desfeux. But each had the same susceptibility: pride of intellect. Each had quarreled in his own way with Papal Authority, each had gnawed away at the doctrine of Infallibility with a rationale inconsistent not only with Vatican Council II but Vatican Council I, in which the doctrine was established as an article of faith.

The difference was that the enemy on the left would stay within the Church when he and the Church would be better if he were out of it, while the enemy on the right would take his sheep out of the Church, and with them would go a part of the heart. It was important for Sicola to reconcile both wings of the Church with the center, but he could not help but feel a sadness for the possible loss of Desfeux, who had represented the devotion of the Church.

He must, please God, prevent it, he thought. But how? He could not accede to Desfeux any more than he could pander to Kugelfinger. Surely, Desfeux knew that if he left the Church he would break with the continuity of Christ's own family. He could but become an apostate pope, and those who would follow him would ultimately face the question as Peter himself did: "Lord, to whom shall we go?"

Even he himself, Sicola was forced to admit, had wondered why the change to the *Novus Ordo* after so long a time. And when he had come into the Papacy, there were few surviving papers of Paul VI to determine the motivation for the change. Paul had been opposed by the venerable Cardinal Ottavierno, but Paul had persisted. Why? Paul had not been a frivolous man. In fact, when the history books would review his time there was every likelihood that he would stand out as martyr to a new spirit that had to be heard, even amidst the cacophony of dissent on both sides. That did not, however, serve to explain to Sicola the mind of Paul at that particular time.

He wondered about it, and he recalled how in early 1959 John XXIII had only talked about calling a Council, saying even that he was certain the Holy Spirit insisted upon it. The furore in the Vatican seemed to shake the tomb of Peter under the Basilica. Everyone had been opposed to it as untimely and unnecessary, and John remained quiet. But then in 1960 he announced that he would, indeed, call a Council. What confirmed his thought in 1960 when he had seemingly vacillated in 1959 with the conviction that the call was from the Holy Spirit? Even popes, it seemed, needed confirmation that the Holy Spirit speaks to them. But what had been the catalyst?

He must go to the archives tomorrow. The question was simply too much for him.

He threw the covers off and knelt beside his cot and prayed to the Holy Spirit for guidance, then to the Holy Mother who had, he remembered, appeared to three small children at Fatima in 1917. They were children with none of the learning or intellect of a pope, yet popes had paid them honor over the years for having carried the words of the Virgin Mother to the world. Among these words he knew was a sealed document given to the Holy Father with instructions to remain sealed until 1960. Why 1960? He had never seen it, and he wondered why he had not, as one of the first acts of his pontificate, asked to read it. It had simply slipped his mind. But, he thought, was there not some coincidence that the document was opened

in the same year in which John had decided to call his
Council? And was it not equally strange that the contents were never revealed to the faithful? Was the document so portentous with catastrophe for the Church
that John believed that its revelation would do more
harm than good, and that, instead, it would be the
better part of wisdom merely to act upon its mandate?
Suppose, for example, that the document had said, in
effect: "Unite . . . or else . . . NOW!" Would that not
explain the currying of favor with our separated
brethren? And knowing that God sees all things from
the view of eternity, that He takes the feeble efforts of
men and converts them to His own final purpose,
would He not also allow the fragmentation that followed the Council to take place for the *sake* of ultimate unity so that harmony could grow from discord as an act of His mercy? What was perhaps important was that the Church take the first steps toward unity. Was this involved in John's decision, and
later in Paul's? It was pure speculation, the circuitous
thoughts of a meandering mind unable to find relief
in sleep. But tomorrow he would find out. The document. He must read it.

Sicola slept.

When he awoke, he awoke as many men do . . .
with the impression of having thought out problems
before he slept, or even dreamed them during sleep,
but now they were washed from his memory. There
remained only the vague impression that he had to
meet with Desfeux, not merely to renew their friendship but to restore the friendship of Desfeux with the
Church.

"Tommaso," he announced over his coffee and
bread, "today I am going to Switzerland to visit with
the lovable renegade, Desfeux."

"You are W-H-A-A-A-T?" Tommaso exploded in disbelief. "Holiness, you cannot do it. He will think that you are crawling to him."

"If I must crawl, Tommaso, I will crawl. But it would be more convenient in the Fiat. Get it, Thickhead!" The September air was crisp and the foliage was burnished with gold and red as the wind bent the trees in a gesture of fealty toward Sicola's course. It was as if he recognized the deference of nature to his position as Vicar of Christ, and he breathed a prayer that Desfeux would be equally bending. Once in the rugged country of the mountains, however, he saw the jagged rocks and peaks that were a fortress against him, and the tiny Fiat strained to overcome the incline and the desolate altitude. What weapons did the Pope possess really, he thought, with all the regal pomp and ceremony. His weapons as they are measured by other institutions were like this little automobile, internally powered but miniscule in appearance. It was the source of power that really mattered, he knew, but just once it would be comforting to know that he could command the mountain and it would crumble before him. But that was a vain thought. He did not need to make mountains crumble. All he needed was the confidence in his source of power to make his words efficacious so that the wills of the recalcitrant would bend not to his will but to the will of God asserting itself in the Church.

His one solace was in the fact that Desfeux was a good man, wrong perhaps, but good, and therefore more easily reached than one whose heart is calcified by evil. They would talk, and Desfeux would soon recognize that his love for the Church was so great that he would be unable to wound her without wounding himself.

The Fiat ultimately meandered down the circuitous drive leading to the Swiss seminary that Desfeux had founded, a seminary that had turned out good priests, totally orthodox short of that point at which they followed their leader in defiance. They, too, were convinced that the Church was wrong, but he thought, how many times have I, too, thought that she was wrong in that part of her that was human, how many times have I grieved that this or that action would lead her to more pain? Yet that very pain had taught her fortitude and made her impervious to persistent morbidity. She was like a mother whose character is deepened more than her husband's simply because it is she who has had to suffer more than her spouse. There, he thought, the simile ended, for as the Church was both the body of Christ and the spouse of Christ, she could not have suffered more than Christ Himself had endured, but in the fusion of Christ with the Church it was as if the Church had become hermaphroditic. She was both male and female. Male in her militancy, female in her love. And it was at this time when the female in her would be called upon to a greater extent than her masculinity. It was a time for gentle understanding and soft caresses.

The young seminarian on reception duty ushered him into the Archbishop's study. The two men shook hands warmly, and Desfeux's eyes seemed to mirror the happier days of the Pope and the Archbishop.

Desfeux offered Sicola claret from a square cut-glass decanter on the sideboard, and the two sipped and stared, fencing with their eyes.

"René," Sicola began, "Tommaso said that I should be crawling to you if I came today."

"I would not have let you, Giuseppe, you know that. Still, I recognize this as a great effort on your part, and I am touched, deeply touched. We have always been good friends. I think that it is unfortunate that this disagreement has renewed itself in your pontificate, but please understand that I do not blame you entirely for the condition of the Church. It would have happened even if another had been elected. It is the times. We thought that Pius X had crushed the modernists with his *Pascendi*, but we know that the enemies of the Church were there all the while, except that they were underground. All it took to bring them out was the libertarianism of the Sixties, a wrong move here, a wrong move there. Then the door was opened and they thrust it wide, crashing into our faces. Still, perhaps you and your predecessors have given them more comfort than they deserved."

"I suppose," Sicola interrupted, "that this is what you meant when you said, referring to me, that the Pope is 'weak, betrayed.' Eh?"

"We must face it, Holiness. The Church is full of thieves, mercenaries and wolves. During the past years the Vatican has become the friend of our enemies. Only recently a Communist leader who had killed many faithful Christians in Hungary was received at the Vatican. Excommunications of heretics, Communists, Freemasons and schismatics have been lifted."

"The Church, René, is troubled, tormented, oppressed, even unsure. . . ."

"Holiness, the Church has always been troubled, tormented, oppressed, but it has never been unsure . . . except perhaps during the Arian heresy, when it was said that the whole Church was Arian. The times are not dissimilar."

"Agreed, René. But have you no confidence in the staying power of the Church? As it overcame

Arianism, or perhaps it would be better to say, as it was delivered from Arianism, do you not have confidence that it will be delivered from this cross also? God tries the Church as He tries the souls of men, and to each He extends His support in their greatest need when goodwill prevails. The Council was the goodwill of men prevailing. If some members have taken the council and diverted its words to their own purpose, their effect will be short-lived. What is important, it seems, is for you and for me to believe in the divine vitality of the Church to cure itself through the lifesaving blood of its founder. We bleed, but we heal, and we walk as giants in our good health. Stay with us that you may walk with us in our day of recovery."

"I am not against the Council, Giuseppe, but I could have wished that the Council bore more resemblance to its preparation. We had great hopes for it. Then there came the maneuvering by the so-called *periti*, the experts, and before we knew it our bishops were acceding to documents, or so-called minor changes in documents, of which we had no knowledge until the smoke had cleared."

"Because it was a pastoral council, René, both of us have admitted that it was not infallible as a doctrinal council would have been, but one must consider that it was all the same guarded from implicit error, for when all of the bishops gather under the head of the Pope, we are assured that what issues from it will be free of error. Moreover, we owe it our assent. You have not given the Council your assent."

"Is there any wonder, Giuseppe? A foolish ecumenism arose from it and has been fostered by the Church, leading to excess in trying to make all religions equal. For instance, the image of Buddha is placed in some Catholic churches in France, which is intolerable. Again, the catechism is being changed. Children are told now that there is no mortal or venial sin, nor original sin, nor angels nor devils."

"You blame the Council and the Church for these things, and I say that these aberrations are as much opposed by the Council and the Church as by you. They have stretched the meaning of collegiality. They are the manifestations of children who have become so enthralled with their new-found puberty that they defy father, mother and peers. Unknown to you, perhaps, I have left the Vatican traveling incognito, and I have seen many of the things that disturb you. They disturb me as well, and they will be corrected to the very best of my ability to do so, with the help of Almighty God."

"It has not escaped my notice that you have played the clown in the streets of Rome as well as the cities of America. You see, I have my sources also. I have been pleased that you have departed from tradition in this sense. I am not so hidebound, my friend, that I do not approve of these actions, for I think that these experiences will contribute to making you a good pope. But when will you start to be a good pope? When the Church is crumbling at your feet?"

"I will be judged by God, René, not by you. You act as if you had a particular role in this regard. But the mission of discerning and remedying the abuses is first of all ours; it is the mission of all the bishops who work together with us. Indeed, we do not cease to raise our voice against these excesses: our discourse to the Consistory of 24 May last repeated this in clear terms. More than anyone else we hear the suffering of distressed Christians, and we respond to the cry of the faithful longing for tradition and the spiritual life. This is not the place to remind you, Brother, of all the acts of our pontificate that testify to our constant concern to ensure for the Church fidelity to the true Tradition, to enable her with God's grace to face the present and the future."

"I have heard you raise your voice, Holiness, but your other actions are contradictory," Desfeux said.

"*Your* behavior," Sicola pointed out, "is contradictory. You want, so you say, to remedy the abuses that disfigure the Church; you regret that authority in the Church is not sufficiently respected; you wish to safeguard authentic faith, esteem for the ministerial priesthood and fervor for the Eucharist in its sacrificial and sacramental fullness. Such zeal would, in itself, merit our encouragement, since it is a matter of exigencies that, together with evangelization and the unity of Christians, remain at the heart of our preoccupations and mission. But how can you at the same time, in order to fulfill this role, claim that you are obliged to act contrary to the last Council, in opposition to your brethren in the Episcopate, to distrust the Holy See itself — which you call the 'Rome of the neo-modernist and neo-Protestant tendency' — and to set yourself up in open disobedience to us? If you truly want to work 'under our authority,' as you affirm in your last private letter, it is immediately necessary to put an end to these ambiguities and contradictions."

"It is strange, Your Holiness, that you who were for so long immersed in the Tridentine Mass, so long engaged in the propagation of orthodox seminaries, now see fit to join your predecessor Paul VI in taking both of these things away from me and the faithful."

"You would like to see recognized the right to celebrate Mass in various places of worship according to the Tridentine rite," Sicola replied. "You wish also to continue to train candidates for the priesthood according to your criteria, 'as before the Council,' in seminaries apart. But behind these questions and other similar ones, which we shall examine later on in detail, it is truly necessary to see the intricacy of the problem: and the problem is *theological*. For these questions have become concrete ways of expressing an ecclesiology that is warped in essential points.

"What is indeed at issue is the question — which must truly be called fundamental — of your clearly proclaimed refusal to recognize, in its whole, the authority of the Second Vatican Council and that of the Pope. This refusal is accompanied by an action that is oriented toward propagating and organizing what must indeed, unfortunately, be called a rebellion. This is the essential issue, and it is truly untenable.

"Is it necessary to remind you that you are our brother in the Episcopate and moreover — a fact that obliges you to remain even more closely united to the See of Peter — that you have been named an Assistant at the Papal Throne? Christ has given the supreme authority in His Church to Peter and to the Apostolic College, that is, to the Pope and to the College of Bishops *una cum Capite*. In regard to the Pope, every Catholic admits that the words of Jesus to Peter determine also the charge of Peter's legitimate successors: '. . . whatever you bind on earth shall be bound in heaven,' 'feed my sheep,' 'strengthen your brethren.' And the first Vatican Council specified in these terms the assent due to the Sovereign Pontiff: 'The pastors of every rank and of every rite and the faithful, each separately and all together, are bound by the duty of hierarchical subordination and of true obedience, not only in questions of faith and morals, but also in those that touch upon the discipline and government of the Church throughout the entire world. Thus, by preserving the unity of communion and of profession of faith with the Roman Pontiff, the Church is a single flock under one Pastor. Such is the doctrine of Catholic truth, from which no one can separate himself without danger for his faith and his salvation.' Concerning bishops united with the Sovereign Pontiff, their power with regard to the universal Church is solemnly exercised in the Ecumenical Councils, according to the words of Jesus to the body of the Apostles: 'Whatever you bind on earth shall be bound in heaven.' And now in your conduct you refuse to recognize, as must be done, the two ways in which supreme authority is exercised.

"Each bishop is indeed an authentic teacher for preaching to the people entrusted to him that faith which must guide their thoughts and conduct and dispel the errors that menace the flock. But, by their nature, 'the charges of teaching and governing . . . cannot be exercised except in hierarchical communion with the head of the College and with its members' (to quote the Constitution *Lumen Gentium*). *A fortiori*, a single bishop without a canonical mission does not have, *in actu expedito ad agendum*, the faculty of deciding in general what the rule of faith is or of determining what Tradition is. In practice you are claiming that you alone are the judge of what Tradition embraces.

"You say that you are subject to the Church and faithful to Tradition, by the sole fact that you obey certain norms of the past that were decreed by the predecessor of him on whom God has today conferred the powers given to Peter. That is to say, on this point also, the concept of 'Tradition' that you invoke is distorted. Tradition is not a rigid and dead notion, a fact of a certain static sort which at a given moment of history blocks the life of this active organism that is the Church, that is, the Mystical Body of Christ. It is up to the Pope and Councils to exercise judgment in order to discern in the traditions of the Church that which cannot be renounced without infidelity to the Lord and to the Holy Spirit — the deposit of faith — and that which, on the contrary, can and must be adapted to facilitate the prayer and the mission of the Church through a variety of times and places, in order better to translate the divine message into the language of today and better to communicate it, without an unwarranted surrender of principles. Hence, Tradition is inseparable from the living magisterium of the Church, just as it is inseparable from Sacred Scripture: '. . . sacred tradition, sacred Scripture and the magisterium of the Church . . . are so linked and joined together that one of these realities cannot exist without the others, and that all of them together, each in its way, effectively contribute under the action of the Holy Spirit to the salvation of souls' (according to the Constitution *Dei Verbum*).

"With the special assistance of the Holy Spirit, the Popes and the Ecumenical Councils have acted in this common way. And it is precisely this that the Second Vatican Council did. Nothing that was decreed in this Council, or in the reforms that we enacted in order to put the decrees into effect, is opposed to what the two-thousand-year-old Tradition of the Church considers as fundamental and immutable. We are the guarantor of this, not in virtue of our personal qualities but in virtue of the charge which the Lord has conferred upon us as legitimate successor of Peter, and in virtue of the special assistance that He has promised to us as well as to Peter: 'I have prayed for you that your faith may not fail.' The universal episcopate is guarantor of this with us.

"Again, you cannot appeal to the distinction between what is dogmatic and what is pastoral, to accept certain texts of this Council and to refuse others. Indeed, not everything in the Council requires an assent of the same nature: only what is affirmed by definitive acts as an object of faith or as a truth related to faith requires an assent of faith. But the rest also forms part of the solemn magisterium of the Church, to which each member of the faithful owes a confident acceptance and a sincere application. You say moreover that you do not always see how to reconcile certain texts of the Council, or certain dispositions which we have enacted in order to put the Council into practice, with the wholesome tradition of the Church and in particular with the Council of Trent or the affirmations of our predecessors. These are, for example, the responsibility of the College of Bishops united with the Sovereign Pontiff, the new *Ordo Missae*, ecumenism, religious freedom, the attitude of dialogue, evangelization in the modern world. . . . This is not the place to deal with each of these problems. The precise tenor of the documents with the totality of its nuances and its context, the authorized explanations, the detailed and objective commentaries already made are of such a nature to enable you to overcome these personal difficulties. Absolutely secure counsellors, theologians and spiritual directors would be able to help you even more, with God's enlightenment, and we are ready to facilitate this fraternal assistance for you. But how can interior personal difficulty — a spiritual conflict that we respect — permit you to set yourself up publicly as a judge of what has been legitimately adopted, with virtual unanimity, and knowingly to lead a portion of the faithful into your refusal? If justifications are useful in order to facilitate intellectual acceptance — and we hope that the troubled or reticent faithful will have the wisdom, honesty and humility to accept those justifications that are widely placed at their disposal — they are not in themselves necessary for the assent of obedience that is due to the Ecumenical Council and to the decisions of the Pope. It is the ecclesial sense that is at issue.

"In effect you and those who are following you are endeavoring to come to a standstill at a given moment in the life of the Church. By the same token you refuse to accept the living Church, which is the Church that has always been: you break with the Church's legitimate pastors and scorn the legitimate exercise of their charge. And so you claim not even to be affected by the orders of the Pope, or by the suspension *a divinis*, as you lament 'subversion' in the Church. Is it not in this state of mind that you have ordained priests without dismissorial letters and against our explicit command, thus creating a group of priests who are in an irregular situation in the Church and who are under grave ecclesiastical penalties? Moreover, you hold that the suspension that you have incurred applies only to the celebration of the sacraments according to the new rite, as if they were something improperly introduced into the Church, which you go so far as to call schismatic, and you think that you evade this sanction when you administer the sacraments according to the formulas of the past and against the established norms.

"From the same erroneous conception springs your abuse of celebrating the Mass called that of St. Pius V. You know full well that this rite had itself been the result of successive changes, and that the Roman Canon remains the first of the Eucharistic Prayers authorized today. The present reform derived its *raison d'être* and its guidelines from the Council and from the historical sources of the Liturgy. It enables the laity to draw greater nourishment from the Word of God. Their more active participation leaves intact the unique role of the priest acting in the person of Christ. We have sanctioned this reform by our authority, requiring that it be adopted by all Catholics. If, in general, we have not judged it good to permit any further delays or exceptions to this adoption, it is with a view to the spiritual good and the unity of the entire ecclesial community, because for Catholics of the Roman Rite the *Ordo Missae* is a privileged sign of their unity. It is also because your use of the old rite is in fact the expression of a warped ecclesiology and a ground for dispute with the Council and its reforms, under the pretext that in the old rite alone are preserved, without their meaning being obscured, the true sacrifice of the Mass and the ministerial priesthood. We cannot accept that erroneous judgment, that unjustified accusation, nor can we tolerate that the Lord's Eucharist, the sacrament of unity, should be the object of such divisions, that it should even be used as an instrument and sign of rebellion.

"Of course there is room in the Church for a certain pluralism, but in licit matters and in obedience. This is not understood by those who refuse the sum total of the liturgical reform; nor indeed on the other hand by those who imperil the holiness of the real presence of the Lord and of His sacrifice. In the same way there can be no question of a priestly formation that ignores the Council.

"We cannot therefore take your requests into

consideration because it is a question of acts already committed in rebellion against the one true Church of God. *Be assured that this severity is not dictated by a refusal to make a concession on such and such a point of discipline or liturgy, but given the meaning and the extent of your acts in the present context, to act thus would be on our part to accept the introduction of a seriously erroneous concept of the Church and of Tradition.* This is why, with the full consciousness of our duties, we say to you, Brother, that you are in error. And with the full ardor of our fraternal love, as also with the weight of our authority as the successor of Peter, we invite you to retract, to correct yourself and to cease from inflicting wounds upon the Church of Christ.

"Specifically, what do we ask of you?

"First, and foremost, a declaration that will rectify matters for ourself and also for the People of God, who have a right to clarity and can no longer bear such equivocations without damage.

"This declaration will therefore have to affirm that you sincerely adhere to the Second Vatican Ecumenical Council and to all its documents — *sensu obvio* — which were adopted by the Council Fathers and approved and promulgated by our authority. For such an adherence has always been the rule, in the Church, since the beginning, in the matter of Ecumenical Councils.

"It must be clear that you equally accept the decisions that we have made since the Council in order to put into effect, with the help of the Departments of the Holy See; among these things, you must explicitly recognize the legitimacy of the reformed liturgy, notably of the *Ordo Missae*, and our right to require its adoption by the entirety of the Christian people.

"You must also admit the binding character of the rules of Canon Law now in force, which for the greater part still correspond with the content of the Code of Canon Law of Benedict XV, without excepting the part that deals with canonical penalties.

"As concerns our person, you will make a point of desisting from and retracting the grave accusations or insinuations you have publicly levelled against us, against the orthodoxy of our faith and our fidelity to our charge as the Successor of Peter, and against our immediate collaborators.

"With regard to the Bishops, you must recognize their authority in their respective dioceses by abstaining from preaching in those dioceses and administering the sacraments there — the Eucharist, Confirmation, Holy Orders, etc. — when these Bishops expressly object to your doing so.

"Finally, you must undertake to abstain from all activities (such as conferences, publications, etc.) contrary to this declaration, and formally to reprove all those initiatives that may make use of your name in the face of this declaration.

"It is a question here of the minimum to which every Catholic Bishop must subscribe: this adherence can tolerate no compromise. As soon as you show us that you accept its principle, we will propose the practical manner of presenting this declaration. This is the first condition in order that the suspension *a divinis* be lifted.

"It will then remain to solve the problem of your activity, of your works, and notably of your seminaries. You will appreciate, Brother, that in view of the past and present irregularities and ambiguities affecting these works, we cannot go back on the juridical suppression of the Priestly Fraternity of Saint Pius X.

This has inculcated a spirit of opposition to the Council and to its implementation such as the Vicar of Christ was endeavoring to promote. . . . This in no way invalidates the good elements in your seminaries, but one must also take into consideration the ecclesiological deficiencies of which we have spoken and the capacity of exercising a pastoral ministry in the Church of today. Faced with these unfortunately mixed realities, we shall take care not to destroy but to correct and to save as far as possible.

"This is why, as supreme guarantor of the faith and of the formation of the clergy, we require you first of all to hand over to us the responsibility of your work, and particularly for your seminaries. This is undoubtedly a heavy sacrifice for you, but it is also a test of your trust, of your obedience, and it is a necessary condition in order that these seminaries, which have no canonical existence in the Church, may in the future take their place therein.

"It is only after you have accepted the principle that we shall be able to provide in the best possible way for the good of all the persons involved, with the concern for promoting authentic priestly vocations and with respect to the doctrinal, disciplinary and pastoral requirements of the Church. At that stage, we shall be in a position to listen with benevolence to your requests and your wishes and, together with our departments, to take in conscience the right and opportune measures.

"As for the illicitly ordained seminarians, the sanctions which they have incurred in conformity with Canons 985.7 and 2374 can be lifted, if they give proof of a return to a better frame of mind, notably by accepting to subscribe to the declaration we have asked of you. We count upon your sense of the

Church in order to make this step easy for them.

"As regards the foundations, houses of formation, priories and various other institutions set up on your initiative or with your encouragement, we likewise ask you to hand them over to the Holy See, which will study their position, in its various aspects, with the local episcopate. Their survival, organization and apostolate will be subordinated, as is normal throughout the Catholic Church, to an agreement that will have to be reached, in each case, with the local Bishop — *nihil sine Episcopo* — and in a spirit which respects the Declaration mentioned.

"All the points to which we have given mature consideration, in consultation with the heads of the departments concerned, have been adopted by us only out of regard for the greater good of the Church. You said to us during our previous conversation: 'I am ready for anything, for the good of the Church.' The response now lies in your hands.

"If you should refuse — *quod Deus avertat* — to make the declaration asked of you, you would remain suspended *a divinis*. On the other hand, our pardon and the lifting of the suspension will be assured you to the extent to which you sincerely and without ambiguity undertake to fulfill the conditions of this request and to repair the scandal caused. The obedience and the trust of which you will give proof will also make it possible for us to study your personal problems serenely with you.

"May the Holy Spirit enlighten you and guide you toward the only solution that would enable you not only to rediscover the peace of your momentarily misguided conscience but also to ensure the good of souls, to contribute to the unity of the Church, which the Lord has entrusted to our charge, and to avoid the danger of a schism. In the psychological state in which you find yourself, we realize that it is difficult for you to see clearly and very hard for you humbly to change your line of conduct: is it not therefore urgent, as in all such cases, for you to arrange a time and a place of recollection which will enable you to consider the matter with the necessary objectivity? Fraternally, we put you on your guard against the pressures to which you could be exposed from those who wish to keep you in an untenable position, while we ourself, all your Brothers in the Episcopate await finally from you that ecclesial attitude which would be to your honor.

"In order to root out the abuses we all deplore and to guarantee a true spiritual renewal, as well as the courageous evangelization to which the Holy Spirit bids us, there is needed more than ever the help and commitment of the entire ecclesial community around the Pope and the Bishops. Now the revolt of one side finally teaches and risks accentuating the insubordination of what you have called the 'subversion' of the other side; while without your own insubordination, you would have been able, Brother, as you expressed in your last letter, to help us, in fidelity and under our authority, to work for the advancement of the Church.

"Therefore, dear Brother, do not delay any longer in considering before God, with the keenest religious attention, this solemn adjuration of the humble but legitimate Successor of Peter. May you measure the gravity of the hour and take the only decision that befits a son of the Church. This is our hope, this is our prayer."

Sicola's expression was grave, his jaw firmly set, and his eyes burned with the fire of his conviction. He

had come to Desfeux expecting to placate and to ca-
jole him, but directness was too ingrained in his character, the Church too important to the world, Christian and non-Christian, for him to temporize with the
whole truth and with the preservation of the Church.
Perhaps, he thought, he might have botched the
whole works by his intractability, even alienated Desfeux for good. But so be it. Whatever he said had to
be said, and the fact that what he said was not what
he had planned to say was evidence of divine inspira-
tion.

Desfeux studied his superior, and it seemed that
his expression had never changed throughout the long
peroration. He sipped the claret and rolled it on his
tongue. At length he spoke without rancor. "Holiness, how much time had you spent memorizing this
castigation of my conduct?"

"It was extemporaneous, René."

"Impossible, Holiness!"

"Why impossible, René? I do not follow you."

"Because what you have spoken is almost word
for word from the letter sent to my predecessor by
Paul VI back on 11 October, 1976. Why can you not
give me your own words?"

"If you say that the words are the same, René, I
will believe you, but you must believe also that on
that date I was an obscure monsignor with no
thoughts of the Papacy. I read the letter in *L'Osservatore Romano* only once and never picked up the letter
again. Do you suppose that there is some meaning in
this that escapes you? If you doubted the action of the
Holy Spirit in these matters, can you continue to
doubt? Is it not saying to you that truth is constant,
that what was true for Paul is equally true for us now,
here, that in this miserable instrument called Sicola

there is a voice that must be heard no matter how often it is repeated? I am as much astonished by your revelation as you are. You attribute my admonition to some unusual trick of the memory, and I tell you truthfully that I have never been marked with so keen an ability. How can you reply to this, René?"

Desfeux was silent, and the perplexity dug furrows in his brow. The two men said nothing for a very long time. Then Desfeux raised his glass to Sicola and said, "How can I reply? you ask. The only reply is in the words of Augustine . . . Rome has sent back her rescripts. The case is finished!' "

Desfeux touched Sicola's glass with his. "I submit, Holiness," he said.

Like Echoes . . .

Sicola loved children because there was so much of the child in him. He was a man of intellect, a theologian, a man versed in canon law, a Bible scholar, and a shepherd in his role as Vicar of Christ. But at heart he was a child.

He was a child in his trust. He was a child in his unquestioning love. He was a child in his submission to his Father. And he had the child's happy faculty of reducing monumental truths to simple statements. Where he lacked urbanity at times, he possessed this capability to reach into the heart of a sophisticated concept, seize its elemental truth and expose it to the view of the beholder. Some intellectuals would smile at his reduction, but the simple-hearted, the angelic spirits in the Church saw this peeling back of profound truths as itself a profundity of rare and exquisite beauty.

And this is how he viewed the disarming wisdom of children.

Now he sat in his study and recalled his visit to one of Rome's Catholic schools. Sister Perpetua had been eager for him to spend more time with the graduating students, but he could not tear himself from the small children who gathered about him, perhaps much as the untainted souls had clung to Jesus in His own day.

"You are like living angels," he had said to them. "And you are among those loved most by God. Do you know, my children, about angels? You, *figlia mia,*" he addressed a little blue-eyed girl, "what is an angel?"

"Holiness," said the child, looking up at him with open awe, "my little sister is an angel. Real angels live in the sky with God. Angels are like echoes. You can't see them, but you know they are there."

"*Mannaggia!*" Sicola grinned. "I must bring you to the Vatican to speak with our theologians. They can learn from you."

"And you, my son, can you tell me about angels?"

"Yes, Padre," replied a boy with a recalcitrant cowlick in his yellow hair. "Angels! Well, angels are just God's wings. When you say your prayers at night, the angels take them right to Jesus to save postage."

Sicola smiled broadly. "They are excellent postmen, child, are they not? And somehow the mail never gets lost. You get a good grade for your answer. And what is your view, *bambina?*" He pointed to another girl.

"An angel," she said, "is someone who flies around and has a soft voice and cries when people are bad. When Jesus sees a bad angel, it turns into a devil and starts biting people."

"Ah, yes, little turnip, you are very wise, for you recognize that there are bad angels. We must always watch for them, for they will try to make us offend God, but there will always be with you a good angel to whisper in your ear and to warn you. Listen always. . . . And you, my son, you with the freckles on your nose, what is your opinion?"

"An angel," the boy began slowly, "well, you see, an angel is . . . well, he's kind of like a spirit. He flies. And he loves you. Angels have wings and a head but no feet, because they don't have to walk. There are no angels here. I suppose they're on vacation."

"On vacation," Sicola seemed to say it sadly as he turned to Sister Perpetua with a nod. " 'Out of the mouths of babes,' does indeed come the simple truth." Then he turned to the child and said kindly, "It would seem that the angels are on vacation, but this is not so, my child. The angels are with us always. Even now one rests on your very shoulder. It is our ears that have gone on vacation, for men have become too busy to think of these angels. And they are heard only by those who think about them, you see."

He chuckled again as he sat at his desk and recalled this memory. "What a beautiful time in which to live," he thought, "when one is so pure of heart, so unsullied by the miseries, the temptations, the exposures to evil. And though it may bring excruciating pain to the heart of a loving mother or father, what a beautiful time to be taken in death. There is no palliative to parents in the death of a child, but if they could only see, only sense the happiness of a denouement that comes before its time. If they could only see that to die in such a state of purity is an *assurance* of eternal happiness denied to those of us who must fill out our appointed times.

"Ah, me! The angels seem, indeed, to be on vacation." Sicola had closed his eyes during his reverie and he seemed to watch the pictures thrust by his memory on a screen inside his eyelids. But his musings were interrupted abruptly by a blinding flash before his translucent eyelids, and he opened his eyes squinting in the effulgence of a white light that bathed him and everything about him "*O Dio!*" he cried. "What is happening?"

A voice reverberated in the room with a booming hollowness that swept him up in a wave of fear and nausea. "No-o-o-o! Not Dio . . . Bu-u-u-u-t one sent by-y-y Him!"

The brilliant luminosity in the room became slightly lessened, or his eyes became more accustomed to it, for now through squinting eyes he was able to see more clearly the vision that was a moment before only a voice. It was as if the words in the book of Daniel had come to life: "His body was like a chrysolite, his face shone like lightning, his eyes were like fiery torches, his arms and feet looked like burnished bronze, and his voice sounded like the roar of a multitude."

"Who are you?" Sicola asked amid his trembling.

"Why do you fear me, Holiness? I am the Angel of your heart's desire, him who has been with you these many years, though even you have not always heard me."

"That's ni-i-i-ce, your Brightness. But do you suppose you could turn the lights down, just a little, perhaps? And maybe you could talk more softly. Do not misunderstand, heh, heh, heh, it is a beautiful voice, so rich, so deep, so melodious. But you come on a little bit — just a little bit, mind you — you come on a little strong. Heh, heh, heh. You know what I mean? *Sotto voce . . . per piacere*, please?"

"I get carried away sometimes, Holiness. I will try. How is that? Better?"

"Much. The headache is dissipating."

"I was able to come to you as I have tried to come for these many years, Holiness, because it was as you said to the child: the Angel comes to him who thinks about angels. It is as if you left the latch out on the door of your mind."

"That is good," Sicola acquiesced, "but I am surprised at your statement, for I have always accepted the existence of angels, but it was my assumption that, in this job, it was the Holy Spirit Himself who guided me. Hence, what need had I for a guardian angel?"

"You misunderstand, Holiness. It is the Holy Spirit who infuses the *Church* with Truth, and in your function as Vicar of Christ you are indeed correct. The Holy Spirit will not permit you to err in the matter of faith and morals, as it is taught to the people of God. But in all other matters you are a man like other men, and in these instances it has been I who perch on your right shoulder, it is I who speak to you. But you are sometimes a very difficult pupil."

"How's that?" Sicola asked, surprised.

"Well, take the time when you were finally able to meet Hans Küng. You were justifiably very angry with him and had made the comment that he took too seriously the fact that his priesthood made him an *alter Christus*, another Christ. And God was amused and pleased when you referred to him as 'Christ the Küng.' That was a good one, Holiness. Did you think it up yourself, or did Tommaso give it to you?"

Sicola drooped his eyelids demurely and humbly. "It was I, your Brilliance, but it was a spur-of-the-moment intellection."

"My foot!" the Angel exploded into Sicola's quivering eardrums. "What do you think guardian angels do, anyway? It was I who whispered the words in your ear."

"I should have known, your Brightness. I am but

a receptacle into which the graces of God are poured."

"But not always, Holiness. Sometimes the receptacle has a leak in it. For example, as Küng was leaving, you gave him an episcopal blessing."

"That was wrong?"

"No, that was right. But why were you compelled to make a fist as you blessed him? And for a moment, just a fleeting moment — I wasn't certain — I could swear that, protruding from the fist was your second finger, straight and quivering, fraught with an implication that does not escape heaven. We've been around, you know."

"I did THAT? *Mannaggia!* You would have been right to punish me."

"Have you forgotten so soon, Holiness? Do you not recall that later you caught that very finger in the door of this very office, and you wore the finger in a splint for several days?"

"You did that, too?"

"None other."

"You were right to do it, then. Have I erred in other matters as well?"

"More times than I can recount, your Holiness. But it is not important to recall all of your peccadilloes at this time. But there was that other time also."

"Other time? What other time? Please do not spare me."

"Do you remember when Father Grievey used his public opinion polls to inform you that there was grave doubt concerning your wisdom, and that the only way in which you could rule the Church was through the voice of the people, making the Church thereby a democratic institution?"

"I remember it well. Who could forget the eminent sociologist, Father Greedy?"

"Grievey."

"Yes. Grievey. My memory is sometimes very fallible."

"Somehow I do not think so, Holiness. You have a way with the slip of the tongue."

"In this, too, I am guilty."

"Do not be offended, Giuseppe. Your satirical use of the *faux pas*, offhanded though it may seem, has a way of touching the truth. There are all kinds of greed, and one is that which seeks to overcome authority. Grievey devours secular truths only to vomit them up as sacred truths. It is understood in heaven that the measurement of what *is* does not qualify it to be the measurement of what *ought* to be."

"Then where was the fault, my Angel?"

"The fault, dear Sicola, was not in the judgment but in your reaction to the poll. Do you recall your message to Father Grievey? You told him, and I quote, 'It would be the wisest course for you to pulverize the poll, add warm water and mix, then pour its contents into a rubber bag attached to which is a lengthy hose, and insert such hose in your anal canal as you release its contents into your intestines.' What a coarse image!"

"Perhaps, Radiant One, I was too severe. But it seemed at the time a more eloquent way to say, 'Shove it up . . .' "

"Enough! Spare me!" the Angel interrupted. "It was better when you were more grandiose in your language."

"Then, my Guardian, I offended God?"

"Well, now, I wouldn't exactly say that. If the truth were known, He shook with laughter until the

tears came to His eyes. You do not remember the tor-
rential downpour that fell upon Chicago at the time?
It is simply that there is a right way and a wrong way
for a pope to act, Holiness, and sometime you act
more bull than pope."

"Perhaps, my Angel, now that you have made
yourself known to me, in future my ears will be more
attuned to your admonitions and advisories and I will
become better as a result."

"What a pity it would be."

"Eh?"

"What a pity it would be, I say. For one thing
you would deprive me of my fun, for I take a perverse
pleasure in slapping your wrists occasionally, gentle
as these disciplinary actions have been. You see, there
is legalism in heaven too, but there is also a twinkle in
the eye of the angels who are charged with maintaining the straight and narrow among the willing. And
you have made heaven thunder with the laughter of
its angels. There is one among us — a newer one —
who has even been known to sing out at your impetuosity, 'Atta boy, Sicola!' We have had to restrain him
while he is learning our ways, though we have secretly
joined him in laughter. There must be some dignity
among the angels, you realize, for imagine if we were
to turn this rookie loose in his present undeveloped
state, untrained and unrestrained. It would bring
havoc to the earth and consternation among the arch-
angels."

"Speaking of havoc, Messenger of the Lord, perhaps heaven should reassign some of its angels."

"Sicola!" the angel sulked. "You are not happy
with me as your guardian?"

"That is not what I meant. All I mean to say is
that many theologians are leading the world away

from a belief in you and your cohorts. Does this not imply that some of your spirits are not doing their job on these theologians?"

"It implies nothing of the sort, Holiness! Do I have to remind you that men were created with intellect and free will, and that one leads the other? The intellect can lead the will or the will can lead the intellect. And we can guide only those who signify a desire to be guided, just as your democratic states govern only with the consent of the governed. God would have it no other way, for if He had wanted to commandeer love, He could have done so long ago. But love that is freely given is true love in the divine sense. Love that is drawn by a halter is not love at all. And when men begin to deny the existence of angels, they begin to show the first signs of alienation from God Himself. To deny the messenger is to deny the message, and oftentimes the sender."

"But, my Angel, there are many good men who do not believe in you or the heavenly choir. One theologian, for example, writes brilliantly on the virgin birth and the perpetual virginity of Mary and yet ascribes the appearance of Gabriel to Mary at the Annunciation as a writer's license in order to convey the idea of her selection by God in a context that would make it believable."

"He is a schnook!"

"To pick up such a colloquialism, my Angel, it is evident that you are assigned to others whose language is even more direct than mine."

"Of course, your Holiness. There are problems of deployment in heaven also. So many angels for so many mortals. Among my charges are even some theologians. And the worst kind of theologian is the kind who is the poorest scholar. True scholars do not allow for personal feelings but only for truth, and they pursue truth so avidly as to be ruthless with their own preconceptions. Then there are those who commence with a doubt and search for any evidence to support the doubt, overlooking vital evidence that would dissipate it. So it is statements such as the one you relate to me that are made by men so filled with doubt that they are unshakable in it. We are only thankful that his doubts did not extend to the reality of Mary's virginity. But there are those, like Father Raymond Brown, who employ the same technique to demolish this sacred and revealed doctrine. Their trap is the historico-critical method, which is a convenience to the acceptance of only selected beliefs, ignoring the divine authorship of Holy Scripture. While it is true that God speaks in symbols frequently, at other times He is most clear. He was, indeed, most direct when He said as Christ, 'Do you think that I cannot appeal to my Father and He will at once send me more than twelve legions of angels?' And even Christ in His very human nature knew the presence of a guardian angel, strengthening Him.' I tell you, Sicola, he who would deny angels is a schnook!"

"There is also another word you can use, most Luminous One, in your future discussions on this subject."

"And what is that, Holiness?"

"Noodnik!"

"Ah, yes. There is something about it that rolls on the tongue, not so much in mellifluousness but in its scorn. I like it. I will remember it. Noodnik!"

The angel was gone, just as suddenly as it had appeared, and Sicola was left to himself, overcome with awe and wonderment. He wanted to be alone to contemplate the mystery of the angel's appearance, to

savor the lightness in his heart and the sense of inde-
structibility, of self-confidence and certitude. He
found himself recalling to mind the prayer of his
childhood, and a shame overcame him that he had ignored it these many years.

> "Angel of God, my Guardian dear,
> To whom God's love commits me here,
> Ever this day be at my side
> To light, to guard, to rule and guide."

And as he repeated the prayer, a wind came into
his office and rustled his papers. He smiled. "You are
quieter, at least, my friend," he murmured. "If we are
to meet again, perhaps you can come with the sound
of a gentle breeze rather than the boom of a cannon.
Yet . . . it was good to visit with you, to bring to certainty that which the Church has proclaimed in her
Councils. Was it not the Fourth Lateran Council in
1215 that decreed, 'God by His infinite power created
from the beginning of time both the spiritual and corporeal creature, namely the angelic and the mundane,
and afterwards the human, a kind of intermediate
creature composed of body and spirit'? And in 1869 it
was reaffirmed by the First Vatican Council."

At length he pressed the buzzer on his desk and
Tommaso entered the Papal Chamber.

"Yes, Holiness?" he asked.

"Sit down, Tommaso, sit down," Sicola said
quietly, as if his thoughts were far away. "Tell me, my
friend, do you believe in angels?"

Tommaso was stunned by the question. "But of
course, Holiness! I have not a doubt. Why do you
ask?"

"Never mind, Tommaso." The Pope studied his
faithful aide for a moment and the questioning frown

increased on Tommaso's face. "And what do you think of these people today who do not believe in angels?"

Tommaso exploded, "They are NOODNIKS!" Then he stopped, amazed, his expression even more quizzical. "I do not understand, Holiness. I have never used this word before. Noodnik! I do not even know what it means!"

'*Mannaggia*!" Sicola gasped. "Is it possible we have the *same* guardian angel? How does he find the time?"

"Wh--wh-a-a-a-t?" Tommaso stammered.

"It is nothing, Tommaso. Nothing. I will explain another time."

Peter's Principle

St. Peter's Basilica was resplendent. The assembled cardinals and bishops of the Church mottled the nave with magenta and white. They had come from all of the continents to meet in this inaugural Mass for Vatican Council III. Some said that the windows that were opened by Vatican II would be as nothing compared to the results of this Council's work. Now the doors would be battered down, for nothing would stem the tide of true unity. Even Hare Krishna would be represented in this pulsating surge of ecumenical oneness.

Others were not so sure. Since Good Pope John had opened his can of worms all sorts of wriggling had taken place, and the talk was that this Pope said that the worms were just snakes with stunted growth, and the time to step on them was now before the worms became adders whose stings would bring paralysis, even death.

The beginning of the Mass went well. Piety exuded from the lutes, the guitars, the tambourines, and even from that great obsolete instrument, the pipe organ. It was observed, ruefully by some, that when the organ roared, the lutes and guitars could be heard no longer. Some others smiled and found in this a hidden meaning.

After the Entrance Song and the Greeting, the celebrant reminded the regional shepherds that they, too, could sin. "My brothers," he droned, "to prepare ourselves to celebrate the sacred mysteries, let us call to mind our sins."

In unison all heads dropped downward in contemplation, as if the celebrant had pressed a button marked, "Release flaps." Some of the assembled leaders still bore on their faces the childlike simplicity of the angels, and their momentary meditation filled them with humility and a sense of unworthiness before the mystery of the Eucharist. Some thought ahead to the agenda, to the intrigues and machinations that would have to be employed in the service of the faithful. Some, like their own parishioners at home, merely stood blankly indifferent, with no thoughts at all to disturb their resignation, their habituated presence, enforced first by parents and later reinforced by their obligation. These were the souls so tepid as to represent the real tragedy of Christ's expiation. And they were legion, in the sanctuary and in the pews. Like the electorate in a great democracy, it was they who allowed the worst to usurp the best. And it was their cry that bleated constantly: "I am a Catholic!" or "I am an American!" and both were spoken with the false pride of the hypocrite who does not even recognize his hypocrisy because apathy blinds him so.

The great ringing beauty of the Gloria swelled the nave with a thunderous exclamation point that capped the Church's latent but true unity in the face of internecine warfare. It was like the poet's "anchor to wind'ard," keeping the buffeting winds from capsizing the bark. And as the winds howled and the waves licked venomously at her sides, threatening to overturn her, there was that humble reassurance: "You alone are the Most High, Jesus Christ, with the Holy Spirit, in the Glory of God the Father. Amen."

The celebrant read the Opening Prayer, and as he did so the lector moved silently and gracefully to the lectern. The Pope, successor to Peter, sat at the high altar as the lector read the reading from the Second Letter of Peter, chapter 2:

> "There were false prophets, too, among God's people. So, among you, there will be false teachers, covertly introducing pernicious ways of thought, and denying the Master who redeemed them, to their own speedy undoing. Many will embrace their wanton creeds, and bring the way of truth into disrepute, trading on your credulity with lying stories for their own ends. Long since, the warrant for their doom is in full vigor; destruction is on the watch for them. God did not spare the angels who fell into sin; he thrust them down to hell, chained them there in the abyss, to await their sentence in torment. . . ."

The reading continued as the lector, puzzled by the selection on so great an occasion, read haltingly and with embarrassment. The prelates buzzed in consternation, asking one another, "Whose selection was this?" Another alluded to Sicola as "That clown!" The din grew so large as to make hearing difficult, but on no one was lost the final lines, ". . . What has happened to them proves the truth of the proverb, The dog is back at his own vomit again. Wash the sow, and you find her wallowing in the mire."

It was said that this Pope would do anything for a joke. Even his orthodoxy was unorthodox, but never had he dared to confront the princes of the

Church with the implication in this reading, a reading nowhere to be found in the Lectionary.

Then there followed the Responsorial Psalm, and the chattering dissipated into the unanimity of the responses. The Alleluia was recited, and it was followed by "My sheep listen to my voice, says the Lord; I know them and they follow me." Now there was no surprised grumbling, merely gasps and arched eyebrows.

All stood for the Gospel reading, and there was an air of expectant inevitability in the great church as the Pope came to the pulpit and his announcement echoed through the room, "Matthew, chapter 16, verses 13-19." He stood for a moment, looked owlishly at the cardinals and bishops, and finally began:

> "Then Jesus came into the neighborhood of Caesarea Philippi; and there he asked his disciples, What do men say of the Son of Man? Who do they think he is? 'Some say John the Baptist,' they told him, others Elijah, others again, Jeremiah or one of the prophets.' Jesus said to them, And what of you? Who do you say that I am? Then Simon Peter answered, 'You are the Christ, the Son of the living God.' And Jesus answered him, 'Blessed are you, Simon son of Jonah; it is not flesh and blood but my Father in heaven who has revealed this to you. And I tell you this in my turn, that *you are Peter, and it is upon this rock that I will build my Church; and the gates of hell shall not prevail against it; and I will give you the keys of the kingdom of heaven; and whatever you shall bind on earth shall be bound in heaven, and whatever you shall loose on earth shall be loosed in heaven.'* "

The Pope read the last part of the Gospel with slow deliberateness at first, then the emphasis became more strident as his voice grew in intensity and fervor. It all began to fit neatly now into the minds of the prelates. Sicola was indeed setting the tone for the Council through the very sacredness of the Mass. This was a buffoon to be reckoned with. "But we shall see," some of them thought, "who shall get the last licks."

"This is the Gospel of the Lord," the Pope said in Italian.

"Praise to you, Lord Jesus Christ," they intoned.

Then they sat for the homily, some uneasily, some with unctuous satisfaction, some with set jaws.

The Holy Father greeted his princes, then began, "My sons, we are pleased to welcome you to the beginning of a new era in the Church. It was only yesterday, it seems, that the holy Pope John welcomed you to Rome with great hopes for a modernization of the Church, and it was within so short a time also that Pope Paul bade you farewell after your deliberations. There were tears in this suffering man's eyes as he blessed you and sent you home to your own countries. At that time we sat among you and wondered about these tears. Were they of joy for the work you had done? Were they of sorrow to see leaving him so many of his very good friends? We did not know then. But today we know. Yes, my sons, today we know! One has to ride the camel to understand his gait.

"So today we also greet you. We ask you to look closely into these eyes, and remember well what you see. If you do not understand what you see, we promise you that before you leave Rome you will understand.

"But enough of cryptic speech. It is for the blessing of Almighty God on you for the work you are about to undertake that we come to you."

Then he raised his right hand above his mitred head and slowly made a sweeping sign of the cross over them, reciting the benediction in Latin: "*In nomine patris, et filii, et spiritus sancti.* Amen."

The Mass ended, and the Fathers filed out of the great church in procession to the Council Room where Monsignor Calucci was finishing his chores, setting pads and pencils before each chair.

When they had reassembled, Cardinal von Tuebingen rapped his gavel for order and the room grew quiet except for an occasional scraping of chairs. He addressed them in formal tones and announced that he would proceed to read the agenda and fill in briefly some of the areas for consideration under each point. They were invited to follow along with the printed agenda before them and to make marginal notes of his suggestions for broadening these points.

One of the areas to be explored, he said, was the ordination of women priests, and if it was so agreed, then it followed that they should wear trousers, (1) so as not to distract the laity, and (2) to mark the symbolism of their complete integration into the priesthood, which would no longer have a gender. There was a nodding of heads as if these suggestions were indeed sensible.

A further area of discussion would center on the new theology, or if one took exception to the term as being disrespectful to theologians of the "Old Church," then some other name could be devised, such as "The Evolving Theology of Christianity." Perhaps, he remarked, it would be necessary to start such a chapter with a debate on whether or not Christ knew who He was, for recent thinking indicated that if He was truly aware of His godhead, then suffering would have been impossible for Him. Knowing that He suffered greatly leads one to the critical assumption that Christ was completely ignorant of His divinity.

Again there were gestures of approval as affirmations ranged from "Ja" to "Si." In the back of the room a weak voice piped out, "No!" but little attention was paid to it.

The third area for discussion, the Cardinal continued, was the need for the Catholic Church to recognize that pluralism of religion — now an accepted fact — extended to pluralism in political affairs, and hence, was it not time now to put an end to our traditional enmity with the Russians, to embrace them and their leaders as children of God, co-equal with us in His love? Care must be taken to discard the notions of men like Solzhenitsyn who speak from a point of view of impractical idealism. As America pursues détente, so also must the Church take great pains to avoid giving offense to those in the Kremlin and in fact to join with them in their efforts to lift up the masses. Was that not what Christ spoke of? What He died for?

There were heard a few bravos and general applause at these statements. Again there was the weak dissenting voice in the rear. But the Cardinal was beginning to warm to his own prophetic leadership of the Council.

Then, he went on, the time had come to deal — once and for all — with the myth of transubstantiation. Must we not face reality squarely in the face, he said, that this had been a tool in the hands of Holy Mother Church to hypnotize the laity. A practical person can see that bread is bread and wine is wine and never the twain shall meet. Was it not sufficient for the people to see this for what it is: a mere symbolic reenactment of the Last Supper, having no mystery, no profundity, no miraculous nature?

Approval was now becoming routine, hence silence gave assent, but the weak voice in the rear was made louder by the silence: "No . . . No . . . No!"

Moderately disturbed, the Cardinal merely peered over his glasses at the lone dissident and continued. It seemed, he said, that Vatican III should lay to rest whatever reverence for the Mother of Christ that was allowed after Vatican II. She was, indeed, a good woman, but she had a penchant for popping up in the lives of the devout with such unbelievable frequency that one began to wonder if, like beauty, she wasn't simply in the eye of the beholder. "I ask you," he addressed the group facetiously, "You are princes of the Church. Have *you* ever seen her? Yet she is reported to come to children and to peasants! Does this not strike you as ridiculous?" There was great laughter, and as it subsided, the weak voice shouted, "Hola da phone!" Then there were only muffled sounds coming from his direction, almost as if someone had clapped a hand across his mouth. There were the sounds of a scuffle, the sliding of chairs, then the man broke loose and strode toward von Tuebingen.

There was about him a kind of majestic air, even with the troubled, angry expression on his face. His beard was a soft brown, like the flowing hair that descended to his shoulders. His soutane, unlike that of the Fathers, was white and as the light struck it he seemed to be surrounded by a glow. Only the Pope wore white, but this was not the Pope. Interloper or priest, he was subverting the consistory.

He was tall and lean, and his strides were long,

determined, swift. He arrived at the lectern and gave
von Tuebingen a gentle shove. The touch was the
merest brush of the hand, but the great Cardinal
found himself thrust to the floor with a thud. He sat
there with his hands on the floor behind him, his legs
straddled, and his jaws agape in consternation. The
intruder made no move to help him to his feet.

He needed no microphone as he addressed the
stupefied Fathers, for his voice had a power and a
ringing strength that filled the whole room. "You
are," he began, "full of the sounds of yourselves, but
your sounds are the sounds of flatulence that give
relief only to the colon and not to the whole of your
body. You have been so inured to the ideal of democratic processes that you lose sight of the fact that you
will not be voted into eternity. It has come to this
through some fault of your own, but through a
greater fault of mine, for I have given you your head
and you believed it to be greater than the Head of the
Church. You have believed falsely that you could
supplant the autocracy of the Church with the democracy of idiots, that the Holy Spirit spoke to you to the
exclusion of Peter."

As he spoke, he tugged at his beard and it became separated from his face. He placed his hand at
the widow's peak of the long, flowing brown hair and
removed it from his head. He stood before them . . .
the Pope.

The Fathers began to mutter at this sudden revelation by that comic Sicola, but there was an ear-
nestness, a seriousness in his manner that seemed to
preclude the possibility of any kind of angry demonstration. The surprise turned to respect, awe, intent
concentration on his words.

"Your inanities today were not unexpected," he

continued. "But I intend no point-by-point rebuttal to the pubescent rantings taking place among you. That rebuttal will appear elsewhere this day. But my dismay at your logic will be summed up in one counterpoint only. In your modernism you have imputed ignorance to Christ, preferring to see Him as an automaton of His Father, splitting asunder the Trinity into parts having no identity to the whole. It is thus, my sons:

"I am I and I am he at one and the same time. You say, 'Who is the Pope?' And I say, 'It is I.' Hence I am I.

"You say to your neighbor sitting beside you now, 'Who is the Pope?' and he points to me and says, 'It is he.'

"Now I ask you, are we not one and the same? And do I not know that I am both I and he? If you prick my finger, it is I who squeals, and your neighbor will confirm that 'he' is in pain. Amen, amen, I say to you: Do not hand me this baloney!"

There was not so much as a murmur in the great hall. In the eyes of many there shone the tears of men who had awaited the firmness of their father. In the eyes of the indolent there was a new fire, a new excitement; in the eyes of the dissident, a tired resignation.

"You have toyed with transubstantiation and with the co-redemptrix of us all, the Holy Mother. Up to that point, I was prepared to permit you freedom in the playground of theology. But now I say to you that your part in Vatican III has ended and my part begins.

"Go home!"

The prelates meekly, with great decorum and humility, filed out of the hall. Outside the huge rococo structure they turned, as the Holy Father followed them, stood before them for a moment, then wheeled about to close the great double door. As he closed the door, the Fathers noted a large parchment scroll nailed to the outer face of the door. The breeze whipped at the corners of the scroll, but it remained flat and undisturbed. The smaller print was not legible from a distance, but clearly visible to all, in large cursive letters, were the words: *"The Ninety-Five Theses of His Holiness Innocent XIV, Pope Sicola."*

The new era had begun.

The Synod

Sicola studied the young man beside him. His intense manner of speaking, his creased forehead, his gesticulating arms underscored his commitment with genuine animation. Why, he wondered, was evangelism in the name of communism so starkly contrasted to Christian evangelism, which dwelt — among the rank and file — so singularly on quiet, pious example without the force of declamation? Here he was, this totally committed youth, full of rhetoric, employing all of his guile and salesmanship in suasion with the unashamed purpose of conversion.

How stupid we are, the Pope thought. If communism waited for mass conversions to take place solely as the result of the quiet example of its adherents, its rally halls would be empty. Yet we, assuming missionary zeal to be the badge of the fanatic cultist, swim lazily in the pool of pluralism. The communist swims upstream, never arriving at the source but making headway all the same, while we float downstream riding the currents that lead to empty churches, or worse, churches trapped in the eddying whirlpools of pluralistic dissension. Possessing but one theology, we cry, "There are many theologies."

He had given in to his advisors in this matter of "Christian-Communist dialogue and cooperation," had interrupted his meeting at the synod of bishops and agreed to meet with the Russian zealot, but he was unprepared for such a frontal attack as he was now receiving. One would think that such heated oratory heaped upon his pontifical ears would cause them to shrivel and block his ear canals in defense against such foolish braying. But the ears were designed by God for hearing, and presbycusis not yet having set in, there was no choice but to listen.

Yevgeny Surov was warming to his role as trumpet of the Kremlin in the Vatican. How many of his comrades would have traded places with him! But this was his plum and his alone, and when he returned to Moscow it would be his proud boast that he had brought Sicola to his knees, penitent for his stupidity and pleading to worship at a new altar over which was suspended the Red Star instead of the crucified Christ. Imagine his glory — to have converted the Pope himself!

"The Jesuit order is, as Marx put it," he railed (quoting comrade Igor Bonchkovsky's classic article in *Trud*) "the 'litmus paper' of the Catholic Church. Watch what is happening among the Jesuits and you have an idea of what is happening in the whole Roman Church today and what awaits it tomorrow. The Roman Church is sick," Surov fairly shrieked, "and the order founded by Ignatius Loyola as a faithful and obedient servant of the Papacy has now become the focal point of the opposition within the Church."

Sicola folded the fingers of both hands together and spread them across his abdomen in a restful pose. A pose indeed, for inwardly he smarted at the biting truth of Surov's words.

"The Jesuits have always been," he returned,

"close to the heart of the Church. Transgressions in their ranks will be dealt with internally and in due course. We hold many of them in high esteem, and be assured that the deviations of the lesser figures do not go unnoticed."

"Deviations?" Surov exploded. "There is dissension among them, political and theological opposition, conflicting attitudes to discipline, criticism of the missionary tradition, growing trends toward secularization of the religious life — all this has in the past decade eroded the order's former solid unity and effectiveness. And you call them 'deviations'?"

"True," Sicola interposed, "we have allowed them some latitude."

"Hah!" Surov laughed, "the Society of Jesus has long allowed its members a comparative freedom of views and expression. For instance, the General — what is his name? Father Pedro Arrupe — himself set an example years ago when he visited the rebel Father Berrigan in prison, thereby giving his Society's blessing to young Americans who violently opposed their country's military policy."

"That was a work of mercy, not a political gesture."

"Reading of atheist authors is allowed in all Jesuit schools, and there is sanction for the study of Marxism in the seminaries. Since 1969 the Papal Gregorian University has had a 'Center of Marxist Studies' which trains experts in Marxism and scientific atheism."

"Very interesting," Sicola commented. "I was not aware that you knew so much of our house by observing our laundry."

"And, my pigeon, I know more, much more. I know of a letter written to one of your predecessors and to the Cardinals Dell'Acqua and Alfrink that begins, 'Now that I am no longer a believer. . . .' Those words are from the letter of a man who attained high rank in the Jesuit order and served Christ faithfully all his life. You know his name, as I do — the Reverend Schoenberger — and he was one of the foremost spiritual leaders of the Jesuit youth. Soon he left the order. The number of younger men in it, he said, is shrinking fast. The youth feel that its day is over.

"And there are others. Father Vrijburg, the confessor of Amsterdam students, broke the Catholic priest's vow of celibacy and married, an action excused by the Jesuit Fathers Oosterhuis and Van der Stap who defended him before the hierarchy. There are many more. But the point is, sir, that more and more members of the order question 'indisputable' tenets of the Church.

"One of your own high-ranking Jesuits has stated, 'We have caught the disease we set out to cure.' Evidently some Jesuits are not too convinced that modern man must at all costs have the Word of God preached to him."

Sicola closed his eyes and seemed to slump in his chair. It was as if this assault, verbal as it was, had showered blows about his head and body so as to drain him of strength, even the will to fight. And in his fatigue there was a paralysis that gripped him. He was unable to speak, and if he had the power no words were framed in his mind to be transmitted to the tongue. Instead, brief pictures seemed to flash across his mind. He felt the weight of the log on Christ's back as the Roman soldier prodded Him and leered, "Carry it!" Then came the first fall, when the cross assumed a weight far beyond its volume and dimensions as it absorbed the sin of man. No man could have carried it, as no man can carry the burden of all the centuries of sin and guilt and indifference. In this agony He was man, for the law of expiation required that only man could suffer for man. But He was God in His sorrow, God in His love, God in His forgiveness. Yet it was the man, Jesus, who was at that moment creating not merely salvation, but the Way, the one Way, to sanctity. It was through immolation, total, self-abnegating, God-centered. And as the cross bent Him low, He dropped to one knee to stave off prostrate collapse. His head turned upward and the blood from the thorns in His head trickled down his forehead and into His eyes, creating a specter of bloodshot misery. He stared, it seemed, into the very eyes of Sicola with pleading. And in the distant corners of his brain at this very instant, Sicola heard the voice of a woman echoing through the years from a little Portuguese village: "The Holy Father will suffer much," she had said. The image flickered and disappeared, and there was silence in the corridors of his brain once again.

He opened his eyes, and the Russian peered at him with that intense commitment. "Can't you see, sir, that you are losing. Tomorrow it will be all over, and you will have lost. The Church will be ours. Come *now*, and we will make a place for you. You will still have your priests and your nuns, though they will be one with the state, as you will be one with us. Nothing can rescue you, for beyond life there is nothing; therefore, you wait for nothing."

Sicola stirred as he felt the searing heat of a great fireball turning in his stomach. Its heat spread to his whole body, and his head grew fevered. He rose to his feet slowly at first, then with a great lurch as he raised a crozier above his head in both hands.

"Demon . . . go to hell! I will not join you. We will not join you. And we will defeat you.

"As you talked I envied your distorted evangelism, and I wished that our people were as dedicated to Christ as you are to Satan. But you, sir, lack our weapons."

Startled by the sudden electric vitality of a man who only moments before seemed stupefied and vanquished, the Russian muttered, "Weapons? Weapons? How many legions do you command? You have no weapon against us."

"Ah, yes, Beelzebub, we do. You cannot pray, for to whom would you pray? To Lucifer? There is more power in the single invocation of the Name of Jesus than in all of your oratory. There is more power in one Mass, one rosary, one act of penance, one holy hour than in your legions."

"Mere prejudices," Surov smiled, "for as Stalin declared, 'We carry on and will continue to carry on propaganda against religious prejudices . . . the Party cannot be neutral toward religious prejudices, and it will continue to carry on propaganda against these prejudices because this is one of the best means of undermining the influence of the reactionary clergy. Have we suppressed the reactionary clergy? Yes, we have. The unfortunate thing is that it has not been completely liquidated.' And our Mr. Khrushchev carried these words further still when he said, 'Those who believe in God are becoming fewer and fewer. Young people are growing up, and they in their overwhelming majority do not believe in God. Public education, the dissemination of scientific knowledge, and the study of the laws of nature leave no place for belief in God.' Are not the words of these great men being brought to life in our own times? You cannot resist longer."

"We will resist," Sicola said angrily. "We will resist until the end of time. Though our ranks become thinned, decimated, we will resist, and in the end I promise you that the Church will not be yours but you will be ours. It is to this end that we will pray. So for now, sir, this interview is terminated. It is ours and yours to await the hand of God, a wave of which is more potent than all of your fulminations. Go. I have God's work to do."

Yevgeny Surov smiled as he turned from Sicola. He had not won the victory he had planned, but there would be another day. It was plain to see that the Pope had been shaken, that he was frightened, and that his very intelligence would force him to see the futility of resisting the flow of his times.

Sicola turned to Tommaso, who had remained silent throughout the discussion. "Again I see the truth in our son Fulton Sheen's observation that 'an atheist is a man without any invisible means of support.' Come, Tommaso, we go to meet with the bishops."

Sicola arrived in the great assembly hall where the prelates of the synod had gathered to discuss their topic, "The Survival of the Church in the Modern World." The bishops stood as the Pontiff entered and strode toward the high-backed chair from which he presided over their deliberations. Instead of seating himself, however, he remained standing before them and extended his arms in a pressing downward motion inviting them to take their seats.

There was a rustling and a clearing of throats as the shepherds took their seats awaiting the words of the Vicar of Christ.

"The topic of this synod is most timely," he began, "for never in the history of the Church has survival been so endangered as today. We look at our children of all ages and see the gleam of hedonism in their eyes. All is the pursuit of pleasure, pleasure that satisfies only the flesh, while the soul dies a fraction at a time from starvation. Our educational systems no longer teach of values, for the question is asked, 'Whose values?' forgetting that all values have their origins in God. Science tells them that nature is amoral, so that all actions that are 'natural' are therefore neither moral nor immoral. All that matters is that one be permitted freedom, total and complete, to operate within the *new* natural law. Among those few who still profess a belief in God there is the ever-present image of a God who is all-loving, all-understanding, all-permissive. That they misunderstand the nature of God's love is evident, but there is something to be learned from their vapid theology. To them God is such manifest love that they see themselves solely as the repository of love, solely as the vessel into which love will be poured by God, and never as the vessel of love that will be poured from themselves into God.

"Many of our priests have encouraged this error, for they have been in the forefront of the teaching legionnaries of self-indulgence. And this is really the disease of the Church. For many years we have heard that the defections and false pedagogy of priests have been the result of an ideological spearhead thrust at the heart of the Church from the Kremlin. Until now, we have discounted these accusations as groundless, undocumented hearsay. But no longer.

"This very day we have talked with an emissary of the Red motherland whose words left nothing to the imagination. Gone is the moment of challenge. The challenge was thrown at the doorstep of the Church long ago and we did not then pick up the gauntlet. Now is the moment of survival. All measures to now have failed, and therefore it is time for actions too long delayed, since the threat of Russia is not an idle boast. It is very real, so real that given the present direction of the world and the Church we will be Russian in a very, very short time.

" 'How is it possible,' Pius XI asked, 'that such a system, long since rejected scientifically and now proved erroneous by experience — how is it, we ask, that such a system could spread so rapidly in all parts of the world? The explanation lies in the fact that too few have been able to grasp the nature of Communism. The majority instead succumb to its deceptions, skillfully concealed by the most extravagant promises.'

"And these promises have reached into the very imagination of our children, lay and religious, exciting them with false hope, stimulating them to preach a social gospel as they see it, frequently even when it is not in conformity with the Church, which has preached true social justice since the time of Christ.

"And who is it that titillates the imagination of our people, who is it that has within its power the control of the minds of our children with one-sided ideas, many of which defy the magisterium? It is the Catholic press of the world — which remains Catholic in name only, but which rides in the saddle imprinted 'Made in Moscow.' What malaise makes them so susceptible to this fever of excitement but the promises of Satan for a better world without authority, as if there were no inconsistency in such a dream. That malaise, my brothers, is the malaise of communism, which strikes at the lesser organs of the Church first and thence spreads to its vital organs as it does now.

"You have doubts? See how the Catholic press controls the mind of our people with its red-tainted doctrines. The *New Catholic World* is a Paulist publication in America and therefore Catholic. But how Catholic? Would one expect, for example, to find Karl Marx's photograph substituted for Christ on the cross hanging over a high altar to illustrate an article in a Catholic magazine? Yet that is how the editors once chose to illustrate an essay titled, 'Marxism Deserves a Catholic Hearing,' by one Joseph Holland. If the Catholic layman had not been informed that the Church condemns Marxism, how would we know from that article, which testified that the Church 'might be enriched by input from Marxian resources,' or that a Marxist 'analysis of capitalism and of class exploitation might help bring solidarity to the distinct U.S. social struggles.'

"The magazine identified the author as a member of the Center for Concern, but it did not say this group was a Catholic leftist organization specializing in promoting women's ordination to the priesthood, the 'relevance of Marx and socialism to the demand for social justice' and activities of the radical People's Bicentennial Commission. And where did it get part of its finances? From the Rockefeller Foundation, the Rockefeller Brothers Fund and International Planned Parenthood — a prime mover behind the anti-life, pro-abortion movement.

"Another magazine, *U.S. Catholic,* heaped further confusion in the minds of the uninstructed by the dissemination of material saying, 'The philosopher Michael Tooley argues that infanticide is morally acceptable for a short time after birth,' and adding that 'Joseph Fletcher, the theologian, takes the position that active euthanasia on a person of any age can be justified.'

"And who, my brothers, was Joseph Fletcher? This perverter of the moral code was serving on the board of the Euthanasia Education Council; he had been affiliated with organizations having a friendly attitude toward the Soviet Union, namely The American Council on Soviet Relations, World Peace Congress, National Committee to Abolish the House Committee on UnAmerican Activities, Victory Committee for Harry Bridges (an identified Communist boss of the U.S. west coast Longshoremen's Union, expelled from the CIO in 1950 for Red domination).

"Most of all, 'theologian' Joseph Fletcher was renowned as the author of *Situation Ethics: the New Morality,* which contended that any act — including lying, premarital sex, abortion, adultery or murder — could be justified depending on the situation. Its message was that 'whatever is the most loving thing in the situation is the right and good thing.'

"In another issue of its magazine, this same *U.S. Catholic,* still adhering to its Fletcherian ethics, asked the question of Euthanasia: 'Can my conscience be my guide?' And their answer was, 'Yes!' 'Catholics have been confused on this key point' that 'dictates of conscience are the ultimate guide.' And, in the same issue, there was an article, 'Abortion: The Moment of Truth.' Let me read from it: 'The ultimate decision to carry a child or to abort it still rests with the woman's awareness of what abortion is and does.' And whom does the author of this article cite as her authority? Paragon of paragons, Joseph Fletcher, preacher of modern-day moral anarchism, by whose standards Adolf Hitler did 'the most loving thing' when he had exterminated millions of Jews in order to preserve the 'master race.'

"And, my brothers, another example. The *Na-*

tional Catholic Reporter, which had in the past suggested that the Pope get off its back, lent credibility to the suspicion of Red influence when it said, 'Much liberation theology employs Marxist thought and concludes that American economic imperialism is the primary cause of oppression and poverty in Latin America. . . . Marxism is not intrinsically atheistic . . . [it] traces back to Frederick Engels.' Students read the authority and reliability of the Church in those statements because they appeared in a Catholic periodical.

"There is much that the Church has failed to do to excise this cancer in its incipient stage — this cancer of communism, which so subtly attaches itself to the entrails of society and the Church. *Mea culpa!* But there is still time. There is time for action: a time when Catholic leaders can exercise their authority by removing from editorial responsibility those journalists who do not conform to the teaching voice of the Church. But there is another solution also, one too long ignored.

"The Mother of God has requested that Russia be consecrated to her Immaculate Heart. Pius XII, fearful perhaps of diplomatic nuances, refrained from naming Russia and instead consecrated the *world* to Our Lady. But this was *not* what she asked, and later pontiffs failed to carry out her wish. We have vacillated too long. The time has come, no, it has passed, but perhaps in her maternal heart there will still be room for compassion. Russia must be converted! Now! My brothers, rise and say after me the following words:

"Almighty God, You who have been affronted by our indifference, soften your view of our weakness and withhold your anger. We follow the example of our beloved predecessor and, once again, consecrate the entire world to Mary, Your Mother, to signify that we are all children of the one Mother and the one God, triune in nature. But — specifically — we commit, turn over, and consecrate to the Immaculate Heart of Mary . . . the SOVIET UNION. Deal with her kindly, for her children have suffered for too long, cloaking in secrecy their filial devotion to the heart of Mary and the heart of Jesus. Mary, Mother of God, into your hands we entrust the soul of Russia."

The prelates began weakly at first, but as Sicola's fervor manifested itself more intensely, the bishops and cardinals spoke in voices increasingly loud and determined. Even those who had been known as favoring close alliances with the Soviet Union saw in this the fulfillment of their wishes. When Sicola had finished, there was a hush in the great room as he stood before the princes of the Church, his head bowed, his shoulders slumping in abject submission and fatigue.

Then Sicola raised his head and looked up at the enormous ceiling and beyond it and his voice boomed through the hall as he recited from memory a former Holy Father's Marian Year Prayer: "Enraptured by the splendor of your heavenly beauty, and impelled by the anxieties of the world, we cast ourselves into your arms, O Immaculate Mother of Jesus and our Mother, Mary, confident of finding in your most loving heart appeasement of our ardent desires, and a safe harbor from the tempests that beset us on every side. Though degraded by our faults and overwhelmed by infinite misery, we admire and praise the peerless richness of sublime gifts with which God has filled you, above every other mere creature, from the first moment of your conception until the day on which, after your Assumption into Heaven, He crowned you Queen of the Universe.

"O crystal fountain of faith, bathe our minds with the eternal truths! O fragrant lily of all holiness, captivate our hearts with your heavenly perfume! O victress over evil and death, inspire in us a deep horror of sin, which makes the soul detestable to God and a slave to hell!

"O well-beloved of God, hear the ardent cry that rises up from every heart in this year dedicated to you. Bend tenderly over our aching wounds. Convert the wicked, dry the tears of the afflicted and oppressed, comfort the poor and humble, quench hatreds, sweeten harshness, safeguard the flower of purity in youth, protect the holy Church, make all men feel the attraction of Christian goodness.

"In your name, resounding harmoniously in heaven, may they recognize that they are brothers, and that the nations are members of one family, upon which may there shine forth the sun of a universal and sincere peace.

"Receive, O sweet Mother, our humble supplications, and above all obtain for us that one day, happy with you, we may repeat before your throne that hymn which today is sung on earth around your altars: You are all beautiful, O Mary! You are the glory, you are the joy, you are the honor of our people! Amen."

Sicola returned to his chambers and stood before the French doors that looked out upon St. Peter's Square, and as he surveyed the piazza below him he saw a tiny figure of a man parading across the stones and coming in his direction, finally becoming discernible. "Surov!" he muttered. "You never give up. Even now, like a labor picket, you carry the red flag at the very door of the Church."

Comrade Surov walked toward Sicola's apartment window and a gust of wind picked at the flag and spread it out so that Sicola could see the Russian emblem rippling on its red field. But now, strangely, it seemed different, for upon the sickle was impaled a crucifix.

Sicola returned to his desk. "*Grazie, Madre mia*," he said. "*Grazie!*"

"*If my people, which are called by name, shall humble themselves and pray and seek my face and turn from their wicked ways, then will I hear from heaven and forgive their sin and heal their land*" (*II Chronicles 7:14*).

Parousia

Sicola sat at his desk in the Vatican and looked down at the floor by his side where the wastebasket was full of false starts. This was to be one of the most important encyclicals of his reign, and he wanted it to combine all of the proper elements of theology and holiness. But somehow it wasn't coming.

Why, he asked himself, was this so difficult? Some of the Protestant denominations had been dealing with the Second Coming of Christ for more than a century. Their predictions, like the reports of Mark Twain's death, had been greatly exaggerated. And was this not, after all, the whole point of his letter, that no one would know the time or the place, but that one should be ready as if this were indeed the time? Certainly the times were ripe for His coming. The world was in a fervor of torment and rebellion. Morality was at a low that rivaled the perversity of the Israelites in the desert. As Moses had been questioned and attacked, so were the institutions of authority — including his own — similarly threatened. There was a hopelessness in the world's atmosphere that pervaded the Vatican itself, almost as if the return of man was beyond the frail coping of mere men like him. It would certainly require only God Himself intervening out of disgust and chagrin, or a love so manifest as to repeat the incarnation of His Son.

Sicola was embroiled in his own despair, and he looked up at the high ceiling of his office as tiny beads of perspiration formed and glistened on his brow. "Lord, Jesus Christ, Son of God, have mercy on me!" he prayed. Then he repeated it countless times in a rhythm that matched his inhaling and exhaling. "Lord, Jesus Christ . . . have mercy on me!" Then he laid his head on his arms folded across the desk, and his white zucchetto slipped off his head to the desk top. He remained like this for a very long time, repeating the invocation over and over.

At length he sat back in his chair with a slump of despair and fatigue, his eyes closed and his head tilted back on the high support in repose. He remained inert for many minutes, then slowly his eyes opened, first in sleepy slits, then as he saw the outline of a man before his desk, they opened wide, and he sprang to his feet. The man was wearing Sicola's zuchetto, and he smiled with a radiance and warmth that made Sicola tingle with new life.

The man was tall and youthful, not a boy by any means, but a strikingly handsome young man dressed in worn khaki with his collar open. His hair was sandy and full, but not long. His face was tanned, and pleasant lines like sunbursts shot from the corners of his eyes. The nose, Sicola wondered, is it Semitic or Roman? One could not tell.

The Pope was aware of a sweet, musky odor in his nostrils, but he gave it little attention as he said, "You walk with the stealth of a cat, my young friend. How did you come to be in my office unnoticed by Tommaso? And, my friend, you are wearing my zucchetto. You wish my job, perhaps? In these days I would willingly surrender it. But come, now, do not remain there smiling at me with so enigmatic an expression. Who are you? What is it you want?

Sicola now became acutely conscious of the man's eyes, brown and piercing, with an openness above them and under the fine eyebrows. It was as if he would sear the very heart of Sicola with a look so direct and devoid of self-consciousness as to create a sense of strong attraction to him. "Giuseppe, My trusted one," he began, "it does not surprise me that even you would not know the Son of Man when His time has come to be with you."

Sicola laughed and said, "Tommaso and his jokes! He knew of my difficulty with this letter to the People of God. But is this not going too far, even for him? Blasphemy is not in such a man as Tommaso. But this! Come, my man, perhaps you have come to repair the chair yonder. Do so and present your bill to Tommaso." Sicola glanced over at the corner of his office where Cardinal Bacciagalupe, the round one, had crushed the chair beneath his two hundred and fifty pounds. The chair stood mended and erect. Only a few moments before he had looked at it and grimaced as he thought of Bacciagalupe and his fondness for Italian pastries. Sicola looked in amazement at the chair, then at the young man.

"I could not have slept," he muttered, "and even if I had, the sound of your work would have awakened me. The chair? You have a magic wand? Lend it to me that I may perform my duties with greater ease."

"Yes, Giuseppe," the man continued, "the chair is repaired. It is time now to give new support and strength to your Chair. This is why I have come."

"You call me Giuseppe, rather than Holiness, and you speak of mending my chair. It is too much for the brain of one so besieged by the problems of the world. Please . . . please to tell me *plainly* who you are."

"It was said two thousand years ago, Giuseppe, that I did not speak plainly, and the problem remains. I speak so that all can understand, but the minds of men have been clouded by thoughts fixed on earth. No one understood then, and you do not understand now. I have come, Giuseppe. I have come."

Sicola's mind began to grasp the reality of what seemed so unreal. The world had waited and known with certainty that He would come, just as Israel had known in another day that He would be the Messiah, but the actual advent was such as to boggle the mind. Although Sicola began to understand, it did not lessen his surprise. "Oh, my God!" he blurted out, more as an ejaculation of astonishment than of fealty.

"Si!" the stranger said. "Now sit and let us talk as friends."

Sicola slumped down in the soft high-backed chair, overcome with awe at what was taking place before him. Then, realizing that his posture might be disrespectful, he sat upright. "My Lord, this is too much for me to assimilate. There is within me a sense of pleasure that is indescribable, as if the joy of Your nearness is so great that it cannot be contained. Yet there is within me also this very great fear. Is it all to come to an end now, my Lord? This is what frightens me."

"There is no end, Giuseppe. Only an end of time. And soon there will be an end of time, but for some a new beginning . . . and when it is seen in its full horror, there will be imprecations to My Father for a final opportunity to put right what has been evil in men. To others, Giuseppe, a new beginning without end 'when every tear will be wiped away,' when all pain turns to radiance, peace and blessedness."

"You say, 'soon' there will be an end of time, Lord. I am familiar with Your use of the word. According to our reckoning of time, Lord, when You have said 'soon,' man has waited for many, many years. Sometimes centuries."

"Measure all things in terms of eternity, Giuseppe. Time is no more important now than ever before, good friend. All that is important is that all men come to know Me. And now they will. They will taste love and anger, and even now the anger will be withheld from full demonstration to those who will bend their knees."

"Where will You start, Lord?"

"I have already started, My son. Just as two millenia ago I was born in secret, spending My early years by the side of Mary and Joseph until the day of My public ministry, so was I born quietly into your times. As in former days I was born in poverty, for it is to the poor that I truly belong in spirit. Once before, also, I was born a Jew, and so am I now . . . a Jew."

"A Jew, Lord?" Sicola asked with disbelief. "But . . . but did You not turn from the Jews and choose in their stead the Gentiles, Lord? How is it that You come back as a Jew when the nails that entered Your flesh must also have penetrated their flesh as an everlasting punishment for their failure to recognize You?"

"Giuseppe, my good friend, even the saints have failed to comprehend the fullness of the Father's love. When the Father loves, it is forever. The Jews have always been and will remain hereafter My chosen people."

"But look at how they have suffered, Lord."

"Did you not know, Giuseppe, that only those who suffer are My friends?"

"Yes, Lord, and no disrespect intended, but was it not Teresa of Avila who said in reply to such a statement, 'Yes, Lord, that is why You have so few friends!' "

"Giuseppe, Teresa is well loved in heaven, and when she said such a thing, My Father whispered to Me so that she would not hear: 'That Teresa! She is quite a card!' We were most amused."

Sicola smiled, satisfied that there was a sense of humor in heaven, all the while recalling his mischief in promoting the Word.

"But, Lord," Sicola said, "after Your death on earth it was said that the Gentiles were newly chosen. What was meant by this?"

"What was meant, successor to Peter, is that I came to the Jews, but through My Word I was intended to walk the earth so that all men would come to know Me. Did not Jews found the very Church that has been My great love? Why then do you assume that I would desert them? That more of them have not followed Peter has been a source of pain — and do not let the theologians tell you that My Father knows not suffering of a certain order — but ever in the forefront of heaven is the tenacity of love. My Father does not know failure, nor will He permit the notion to be spread that He does.

"Let me ask you, Giuseppe: If My Father created the world from the depth of His love, would He permit the world to end in such a disaster of failure as to be a mockery of that love, that creation? God created the world in triumph, and it will end in triumph. What God creates in love is consummated in love.

Hence the tenacity of God's love for the Jews does not permit Him to turn from them. As a final act of love the Jews and the Apostles will be one. It is for that reason that I have chosen to be one of them again. *Capisce*?"

"Yes, Lord." He could not recall such a view as this in Theology 101, but who could dispute what he was now hearing? What would You have me do, Lord?" he asked.

"Nothing, Giuseppe. The world has known from the beginning first the reign of God the Father, then for thirty-three short years, the reign of God the Son, then for two thousand years the reign of God the Holy Spirit operating through His Church, which you now head. Now, because thirty-three years was so brief an introduction to the world, the Son returns. And as before, He comes not to change the law, but to affirm it. And the law you have established has been done through Us. I come now to witness the fulfilment of your law. To you I have come first. Now I will go to your people, and they will know that it is not a new Power that comes, but the old Power, adjuring the espousal not of a new theology but an old theology. For what was truth yesterday is the truth today, eternal and unchanging."

"How will You do it, Lord?" Sicola asked.

"Through the power My Father gives Me, and I will share this power with you so that — unorthodox as your methods have been — your associates will have seen but the foreshadowing of abilities yet to come. I will work in the pastures herding the sheep into your corral, My friend. For it is not my wish that men look to Me as a new king of earth, as was their hope, but that men will follow Me to the sacraments you are empowered to dispense.

"It is a return to the sacraments that I seek first. For when men learn reverence for the sacraments they will revere all of life and thereby be made ready for all eternity. It is easy for sheep to follow, but they must not follow false shepherds. They must not simply be followers of men, but they must follow the truth above the man, so their truth does not fall when the man falls. Do not misunderstand. When I am finished, they will know indeed that the Son of Man returned to earth, but during My ministry My purpose will be to use the Church as the conduit to heaven."

"Was it not always so, Lord?"

"Indeed, Giuseppe."

"And that is all that is involved in the parousia, Lord, to find God through the Church?"

"Precisely."

"*Mannaggia*, You had to make such a long trip just to tell them again what You told them two thousand years ago."

"Yes, Giuseppe."

"What a shame, Lord! What a shame!"

"Somewhere, one or more of you Popes forgot that it was really very simple. Your mistake was to forget that I referred to souls many, many times as sheep, and sheep must be guarded, guided. Left to themselves, sheep will stray from the fold. It is too late for you to herd them, hence I must do so. But have no fear, Giuseppe, they will be directed to you for the dipping and the shearing. I go now to be about My Father's work. You will hear from Me."

"*Grazie*, Lord. Please drop in when You are in the neighborhood again. *Arrivederci*!"

"Until we meet again, Giuseppe."

The Lord left as suddenly as He had arrived,

without so much as opening a door on His way out. Sicola scratched his head in amazement at the whole experience, and as he did so he realized that the Lord had taken his zucchetto with Him. He reached into the desk drawer for another, plopped it on the back of his head, and leaned back in his chair with a happy grin. He muttered to himself, "That's a ni-i-i-ce a boy!"

"Awake,
arise,
or be forever
fallen!"

John Milton, *Paradise Lost*

A GLOSSARY FOR GREENHORNS

The writer has used words throughout this book that may not be known to some readers. Many of these are Italian words, and those who are strangers to the language, or those without an Italian dictionary, may be left questioning their meaning. At least one other word is a medical term used in the book as a proper name. Therefore, some comment about the meaning of these words is in order:

Buono. Good. "Hokay," or "Thatsa nice."

Cafone. Do not pronounce the *e* ending, and in order to give the impression that you are cultivated in language, give the *c* a slight *g* sound, which makes it Ga-PHONE! It means a rustic, a rube, a yokel, a babe in the woods. Take a you pick.

Caro. Darling or dear.

Compagno. A comrade, but not as in Russia. Though communism has made sharp inroads in Italy, one is brought more to pity for the Russians than for the Italians, for *campagno* has just the right touch of brotherhood in it, a quality missing from its Russian equivalent.

Curare. A dried aqueous extract of a vine used in arrow poison, or medically as a muscle relaxant. Your conclusions on the context of its use herewith are your own. Ahma say no more.

Faccia tosta (Fach-a tossed-a). Brazen-faced. Italian parents like to call their teenage children by that term. I heard it frequently.

Grazie. Denka you.

Ha capito? or *Capisce?* Understood? or Understand?

Mannaggia! It has no more meaning than the word ¡*Carramba*! to the Spanish. It is like saying, "Holy Smokes," only stronger; like "Son of a gun," only stronger; or like "Damn!" only much, much stronger.

Mezzo-mezzo. Some dialects in Italian would say it as "menza-menza," but it is the same. It is like saying "half and half," or "mebbe-yes-mebbe-no." It is a good word to vacillate over.

Pazienza. Sicola might translate it as, "Holda you water!" If you insist on being so prissy, then it means "Patience!" or "Be patient!"

Per piacere or *Prego.* Please.

Ponza. Here again you will sound more authentic if you are not so precise in your pronunciation. Give the *p* a *b* sound. The *ponza*, or *la ponza*, is the breadbasket or the belly, which is the "seat" of an Italian's pride.

Smegma. Ask your family doctor. If you are a lady, it will require a lot of nerve. In any event, the meaning will turn your stomach, so why not simply accept it as a suitably descriptive word for the foul character I have so named? Even I, who am your friend, will not tell you what it means. Don't ask.

Sta te buono. This phrase would be appropriate on the Papal Coat of Arms, or as a replacement for "Sincerely yours," or "Cordially" at the end of a letter. It means "Be good." It should not, however, replace "Yours in Christ." Dottsa more better.

Sta te zite. "Be quiet." Or as it is also said, "Shut uppa you face!"

Tesoro. Treasure.

Testa dura. "Hard head," stubborn. A cafone with more education perhaps, but not much more sense.

Vigile. Street-corner cop or *poliziotto*, as distinguished from a more gravely official *carabiniere*.

Finally, there is a phrase used nowhere in the book, but one that should be used to describe my efforts in this fantasy. It is *in buona fede*, and in these days of ecclesial torment it suggests that each of us always hold the Church aloft . . . in good faith.